A Sham Engagement

The Mismatched Lovers
Book One

Fil Reid

ARE YOU SIGNED UP FOR DRAGONBLADE'S BLOG?

You'll get the latest news and information on exclusive giveaways, exclusive excerpts, coming releases, sales, free books, cover reveals and more.

Check out our complete list of authors, too!

No spam, no junk. That's a promise!

Sign Up Here

www.dragonbladepublishing.com

Dearest Reader;

Thank you for your support of a small press. At Dragonblade Publishing, we strive to bring you the highest quality Historical Romance from some of the best authors in the business. Without your support, there is no 'us', so we sincerely hope you adore these stories and find some new favorite authors along the way.

Happy Reading!

CEO, Dragonblade Publishing

Additional Dragonblade books by Author Fil Reid

The Mismatched Lovers Series
A Sham Engagement (Book 1)

The Cornish Ladies Series
The Cornish Mermaid (Book 1)
The Cornish Bride (Book 2)
The Cornish Inheritance (Book 3)
The Cornish Widow (Book 4)

Guinevere Series
The Dragon Ring (Book 1)
The Bear's Heart (Book 2)
The Sword (Book 3)
Warrior Queen (Book 4)
The Quest for Excalibur (Book 5)
The Road to Avalon (Book 6)

CHAPTER ONE

NINETEEN-YEAR-OLD ELENORA WETHERBY gazed around at the sea of people attending the Amberley House ball in something akin to terror. Beside her, Cousin Petunia, whose first ball it was as well, drew in a deep, awe-laden breath. "Just look at all these sumptuous gowns, Ellie. Although none are as fine as ours. And the gentlemen, too. Look at their fancy waistcoats and their hair. And how handsome the soldiers are in their regimentals. I think I shall swoon with happiness." She gave a little squeal of excitement which made Aunt Penelope turn her head with a warning frown, and Mama give her a frosty look.

Elenora regarded her cousin, of whom she was fond, but in the rather tolerant manner she would have been fond of a puppy, and huffed. "I suppose they look well enough." Why Petunia was getting herself in such a state of excitement, she had no idea. Although the same age as Petunia, from time to time she felt as though she were much the older and more sensible of the two. And this was one of those times.

Petunia gave a snort of disgust at Elenora's lack of enthusiasm. "Oh, pooh and fiddlesticks. Even you have to agree that nowhere could be gathered a more beautiful assembly. And we are part of it, at last! Our first ball. I've waited so long for this day, and it's a dream that we should both come out into society together." She gave a little skip, but neither Aunt Penelope nor Mama noticed this time.

Elenora did not join in. The crowd of these noisy, brightly colored birds of paradise was hemming her in far too close on all sides. Too many people for comfort. Far more than she'd imagined would be at a ball in London. Her first proper ball, because, according to Mama, you couldn't count the country affairs at the Winchester Assembly Rooms. Petunia was different, though, being as determined to enjoy it as she was with everything. Something that could be more than annoying.

The sound of garrulous chatter rose in the warm air toward enormous glittering chandeliers where they hung from the stuccoed ceilings, and the scent of perfume, oozing in an almost visible fug from both men and women alike, cloyed in Elenora's sensitive nostrils, inducing a vague sense of brewing nausea. Laughter echoed, raucous as a tin shed rattling, and the dreaded sound of dance music tumbled in from a room she couldn't see. Oh, the torture of having to dance with people she didn't know. *Men* she didn't know. A little nervous shiver ran through her.

Unlike her cousin, Miss Petunia Dandridge, Elenora did *not* want to be at the Amberley House Ball.

She glanced down at her own gown, which was indeed worthy of examination. Nothing she'd ever owned had been as beautiful as this. Delicate gauze covered a pale blue silk underskirt, both richly decorated with blue and silver embroidered roses. All around the low neckline, tiny, matching-silk roses had been attached by the dressmaker in Albemarle Street. The woman's name, Mrs. Bean, had made Elenora want to burst out laughing, which Mama would have frowned upon, while Aunt Penelope would have added it to her list of her niece's many perceived eccentricities. It must be a long one by now.

On her feet sat delicate, pale-blue slippers, and her long gloves were of the same hue. She was a vision of exquisite innocent beauty, Mama had said with pride, on looking at her just before they set out. Men would fall in love with her at first glance.

Elenora and Petunia had exchanged glances but stayed silent, because both Aunt Penelope and Petunia knew very well how much hung on Elenora finding herself a rich husband, although only Petunia was privy to how she felt about that prospect. How she was praying this season would be both short and her last, and not because she'd have found herself the required husband. To do her credit, Petunia had tried to understand her cousin's reasons, but, like Elenora's four younger sisters, she'd failed. She did know, however, that the last thing Elenora wanted to be was a vision and have people look at her, much less fall in love with her.

Elenora sighed. None of this was helping her cope with the unnerving sensation that everyone was indeed staring at her. That if she looked up from studying her entwined hands, she'd find hundreds of pairs of eyes fixed on her, prickling her skin with their accusing gaze like so many irritating arrows.

If only she hadn't been cursed with a mane of luscious blonde hair (her sister Augusta's slightly envious description), a pink and white complexion worthy of a goddess (Mama's words) and wide eyes of a deep, cornflower blue (Papa's delighted description, as they were just like his). If she hadn't, life would have been a lot easier. But she was the only one of Mama and Papa's seven children to have inherited dear Papa's tall, golden good looks. All the others, from her oldest brother Jolyon down to darling little Phoebe, who was only eleven, looked as much like their short, dark-haired mother and each other as to have been described as peas in a pod.

Luckily, she hadn't also inherited Papa's propensity for gambling. No, that had gone exclusively, as far as they all knew, to Jolyon, who was continually on his uppers and dunning Papa for money he didn't have. Didn't have because he'd already lost it at the gaming tables himself. As oldest daughter and Mama's unwilling confidante, Elenora knew all about her father's gambling losses. How much easier to have been Phoebe, still in the schoolroom and, ignorant of the family's money troubles, without a care in the world.

Instead, here she was in London at her long-dreaded first ball, with Mama determined she should make a match with the richest man there in order to shore up the ailing Wetherby coffers. Or, if not the richest, then the most titled, but preferably one who was also in possession of a sizeable fortune of some kind. Mama had been very explicit about that. Elenora cringed inside at her own similarity to the mythical fatted calf that was always sacrificed for the good of others. Because not only did she not want to be married off for money to the highest bidder, she also didn't want to ever get married at all. She wanted to remain at home at Penworthy with nothing changed. Forever.

"Elenora, my dear," Mama cooed, making great play with her ivory fan, a skill she and Aunt Penelope, with the assistance of a resigned Petunia who considered it a pointless undertaking, had been endeavoring to drum into Elenora for over a month. "Do lift your chin a little and stop gazing at your feet. You make your shoulders look quite stooped. Look over there. I see Lady Routledge herself. I must introduce both you girls to her. She's one of the most influential hostesses in London, and, if she takes to you, all sorts of invitations will follow. And dear Lady Sedgemoor as well. We came out together as young girls. It'll be such a pleasure to renew our acquaintance. Come along."

What Elenora would have liked to do right now was bolt, decorously of course, back outside into the damp and foggy London night air, to find their carriage and have Aunt Penelope's coachman drive her home. Preferably not to Aunt Penelope's elegant town house, but to Penworthy, Papa's small estate in Hampshire. Posthaste.

It had been bad enough being expected to smile sweetly and curtsy to their host when they arrived. Meeting new people always made her nervous and on edge, and as he was an earl, no less, her fears had multiplied. On top of that, she'd been sure that Lord Amberley, a tall, stiff-backed and white-haired gentleman, had peered down his long aristocratic nose at her and Mama and Papa, and thought them jumped-up little country squires. He'd had the sort of look on his face that said he knew to within a penny how near to ruin Papa was, and didn't want Mama husband hunting at his ball.

As if all the other mamas here weren't doing the same thing. Aunt Penelope certainly was, but in Petunia's case it was because she wanted to get married, not because she had to in order to save the family fortunes. Uncle George had left Aunt Penelope a very nicely off widow, or so Papa kept saying with a decided air of resentment whenever he was out of his sister's earshot.

With an inward sigh, and keeping her head lowered so she wouldn't have to look anyone in the eye, Elenora followed her mother and the ever-enthusiastic Petunia through the crowd to where two imposing elderly ladies stood near the doors into the next room, fans fluttering as they surveyed the press. One was tall and stately as a galleon in full sail and possessed of jowls a bulldog would have been proud of, the other short and as scrawny as Parson Dobbs' underfed wife at home in Penworthy, but both were so bedecked in jewelry and ornate gowns that nobody could mistake either of them for anything less than a duchess.

Although, in fact, only Lady Routledge was a duchess, and a dowager duchess at that. Mama had spent a long time going over the names and titles (and desirability as husbands or mothers of prospective husbands) of everyone Elenora was likely to meet during her first season. Aided and abetted by Aunt Penelope's encyclopedic knowledge of the upper echelons of society, of course. Most of this information had passed directly through Elenora's disinterested head, but a few bits had stuck, and Lady Routledge was one of them. Because Lady Routledge was in possession of a Mama-approved son, the young Duke of Routledge, a person Elenora intended to avoid as though he was suffering from the plague.

Two sets of appraising eyes fixed for a moment upon Mama, perhaps in surprised recognition, before switching to stare at Elenora. If only she could just vanish. No, if only everyone else but her could vanish. That would be best. She'd be fine here if it was empty of people.

As if suddenly remembering their manners, the owners of the eyes, in unison, reverted their gazes to Mama.

The stately galleon extended a beringed hand to Mama. "Lady Wetherby, dearest Fanny, how delightful to see you here. I had no idea you'd come up to Town for the season. And Lady Dandridge, as well. When last I saw you, Penelope, I believe you mentioned to me how settled Fanny was in her rustic surroundings. Where was it? Hampshire, I think you said. Quite charming and bucolic, I imagine, and I'm sure it suits you well, Fanny."

Elenora frowned. Was this pompous lady being rude to Mama and hinting that Penworthy was in the back end of beyond? Hard to tell, but an insult to Penworthy was not one Elenora was about to forget. Although its proximity to "the back end of beyond" suited her very well.

Mama clasped the tips of the stately galleon's gloved fingers briefly and smiled her sweetest smile. "Lady Routledge, Lady Sedgemoor." She and Aunt Penelope swept graceful curtsies to which were returned the barest of nods.

Mama ploughed on. "Of course, you couldn't know that I'm visiting dear Penelope for the season in order to present my oldest daughter at the same time as she is presenting her own delightful offspring." Her own fan worked in overtime. "One has to abandon one's rural idyll whether one likes to or not, eventually, and the entertainments in Hampshire are nothing as compared with the balls and soirées of the Beau Monde. May I present my daughter, Elenora. You will see how fresh she is from the schoolroom. Such a delicate flower. And I believe you already know my niece, Miss Dandridge?"

The stately galleon bestowed a condescending smile on Elenora and Petunia. "Quite charming, and such a modish gown your daughter has. Country dressmakers must be improving, Fanny."

Elenora cringed as she made her own respectful curtsy, wishing the ground might open and gulp her down. Again. Her and her expensive gown. This, of course, was why Mama had insisted on a wardrobe of new gowns ordered and made in Town over the past month. None of the old ones she'd left behind at Penworthy, ones that had passed muster to attend a few local events, would have done for London society, or so Mama had pronounced to an increasingly horrified Papa.

Acutely aware of how much her new wardrobe must have cost, Elenora rose from her curtsy with warm cheeks and took a better look at the two most well-known hostesses in London.

Lady Routledge, a redoubtable dowager—Elenora had read the gossip papers as well as listened to Mama's gazetteer of the Ton—was the stately galleon. An amazon of a woman, she'd produced no less than twelve surviving children for her husband, although only one of them had been a son, the young duke—also gleaned from the gossip papers. This lady wore a thick layer of makeup she must have intended to disguise her age. It hadn't worked and the powder she'd dusted her cheeks with only served to emphasize her wrinkles.

Don't stare and don't mention the wrinkles. Remember what Mama said in the carriage. Think before you speak.

Mama smiled all the more sweetly. "We came to London for Elenora's gowns, of course. And Elenora has been such a pleasure to dress, with her good looks. Everything looks perfect on her with her figure and coloring." Mama had not neglected to mention that Lady Routledge's eleven daughters all resembled their mother in build—quite a fleet they must look when assembled together.

However, Elenora cringed. Why must Mama mention her looks—which in all truth she'd rather she didn't possess. Oh, to be more like her sisters and melt into their homogenous background, and less like dear Papa.

Lady Sedgemoor, the dowager's miniscule companion, thin as a leafless twig with rather sallow, unhealthy skin, was also the younger of the two, and in possession of a living husband, although he wasn't as exalted as a duke. The fact that both of her sons were already spoken for had irked Mama, as apparently both were exceedingly well off and the elder due to inherit his ailing father's earldom sometime soon.

"What a charmingly pretty daughter and niece you have, Fanny," Lady Sedgemoor said, the look on her face rendering her praise insincere. "Almost like sisters. I am sure they will be a great success this season. Quite the belles of the ball tonight."

Why did Elenora get the impression both these ladies knew exactly why she and Mama were here? That their every secret was well known to everyone, in fact? A tickle of apprehension ran down her back, making her want to fidget her shoulders. Mindful of Mama's strictures not to wriggle, she resisted the temptation with difficulty.

But belles of the ball? *Over my dead body.* She cringed some more. She didn't want to be the belle of any ball, nor have people say she was, nor have them look at her. She didn't want to be flaunted by Mama in the hopes some eligible man's roguish eye would settle on her. And most of all, she didn't want to be found a husband. However, she smiled demurely, as she'd learned to do long ago, and cast her eyes down again as though she might possibly be a respectful and modest daughter.

"Indeed they are," Lady Routledge joined in. "I should say neither of them will have any trouble filling their dance cards." Her gaze ran up and down Elenora as though studying the conformation of a horse she was thinking of buying, and making her once more wish for that elusive hole in the ground to open up and swallow her. "She looks nothing like you, my dear Fanny. One would think she and Miss Dandridge were sisters in truth, if one didn't know better."

"She takes after her papa," Mama said, with more than a hint of truculence, as though this might be a bad thing, which, of course, in Jolyon it was.

Aunt Penelope interrupted. "And of course, dear Petunia takes after me, as you can see, and I am very like my dear brother. Fanny will tell you that Elenora has four younger sisters who all take after her, though."

Lady Routledge raised a perfectly penciled eyebrow. "Indeed? How charming for Fanny's other daughters to have inherited her... looks."

Elenora had to bite her tongue. Her sisters had often bemoaned the fact that they all took after Mama, and Elenora, conscious of what they saw as her own good fortune, had hastened to inform them good looks were not that important in life. She'd have swapped places with any of them if given the opportunity. None of them had believed her.

Mama smiled back as though she hadn't just heard a thinly veiled insult, putting into practice the advice she'd given Elenora before they'd left Aunt Penelope's house in Arlington Street. *If someone insults you, just smile politely and ignore it.* She patted Elenora's elegantly coiffed hair. "I know. I'm blessed with having five such delightful daughters, as well as two handsome sons, all of them different. Elenora is the apple of her papa's eye."

"I see not quite enough that he is here to escort her to her first ball," Lady Routledge said, her piggy eyes narrowing as though she were a hook-beaked eagle coming in for the kill. Did they all know about Papa's propensity for gambling? Elenora felt her cheeks begin to warm and dug her nails into the palms of her hands in an effort to prevent herself blurting out some rude retort. How hard it was to follow Mama's advice.

"Oh, he's here tonight, of course," Mama said, a trifle too breezily. "He's just gone off with Jolyon, our oldest, to find us refreshments. So kind and thoughtful of him."

Gone off to the card room was what she really meant. How to rescue Mama from this painful interlocution and get away from these two old harpies?

Fate came to her rescue. "Oh look, Mama," Elenora said, tapping her mother's arm with her folded fan, the only use she could see for it. "I see Matthew over there with several of his friends." She pointed the fan in Matthew's direction only to have it pushed down.

"Do not point, Elenora. That's so common." But the words

had been muttered behind her mother's fan, not meant for her two old friends to overhear. "You are quite right. I fear, ladies, that we must leave you. My younger son has just come down from Oxford and I've not spoken to him as yet." With another elegant curtsy, Mama swept Elenora away in the direction of her older brother. Aunt Penelope and Petunia followed in their wake.

Mama leaned close. "Thank you, Elenora. Elegantly done."

Praise indeed. Elenora wasn't used to being told she'd done the right thing, especially not that it had been elegant. Perhaps, at last, her mother's and governess's influences were rubbing off on her.

CHAPTER TWO

S ELENORA AND Petunia followed Mama and Aunt Penelope toward the little group, Elenora's brother, Matthew, turned to greet them, a wide smile on his rather homely face, his brown eyes dancing with mirth, as usual. Yes, he resembled Mama too, although no hint of the frivolity he possessed attached itself to her.

"Ellie, Mama! I was hoping to see you two here. I heard from Jolyon that you're staying in Arlington Street so Ellie can come out at the same time as Petunia. Aunt Penelope, you're looking as lovely as ever. Pet, you look charming, lemon suits your coloring. Ellie, cheer up, it could be worse. Jolyon's about somewhere, I think. We came together as he's been so kind as to put me up in his rooms in Jermyn Street since I was sent down. Let me introduce you all to my best friends, Adam Thoroughgood and Timothy Brightwell. We were all up at Oxford together." He grinned. "And all rusticated together I'm ashamed to say."

Matthew didn't look in the least bit ashamed. Even Elenora could see that.

"What have you done this time?" Petunia asked, sounding just a little impressed at his daring. She'd confided to Elenora in bed last night that she thought Matthew the better looking and the more interesting of her two male cousins. Had Elenora been bothered, she might have taken the opportunity to tease her, but thoughts of the coming ball had occupied her mind.

"Adam, Tim, this is my dear Mama and the oldest and best of my brood of many sisters, Elenora. Oh, and this is Cousin Petunia."

The two young men, who from their youthful countenances must have been of the same vintage as Matthew, who was six months off his majority, swept bows to Elenora, Petunia, Aunt Penelope and Mama, both of them with appreciative stares for Elenora that made her want to hide behind Mama. Or that pillar over there. Or that enormous vase of hothouse flowers.

Mama fixed her second child with the sort of hard stare that had terrified her brood when they'd been in the schoolroom. Alas for her, it had less effect now Matthew had been out of her control for several years. "Yes," she said, her tone dry. "Your father and I heard you'd been sent down. What was it for this time?"

Matthew waved a negligent hand. "A mere trifle. Nothing I can mention in front of the girls, at any rate." He gave a self-deprecatory smile. "Don't want to shock 'em."

"We won't be shocked," Petunia said.

"Yes, you will," Aunt Penelope snapped. Perhaps she already knew what Matthew had done.

Elenora suppressed a frown, which Mama would doubtless censor as being detrimental to her looks. As this was the third time Matthew had been rusticated, it did seem as though he hadn't learned anything from the first two occasions. If she'd only had the chance to go to Oxford to study, she'd never have done anything to jeopardize her place. But girls weren't allowed to attend any university. So frustrating, as it was the only place in the world she'd be happy to go to, if she had to leave Penworthy. Another thing Petunia couldn't understand.

"Your Papa is here too," Mama said, her tone brusque. "No doubt he'll be anxious to hear your side of the story, Matthew. He received a letter from your college giving their point of view on the subject a few days since."

Matthew's amiable expression fell a little. "Oh. Right. I

daresay they've colored it in their direction. I'll let him know the truth when I catch up with him."

"He's in the card room," Elenora said. "Why don't you go there now? I daresay he'll be glad to see you."

Matthew bridled. "In a while, Sis. Can't leave Adam and Tim on their own, not with all these predatory mamas out and about." He waggled his eyebrows at her in the way he'd been used to do when they were children together at Penworthy, and she had to suppress a giggle. She'd worm the reason for his latest rustication out of him later.

His two friends, however, to her delight didn't look much like desirable catches. Mr. Thoroughgood's plump face boasted a fine display of pimples while Mr. Brightwell's singular most noticeable feature was his bright red hair—the sort of hair the unkind might describe as carroty.

"I say," Mr. Brightwell ventured, having found his tongue at last. "Might I trouble you to put me down on your card for a dance, Miss Wetherby? Now we've been introduced, that is." The rosy color creeping up his face clashed terribly with his hair.

Mama opened her mouth to say something that would inevitably be a refusal to this poor young man as he didn't conform to the list of requirements for dance partners that had been hammered home to Elenora before they set out. But Elenora was already opening her dance card and licking the end of her pencil. Mama's words rang in her head. *The men you dance with must be of marriageable age, they must be rich and they must be titled.* Looking more closely at Mr. Brightwell, she wasn't sure he was even of marriageable age. And she doubted very much if he fulfilled either of Mama's other requirements. Which made him the perfect dance partner.

As they'd only arrived a short while since, not a single name so far had been written in the card. "Do you like to dance the cotillion?" Elenora asked, surprised at her sudden onset of confidence. "I see it is the very next dance." If she had to dance with someone, let it not be anyone of whom Mama might approve.

Mr. Brightwell, looking as though his birthday and Christmas had both arrived at the same time, spluttered out a yes, and, after she'd written his name down, held out his arm to her, his pink face glowing with pride.

As if inspired by his friend's success, Mr. Thoroughgood bowed to Petunia and asked her for a dance as well. That made the prospect of dancing less of an ordeal than Elenora was expecting, as much of her practice had been with her sisters at Penworthy and with her cousin here in Town. She could almost view it as another practice day if she tried hard enough.

Heart hammering against her stays, she allowed Mr. Brightwell to lead her out onto the crowded dance floor, as Mr. Thoroughgood led out Petunia, leaving Mama with Matthew and Aunt Penelope, where no doubt they would take the opportunity to grill him about his Oxford indiscretions. A delightful thought occurred to her. If she could fill her card with unsuitable matches, then that would thwart Mama's plan to marry her off to some inbred member of the haut Ton. Let Augusta, who at sixteen was already itching to have her first London season, save the family fortunes. And then maybe she, Elenora, could get on with doing what she really wanted, which was studying history.

Mr. Brightwell was not a good dancer. Or perhaps he was, but dancing with Elenora brought out the clumsy, two-left-footed side of him. Every time he trod on her toes, which was often, he apologized in the most exaggerated fashion, and so loudly that heads turned. Which only succeeded in bringing a flush of hot embarrassment to Elenora's cheeks at being made a spectacle of. What was the betting Mr. Thoroughgood would be just as bad a dancer, although he appeared at the moment to be getting on swimmingly with Petunia as a partner. However, bruised toes were a small price to pay for avoiding Mama's matchmaking plans.

Mr. Brightwell's lack of any other kind of conversation than apologies enabled Elenora to study the other dancers in their eight. She hadn't expected to know any of them, except, of course, for Petunia and Mr. Thoroughgood, but one of her favorite occupations was people watching, so, as she knew the dance steps intimately, that was what she did.

One of the men, a fair bit older than the other dancers, kept glancing in her direction, a wicked glint in his eye indicating he had perceived her problems with Mr. Brightwell and his uncontrollable feet. Tall, powerfully built, and with just a few flecks of silver adorning his unostentatious dark sideburns, he had an air of being amused about him that set her hackles rising. Was he presuming to laugh at her?

And what about the woman he was partnering? Nearly as old as Mama, which was positively ancient, her gown was of a deep ruby red and her face had been painted to perfection, unlike Lady Routledge's, giving her the appearance of a beautiful and voluptuous statue come to life, despite her advanced age. As the ladies came together, the woman's eyes met Elenora's and for a moment held them, as though in a challenge. Taken aback, Elenora stumbled, and, when she looked up again, the dance had moved on. The woman was no longer looking at her but laughing up at her handsome partner.

Because even Elenora, uninterested as she was in marriage, couldn't deny that the tall gentleman was handsome in a devilish kind of way. Even a dangerous kind of way. And that did make him interesting from the point of view of people watching, just as his dazzling partner was.

As she and Mr. Brightwell came together again she had time for a question. "Do you know who that woman is?"

He followed her gaze, more color rising up his cheeks as he saw who she was referring to. His reply came out as a mutter. "Um, I believe that's Lady Raby."

"Why did she look at me as though she hates me?"

The blush kept on rising. "Really, Miss Wetherby, I have no idea at all." He glanced about furtively. "I've heard she's a woman to be avoided at all costs. Do not let her make a friend of you."

As if that would happen after the look she'd given Elenora.

The nature of the cotillion meant that as the dance progressed, she kept finding herself momentarily having to dance with all the other ladies. When she did, she now deliberately kept her gaze away from the flamboyant Lady Raby, assuming the demure behavior that Mama had hammered home was to be expected of a newly-come-out young lady.

But the dance also meant she was every so often partnered with Lady Raby's escort, the man with the devilish look and the amused gaze. The first time this happened, she took his proffered hand in the lightest of holds and let him twirl her around, her head pointedly turned away from him. The second time, though, he caught her unawares. "Is there something about me that you dislike, Miss Wetherby?" He possessed a deep and undeniably attractive voice.

Her head snapped around. How did he even know her name? Did gentlemen also study the members of the Ton the way Mama had made her? Not that she knew who this particular gentleman was. From the look of him he wouldn't have figured on Mama's list of prospective husbands. "No, there isn't." Caught unawares she'd reverted back to her old forthright ways—ways that Mama had spent years trying to groom out of her. "Sir." Or was he a "my lord?"

The dance led them apart, and it was a short while before they were once again paired. He started up exactly where he'd left off. "Then why is it you refuse to look at me when we dance?"

She took a quick peek up at his saturnine face. Dark hair curled around his forehead and the shadow of dark stubble outlined a strong jawline. Winged eyebrows framed eyes so dark they were almost black in this light. A face to be afraid of, if you were of a more missish disposition than Elenora. "You wish me to look at you?"

"It's only polite while we dance together."

They parted again, and now Elenora did indeed look at him

as he danced with Lady Raby. The dance called for minimal touching of more than hands, and yet Lady Raby seemed to imbue every touch with something Elenora had never seen before. A languidness adhered to the woman, to both of them, as they danced the same dance as everyone else, yet in a way that seemed to exert a strange pull on Elenora, making her feel warm all over. The stranger had an elegance about him that pleased the eye, although his face possessed a distinctly devilish look even from a distance. To her surprise, she found that something more than just her idle interest in people watching fascinated her.

They came back together again. "Do you like what you see?"

Had he noticed her watching him? Even though he'd seemed so engrossed in partnering Lady Raby? Goodness, but he was forward. Was he one of those men Mama had warned her about? A rake? She couldn't deny that the thought was quite delicious. She'd always wanted to meet a rake, just because they sounded more interesting than most young men. Augusta would be green with envy and so would Petunia. She sought amongst the phrases Mama had drummed into her for a clever reply. "You are not displeasing to the eye."

He gave a deep rumble of a laugh that had heads turning. "I'm glad to have your approval, Miss Wetherby."

"You have the advantage of me, sir."

"Jack Deveril."

Did she know that name? But they were apart again before she could decide whether he'd featured in Mama's lists, unlikely as that seemed.

"I wouldn't talk to that man if I were you," Mr. Brightwell said as she rejoined him.

"Why not?"

"That's Lord Broxbourne. He has a terrible reputation."

Much like Lady Raby. No wonder the two were dancing together. But was his a name she should recognize? "A reputation as what?"

Mr. Brightwell blushed yet again, his face an unprepossessing shade of puce that clashed appallingly with his hair. "Um, er. I can't be more specific, but I've heard his nickname is Satan, and not just because of his looks. He's not a man any young lady should be talking to. If I'd known he'd be in this eight, I'd have stepped down."

This scarcity of information had Elenora intrigued.

When she and Deveril came together again, she peeped up at him as she took his hand, warm in hers. This might turn out to be fun, as he more than likely wasn't on Mama's list of possible bridegrooms so could be encouraged. "My dance partner tells me you have a terrible reputation."

He laughed and heads turned again. "He's right, Miss Wetherby. You'd do best to steer clear of me."

"How can I when we have to keep dancing together?"

"Perhaps you'd like to partner me in the next dance then? So we can talk some more. If, that is, you would like to shock your Mama. I suspect that is her over there, with the determined scowl on her face watching me dance with you."

She nodded and they parted again. Two callow youths and a rake. That would make Mama sit up and look, and diminish the number of dances left for approved young men to claim.

The next time they were back together was the last. As she left the dance floor with Mr. Brightwell, Deveril approached with Lady Raby on his arm, her perfect face curved into a smile that might not have been as friendly as it seemed. "Miss Wetherby. May I introduce you to the Countess of Raby. Sir, I don't have the pleasure of your name." He made a bow to Mr. Brightwell, who spluttered wordlessly and went even redder, but managed to remember to bow back.

Elenora curtsied to Lady Raby. She'd better make the introductions herself. "My lady. This is Mr. Brightwell, a friend of my brother's."

Lady Raby held out a dainty, gloved hand to Elenora. "Charming, my dear. You make such a pretty picture dancing with your handsome beau."

Now, that wasn't at all true, was it? Even Elenora could recognize this as a lie.

If only she could read people better. For all her people watching, Elenora was a slow learner. That something lurked beneath Lady Raby's seemingly friendly words and charming smile was obvious, but what it was she had no idea.

Mr. Brightwell, who seemed somewhat recovered, made a tentative bow to Lady Raby. Being introduced to two people with such dastardly reputations seemed to have quite upset him. "My lady, my lord."

Mama hove into view, a determined glare on her face, with Mr. Thoroughgood and Petunia trailing behind her. "Mr. Brightwell. Elenora, my dear. Come along." She directed her fiercest glare, that had been known to make brave men quake in their shoes, at Deveril.

He swept her a bow. "Broxbourne at your service, Lady Wetherby. I came to stake my claim on your daughter's dance card."

Mr. Thoroughgood's face fell. No doubt he'd been planning on asking for the next dance. Elenora felt a sudden, inappropriate urge to giggle.

Mama's face fell too. That reputation of Deveril's must be widespread. The urge to ask more about it rose but had to be dismissed. She'd ask Petunia later. She had nearly as wide a knowledge of everyone as her mother did.

Elenora moved to retrieve her dance card from where it hung on her wrist, but Mama was too quick. "I'm afraid my daughter's dance card is quite full already, Lord Broxbourne. Come, Elenora, let us go and find some refreshment." And with that, she whisked Elenora away.

CHAPTER THREE

"BUT, MAMA, LORD Broxbourne asked me to dance so politely. Wasn't it a little rude to lie to him about my dance card?"

Mama seized Elenora's hand as she hurried her away, Aunt Penelope and Petunia trailing in their wake. "There are some gentlemen it isn't wise to dance with, Elenora. You are too young and naïve to understand."

"It's only a dance. And he does have a title. I thought that was what you wanted for me." The impulse to provoke her mother was proving too strong.

"Have I taught you nothing? It's not *only* a dance. Nothing like it. This is the marriage mart and, as I've repeatedly told you until I was blue in the face, all the young unattached ladies are here for one thing only. And they won't be finding it with Viscount Broxbourne, even if he is as rich as Croesus."

Her interest more than piqued now, although not in a way Mama would have liked, Elenora persisted. "Mama, you're rather presuming that, aren't you? He seemed perfectly pleasant when he was talking to me as we danced the cotillion." Not quite true, but what did a little white lie matter? And as for the way he'd danced with the disreputable Lady Raby... the way watching them move together had made her feel...

Mama turned to Aunt Penelope. "You see, Penelope, what it is I have to put up with. And I have four more of them I have to deal with after this one. The thought's enough to put me into a decline. You are so lucky to have just the one daughter."

Aunt Penelope nodded sagely, and, it had to be said, a tad smugly, while Petunia stood beside her endeavoring to look like the sort of perfect daughter Mama obviously thought she was, but at the same time trying not to giggle.

"It's no good, Penelope." Mama heaved a heartfelt sigh. "You go on. Elenora and I need to have *words*. Again. We'll join you in a little while."

As Petunia pulled a commiserating face, Mama drew Elenora into a curtained alcove by a window and they both sat down on a cushioned bench. Outside on the terrace, lanterns shimmered in the darkness, casting pools of golden light across the paving. Chill air, a reminder that it was still winter, filtered in around the edges of the window in little eddies, and Elenora shivered.

Mama shook her head as if in despair. Mama was always doing this for reasons Elenora couldn't fathom, but what was she supposed to have done now?

"Oh, you are such an innocent, Elenora. I don't know how I'm going to get you married off successfully. Men like Broxbourne ask pretty girls with no fortunes to dance because they're after one thing only. And it is not marriage." Mama lowered her voice to a hushed whisper. "You saw that dreadful Lady Raby he was with, in that shameless scarlet gown, no less—rumor has it she's his mistress. That's the sort of man he is. Flaunting his affairs in public. No shame at all. And neither has she."

Was there a cuckolded Lord Raby somewhere? Elenora's mind spun off for a moment down a rabbit hole of enquiry, but common sense prevented her from sharing this with her mother in case it caused a fainting fit. Long years of experience had taught her that neither Mama nor her sisters, nor her brothers either, thought the same way she did. She folded her arms. "Well, as I don't wish to marry him, I'm unlikely to come to any harm if I dance with him, am I? And as he clearly has a mistress already, he's not going to be on the look out for another one, surely?"

Now she'd done it. Mama's face achieved a shade of puce that rivaled poor Mr. Brightwell's. "Elenora Wetherby! Stop talking in such an unladylike manner. Thank goodness your father's in the card room and can't hear you. His toes would curl."

As Papa's own language, frequently to be heard around Penworthy, was far more toe-curling, Elenora just compressed her lips and frowned at Mama. She loved her dearly, but she could be so frustrating. In fact, her whole family could be frustrating.

"And there's no point in dancing with young men like your brother's friends," Mama went on, with a dismissive wave of her hand. "They have as little money to their names as he does. And that goes for Jolyon's friends as well. All of his friends are hardened gamblers and what money they do have they fritter at cards or on the horses. You are not to dance with young men like that."

As this was precisely why she would have chosen these young men as dancing partners, Elenora forbore from answering. Coming out during the London season was turning out to be more of a minefield than she'd expected, and she'd not entered into it blindfolded. Even though Mama had given her that long lecture before they'd come up to London after the New Year celebrations at Penworthy, she hadn't really absorbed exactly what it would be like, nor how much Mama might try to control her choices. Being nineteen might make her feel like an adult, but in Mama's mind she was clearly still a child to be told what to do. And that included whom to marry. She'd made up her mind back then that she wouldn't just knuckle under and obey, and she had no intention of wavering. Mama could present her with as many eligible men as she wanted; she wasn't going to be marrying any of them.

Mama took her arm. "Now, let's go and introduce you to some much more suitable young men. We won't meet any sitting here. We need to find your Aunt Penelope and Petunia again and circulate. No need to bother with anyone we're not considering for marriage." She drew Elenora out of the alcove. "The more people who know we're here, the more invitations you're likely to get to other balls and parties and the more likely you are to meet someone you could like as a husband."

Oh no. That was just what Elenora didn't want.

JACK DEVERIL RELINQUISHED the charming Lady Raby's company at the earnest request of his friend Lord Thomas Mayhew, who whisked her off onto the dance floor, leaving Jack with a thirst that required quenching. The ballroom at Amberley House was more than warm, despite the chill of winter prevailing out of doors, and sweat stood out on his forehead after the vigor of the cotillion.

His eyes followed the intriguing blonde girl, Miss Wetherby, as her mother hurried her away, waiting for her to look back at him over her elegant shoulder. When she didn't, he experienced a sag of disappointment. He must be losing his touch. She was the prettiest girl here tonight and it would have been fun to have squired her out onto the dance floor. Not to mention she had a direct attitude about her that fascinated him. Purely from the point of view of liking the company of women in general, that was. Nothing else. Of course.

She and her battleaxe of a mama disappeared into one of the curtained alcoves along the right hand side of the room. Perfect for a gentleman's rendezvous with a lady, but as they'd both gone in there, their tête-à-tête must be for a quite different purpose. In all probability, Lady Wetherby was outlining to her delightful daughter the many reasons why she shouldn't dance with a man like Jack. He smiled to himself. It would be fun to pursue the young lady, if only to annoy her ambitious mother.

And besides, used as he was to young ladies setting their caps at him, her apparent lack of interest piqued him. He liked to think he could have any young lady he fancied with a click of his fingers. God hadn't blessed him with this countenance and this physique for nothing. It might also be fun to make her want him, something at which he considered himself gifted.

He frowned. Perhaps not. Of course, her dance card wasn't full. Her mother just didn't want the girl to dance with him. Unsurprising really, although a lot of mamas seemed to see him as some sort of challenge they were sure their daughters could conquer. The frown softened into a smile again. No. He wasn't interested enough to put himself out. After all, he had Louise, didn't he? And wasn't she the most accommodating mistress he'd had so far? Just thinking about her lying naked in her silk sheets had him uncomfortable in his breeches. He'd have to go and find an alcove or a quiet corner himself if he couldn't get his body under control.

Anyway, he'd only wanted to dance with the girl to make Louise jealous. Because she was such a pretty girl, and he'd seen Louise's face when she'd spotted him talking to her during the changes. And because he liked to tease. He had to admit, though, that at ten years his senior, Louise's looks were beginning to fade, the contrast made more noticeable when he'd looked at her beside Miss Wetherby. He shrugged. Miss Wetherby was a pretty girl whom he might have wanted to seduce had she not such a ferocious guard dog of a mother. Just for the fun of making her want him when she so clearly didn't.

Shrugging off thoughts of the annoyingly disinterested Miss Wetherby, Jack strolled through into the refreshments room and secured himself a glass of lemonade. Whisky was on offer, of course, but his thirst kept him away from it. And besides which, if he was going into the card room he'd need his wits about him. Only a fool played cards while drunk, and Jack was no fool.

In the card room several tables had already been set up and a fair number of gentlemen were playing. The scent of fine whisky filled the air. No one should notice that he wasn't drinking, a fact he was adept at hiding. At a table over by one of the windows, Sir Nicholas Wetherby was playing loo, an unwise, half-full glass of whisky by his right hand. Jack knew him by name only, although he'd seen him a number of times at White's and Almack's, always seated at a gaming table with a hand of cards in his grip. He was a tall, rather willowy gentleman with a shock of blonde hair just going gray and startlingly blue eyes. Too much of a coincidence for the fair Elenora not to be his daughter.

Jack ambled over and stood watching for a minute or two while Sir Nicholas lost again. Unwise to gamble what you didn't have, and if rumor was correct, Sir Nicholas was dished up. Why was it men who'd lost everything persisted in the fallacy that their luck was about to change if they kept on digging deeper? He almost felt sorry for the girl, as clearly her mama was out to snare a rich husband for her, something she might succeed at thanks to Miss Wetherby's looks, and turn about the family fortunes. A man would have to be desperate to choose to end up leg-shackled to a girl with a family like hers.

"Jack, old chap." An arm was slung around Jack's broad shoulders. "Found you at last. I might've guessed you'd have hidden yourself away in here, away from all the predatory mamas. Come and sit over here—we're just starting a bank for a game of Faro. Sssh. Don't tell anyone, or we'll be in trouble." The encircling arm of the Honorable Oliver Fairley, one of Jack's closest friends, guided him away from his contemplation of Wetherby's table and toward a fresh one that was just being set up. "Westlake and Dugdale are going to join us when they're back from the refreshment room."

Jack sat down on a seat richly upholstered in deep pink velvet. "I wondered if I'd see you in here."

Fairley grinned. "Can't keep me away from the card room, which means you can't keep me away from any ball I'm invited to. I think the matchmaking mamas still believe their daughters can catch me." He chuckled. "Good luck to them on that. Why would I swap a new mistress every few years for being leg-shackled to one woman for life?"

Jack chuckled back. "I suppose marrying wouldn't necessarily mean you'd have to give up your mistress. A lot of men have both, keep each apart from the other, and live in perfect harmony."

Fairley snorted. "Would you give up the joys of a mistress for a missish girl ruling your household and a nursery full of squalling brats?"

Jack shook his head. "Not for a moment." Not even if the wife in question resembled the beautiful Miss Wetherby. Definitely not.

Fairley leaned closer. "Which reminds me—do I hear you've been escorting the exquisite Lady Raby about town?" He waggled his eyebrows up and down a few times, something he clearly thought suggestive of intent.

Jack tapped his nose. "Wouldn't you like to know."

Fairley laughed out loud. "Not just me but the gossipy old harridans who rule over the Ton. They'd all like to know if you've breached the walls there."

"And I suppose if I told you, you'd rush off and spread the story to everyone here." Jack lowered his voice to an urgent whisper. "Hey, did you hear, Broxbourne's scaled the heights of Raby." He finished with a laugh.

"Damn you, Jack, I can never tell if you're gulling me or not."

Jack shrugged. "Take it whichever way you wish."

Fairley's eyes lit up. "Does she? Take it whatever way you wish?" He licked his lips. "I've always had a fancy to broach that lady's defenses. Such as they are. I hear she doesn't fight hard to defend her virtue."

"Lord Raby might have something to say about that, as you're not the most discreet of lovers, even though he keeps to his country estate nowadays. We can all tell which lady you're trailing after, every time. And so can their husbands."

"Probably why I've never tried." Fairley paused. "But you're hardly the soul of discretion yourself, so don't tell me off for my inability to hide how happy I am each time I find a new light o' love. And we all know Raby won't come up to Town and doesn't give a fig what his wife gets up to as long as he has his hounds to ride to."

They were interrupted by the arrival of Sir Simon Westlake

and Lord Arthur Dugdale, each bearing two glasses of lemonade. They sat down.

"I'm determined not to drink while I play this time." Dugdale, a sturdy man whose carefully upswept sandy hair hid a growing bald spot, handed a glass to Jack. "Or I'll be lured into playing too deep and you'll fleece me again. No one with your breeding has a right to be so damned lucky at cards. You're meant to lose sometimes, you know."

Westlake, a lugubrious fellow with the visage of a disappointed undertaker, snorted with laughter. "Staying sober won't help you any, Arthur. Playing you is like taking money from an old lady. In fact, you play like an old lady at an afternoon tea party."

Dugdale huffed. "It's a jolly good thing you and I are old friends or I'd have to call you out for that. At the very least plant you a facer."

Westlake pulled a disbelieving but good-natured face and turned to Jack. "I say, didn't I see you dancing with the most gorgeous girl in the room just now?"

"Did you?" Fairley asked, ears pricking. "What girl was that?"

"Not one to interest any of you," Jack said. "I only managed to dance a few steps with her in the cotillion. She has a bulldog of a mother who refused to allow her to dance with me and a father who's on his uppers, so her face is her only fortune. I suspect the mother knew quite well who I was, and that she's relying on the girl's looks to snare her a rich husband."

"A diamond of the first water, I'd say, by the look of her," Westlake said. "Prettiest girl here tonight. If I were a bit younger and not hog tied to Amelia's apron strings, I'd be out there pressing her for a dance." Eyes suddenly furtive, he glanced at the door. "Amelia's not there, is she, spying on me to make sure I behave myself?"

His three friends laughed in unison, and Jack picked up the new pack of cards that had been left ready on the table by their hosts. "No, she's not, but if it keeps you out of trouble, let's keep the bets to below five guineas."

"Oh, the ignominy of always having to do as my wife says," Westlake moaned, turning back to the table. "You three are wise to steer clear of tying yourselves down to a chit." He paused. "Well, I thought that was what I was doing when I asked Amelia's papa for her hand in marriage, but it turned out that what I was really marrying was a hard-nosed accountant."

Dugdale poked him in the arm. "Methinks you protest too much. You know you like being married to Amelia." He reached into an inner pocket of his frock coat and drew out a snuff box. Having taken a pinch himself and snorted it, he offered the box to his friends.

Jack, who rarely indulged, shook his head, his gaze wandering back to where, from the sound of it, Sir Nicholas was losing heavily. Again. His thoughts returned unbidden to Miss Wetherby and her termagant of a mother. He'd seen that look in the eyes of enough mothers of daughters to recognize it when he saw it—she was a woman for whom only the most advantageous match would do. To his surprise, a tiny pang of pity rose in his breast for Miss Elenora Wetherby. Too many mothers were willing to sacrifice the happiness of their daughters for the cachet of saying they'd snared a title for them. He glanced about the room. How many of the men here possessed unhappy wives? The relief that he would never be father to a daughter washed over him. "Shall I be banker?"

CHAPTER FOUR

A S THE EVENING wore on, Elenora found it increasingly difficult to hold her tongue with her mother. She'd already had the argument she envisioned repeating itself here several times prior to this, her first ball, and on every occasion she had come off the loser. Only this kept her from voicing her objections to this cattle market of a ball.

The argument had begun at home in Penworthy when Mama had announced she'd decided it was high time for Elenora to come out. She'd clearly been expecting her oldest daughter to be ecstatic and had been less than impressed at the reaction she'd received. Elenora, wondering how her mother had lived with her for nearly twenty years yet still didn't know her, had expressed her ardent desire, in rather too explicit terms, to forego such an ordeal.

Mama, in high dudgeon and appealing to Papa for support, had pointed out all the reasons why it would be advantageous not just to her but to the whole family if she acquiesced meekly and found herself a rich husband. Mama had been frustrated and sadly disappointed at what she called Elenora's "selfish obduracy," quickly followed by anger, and had demanded that Papa inform Elenora of her duty with a capital D. Papa had done this with reluctance and retreated into his study, the door of which he'd locked behind him.

The fact that Augusta, three years her junior, and Frances,

only one year below that, had been present had not helped Elenora's argument. Both of her sisters had been not just green with envy but also wildly enthusiastic for her prospective debut on the London social scene. Because, with her married off, they could see it would soon be their turns to be presented and for both of them, perplexingly, this seemed to be their one aim in life. Empty-headed feather-brains that they both were.

So no support had come from either of them. In fact, they'd acted as though they couldn't wait to see the back of her, which had seemed a little unfair. All that had resulted from that first, heated confrontation was that Mama had come down with a megrim and taken to her bed with her much-used smelling salts and Elenora had been left feeling guilty. She hadn't wanted to, because she felt it was Papa's fault she needed to be married off advantageously, and if he hadn't had such an addiction to gambling, she could have remained happily at home in the country forever.

On arrival in London, any hopes Elenora had cherished of appealing to Aunt Penelope had come to nothing, as Papa's only sister was overjoyed to be bringing out not just her own daughter, but her prettiest niece as well, especially as both girls were so similar in appearance. Well, Petunia had inherited her late father's sturdy figure whereas Elenora was more like her tall and slender father, but they were alike in coloring at least, a fact which Aunt Penelope was wont to repeat ad infinitum to anyone who would listen and even those who didn't want to.

Aunt Penelope had been left a rich widow three years ago, something which seemed to rankle with Mama. She had been overjoyed that she could, for a second time, as Petunia already had her wardrobe assembled, traipse around London's best couturiers and mantua makers and shoemakers and hat shops and all the other establishments Mama swore were necessary for a girl making her debut with the Ton. After all, as Mama pointed out more than once, dressing a girl as rewarding as Elenora was delightful.

Elenora had tried again at every opportunity to put forward her reasons for not wishing to come out, especially the amount of money they were spending on gowns and gloves and spencers and cloaks and slippers and hats and… well, too many clothes for one girl, especially one who preferred messing about in the country and shooting with her brothers. And, of course, Mama had to have new gowns as well. Her protesting was to no avail. Aunt Penelope, unfortunately for Elenora, had already offered to help Papa pay for Elenora's gowns, so there was to be no argument.

She'd tried again that very evening, before Aunt Penelope's carriage had arrived at the front door, ready to take them to the Amberley House Ball. Mama had already been in an ecstasy of anticipation. "We're so lucky dear Penelope lives in London for most of the year. She knows everyone who's everyone and we'll reap the benefit of that with invitations from all her friends and acquaintances."

Elenora hadn't shared Mama's enthusiasm and made the mistake of airing her thoughts. Mama had not been amused. And here they were, after midnight now and an excruciating supper in the company of the tubby and middle-aged Lord Shinfield, the recently widowed heir to a dukedom. He featured high on Mama's list of suitable gentlemen, despite his pot belly and nascent bald spot, and the fact that he was three inches shorter than Elenora. She was sure she'd heard Aunt Penelope whisper her congratulations to Mama when he'd edged his way across the ballroom to request a dance.

Elenora had been quite relieved when, as they emerged from the supper room, a younger gentleman arrived to claim the next dance with her. Lord Shinfield, who had regaled Elenora with tales of his seemingly numerous motherless children, and not once asked her a question about herself, glowered at the newcomer, but etiquette required him to stand back and cede the day.

However, this young man had proved no more interesting a

conversation maker than his predecessor—did no one in London have anything worthwhile to talk about? As the dance ended, Elenora wished him a brusque good evening and slunk away into the mêlée of people around the refreshments before Mama could pounce. Surely there must be somewhere she could get away from this crowd of noisy, tipsy if not outright drunk gentlemen and their imperious ladies.

She found herself almost bundled to the side of the room, where a closed oak door beckoned her. Glancing around in case the young man to whom she'd been consigned for the next dance might be approaching, she opened the door and slipped inside.

The oasis of peace that was the room she found herself in surprised her. Only a faint buzz of noise managed to penetrate the heavy door and paneled walls of a large library. Of all the places in Amberley House, this was the one she would have most wanted to find herself in if she'd been asked. What luck. A little sigh escaped her as she surveyed the floor to ceiling shelves of leather-bound books. Heaven on Earth. And nobody knew she was here. Perhaps she could hide in a quiet corner until it was time to return home. With a book.

A coal fire burned with enthusiasm in the large fireplace on the far side of the room, in front of which stood two large wingbacked chairs, facing the heat. If she sat in one of them, with a book of her choice, no one would even see her from the doorway, and in her somewhat limited experience, most people were not fond of the actual books in libraries so wouldn't linger even if they found their way here. Perfect. Now to choose a book.

No easy task. Whoever owned this library had the books ordered by subject, so that was a great help. She navigated her way down the shelves to the right of the door, searching for the history section, if there was one. History was a subject that had always interested her, but she'd long since exhausted the small supply of such books in the library at Penworthy. A library that had been purchased by Papa's father by the linear foot, for the way it looked and not for its content. A library only she and Papa frequented.

The pleasingly large and well-stocked history section resided on the mahogany shelves on the right side of the room. Elenora perused the spines, reading off title after title in an awed whisper as she went, as spoilt for choice as Mama had been last week in the couturiers when choosing the fabric for her new gowns.

She paused, her breath catching in her throat. *Antiquities of Athens Measured and Delineated* by James Stuart and Nicholas Revett. All three volumes, the last published in 1794, when she'd been a little girl, just starting out with an obsession for history the rest of her family couldn't understand. She let her fingers run over the embossed leather of the books' spines. How often had she begged Papa to purchase a copy of these books, offering to forego new gowns for several years should he be so kind as to agree. An easy thing to offer, but all to no avail. And now here were all three, and she had time only to skim their surface. Better not waste any time and start with the first one.

She pulled the first volume from the shelf, and, hugging it to her breast like a beloved child, headed for the leather wingbacked chairs by the fire. It would be so cozy to sit in silence with her feet up on the fender, warming her toes, with the book she'd longed to read for so long in her lap.

She rounded the seats and stopped in her tracks. A man already occupied one of them, and he wasn't discreetly asleep, or even feigning sleep, which would have been polite. Instead, he was looking at her with one dark eyebrow raised in open enquiry and a sleek, sardonic smile on his lips.

Jack Deveril, Lord Broxbourne. The man with the reputation.

"Oh," was all she could think of to say.

He steepled his fingers. "I was wondering whether you intended to purloin that book or come and sit with me before the fire to read it."

"Sit with you? Good heavens, no." Shock made her more honest than she would have liked. "I shall put it back forthwith and leave you to your thoughts, Lord Broxbourne." Damn it.

How dare he be here spoiling her escape from the ball? Spoiling her chance to read this book. She made to turn away, but he shot out a hand and caught hold of her gown.

"Pray don't depart on my account. If you wish to read that book, then please do so."

Oh no. She pulled away from him, expecting him to let go of her gown, as any gentleman would. He didn't. The delicate, and eye-wateringly expensive, fabric tore.

She did stop then, in case the gown tore even more, which would be a disaster and take a lot of explaining. "Please release your hold on me. I must return to the ballroom. You may have the book back and return it to the shelf yourself." She held out the book.

He ignored her.

The book was heavy and holding it out made her arms ache. She drew the book back to her breasts again, holding it like a shield between her and this ridiculous man who seemed to think he could tell her what to do. Just like Mama. Just like everybody she knew. "At least, my lord, unhand me so that I may return the book myself."

He nodded his head at the other chair. "Nonsense. I'm bored and you interest me. Sit down and tell me why you chose that particular book, when there are others of a more feminine taste over there. Novels. I never met a woman yet who didn't like a romantic novel."

Well, he'd met one now. She didn't say so though.

She didn't move. "That is really none of your business. Now please let me go before someone comes."

He didn't let go, a rather wicked smile lighting up his face, as though he were finding this whole thing entertaining. "Afraid of the consequences, are you? You know you like me. I could tell from the look on your face when your erstwhile mother lied to me that your dance card was full."

On sounder ground now, Elenora could answer this one. "You mistake me, my lord. I was not pleased you'd asked for a dance because I liked you, but because you are so unsuitable a partner. And if you had secured a dance with me, that would have been one less dance for me with someone my mother sees as a possible son-in-law."

He had unusually dark eyes, in which the dancing flames of the fire flickered, giving him an undoubtedly devilish appearance. Hadn't Mr. Brightwell said his nickname was Satan? Lord Satan, would that be? And his family name, Deveril, was close enough to the word 'devil' to be more than a coincidence. Perhaps.

He laughed. "Are you telling me you wanted to dance with me because I'm considered an unsuitable match? Don't you want to be married to some scion of a noble house?" His laugh hardened. "To save your family from ruin?"

Indignation surged up through Elenora's body at his insinuation, and she took another step, tugging at her gown. More worrying ripping followed. "My family is not ruined, and it is very rude of you to imply that." Lying didn't come easily to her.

Broxbourne's lips curled in a mirthless smile. "Your father is in the card room now trying to win back everything he's lost, writing vowels out to those he owes money to. And your brothers are no better, if smaller losers. Don't think this has gone unnoticed."

Heat washed up Elenora, flushing her from her breasts to her cheeks, and with it, anger. "I must point out that it is very ill bred of you to draw this to my attention. It is not the done thing to speak of such things in public. You might be a lord, but you are clearly not a gentleman… my lord." Obnoxious man. How dare he speak to her like this?

She looked back down at her gown, rage bubbling inside her. What she would have liked to have done was punch him. Matthew had taught her how to box a few summers since, and she'd once knocked him out. How she'd relish doing that to this dreadfully rude man. How she'd like to wipe that smug, self-satisfied, I'm-cleverer-than-you look off his face.

However, she had other things to think of, like how she was

going to hide this rip in her lovely gown from Mama. From everyone in the ballroom who would really have something to stare at if she emerged like this. Then she remembered that, in her reticule, thanks to Mama, she had a needle and thread, a hussif, for just such an incident. Well, not an incident of this actual sort, more perhaps a catching of a gown on something sharp. She could mend it herself with a few stitches.

She looked down. A lot of stitches. And stitches were not her forté. "None of this is any of your business. You ask far too many questions about things that have nothing to do with you. And you need to release your hold on my gown, my lord, or… or I'll scream."

"And have people rush in here and find you in such a compromising position?"

She opened her mouth to speak, but words failed her, so she shut it again. How it pained her to admit he was right. She shouldn't be alone in a room with a strange man, still less one who had ripped her gown and didn't seem to care. Mama would say she was ruined which was most unfair as apart from the rip, nothing at all had happened.

His eyes narrowed. "You are a strange girl indeed. Not wanting to be married, and choosing this particular book." Here he pointed his free hand at her book, still clasped in defense against her breast. "Out of all the books you could have selected you chose one on the antiquities of Greece."

"That's because I haven't read it."

"Nor have most girls your age. No, I doubt any girl your age has. In fact, I'd wager I could count the number of women of any age who have read it on the fingers of one hand. What makes you want to read it? It's hard going, you know."

"You've read it?" Elenora's limited experience of young men, which mainly meant of her two older brothers and their friends, had not led her to assume any of them read any books at all. Not even those up at Oxford, as Matthew had been until recently. Her surprise at his claim to have read it distracted her from his slur on womankind for the moment.

He nodded. "Of course. My father bought me this particular volume when I was twelve. I've read them all."

"Oh."

A smile curled his lips. "No need to look so surprised. You can't be as surprised as me, finding a girl as pretty as you are raiding my father's library and choosing a book describing in great detail the antiquities of Athens and beyond."

"Your father?" If this was his father's library it must also be his father's house, and his father must be the intimidating white haired old gentleman who had greeted them on their arrival. Lord Amberley. The Earl of Amberley in fact.

As he nodded, she managed to gather her wits. "I can see, my lord, that you have fallen into the trap of assuming all young ladies have the same shallow aims in life—namely playing the pianoforté, painting and finding themselves a rich husband."

"And you do not aim for any of that?"

She shook her head with more than necessary vehemence. "Not at all. My mama and sisters will tell you that my musical skills are appalling. I cannot even sing in tune. And as for my artistic abilities—well, if I have to draw something historic, then I can do it, but young ladies aren't schooled for anything more than demure watercolors, which I abhor. And I do not wish to be married—ever."

"Why don't you sit down?" He gestured to the seat opposite his. "That was what you had in mind when you came in here, was it not?"

She compressed her lips. "You are right. It was. But I did not for a moment think I would be sharing this room with anyone else."

"It is my father's library. Where else would you like me to sit?"

She perched herself on the edge of the second seat and he at last released her torn skirt. "In the card room, I think. Yes, that would be perfect. Perhaps you might go there now and we can forget we ever met?"

He leaned toward her and out of instinct she drew back. "How can I possibly forget I've met you, Miss Wetherby? I don't think I've ever met a young lady quite like you before. One so charmingly pretty, but with no intention of marrying and a penchant for dusty books."

She frowned. Was he referring to her blonde good looks, the bane of her life? Best to ignore this remark. "If you don't mind then," she said, opening the book on her lap to the dedication to the king, "I'll get on with reading. I daresay I have a good three hours before all the guests depart, and I can read a lot in that time. I prefer silence while I'm reading."

He burst out laughing. "And do you not think someone will start to wonder where you are? I daresay at this very moment your mother is scouring the ballroom wondering where her prize sacrifice on the bonfire of her family has got to. She's probably even gone into the card room to tell your father you've vanished. Your brothers and your aunt are even now joining the search."

"I didn't think of that."

"I can see that."

She closed the book with a sigh. "Then I had best return your book to you and go back to the ballroom. No doubt my mother has found several more prospective husbands for me to meet and have trample on my toes." She laid the book on the table between the chairs and stood up. Her gown flapped where it had been torn. Oh no. She'd have to patch it first and hope no one would notice.

Broxbourne rose to his feet as well. He towered over her, a distinctly masculine presence so unlike those of her much shorter brothers. He nodded at her skirt. "I see you hadn't thought of that, either."

She fished in her reticule. "I have thread and a needle. Mama says always to be prepared wherever you go." And the needle was even threaded, ready for use.

He held out his hand. "Here, give it to me. It'll be easier for me to sew it than you, and after all, it *is* my fault it's ripped."

Without thinking, she handed him the needle and thread. How was it a man such as he could sew? How unexpected. Especially considering she was so bad at sewing herself.

He dropped to one knee beside her, head bent, and began to sew, using small, neat stitches—better than any she could have done herself, particularly whilst wearing the offending garment. Quite at odds with his reputation.

The rip was large, though, and he was only halfway through it when the library door swung open and three people came in. Mama, Papa and the white haired old gentleman who'd welcomed them to his ball. Broxbourne's own father, the Earl of Amberley. Behind them, a fourth figure loomed, staring through the open doorway. Lady Routledge.

Elenora's head snapped around as her eyes widened in shock. Not quite so much, though, as the eyes of her audience.

CHAPTER FIVE

"ELENORA!" MAMA'S VOICE rose to a horrified squeak, as Lady Routledge almost elbowed past her and into the library and Papa hurriedly slammed the door behind them all.

"Mama!" Elenora's hand shot to her mouth and unwanted heat rose to her cheeks.

Oh no. This was too terrible for words. And that condescending old harpy who'd looked down her aristocratic nose at them and cast aspersions about Penworthy as well. What could possibly be worse than being caught in what was undoubtedly a compromising position? Being caught by that arbiter of the Ton, that was what.

Lord Amberley's face purpled as though he were in danger of suffering apoplexy as he glared at his son. "Jack!"

"Father." To do him credit, Broxbourne didn't get up, but continued sewing. "Give me a minute or two. I'm just mending Miss Wetherby's gown."

Admirable sangfroid in this awkward situation.

"What's going on here?" Papa asked, coming farther into the library, his accusing gaze snaking between Elenora's blazing hot face and Broxbourne still on his knees in front of her.

"M-my gown tore," Elenora tried, twitching with desperation to move away from the man on his knees in front of her. If before she'd longed for a hole to swallow her up, that had been nothing compared with right now.

"It doesn't look as though you were doing nothing," Lady Routledge almost crowed. "You look as though we've surprised you in a tryst." She couldn't have looked more delighted if she'd tried. She'd have been the sort to sit watching the French aristocracy going to the guillotine and congratulating herself as each head fell into the waiting basket.

Mama turned anguished eyes on Papa. Elenora, unable to put up with Broxbourne's attentions any longer, snatched her gown away from his nimble fingers, the needle left hanging loose by its thread. Her unavoidable eye for the smallest detail had her admiring his stitchwork. "Nothing whatsoever has happened here," she tried, keeping her voice as calm as she could but uncomfortably aware that the heat of her face, which had to rival Lord Amberley's, might be giving the lie to this.

"My boy," Lord Amberley said, his voice a deep rumble replete with heavy threat, "This young lady is of good breeding. You can't go bringing your back street morals into my ballroom."

"This isn't your ballroom, it's your library," Broxbourne said, with some asperity, as he rose to his feet. "And I have not brought my 'back street morals', as you call them, here. All I was doing was assisting Miss Wetherby in her hour of need."

Lady Routledge stepped forward like an actress taking center stage. "And how exactly did Miss Wetherby's dress become ripped?" She fixed Elenora with a gimlet stare.

Elenora swallowed, her mind wiped clean of all coherent thought. She'd always found it impossible to lie, and a lie was what was needed here, but one would not come.

"She—" began Broxbourne, only to be silenced by an imperious hand.

"I am asking Miss Wetherby," Lady Routledge intoned, sounding like a judge about to pass sentence of death, or how Elenora imagined one might sound.

Her eyes going from her mother's face to her father's, Elenora groped blindly for some excuse. Her parents stared back at her, but their expressions gave her no confidence that she would be believed.

Lady Routledge took a step closer. "Did Lord Broxbourne tear your dress, Miss Wetherby?"

Caught like a mouse in a trap, all Elenora could do was give the tiniest nod.

"Oh, my dear, sweet, innocent child." Mama ran forward and enfolded Elenora in her arms so tightly she almost choked the breath from her. "She's been violated by this odious man. I don't care if he's your son, my lord, he's a vile cad. A rake. He's defiled my daughter's honor."

"Mama, he didn't…" Elenora tried, her face embedded in her mother's fragrant shoulder.

"Is this true? Lord Amberley blustered. "You ripped Miss Wetherby's gown, Jack?"

Elenora couldn't see Broxbourne now, clasped as she was to her mother's heaving bosom, but she could hear him. He sounded as shocked as she was. "No, well, yes, I suppose I did, but not the way—"

"Then you must marry her," his father bellowed, turning a darker shade of puce, if that were possible. "Make an honest woman of the chit. There's nothing for it. You have no other way out of this." Was there a touch of satisfaction in his tone?

Elenora wriggled free of her mother's hold.

"I agree," Lady Routledge boomed. "Announce their betrothal forthwith and you'll be able to avoid the scandal this will cause."

"I can rely on your discretion, Horatia?" Lord Amberley said, taking Lady Routledge's hands in both of his.

"You can."

"Then offer for Miss Wetherby forthwith," Lord Amberley snapped, glaring at his son.

Broxbourne heaved a deep, resigned sigh. "Miss Wetherby, would you be so kind as to accept my offer of marriage?" He had the distinct look of someone to whom the utterance of this sentence brought pain.

"There," Mama said, unmistakable triumph in her voice. "That's settled, then. They are betrothed."

Elenora stamped her foot. "But I don't agree. I refuse his offer. You can't make me marry someone I don't want to marry, and I won't do it."

Everyone stared at her, including Lord Broxbourne, whose expression could almost have been described as comical, so full of surprised shock was it.

"Elenora," Mama fairly gasped out on a strangled breath. "You don't understand the gravity of your situation. You have been surprised in a most compromising position with a man whose reputation goes before him. Your only way out of this is through marriage." She shot a glare at Broxbourne. "To the man who compromised you, distasteful as that might be to your family."

Elenora wasn't fooled by this outburst. The steely glint in Mama's eyes betrayed her satisfaction that Elenora had managed to snare herself an earl's son at her first ball. A man with a considerable fortune.

She clenched her fists. "But I don't want to marry anyone." Despite a longing for self-control, Elenora's voice rose in desperation, the distinct impression of being carried along on a wave of triumph by her mother swamping her. "I don't understand. Four hours ago you didn't want me even dancing with Lord Broxbourne and now you want me to marry him?"

Mama shook her head. "Nonsense. Marriage is quite different to what I'd feared he might be after from you. And clearly I was correct in my assumptions. But as luck would have it, he has been caught in his vile addiction and you have been saved from further degradation." She paused, her brows knitting. "You have been saved, haven't you? He didn't do anything more than tear your gown... did he?"

Despite her aversion to lying, an awful longing to tell her mother Lord Broxbourne had done something much worse than tear her dress swept over Elenora. Just to shock her. But shocking her like that would only make this situation worse. If that were possible.

"No," she said. "He did nothing else."

Lady Routledge, who still had hold of Lord Amberley's hands, nodded firmly. "You were lucky enough to have been in time to save your daughter from a fate worse than death, Fanny. And in the process have gained her a far better match than you could have hoped for, for the daughter of a simple baronet." Was that a hint of resentment mixed in with the satisfaction of having witnessed the situation?

However… "Papa is not a simple baronet," Elenora burst out, fury getting the better of her. "He's a wonderful baronet."

Papa, whose part so far had been negligible and whose appearance could have been described as flustered, had the grace to look flattered and happy for a moment at this extravagant praise.

"Be quiet, Elenora," Mama ordered. "This is not for you to interfere in." Nor Papa, so it seemed.

"But it's my future you're talking about."

"And that will be decided by your father and me." What she meant was by her. Papa would have no say in the matter at all.

Elenora turned to Lord Broxbourne. "Please explain that nothing happened and that you don't want to marry me."

He shrugged, an annoying twinkle in his eye. "I don't think it's up to me."

What was he saying? Did he not care? Was he about to allow himself to be bullied into a betrothal to someone he scarcely knew? Someone he'd been so rude to so couldn't possibly even like? Was he mad? The suspicion that he might be rose. Was she to be forced into marriage with someone who belonged in Bedlam?

"You are absolutely right when you say it's not up to you," Lord Amberley, whose snow-white hair had somehow become wildly disarranged, declared. Had he been running his fingers through it? No, he couldn't have been. Lady Routledge still had his hands firmly in hers. Did hair truly stand on end by itself, then, when someone was shocked? Its state was very diverting.

"Told you," Broxbourne said to Elenora. "You'd best consider yourself an engaged young lady."

Elenora might have been lost for words had she been less determined. "But you don't love me. I don't think you even like me. Why are you letting them force you into marriage?"

Her mother snorted like an angry bull. "Elenora! Cease from this. Of course, he likes you or he wouldn't have importuned you so violently." She swung round on Papa. "Nicholas, take your daughter and keep her silent. She can have no part in this."

What? Elenora opened her mouth to continue complaining, but Mama's angry glare silenced her.

Papa, ever obedient to Mama, wrapped a commiserating arm around Elenora's shoulders. "Come over here with me. We mustn't interfere with your mother's arrangements. You really will be ruined if this comes out and you're not engaged to Broxbourne, you know."

"But he's a rake, Papa." Surely he didn't want her forced into marriage with a rake?

"There, there." He patted her arm. "Don't take on so. I'm sure you'll rub along quite well." Always one for the easy way out. How typical.

Elenora pressed her lips together. This was terrible. Her very first ball and nothing had gone right. She'd known in her heart that it wouldn't. When did anything ever go right for her? And now everything and everyone was conspiring against her. Even Lord Broxbourne, who couldn't be any happier than her at the outcome of this evening's events. If only she'd sent him away and sewn up her gown herself. Then she could have told them she'd ripped it on a table or chair and no one would have been any the wiser.

"Well?" Mama was saying to Lord Amberley. "Do we have an agreement?"

"He'll marry her or be damned," the elderly earl snapped, as though his son had offered up a major objection to his proposed engagement instead of quietly acquiescing.

JACK, WHO'D GONE over to the fire, turned and leaned against the mantelpiece, the flames warming his backside admirably. "I've said I will, haven't I?" Why on earth were all these people treating him as though he hadn't done the right thing and said he'd marry the girl. Not that he intended for it to get any further than a betrothal. But for now, he could agree to an engagement—one that could be called off in a few months' time, once everyone had forgotten about this incident.

His father stared at him out of angry, dark eyes that, had Jack but known it, were the exact image of his own. Was that a hint of triumph in them as well? The Old Man had been trying for long enough to get his son and heir married off. Perhaps he thought this way was the best he could hope for and that the daughter of a minor country baronet with a gambling problem was better than an actress or an ageing countess.

"Good, then," the earl said with a harrumphing snort. "We'll get the contracts drawn up."

Oh God. The contracts. Well, he should have been expecting that. And the girl's mother would no doubt want to boast about having secured an earl's heir for her daughter. There was no way this engagement was going to be kept quiet. But that still didn't mean they couldn't break it after a discreet amount of time, especially as Miss Wetherby, Elenora, didn't seem at all pleased by it. She'd be as pleased as he was to call it all off at some point, wouldn't she?

He directed a somewhat hostile stare at her, his male pride more than a little piqued by her confusing attitude. Why on earth was she protesting so loudly about becoming engaged to him? Wasn't that something most of the Ton's predatory mamas would have gone out of their way to obtain for their daughters? The sensation that he'd somehow been insulted by her turning up her nose at him arose. Was he really that abhorrent? Every other woman he encountered didn't seem to think he was.

Lady Routledge, a woman he had long nurtured a strong dislike for, smiled with smug satisfaction. And what did *she* have against him? He was beginning to feel a bit hemmed in by enemy forces. He'd never allowed himself to betray his dislike for Lady Routledge, so she could have no idea of his feelings. If the nosy old woman hadn't been passing the library door as Sir Nicholas, his wife, and his own father, had been entering, this whole thing could have been passed over with much less of a kerfuffle. Trust her to be in at his perceived downfall.

However, he smiled back at her with careless grace, as though this was just another normal day for him. Above all things, he had to put on a good show. Though why he'd grabbed Miss Wetherby by her gown in the first place he now had no idea. He nurtured no amorous feelings for her. Did he? She was just an ordinary chit of a girl, too young by far for him, and yet… he couldn't deny something about her intrigued him. In particular, her extreme disgust at having to become engaged to him. It might be quite fun to play along with this.

He abandoned the fireplace and approached where she was standing with her father. "Miss Wetherby." He made a flamboyant bow, calculated to impress any lady. Not her. She regarded him out of stony blue eyes that held more than a little annoyance. "Perhaps the first time I asked you, you formed the wrong impression of me, and considered that I was only asking you out of deference to the wishes of our parents. That is not so. I will ask you again, and do it better this time." He benefitted her with his most engaging smile. "Will you be so kind as to do me the honor of accepting my offer of marriage? This time?" Prettily put. He could do pretty when he had a mind to it.

Her nose wrinkled. Yes, wrinkled. Damn it, but the chit was going to turn him down again. "No thank you, Lord Broxbourne. I would prefer not to."

"Elenora!" This was a chorus from her mother and Lady Routledge. The girl's father remained mute. Perhaps he agreed with her.

"Well," Elenora snapped. "In all honesty, I have no wish to be married at all, if anyone ever took any notice of anything I have to say."

"Nonsense," her mother said. "If you don't agree to this you'll be ruined and then no one will marry you."

"Good," retorted his prospective bride. "That's exactly what I want."

Realization began to dawn upon Jack, and with it the germ of an idea. He turned to the other three. "Might I have just a few minutes alone with Miss Wetherby?"

They all regarded him as if he'd asked to take her to his bed for a few minutes.

Sir Nicholas came to his senses first. "I don't see why not. He's been alone with her already. What more can he do?"

Lady Wetherby opened her mouth, undoubtedly to point out where he was going wrong here, but Lady Routledge interrupted her. "A splendid idea. Let the two of them come to an understanding. We can wait outside and make sure no one disturbs them." She held up a gloved finger. "Five minutes. That is all."

And before anyone could object, she herded Elenora's parents out of the library.

As soon as the door closed behind them, Jack turned back to Elenora. "Dare I enquire as to why you find marriage to me so distasteful?"

Her eyes widened as though he'd asked a ridiculous question. "Many reasons, not least the fact that I don't know you. And that I have no intention of marrying anyone."

He felt a smile trying to twitch the corners of his mouth. "So, I am not repugnant to you, just the thought of marriage to anyone is?"

She nodded. "You are not repugnant at all, I can assure you. Were I a romantic sort of a girl, I might be swayed by your good looks." She paused. "Even though you are really quite old."

"Ouch. I'm not as old as all that, you know."

She raised her light eyebrows. "I suppose you can't help your age."

Now he did laugh. "But you seem to forget that your mother has brought you to London to find you a husband. Did you not think to inform her of your aversion to marriage before you set out, and thus save her some time and expense?"

"Of course I did, but as usual, she took no notice. And my sisters are no help because they are straining at the bit to have a season of their own and find themselves empty-headed young men who they mistakenly think might make them happy."

"And this is your first ball of the season?"

"It is. I wish it could be my last."

The germ of an idea began to solidify. "What if we could dispose of the necessity for you to be found a husband?"

Interest flickered in those candid blue eyes—not quite so stony now. "And how would 'we' do that? I take it you are offering your assistance?"

"I might be. Let me explain. Sit down in front of the fire again." He gestured at the two wingbacked chairs.

Much to his surprise, she offered no resistance and sat herself down. This time, instead of perching on the edge, she sat back in her chair, staring at him out of oddly intense eyes. They really were the loveliest shade of blue. If he'd been minded to, he could have lost himself in them all too easily.

He took the other seat. "Do you always stare so?"

A little smile touched her lips. "I'm afraid I do. I don't like to look someone in the eye. I find it very difficult. Mama taught me to look someone in the mouth instead—so much easier. You will see that what I'm really looking at is your lips. Does it discomfort you?"

He shrugged. "Not now you explain it."

"So, what is it you were going to suggest? I fear we have only a minute or two left before my parents and yours return."

He steepled his fingers, something he was wont to do in times of stress. And yes, this was stressful. He needed to tread carefully. "Your parents have brought you to London because they wish you to be married to a rich man, preferably with a title, who will save their family fortunes out of obligation for receiving such a beautiful, but portionless wife. True?"

She nodded. At least she seemed to have got over her initial offended huff when he'd first mentioned her father's problems. "True."

"But you don't wish to marry at all. I have no idea why, and that is your own private matter. However, if you were engaged to someone, they would have to stop looking for a husband for you. Also true?"

Her eyes narrowed. His intimation must be sinking in. She nodded. "True." She strung the word out as though thoughtful.

He smiled. "My father, and my mother, would like me to marry and provide an heir for the earldom. I'm their only son and they view my profligate ways with distaste. I generally steer clear of Amberley House because I want to avoid them badgering me to find some blue-blooded young woman without a brain in her head to marry. So long as she has good childbearing hips, my mother will be content. Brains do not count with her."

Elenora's blue eyes flashed in a rather becoming manner. "Let me tell you right now that I'm not providing you with an heir."

The thought of making one with her proved a tad distracting. She was very pretty, after all. He shook his head to clear it of that image. "And nor do I want you to. But my father is clearly rather pleased with me tonight for having put you in a compromising position. I know that look on his face. He is pretending anger because he thinks he has me backed into a corner I cannot escape from. Marriage."

A frown crinkled her brow. "So, are you saying that if we both agree to an engagement, it will be mutually beneficial?"

"Exactly. My parents will be silenced for a while. Yours will cease to push you into the arms of young men who are your intellectual inferiors." Which was most of the men at present dancing at the ball.

She nodded, and a slow smile crept across her face. "I think that's an excellent idea. But what do we do when the wedding day comes around? Don't think for an instant that my mother will want a long engagement. She'll be so eager to get me up the aisle she'll be behind us both with a pitchfork. And I suspect your parents might be the same, from what you've said."

"We shall insist on a long engagement, bolstered by the fact that I intend to settle your father's debts straightaway, as they seem to be of most pressing importance to your family. Once those are settled, I think your parents will be more willing to wait for the actual wedding. When they ask, we'll say we both want time to get to know one another. And then, a discreet few months from now, by mutual consent we'll quietly abandon the engagement, having discovered we are incompatible. How does that sound?"

This time she looked into his eyes. "Like an excellent idea. I agree. Although I fear I ought to point out that from the financial point of view, you appear to be going to end up out of pocket."

He shook his head. "That's of little matter to me. I have sufficient blunt to cover the debts of many of the men out there on the dance floor. And I feel it will be worth it to have my parents drop the subject of my marriage. At least for a while. It is my mother's constant complaint when I see her. When she sees you, she will be content."

Elenora nodded slowly, her lips pressed together. "Very well. I accept your offer. Now we'd better tell our parents it's all settled, I suppose."

CHAPTER SIX

T HE THUD OF running feet woke Elenora from her sleep. Two people landed with a thud on her bed. She opened her eyes.

Bright winter sunshine was streaming in through the gaps between the heavy brocade curtains of Cousin Petunia's bedroom, illuminating the excited faces of her two younger sisters. Both of them were already up and dressed, wearing dimity frocks that had once been Elenora's. Papa, who found it as difficult to resist his daughters as he did his wife, had, in a moment of weakness, given in to the two girls pestering to accompany the husband-hunting party to Aunt Penelope's house. Although, of course, they were too young to attend any of the balls and soirées Mama had lined up for Elenora.

"You're awake!" squealed Frances, the younger of the two, a slight fifteen-year-old whose long brown hair hung almost to her waist. Her crowning glory, Papa was wont to say, whenever he emerged from his study and showed any interest in his brood.

Elenora pushed herself partly upright on her pillows. "Well, I am now. What time is it?" Hard to be annoyed with these two.

Augusta, the elder by barely twelve months, bounced up and down. "I believe it's gone ten. We couldn't wait any longer to find out about the ball. We just had to wake you. Mama is still in bed and you know what Papa's like. He'll have spent the entire evening in the card room."

Not quite.

Elenora rubbed the sleep out of her eyes. What time had she gone to bed? After four, that was certain, and as bed had not brought sleep for some time, the thought that she could have done with remaining undisturbed until at least midday arose. But she loved her younger sisters, despite having little in common with them. "Where is my wrap?"

In the other bed, Petunia pulled the covers over her head and groaned. She too must be as tired as Elenora.

Frances bounded off the bed and seized Elenora's favorite shawl from where it lay spread over a chair near the window. "Here it is. Now put it on and tell us all about the ladies' gowns."

"And how handsome the men were."

"And who you danced with."

"And what you had for supper."

"Can't you talk a bit more quietly?" Petunia's muffled voice emerged from her covers, but not her face. "Some of us are trying to sleep."

Elenora wrapped the shawl about her shoulders. After all, this was February, and as no one had been in as yet to light the fire, a chill hung in the air. Neither Augusta nor Frances appeared to have noticed though. She surveyed the two eager faces, staring at her in anticipation. What should she tell them? "I suppose the ball was quite nice. Not nearly so jolly as the ones at the Assembly Rooms in Winchester. Much more formal, I'd say." Not that she'd ever enjoyed her outings to the Assembly Rooms, but at least there she'd known a few other people.

Both girls assumed disappointed expressions. "Gowns," Augusta said with a sigh. "You must have seen lots of beautiful gowns."

Elenora sighed. She hadn't really been looking at the gowns, but she'd better make something up for her sisters. "Lady Routledge's gown was gorgeous." But what color had it been? No idea. Better make something up. The only gown that sprang to mind from last night was the one worn by Lady Raby in that deep red. A red that had seemed a little improper, especially when combined with the sinuous way she danced. "She had a crimson gown with gold embroidery, and gold jewelry."

"Was it a terrible press?" Frances asked, bouncing a bit more, presumably having given up on extracting gown descriptions from her sister. "And did you dance every dance? With handsome young men? Were there lots of handsome young men?"

"Officers in their regimentals?" Augusta clasped her hands together. She'd been allowed to attend the Assembly Rooms in Winchester, so she'd met a few young men such as these. "I do love their red uniforms. So dashing."

Elenora bit her lip. If only her sisters would leave her alone. Now she was properly awake, all she wanted to do was think about the events of last night, and how somehow she'd ended up an engaged young lady. To the heir of an earl. Not something she'd expected to happen on her very first outing into society. Not something she was even pleased about. How had she allowed him to talk her into this sham engagement? Was she a fool? Had she had too much to drink? "Yes, yes and no. Everyone who's anyone was there, I think. And the men Mama wanted me to dance with were definitely not handsome. Rich and titled, but not handsome."

Frances's face fell. "Were the handsome men not rich and titled then?" She sounded deeply disappointed.

Augusta ignored her. "Was the Prince of Wales there?" She liked to follow the court news.

Had he been? Elenora had no idea. She shook her head. "No, he wasn't."

Augusta pulled a face. "Imagine if he'd danced with you. How exciting that would have been."

Elenora frowned. "I have heard he's very old and corpulent now, so no, I would not have liked to have danced with him and refuse to imagine it as it's repellent to me."

Augusta gave a little screech. "Ellie! You can't say things about the Prince! He'll be king himself one day and no one should say bad things about him."

"Oh, do stop talking about the Prince of Wales," Frances said. "I agree with Ellie that dancing with him would have been awful. Like dancing with a fat old uncle. Dreadful, and I would have said no to him. But do tell us who you did dance with, Ellie dear. Weren't any of them even a little bit handsome? Were they all titled? And most importantly, were they rich?"

"Most important would surely be, did she like them?" Augusta snapped, clearly miffed at her sisters' disdain for her hero.

The covers in the other bed shook. "Do be quiet, can't you?"

Everyone ignored Petunia.

"No, I didn't like them," Elenora managed to insert into her sisters' conversation. "And now I'd like to get up. Frannie, can you ring for my maid, please, to come and help me."

Augusta gave a deep sigh. "You are a sad disappointment to us, Ellie. I'm sure when I go to my first ball I'll take notice of everything I see and come back and give Frannie a detailed account. And I'm sure I'll meet some handsome young men to dance with. I sometimes wonder if you go around with your eyes closed."

Frannie was tugging the bell pull. "Me too. I can't wait for it to be my turn. You're so lucky being the oldest. Well… the oldest girl."

Augusta seemed to recall something. "Were Joly and Matt there? I heard Mama and Papa talking about Matt having been sent down from Oxford."

"Again," put in Frannie. "They were very specific that it was again."

Elenora pushed the bedclothes back. "They were. I danced with some of their friends who I'm sad to say were also not handsome enough for you two. Now, off you go, because I think I can hear Agatha's footsteps outside in the corridor."

She was right about the footsteps, but when the door opened it was not to reveal her maid, but rather her mother and Aunt Penelope, who looked to be all of a flutter.

Aunt Penelope was fully dressed in a demure gray gown, but

Mama swept into the room resplendent in a purple silk peignoir over her nightgown. "Elenora, have you been telling your sisters all about your success last night?"

In the other bed Petunia threw back her covers and sat up, hair awry. "I give up. Why don't we invite all the servants in here too and have a party?"

She was again ignored.

"Success?" Augusta, who'd been about to leave the room, reversed at speed and swung around. Frannie had no need to as she'd not moved from the bell pull.

Aunt Penelope clasped her hands under her chin and seemed to swell like a bullfrog in the pond at home in Penworthy. As if she'd had something to do with it herself.

This morning, Mama had a definite cat-in-the-dairy-finding-a-big-pot-of-cream look about her. "I see you've been too shy to do so. Bless you, darling girl. You should be shouting it from the rooftops. Well, not quite, but I think you know what I mean."

Augusta closed the door and fixed Elenora with an accusing stare. "What success, Ellie? Did you neglect to mention something?"

Elenora turned her back on them and whipped the curtains open with unnecessary force.

"Don't pull them down, Elenora," Aunt Penelope said, ever with an eye open for the safety of her furnishings. "Open them gently."

"Is anyone going to tell us?" Frannie asked. "Or do we have to guess?"

"We know she didn't dance with the Prince of Wales," Augusta put in with a sniff. "So what could it possibly be that would trump that?"

Mama positively swelled with pride. "Of course, it's not something like that. Although it would have been an honor had he been there and chosen to dance with your sister. No, girls, you see before you an engaged young lady, who one day will be a countess, no less."

Augusta's and Frannie's mouths fell open in unison.

Aunt Penelope let out a chortle of glee.

Petunia, who'd been more than a little disgusted last night on being told of her cousin's precocious triumph, as Mama had put it when they told her about it, harumphed.

Mama glowed with pride.

Elenora scowled. "I can see right down your throat, Gussie."

Augusta shut her mouth. "Don't call me Gussie. You know how I hate that."

Frannie, ever the romantic, clasped her hands. "A countess? She's going to be a real countess?"

Mama and Aunt Penelope nodded in unison.

The door opened yet again, this time to let in Agatha, Elenora's maid who not so long ago had been just a housemaid at Penworthy. Her cheeks shone as though she'd been hurrying. Seeing how crowded the room already was, she dropped a curtsy to Mama and Aunt Penelope and remained by the door, her fingers twiddling with her apron. "Miladies."

"Come in, Agatha," Elenora said. "I'd like to get dressed if the rest of my family will give me leave to. They seem to think my bedroom is some kind of Assembly Room."

"It's my bedroom, actually," Petunia said, but was yet again ignored.

"You're really, truly getting married?" Augusta at last managed to enunciate. Perhaps shock that her awkward older sister had snared a man first time out had rendered her mute for a moment. That she thought her odd, Elenora was well aware.

"Married, miss?" Agatha echoed. "Ooh, that's proper good news." And she too took on the demeanor of someone who'd lost a farthing and found a guinea. Why was everyone so overjoyed at the news? It was a good thing it wasn't a real engagement.

"Just engaged," Elenora said, beginning to feel a tiny bit anxious about all this unwanted attention. "A long engagement, as we hardly know each other."

"Nonsense." She might have known Mama would take this

attitude. "The sooner the two of you are married, the better. Your papa will be sorting out the marriage contract this morning, and then we can set a date."

Not if Elenora could help it. Or Lord Broxbourne. The urge to burst out laughing washed over Elenora. What would her affianced have to say if he were a fly on the wall right here? He might feel his liberty threatened, that was for certain. She was feeling threatened herself. Mama could be like an advancing army when roused—an unstoppable advancing army of one.

Augusta stamped her foot. Was there a hint of jealousy there? "But who is she marrying, Mama? You've neglected to tell us the most interesting bit."

Mama gave a little tinkle of laughter. "Oh, I had quite forgot that none of you know. She is to marry Viscount Broxbourne, the heir of the Earl of Amberley."

A rather stunned silence fell. After a moment or two, Augusta narrowed her eyes. "But isn't he a dreadful rake?"

How on earth did Augusta know this? Elenora had hardly known it herself and she was the one coming out. But then, Augusta had always been the one of the five sisters to know everything that was going on at Penworthy. So why would she not have somehow soaked up the Town gossip over the last few weeks here in London?

"Just a little, but he clearly wishes to settle down now," Aunt Penelope said, almost as if she believed it.

As if anyone could be "just a little bit a rake." Ridiculous.

"He's definitely a rake," Elenora said. "He compromised me, and now he has to marry me. Mama and his father have made him offer for me."

"Elenora!" This was Mama and Aunt Penelope in unison.

Mama gathered Augusta and Frances to her and started ushering them toward the door. "Ignore her, girls, she doesn't know what she's saying."

"You were compromised?" Augusta asked, gawping over her shoulder. "What did he do to you?"

"Did he kiss you?" Frances, this time, but by now Mama was pushing the two of them out of the door. She closed it with a bang behind them and rounded on Elenora.

"Did you have to tell them that? The fewer people who know the circumstances of your engagement, the better." Her gaze fell on Agatha, who was busy trying to make herself look small and inoffensive beside the wardrobe. "And as for you, if I hear a word of this anywhere I'll know you've spoken of it below stairs. Consider yourself sworn to silence."

Agatha, shrinking still further into the wardrobe, bobbed another curtsy, eyes firmly down. "Yes, milady. Of course, milady."

"Mama." Elenora wrapped her shawl more closely around her and wished she had slippers on her cold bare feet. "I wasn't going to tell Gussie and Frannie anything about being engaged. I wish you hadn't. And I thought we were only engaged because of what people would say when they find out I've been compromised. Now you're saying no one should know. I don't understand. If they don't know, why do I have to be engaged?"

Mama shivered. "Never you mind. No need for you to bother your head with all of this. It's too full already with the books you insist on reading."

Aunt Penelope nodded. "She's quite right. Nothing to concern yourself with, my girl." She waved a hand at the empty fireplace. "This room is too cold. Why hasn't the fire been lit? It's winter, for goodness sake. Whose job is it to light the fires? Agatha, ring that bell please and we'll have a maid up here to light it straightaway. Insupportable that my daughter and my niece should have a cold bedroom to wake up in."

Mama nodded at poor timid Agatha. "And you can start getting my daughter dressed, while Lady Dandridge and I talk to her, or she'll die of cold and we can't have that, not now she's made such a catch."

"That would be a dreadful misfortune," Aunt Penelope said, as though she thought Mama had meant it.

Agatha hurried to obey.

"I've the constitution of an ox. Papa says," Elenora put in, but was ignored.

"Lord Broxbourne will be calling on your Papa this afternoon, I'm sure," Aunt Penelope said, going to the wardrobe. "And then afterwards on you. Which gown will you wear, I wonder, to look your best?" She started flicking through the new gowns as Agatha assisted Elenora out of her nightgown and into her underclothes. "What about this one with the tiny lemon flowers embroidered on it? I liked this one in particular when we ordered it. Or this one with the blue on it that so perfectly matches your eyes. You are so lucky to have the Wetherby eyes, just like dear Nicholas and me. And Petunia of course. Such a shame your sisters don't have your looks. Lord Broxbourne must have been quite overcome by them."

Elenora, now clad in her stays and petticoats, reached into the wardrobe and pulled out one of her old Penworthy gowns in a dove gray. "I'll wear this one." If Lord Broxbourne had been so shallow as to have fallen for her eyes and her looks, then he'd have been an intolerable fool. Luckily, he'd fallen for neither.

"No, no, no," Mama cried, real tears in her eyes. "What will Lord Broxbourne think when he sees you in this shabby thing? That we cannot afford to trick you out in modish gowns, that's what."

"Well, we can't," Elenora retorted, hanging on tight to her chosen gown. "And I don't care. This is my favorite gown, and I'm wearing it. He's hardly in a position to complain or renege on his offer, is he?"

Mama made a lunge for the gown but Elenora stepped back out of reach. "Now, kindly leave me alone with Agatha so she can do my hair. She can't possibly concentrate with you two arguing over me. Look at her—you've turned her into a nervous wreck."

Aunt Penelope huffed. "Well, I never. I'm sure Petunia would never speak to me like this."

Mama sighed. "She would do were she anything like Elenora." She shot Elenora a hard glare. "I never met a more recalcitrant child. The only thing to do when she's like this is to ignore her. Come, Penelope, we'd better leave her to get her hair done nicely to meet her betrothed."

And they went.

"Thank goodness for that," Petunia grumbled, snuggling back down into her bed. "Perhaps now I can go back to sleep. Wake me up tomorrow."

CHAPTER SEVEN

JACK DEVERIL TOOK breakfast at half past eleven in his bedroom, having slept late due to the hour at which he'd returned home to Portland Place from the ball at his parents' house. Dressed in breeches and shirt under a silk banyan, and with his Turkish slippers on his feet, he ate in silence while considering the events of the night before. Technically, of the early morning. Had he been so drunk as to have agreed to an engagement to the daughter of an impoverished nobody, possibly just because of her combination of a pretty face and an intriguing disregard for matrimony? No, he couldn't blame it on that because he'd scarcely drunk anything, as was his habit.

So why had he done it? A whim. With just the six of them knowing what had happened, which admittedly was rather a lot, especially when one was Lady Routledge, he could perhaps have smoothed things over, but he hadn't. Why? He kept coming back to that question. Had he been piqued that the girl so plainly saw him as an unsatisfactory object only good for being refused? Or was it, heaven forbid, that a noble sentiment had arisen in his hardened heart to help this girl who didn't appear to want to marry anyone.

He'd told her it was her business as to why she didn't want to marry, but in truth, it wasn't. Or it wouldn't be soon, because he wanted to prise that secret from her. Out of curiosity if nothing else. He'd not met a girl yet whose main aim in life hadn't been to marry, and marry well. That the girl he now found himself engaged to didn't fit into that mold intrigued him. A mystery. One he intended to solve. Plus, she seemed to have more about her than any other girl he'd encountered, and that included the lovely Lady Raby, whose charms this morning didn't seem quite so fresh when compared with Miss Wetherby's.

He pushed aside his plate of deviled kidneys hardly touched, which was most unlike him. Normally, he partook of a hearty breakfast which would be enough to see him through to dinner at six. Instead, he poured himself another cup of treacly, dark coffee, added several spoonfuls of fortifying sugar, and drained it in seconds. Time to go out paying calls on people, and he had one particular person in mind.

A little over an hour later, togged out like a Bond Street Beau in immaculate tailcoat, hat, breeches and topboots, and holding his favorite cane in one gloved hand, he emerged from the front door of his house in Portland Place.

Last night, after he and Miss Wetherby had reached an amicable agreement, Sir Nicholas had provided the address of where he and his wife were staying with his widowed sister, Lady Dandridge. Arlington Street. A less splendid address than Portland Place with its enormous houses and wide views down toward the farms and woodland of Marylebone Park, it lay in a smaller side street down toward the river, but very handily placed for St James's Street and White's. No doubt that was why the late Lord Dandridge had chosen it. A mere hop, skip, and a jump to his club. The distance from Portland Place was a little over a mile, which, as it was not raining, he felt inclined to walk. He could use the time to think about what he would say to the attractive stranger to whom he'd so precipitately engaged himself.

The streets thronged with all manner of traffic—coaches, private vehicles, a few people on horseback heading for Hyde Park, and numerous individuals such as girls selling matches, men loitering on street corners chewing tobacco, and women hawking such varied foodstuffs as oysters and gingerbread cakes crowded the pavements. *Come to London and see the world*, caught in a nutshell. His father had once said that to him and it remained true.

He didn't hurry. No one rose early on the morning after a ball as they always finished so late, often when the sun was just rising. Not in February though, with the short daylight hours and dark mornings. He glanced up at the cloudy sky. If he arrived too soon to pay a call on his putative future in-laws, he might find them unprepared for his visit. Although they must assume that he would be arriving, as his betrothed's father would no doubt be keen to draw up the necessary papers detailing the conditions of the engagement. His betrothed's rather fearsome mother would be slavering at the bit to get that out of the way.

Thoughts of the marriage contract rendered him a little uncomfortable, smacking as it did of something legal and binding. But he'd said he'd do it now, and if both parties eventually withdrew from an engagement, little would be lost, not even face. Hopefully. In the cold light of day, he found he needed more than a little convincing of this.

To his surprise, he found himself more concerned about the effect reneging on their agreement might have on Miss Wetherby's future prospects, rather than on his own. He wasn't used to considering others above himself, and he seemed to be doing a lot of that just now. What was happening to him? Was he, perhaps, getting old?

Louise would be horrified by his sudden, and unusual, attack of conscience.

Louise.

She wasn't going to be pleased about this, and he couldn't risk telling her it was all a ruse. She wasn't the sort of woman to be snubbed and keep silent.

He stopped in his tracks. Snubbed was definitely how she would see this. How had he not considered what she would think if he became engaged to some previously unknown young woman? An ingenue. His only thought of his mistress this morning had been in passing—and it had been in comparing her appearance to the dewy, flawless skin and fresh-faced beauty of a nineteen-year-old. He'd thoughtlessly condemned Louise as appearing jaded and old. If he was commencing a period of thinking about others, perhaps he'd better start with her. He swiveled on his heel and turned left down Weymouth Street. She must hear the news from him first, before the gossipmongers got hold of it.

Lady Raby owned a house in Upper Wimpole Street, a house she mainly inhabited on her own, as her husband, who was a lot older than her, preferred to remain in the country at Raby Castle in Northamptonshire nursing his gout and, when well enough, riding to hounds.

Her butler, Trevose, opened the door. She'd brought this lugubrious elderly retainer with her when she married, and his unswerving devotion to his mistress enabled her to carry on with whatever member of the nobility, or sometimes someone from the lower echelons of society, she happened to favor that month. She'd been favoring Jack for the last four weeks, and it had been most enjoyable.

"Ah, Trevose, is her ladyship at home?"

"She is, my lord, if you'd care to come in." Trevose stood back to allow Jack into the sumptuously decorated hallway. Like the rest of the house, only some of which Jack had seen, their interactions having taken place mainly in the bedroom, it reflected her ladyship's exotic tastes. Her husband had given her free rein to decorate it as she wished when he'd married her twenty years ago. He'd been fifty then, a good twenty five years her senior, and perhaps overindulgent having snared himself so attractive a young wife to replace the one who'd died.

No longer quite so young, Louise's taste for younger men had grown as she matured. Whether her husband knew of her many dalliances, Jack had no idea, and he didn't care.

"Her ladyship is in her boudoir." Trevose led the way up the wide oak staircase and Jack followed, his boots tapping on the richly figured wood.

Opening the boudoir door, through which Jack had entered many times, Trevose stood back in deference. If they wanted anything, a simple tug on the bell rope would bring him.

Feeling as though he had to gather his courage, which was a ridiculous notion, Jack stepped through the doorway.

Louise was seated on a chaise longue by the window, wearing what appeared to be a tawny silk peignoir and nothing else. Her auburn hair, which Jack was certain she used henna on to disguise the increasingly obvious gray hairs, hung in a luscious mane down her back and over her luscious breasts, which the peignoir barely concealed. What a woman. All thoughts of her advancing age vanished as his body responded to the sight of what was on offer.

"Jack, my dear." She held out an elegant hand to him, the silky fabric slipping back to reveal her softly rounded forearm. "What a pleasure it is to see you at this hour of the morning. I hadn't expected your company before tonight. We are still going to the opera, are we not?"

Damn it. He'd forgotten all about the opera. His life was getting unexpectedly more complicated by the minute.

He took her hand and pressed his lips to it, his eyes fixed on her face. Better start with a few compliments. "You look ravishing."

He straightened, still holding her hand, and she laughed, a deep, attractive gurgle that slithered into Jack's brain down to where his friends swore he kept it—in his trousers. If only she weren't so damned alluring. Any remaining thoughts of her age vanished.

"And it's so early, you find me in deshabillée." She let the peignoir slip from one plump, alabaster shoulder. "Unless you have in mind something that requires less clothing?"

What a temptress she was. But he was now an engaged man and part of that had to include abstinence from the lures of other women. At least for now. Even at his most discreet, he couldn't keep a dalliance from the hotbed of gossip that was the Ton. His parents would hear about it, and so would Elenora's, which was worse. For some reason he couldn't fathom, he didn't want to cause her anguish or embarrassment. Looking at the scantily clad Louise, it dawned on him how hard this was going to be. But he'd given his word, and even if no one had actually specified that he could have no other liaisons, it would be an assumed part of the contract Elenora's father was no doubt having drawn up right now.

"I'm afraid I don't have the time, tempting as your offer is." He turned around the chair she kept in front of her dressing table and sat on it, crossing his legs to hide his discomfort, and keeping at a distance of ten feet from her chaise longue, lest temptation got the better of him.

She pouted and didn't rectify her slipped peignoir. No doubt she doubted his determination and had faith in her own attractions. Any other day and she'd have been correct.

"Then what is it you've come for?" The words purred out of her mouth, slithering into his brain and making him wish he were here for another reason.

Best to come out with it. "I've got myself engaged to be married."

Silence. Her cat-like eyes sharpened and her breasts heaved as she took in several deep breaths.

He waited.

"Married?" Gone was the purring allure to be replaced by a sharpness that could have etched glass.

"Married. I'm thirty-eight. It's time I thought about providing an heir for the earldom that will one day be mine." He kept his voice measured and matter of fact, while watching her closely. He'd had experience of several of her rages before, which both times had ended up with them in bed together. That couldn't happen this time.

She hitched the peignoir up to cover her shoulder. "This is very sudden." Now she was cold and calculating, and, with her smile gone, annoyance dragged her features down, ageing her in an instant.

His resolve hardened, and the opposite happened to his cock.

Perhaps he was wise to break off this liaison. He nodded. "I wanted you to be the first to know. Well, after the girl and her parents, and mine, of course."

"How thoughtful of you." Words she didn't mean. He'd always been aware of her lack of consideration for anyone else's feelings, including his own, but other, more carnal things had outweighed her selfish nature, and she'd rarely shown him her true self.

Silence fell again. What was she thinking? Probably that this might mean the end of their relationship. Well, she was right, and he was beginning to think it would be a good thing. He couldn't abide clingy women and she was fast mutating into one if he wasn't mistaken.

"To whom have you become engaged? I'm curious to know what attributes the lady in question possesses that have allowed her to snare the most confirmed bachelor I've ever had the opportunity to pleasure."

"Miss Elenora Wetherby."

Louise's brow furrowed and her upper lip curled. "Never heard of her. She sounds like a nobody."

"She is."

Her brow furrowed some more. If she took a glance in her mirror she'd be horrified by the lines on it. "Then why on earth have you chosen her as a bride? You're an earl's only son, you're devilish handsome, by gad, and far too charming when you want to be. You have a more than substantial income and a house here in Town as well as an estate in Wiltshire. You could have the pick of the Ton, a diamond of the first water, the daughter of a duke. In fact, I can think of several duke's daughters who would be falling over themselves to snare you."

He smiled. "Have you taken a look at the young ladies you are referring to? I am not attracted to horse-faced girls, as you well know."

Her face softened into a knowing smile. "I do indeed. But I also know your tastes don't run to innocent ingenues. Your tastes," and here she stroked her hand down her thigh, "run to women who know what to do in bed, and who have old husbands who can't satisfy them. Women like me."

"Women like you are not the sort my mother would have me marry. And to put it bluntly, you're too old to give me the heir my father thinks I need."

She laughed, the sound deep and provocative. "I would very much like to see your mother's face if you told her you were marrying a woman like me. I can only presume that the lady of your choice, despite being a nobody I've never heard of, has attributes your mother, and of course your father, would find satisfactory, although I doubt you will. A meek little mouse, I imagine."

He nodded, ignoring her last words. "She does indeed pass muster with my father. And you've met her. She's not a meek little mouse." Anything but.

The frown returned. "I have?"

"The girl with the rather lovely blonde hair and eyes of a cornflower blue with whom we danced the cotillion last night. She was partnering a red-headed oaf who kept trampling on her feet."

The moment realization sank in, Louise's eyes changed, hardening like a pair of diamonds. "That girl? You've affianced yourself to that chit?" Her voice rose. "She can only just be out of the schoolroom. And her parents have accepted your offer? Don't they know your reputation?" Indignation filled every syllable. Perhaps he shouldn't have revealed Elenora's identity.

"She's nineteen."

Louise's breasts heaved as her breathing quickened. "A child. And you're throwing me over for a chit like that, a chit half your age, just because she has blonde hair and blue eyes? I'll wager that blonde coloring isn't natural. Her collar and cuffs will betray her."

This was not going well so far. Jack rose to his feet, keen to make himself scarce. "So, due to my newly affianced state, I regret that I shall no longer be available to squire you about Town."

Her eyes flashed in fury, but if he knew her at all, this wasn't due to any kind of sentiment she felt for him, but rather to the fact that she felt she'd been scorned. And for a girl such as Elenora. That he was feeling defensive about his supposed fiancée surprised him.

He took a step toward the door. "I'm sure you'll be able to find someone else from your wide circle of friends to attend the opera with this evening. I wish you well. Good day to you… my lady."

Louise surged to her feet, the peignoir, that had not been tied, gaping open to reveal her opulent body and heavy breasts. If she'd done that just a day ago, Jack would have been across the room and sweeping her up in his arms, unable to resist. Now, that overblown body suddenly seemed repulsive to him, the stomach too full, the breasts too pendulous.

But she still deserved his compassion. He bowed. "I'm sorry, Louise, if I've hurt your feelings."

She sprang at him, hands clawed, but he caught her by the wrists. "Calm yourself and think sensibly. I can't continue to see you when I'm engaged to be married." This was beginning to look like a wise decision. Her previous rages had never been directed at him, and this new experience of facing a woman spurned disturbed him.

"You've made a huge mistake," she snarled. "Throwing me over. And you'll live to regret allying yourself with a nincompoop of a girl for the rest of your days." She gave a wild laugh. "You'll be back knocking on my door less than a month after you marry, begging for the crumbs off my table. You mark my words."

Jack released his hold on her and she sagged down, pulling the peignoir about her nakedness. Were those tears in her eyes? He'd never seen her cry. Never thought she could. Might this mean she'd felt more for him than he'd ever suspected?

She glared up at him. "Get out of my house. Now."

He needed no further telling.

CHAPTER EIGHT

ONCE MORE OUT in the street, Jack halted beside a lamp post, one hand out for its support, and the scruffy man who'd been leaning on it hurried away, pulling his matelot hat down over his eyes. He'd been expecting Louise to only be annoyed, because he'd always imagined their little affair to be nothing more than a casual dalliance. It certainly had been on his part, as had all his affairs, since... He shook his head, to clear it of thoughts of his past. Her reaction suggested she might have seen it otherwise.

Without wishing to, he'd hurt her and those tears had been real. He'd been so anxious not to hurt a girl he didn't know, he'd not even considered how his mistress might feel to be cast aside. And cast her aside was what he'd done, callously as though she didn't matter to him. The thought that other men might have done the same in her past troubled him. Was he just as bad as they'd been? Too late now though.

"Matches, milord?" A waif of a girl with a small, pinched face broke in upon his self-flagellating thoughts, edging closer to him with her tray of matches. Her mousy hair hung in rats' tails, and gray eyes gazed at him from shadowed sockets. She looked in need of more than just a penny for a few matches. The image of another child leapt into his head. A clean child with plump cheeks and freckles on his nose. There, but for the grace of God...

He fished in his pocket for loose change and came up with a

crown. If he gave her that, would she even be able to spend it? Would someone steal it from her or accuse her of having stolen it herself? What he needed was smaller coins, and what she needed was food. On the opposite side of the street a man in a dirty apron had set up a pie stand. Just a barrow really, but it had "hot pies" written on the side of it, and their appetizing aroma wafted across the traffic. Something should be done to help this child, despite the urgency of his visit to Miss Wetherby's parents. "Wait here," Jack said.

Dodging a few carriages and the plentiful horse droppings that decorated the cobbles, Jack made it to the other side of the street and approached the man. "Two pies please." A few moments later, having left a rather discontented pie seller who'd had to give up most of his change in return for the crown, he was back beside the match girl, who stood just where he'd left her, eyes round with awe as she saw him returning holding two pies.

He held one out to her. "Careful. It's hot."

She took it in a far-too-thin hand, the skin almost translucent over the bones, eyes wide with awe. "Fank you… milord."

Well swept steps rose behind them past a basement's railed area to a splendid front door. The house of one of Louise's well-to-do neighbors. Sweeping his coat tails out of the way, Jack sat down and indicated for the child to do so too. With as much delicacy as a duchess taking her seat at a dinner party, the child sat a few feet away from him and began to eat the pie. He watched her in silence until she'd finished. As she licked the last of the crumbs from her fingers, a resounding burp escaped her. She clapped her hand over her mouth, eyes brimming with embarrassment and even a hint of mischief. A hint that within that sorry exterior lurked a real, fun-loving child. Someone must have taught her manners at some point. A mother, perhaps.

Smiling, Jack held out the other pie.

"Don'tcher want it, milord?" Her voice had gained in volume, perhaps strengthened by the consumption of the pie and the suspicion that he meant her no harm.

He shook his head, although in truth, the pie's alluring scent had him salivating. He hadn't eaten his breakfast, after all. "I bought it for you."

She took the pie. "I'll save it fer later, if that's all the same wi' you." And it vanished into a fold in her clothing.

Jack reached into his pocket for the change he'd received from the pie man. He found two shillings and handed them to her. "Here, take this and buy your mother, or your family some food."

"I ain't got no fam'ly."

He sighed. He didn't really have time for this, as his aim this morning had been to call on Sir Nicholas, and Miss Wetherby, of course, and settle the conditions of the betrothal. He'd already been made late thanks to his visit to Lady Raby. Things seemed to be conspiring to get in his way. But his conscience wouldn't allow him to ignore this child. "No mother?"

"No."

"No father?"

She shook her head.

An orphan. Another waif he could help. Damn Miss Wetherby and her family. What was more important? Settling a betrothal or saving a child from starvation on the streets? He should take the time to help this waif and the Wetherbys would have to put up with him being late. Her stick-like limbs wrung his heart, and her gray eyes, devoid of hope, didn't help. He kept his voice as gentle as he could, despite his fury that a child so young could be left to fend for herself. But apart from the streets, what else was there for her other than the workhouse? "What's your name, child?"

She sniffed and wiped her nose with the back of her hand. "Josie."

"Just Josie? No surname?"

She shook her head. "I fink I had one once, but I don't recommember rightly. No one calls me anyfin but Josie now." She thought for a moment. "Or mostly jus' 'girl', when they wants me."

"Well, Josie, can you tell me where you sleep at nights, then? Does someone other than your mother take care of you? Perhaps an older sister?" Surely someone had her under their wing and he could class her as "looked after." She could only be eight at the most, hardly any older than…

"I ain't got no one. I finds meself a corner, outta the way. There's dange'rous people about at nights. But I'm real good at hidin'."

A corner. A child sleeping in a cold corner in February in these inadequate rags, hoping not to be discovered by the scum who roamed the streets under cover of the darkness. He knew all too well what sort of men peopled the back streets at night. Seeing street children dead from the cold, or dead from other things, had started all this for him. That and…

He shook himself. He wasn't about to let this child become one of their number, not when he had the means at his disposal to save her. "Will you trust me, Josie, when I say that I mean you no harm?" There were plenty of men, even gentlemen, about, who would take advantage of an orphan like her for their own pleasure, and he had no idea whether she'd been subject to their attentions.

The gray eyes gazed up at him. "You bought me a pie. I trusts you." Perhaps she was innocent of such attentions still. She was very small. Savable.

The longing to warn her not to trust men who bought her things arose, but he pushed it away. It would only scare her off, and where he was taking her would be her salvation. He stood up and held out his hand. "Then come with me, and I'll take you somewhere warm to sleep tonight and where you will be looked after. You won't need your tray of matches. I know a house where a kind lady looks after children who don't have their mothers anymore. She'll give you warm clothes and food and a bed to sleep in."

He'd already decided not to tell her how she would be taught to read and write and reckon, and then trained for a proper employment in millinery, or as a housemaid. Good employment for a girl like her. Honest employment. Blinding her with what the future could hold might frighten her off. But it was all work she could have no hope of attaining if he abandoned her to her fate.

The little girl, eyes full of touching faith, scrambled to her feet and slipped her tiny cold hand into his large warm one. An odd couple, drawing the glances of passersby, they set off down the street together.

THE REDOUBTABLE MRS. Sharpe kept a house that Jack paid the rent on, or rather two houses, for Jack had taken the one next door when necessity had arisen and had a door knocked between the two. They were located in Betterton Street, which lay somewhere around the rather indeterminate junction between the houses of London's middle class bankers, shopkeepers and businessmen, and the slum area of St Giles that crowded so close behind the homes of the better off.

Numbers 23 and 24 lay halfway along a narrow street of terraced houses, each in possession of a paved yard, with outside water closets, rather than gardens at the back, and with neighbors Jack knew to be respectable shopkeepers and clerks. Not far away from the tenements and rookeries of St Giles that many of the children he'd installed there had escaped from. As had Mrs. Sharpe herself, whose own rescue from her bully of a husband, an out and out villain, he'd effected some years since.

He'd chosen Betterton Street for its quiet neighborhood and lack of interest for the sort of people these children had escaped. And he'd chosen Mrs. Sharpe, thanks to fate, for her motherly demeanor and sensible outlook on life. Plenty of orphanages existed, not least the workhouse, where children were poorly fed and badly treated, mainly due to the corruption of those that ran them, but this was not one of them.

Mrs. Sharpe, whom Jack would have trusted with his own

life, had raised seven of her own children, two of whom continued to live with her, acting as surrogate big sisters to the orphans in their parent's charge. All three of the Sharpes treated the children with kindness and understanding, and the necessary firmness that would transform Jack's rescued waifs into useful members of society.

He'd forgotten how far it was though. His own long legs were up to the journey, but it soon became obvious that Josie's malnourished ones were not. By the time he arrived in Betterton Street he was carrying a rather malodorous little bundle clasped to his chest and attracting further curious stares from respectable passersby. The sort who would cross to the opposite side of the road rather than look at a child in need like Josie.

Whenever Jack thought of how blind most people were to the suffering of a large proportion of London's population, he felt as though his blood might boil. What he'd set up in Betterton Street, although it remained on a small scale, went a little way to assuage his conscience about the opulent lifestyle he'd had the luck to be born into.

On his knock, the door was opened by Lucy Sharpe, the youngest of Mrs. Sharpe's brood, a sturdy, apple-cheeked girl of twelve. Seeing Jack, she smiled and bobbed a creditable curtsy, something her mother had made sure all her young charges could do. "Milord Jack."

Jack deposited Josie on her feet once more and took hold of her hand again, lest her presentation at such a splendid house frighten her into flight. A wise move. She hung back, trying to hide herself behind his legs.

"As you can see, I've brought you a new sister." He bent to the child. "Josie, this is Miss Lucy Sharpe. She's one of the kind ladies who will be looking after you here."

Josie peeked at Lucy, who smiled back at her with her usual open bonhomie. "Hello, Josie. You're a very lucky girl that Lord Jack found you."

Jack glanced at his fob watch. "I'm afraid I can't stop, Lucy.

Will you apologize to your mother for me. I'm rather late for an appointment already. I happened upon little Josie selling matches in Upper Wimpole Street and just couldn't leave her there. Not in this cold weather. She's had a hot pie already and has another tucked somewhere about her, but she'd benefit from a bath, a delouse and some clean clothes. I'll leave her in your tender hands if I may."

Josie clung onto his hand. "I ain't goin' wiv her."

Jack bent again. She was so tiny. Perhaps younger than he'd at first thought. A lot shorter than…

He smiled at her. "You will be quite safe here, Josie. The lady who runs this house for me, Mrs. Sharpe, is the kindest lady you could imagine. Lucy is her youngest daughter. She has seven children of her own, but only the two youngest live here with her. You'll like them very much as they're just as kind as their mother."

Lucy held out her own plump, well-fed hand. "Come along, take my hand and come inside with me, Josie, and let's get you warm. You look perished to death nearly out here on the step. There's a warm stove in the kitchen with the kettle ready to sing on it."

Josie looked up at Jack. If he wasn't already running so late for his call on the Wetherbys, he'd have stayed, taken her inside, introduced her to Mrs. Sharpe himself, but he didn't have time. "I have to leave you here, I'm afraid." He smiled again, guilt at abandoning her looming large. "However, I don't do any of the care here myself. I leave that to Mrs. Sharpe and Lucy, and her older sister. Mrs. Sharpe will be like a mother to you, I promise, just as she is the other children here. Right now, you need to go with Lucy."

Josie tentatively released his hand and slid hers into Lucy's outstretched one.

Jack stepped back.

Lucy drew Josie to her, slipping a supportive arm around her shoulders. "Brave girl."

Jack took another step back.

Josie's head swiveled and, chin on shoulder, she stared back at him. Accusingly. Poor little mite. She only had his word that this was a good place in which he was leaving her. Perhaps she'd heard tales of what happened to little girls who went off hand in hand with strange gentlemen. "I will return tomorrow to see you." A rash promise, with all he had to do, but it would be good to sit with Mrs. Sharpe in her tiny front room and hear how her little charges were doing. At least one of them had recently left to go into service as a housemaid, and he'd like to hear how she was getting along. He lifted his hand. "Until tomorrow."

Lucy closed the door and he was left standing on the street, a further sensation of guilt at having abandoned the child too soon settling in his heart. But he couldn't stand here all day. He had a marriage contract to go over and a fiancée to pay a call on. He turned on his heel and almost fell over a man just passing on the pavement. A man with a sailor's hat pulled forward over his eyes and a hunch to his shoulders as he hurried away, leaving a trail of pipe smoke behind him.

Tucking his cane under his arm, Jack set off to retrace his steps back to the more salubrious areas of London that were his usual haunt.

ELENORA AND AUGUSTA, along with Mama, Aunt Penelope and Cousin Petunia, were seated in the drawing room of the house in Arlington Street when Frances came hurrying in, face flushed with excitement, to inform them that Lord Broxbourne had just arrived to call on Papa.

"Hemmings has taken him into the study," Frances blurted out, her eyes alight with excitement. "I was watching from the top of the stairs." She giggled. "He looks very handsome but positively ancient, almost as old as Papa. But I can vouch for him having an excellent head of hair—no bald spot to be seen."

"Good heavens! He isn't as old as Papa, is he?" Augusta asked, setting down the needlepoint she'd been doing, eyes wide with surprise. "Tell me he isn't." Then she seemed to think better of her outburst. "Although an older husband would be good for Ellie, as you've always said, Mama."

"Augusta!" Mama frowned at her. "You don't ask questions like that. Your papa is not old and nor is Lord Broxbourne."

Elenora, who had only been pretending to sew, as it was one of her least favorite of ladylike activities, also laid her sewing aside. With relief. "I have to say that he is indeed quite old, for at his ears," she touched the side of her face, "I noticed he already has a few gray hairs."

"I'm sure I could never marry someone as old as that, title or no title," Petunia said, prim faced. Her attitude to Elenora had changed since the announcement of the engagement.

Everyone ignored her.

Mama shot Elenora a frown and indicated the spare chair near the long window to her youngest daughter. "Sit down, Frances, if you are staying, and get out your sewing. We must make an industrious picture when your papa brings him in here to see Elenora."

Elenora patted the seat on the sofa beside her, and Frances went to take the space.

Mama's imperious raise of the hand stopped her. "Not that one, child. Elenora must have a seat available beside her for her betrothed."

Elenora bit her lip. Drat it. Mama knew all the moves required of courting. She was going to have to sit beside Lord Broxbourne—or rather, he was going to have to sit beside her—because nowhere else remained for him. A little smile tickled her lips, quickly controlled, at the thought of the discomfort he was about to suffer at the hands of her family. Because suffer he would. And, if she could, she would enjoy it.

Augusta picked up her needlepoint again, eager, as always, to oblige Mama. No doubt she was crowing inside at the thought of so swift a marriage for Elenora, as that could only mean her own debut in society must be soon. Elenora frowned. Probably her impatient younger sister would have had her marry anyone, just to get her out of the way. Even some white-haired old cit.

"I believe Lord Broxbourne has a tidy fortune and a sizeable estate in Wiltshire," Aunt Penelope, whose husband had been parsimonious and who, since his death and her acquisition of his fortune, had become something of a spendthrift, remarked. She made it her business to know the worth of every member of the Ton, something Elenora suspected Mama had been exploiting in her list making of prospective bridegrooms.

"Of course he has," Petunia muttered into her sewing. "I bet Elenora snared him on purpose."

Aunt Penelope shot her daughter a quelling glare, which Petunia ignored, glowering over her sewing as though it had offended her.

Mama, who was embroidering a handkerchief she'd already labelled as being part of Elenora's bridal trousseau, smiled in satisfaction. "He is everything one could want in a husband for a daughter with the looks Elenora has been blessed with. Rich, titled, and devilishly handsome." Her cheeks flushed as though she might herself be finding Lord Broxbourne attractive. A bit of a change from last night.

Elenora's brow furrowed. What? A self-centered, middle-aged rake in possession of a notorious mistress? That was what Mama had been dreaming of for her? A man who couldn't give two hoots for anyone but himself? Although, it had to be admitted, his actions were going to be a great help to her in staving off any suitors Mama might have been likely to thrust under her nose. He probably felt he was benefitting more than her, though, or he wouldn't have done it.

"Is he very handsome, Frannie? Did you manage to see?" Augusta put in. "I quizzed Ellie on his looks, but she said she was sure she didn't know and beauty was in the eye of the beholder. So boring of her and so typical."

"For such an old man, very, I suppose…" Frances said, her head tilted to one side like a little brown bird's. "Tall, well-made, and wearing the most highly polished boots I've ever seen. And such a well-cut coat." Frances was a keen follower of fashion, both for young ladies and for gentlemen, or at least as keen as she could be living in Hampshire. Being brought to London with her two older sisters had almost given her a fainting fit from delight.

"He's not so old as all that," Elenora put in, a trifle stung that her supposed future husband was being compared to Papa, who really was old.

"I believe Viscount Broxbourne is thirty-eight years old," Aunt Penelope said. Another of her obsessions was keeping account of the age of everyone who was anyone. She knew the birthdays of all her friends and acquaintances and a lot more people besides.

Augusta wrinkled her nose. "So indeed quite old then."

"Twice Ellie's age," Frances added.

"Ancient," Petunia put in, stabbing her needle into her sewing.

"I'm surprised you can divide thirty-eight by two so successfully," Elenora snapped at her sister, still a little miffed. Thirty-eight did sound quite old though, even she had to admit it. But only to herself, not her sisters.

"Get on with your sewing, girls," Mama said. "I want his lordship to see what quiet, well-behaved girls I have."

Augusta sniggered. "If you wanted him to think that, you shouldn't have let him offer for Ellie. She's the least quiet and well-behaved of all your children."

Mama's chest swelled like that of an angry hen. "Be quiet, Augusta, unless you have something nice to say. I will not have you saying things like that about your sister. When Lord Broxbourne arrives, both you girls are to remain silent. Have I not told you often enough that children should be seen but not heard?"

Augusta dropped her gaze to her sewing. "Yes, Mama." But she was not contrite.

"Am I to remain silent too?" Elenora asked.

Mama opened her mouth to make what looked as though might have been a tart reply, but the opening of the drawing room door cut her off. Papa came in, a little red in the face and nose, followed by Lord Broxbourne.

Elenora took a good look at her betrothed, having managed to forget his precise appearance overnight, trying to see him through the eyes of her two silent sisters. Yes, he was no longer in the first flush of his youth, like Jolyon and Matthew, but he had about him an air of maturity that wasn't displeasing. Tall, lean, broad-shouldered, well-dressed, and even rather handsome. Well, very handsome in a devilish way, as had been mentioned earlier. For just a moment, she forgot that theirs was a pretend engagement and she wasn't weighing him up as a prospective husband, and almost thought she liked the looks of him. But that was far too silly for words.

Lord Broxbourne made an elegant bow to Mama and Aunt Penelope. "Lady Wetherby, Lady Dandridge, how charming you ladies look, and how industriously occupied you and your charming daughters are." Mama's plan had worked. Just for a moment, Elenora remembered how well he'd effected the repair on her gown and wondered how he'd learned to sew so well. That skill seemed very much at odds with being a rake.

He turned to Elenora and made another bow. "Miss Wetherby, what an… exquisite gown." A twinkle of mischief shone in his eyes.

Elenora bit her lip trying not to chuckle, as she was still wearing the old, dove-gray gown she'd insisted on donning earlier, while Augusta and Frances both had on the new ones Aunt Penelope had bought for them.

She got herself under control in time. "Lord Broxbourne, what an unexpected pleasure." She held out her hand, conscious of the expectant, if slightly envious, gazes of Petunia and her sisters, who'd abandoned all pretense at sewing. Broxbourne took her hand in his, bent over it and bestowed a kiss upon it. No one had ever kissed her hand before and before she could steel herself to control her reaction, heat had swarmed up her cheeks.

"Do pray sit down," Mama said, indicating the space beside Elenora. It looked like Papa would be standing up.

Lord Broxbourne, ever obedient, sat down next to Elenora and turned to face her. "Your father and I have just been sorting out the details of our engagement, Miss Wetherby. I think you would like to know that I have requested a long engagement so that you and I can get to know one another before our nuptials."

Whew. At least he'd been good to his word. Not that she'd thought that he wouldn't.

Elenora forced herself to lift her gaze from his mouth to his eyes for a moment. "Thank you, my lord." How dark they were, and full of something she didn't quite understand because reading people's expressions had never come easily to her. She frowned.

"Now girls," Mama said. "I think it's time you younger three had a little rest in your rooms." She rose to her feet. "I'm sure Lord Broxbourne would like a few moments alone with dear Elenora, his betrothed."

"And I shall go and talk to Cook about dinner this evening," Aunt Penelope said, standing up in haste.

Elenora glared at Mama. "Are you sure it's quite proper for me to be alone with Lord Broxbourne?"

Papa opened his mouth.

Mama got in there first. "Of course it is now you're properly affianced. Just for a few minutes, of course, and perhaps you'd like to take a turn about the garden together? That would be very proper and correct. The garden is not large and wholly in sight of the house at all times."

In February? Was Mama mad?

Augusta and Frances, looking disappointed, followed their mother and aunt out of the room, Papa trailing after them like a lost puppy. Poor Papa. What say did he have in anything? Petunia was last out of the door, casting an envious gaze at Elenora as she went.

The door closed behind them.

Silence fell.

Elenora regarded her hands and her awful sewing. His had been much better than hers was ever likely to be.

Lord Broxbourne cleared his throat. Was he as nervous as her? "You like sewing?"

Elenora smoothed out her work. "Does it look like I do?" The stitchwork was blotted with blood spots and the stitches were everywhere.

He chuckled. "I know very little about such things, but it does seem to me that perhaps whatever you're making could do without being dotted with blood."

She nodded. "I am a very poor hand at sewing. If you were truly going to marry me, you would be sadly disappointed by my lack of useful skills. My mother despairs of me." A little smile twitched across her face. "Although you have already proved to be an efficient stitcher of tears yourself so cannot be so ignorant as you claim."

He chuckled. "Perhaps just a little. I daresay you, though, possess other skills that are commendable."

She dared a peek at him. "Well, if you could count my interest in all things historical as a skill, I suppose so. Mama says it is not at all a feminine attribute. And I am said to be a veritable Valkyrie in the saddle."

"So you like to ride?"

She nodded. "Not here, of course. Why would anyone wish to ride in Town? I hear Rotten Row is where everyone goes to do so, but it's in a London park, and when you're used to the open countryside as I am, that would be a poor substitute."

He shifted on the sofa, leaning back. "You are very candid."

"Another of my faults. Mama constantly cautions me not to speak my mind, but I'm afraid I find it very difficult to dissemble."

"As do I."

She studied his boots. They were indeed as highly polished as Frances had reported. "You have very shiny boots."

He laughed, a deep throaty chuckle that was rather attractive.

"Do you always say what comes into your mind?"

She clapped her hand over her mouth. "I'm sorry. I try so hard not to. It's another of my faults. Please don't tell Mama I was rude to you."

"Of course I won't. And I'm not in the least offended by your bluntness. I do indeed have shiny boots—courtesy of the boot boy, I imagine, at my establishment. Nothing to do with me. I don't think my valet stoops to shining boots."

Relief swept over her.

He stood up. "Your mother suggested you might like to walk in your aunt's garden and I have a longing to see it myself, despite the time of year. The sun has deigned to come out at last, but it's a little chill. Do you have a shawl?"

Of course, Mama had seen fit to make sure a thick shawl was on a table in the corner. For this very reason. Lord Broxbourne fetched it and held it up for her. Was she to let him wrap it around her? That felt too intimate a gesture. She took it out of his hands and folded it about her shoulders. "We can go out this way."

As he held out his arm to her, she hesitated. Somehow, touching him now felt quite different to having him touch her hand or waist while they'd been dancing last night. Now it felt like an imposition. She'd never liked to be touched, and that whole feeling came thundering back. But if she didn't take his arm, he would think her rude.

Very delicately she set her hand on his coat sleeve. Minimal contact only. And they went out through the double doors into the wintry garden.

CHAPTER NINE

A T THREE IN the afternoon, Aunt Penelope's small garden was already in the shade of the houses surrounding it, and an uninviting chill hung over the drab flowerbeds and evergreen shrubs. Jack closed the drawing room doors behind them, and led Elenora down from the paved terrace onto the gravel pathway that traversed the garden. Lady Wetherby had been right when she'd said it was quite a proper place for a walk, as it possessed not the least nook or cranny to be private in. Not that he had any wish to tarry with Miss Wetherby in a discreet corner. Of course he didn't. No. Definitely not.

His own defensiveness surprised him. Did he want a nook or cranny in which to be alone with this strange girl with her barely present hand on his arm? Was he interested in her further than as a lighthearted amusement? Absolutely not. Why on earth was he even letting this thought intrude into his mind? He gave himself a mental shake. In a few months their charade would be over and he could go back to what he did best—enjoying himself. Only... wasn't he quite enjoying this? Ridiculous.

"I'm afraid Aunt Penelope's gardens are nothing to write home about," Elenora said, her tone a mixture of the matter of fact and apology. She kept her head turned away from him as she spoke, possibly deliberately. She seemed to have a strong aversion to looking him in the eye, as she'd already admitted, and even, now, to looking at the lower portion of his face. What a conundrum she was.

But she was right about the garden. And it was cold. He smiled. "I'm not walking in it for the pleasure of admiring its appearance."

She stayed silent, perhaps trying to work out what he'd meant by that, and they reached the end of the garden, which did not take long, and the high brick wall that must separate it from the garden of the house behind, or maybe from the mews.

However, silence did not seem to suit her, and clearly she hadn't worked out his meaning. "Then why are you walking in it?" She paused and he was forced to halt as well. Her head turned and she appeared to be regarding his chin. "And why have you chosen to walk in it with me?" Her rather blunt way of talking was not unattractive. Refreshing after the dissembling of every other young lady he'd ever met. It seemed that if she wanted to know something, she wasn't going to beat about the bush.

However, now she'd asked the question, he wasn't at all certain of the answer. "We are an engaged couple now." Stating the obvious. "And we need to satisfy certain requirements in order to maintain the illusion. One of these is that I should call on you here at your aunt's in order to spend time with you. And that is what I am doing now." How stuffy and pompous that sounded. So unlike the open way she talked.

Her eyes rose for a moment to meet his, then dropped again to somewhere around his lapels. "Pray don't feel that you must do this, Lord Broxbourne. I am quite certain that the fact you have requested my hand in marriage will be enough for my mother. She will think no less of you if you absent yourself from my aunt's house for long periods."

A sense of feeling affronted arose in Jack's chest. Did she not want to spend time with him? Unused to this sort of reaction from women he met, whether ladies of the Ton or not, Jack felt piqued. "I fear your mother is not the only one who will be observing our behavior, Miss Wetherby. The eyes of the Ton will be upon us, for you have snared for yourself, or they must think that you have, one of the most sought after of bachelors. I bring you an earldom, or I would if our engagement were real, and they are few and far between. Many an ambitious mama will be watching the progress of our engagement with an envious eye. If we deviate from the normal, they will be quick to gossip. And I have no desire, as yet, to be the subject of the gossip of the old biddies who fancy themselves as arbiters of taste and good behavior." As if he wasn't already, with his so recently ended liaison with Louise and all that had gone before it. But best not to mention that.

"That is a very long speech to say you'll be calling on me just to keep up appearances."

Was she finding the situation amusing?

He shrugged and they set off again along the bottom of the garden, where the stunted, heavily-pruned rosebushes bestowed a sad appearance on the flowerbeds. "I am known for my long speeches when in my cups."

Her eyes rose again, this time with a definite twinkle in her blue eyes. "And are you in your cups now?"

He burst out laughing. "You are a most original young lady. I begin to think that being engaged to you for the length of the season might be quite amusing."

A frown marred her brow and the thought that perhaps her openness was rubbing off on him arose.

She pursed her lips before speaking. "Are you laughing at me? I must inform you that I do not like to be mocked." Anxiety filled her eyes. Had others mocked her in the past, perhaps for the attributes he found the most attractive? How unkind. The longing to be kind to her, much as he had been kind to little Josie, swept over him. Good heavens. He must try to keep it in check. With children like Josie he could allow himself free rein with kindness, but with an impressionable girl like Miss Wetherby, he must be more circumspect. Josie might repay his kindness with trust, but a girl of his new fiancée's age might take it quite the wrong way.

They turned the corner and started back toward the terrace,

past a small pond with a Grecian statue at its center. He shook his head. "Heaven forbid that I should do that. My intention was to flatter you, Miss Wetherby." He paused. "Although, as we are engaged now, perhaps you will allow me to address you as Elenora?" Such a pretty name, the desire to say it aloud waxed in his breast. He pushed aside the part of him that questioned the wisdom of such a move.

Her eyes twinkled again, the hunted look dispelled. "I think perhaps that would please Mama. She would see it as a 'good sign'." She paused, drawing in her lower lip over her teeth as though in deep thought. "And," she ventured, "if you are to call me by my name, might I also call you by yours? It's Jack, isn't it? A delightful name, I think, redolent of the countryside and bucolic idylls. I love the countryside far better than London."

He laughed. "You have some novel ideas. I had no idea my name held such connotations. Please call me by it... Elenora." Her name flowed off his tongue like water burbling in a little waterfall.

Wait. What was he thinking? This smacked of romantic thoughts. No, he had to stop this. He couldn't possibly be cherishing those sort of thoughts about her, despite the loveliness of her name and her blonde beauty. She was not at all the sort of young lady who should promote those sort of feelings in him. No, he preferred women of experience who liked to play the game of love with him, and who didn't come with the threat of marriage. Although, he had to admit Elenora didn't come with that threat either, despite what her family thought.

She nodded. They were climbing the three steps to the terrace by now. "Jack. I shall definitely call you Jack as I like the name so much. Although... it does occur to me, now I think of it, that it would be an excellent name for a dog."

They were at the door. Through the glass Jack could see the drawing room now held Lady Wetherby and her sister-in-law, although etiquette had kept them from pressing their noses to the window. Thank goodness. He burst out laughing. "And now I think you are mocking me."

She stopped, raising her eyes to his for a moment. He could see the effort it cost her. "Why, Jack, I would never mock you." She kept her face straight, but her eyes were laughing as she reached for the doors.

The sudden realization that this season was going to be quite fun washed over Jack as she opened the door and they stepped back into the drawing room. Still laughing.

ONCE JACK HAD taken his leave, Elenora, much to the annoyance of Mama, who seemed inordinately pleased to have caught the engaged couple laughing together, repaired to the late Sir George Dandridge's library. This was where Mama had decreed the book she'd borrowed from Jack should be kept. If Mama had her way, it would have rested unopened and inviolate on the large desk under the tall sash window as some kind of symbol of their engagement. However, Elenora was not about to waste the chance to read it by sitting sewing with the other ladies in the family. Not when a fascinating book about the antiquities of Athens was available.

It was there that her two brothers found her some two hours later, when they called to dine with the family.

Matthew, ever the more boisterous of the two, flung the library door open and fairly catapulted into the room, his gangly limbs reminiscent of Bluebell's latest foal at home in Penworthy. "What's this I hear, Sis?" He flung himself into one of the high-backed leather chairs by the blazing fire and set his booted feet on the fire surround. "Papa tells me you're hitching yourself to an earl."

Jolyon, the elder by two years, strolled in with more decorum, as befitted Papa's heir.

"Not an earl, you nincompoop. Do you never listen? The heir of an earl."

"Makes no difference." Matthew gave a derisive snort. "An earl one day, that's for sure. And our little sis to be a countess, no less. That's a few steps up on a mere baronet, Joly."

Jolyon sat down on the window seat, stretching his not-so-long legs out in front of him. Both young men stood a head shorter than their tall father, having inherited their stature and rather sallow looks from Mama. Elenora was herself only an inch shorter than Matthew, the shorter of the two. Jolyon tapped his nose at his brother. "It's not so much that she's betrothed to an earl's heir, you numbskull. More which earl's heir she's to marry."

Matthew's dark brows rose but he didn't stir himself from his seat in front of the fire.

Oh dear. Elenora had an inkling where this was going. Both her brothers suffered from the totally unnecessary desire to protect her. It had been the same all her life. For some reason they saw themselves as her champions. This had been a nuisance to her on numerous occasions, such as when she'd been teaching herself to swim in the lake at Penworthy and they'd thought she was drowning and dived in to save her.

"It matters nothing to which earl's son I am engaged," she snapped, closing her book with a thud. Now her brothers were here, she was unlikely to get the peace required to read it again. And besides which, she should be going upstairs to change for dinner soon. Perhaps she could escape their attentions that way.

"Which earl's son is it, then?" Matthew asked.

Jolyon sighed. "As I said, you never listen, do you? Papa told us not ten minutes since when you were staring out into the garden like a sap, probably thinking about that actress of yours in Oxford. It's Lord Broxbourne she's engaged to. The Earl of Amberley's heir."

Realization dawned on Matthew's plain face, as well as a self-conscious flush. He was not the brightest spoon in the drawer, that was certain. "Oh. *That* earl's heir."

Annoyance washed through Elenora. Why were her family picking holes in her engagement? The fact that it wasn't real was forgotten. She needed to defend Jack. "And what is wrong with being engaged to Jack Deveril?" she snapped. "He's very eligible and Mama is overjoyed."

"Thought you weren't going to marry anyone?" Matthew, who was only a year older than her, so her closest sibling, asked. "Last summer, before I went off to Oxford, you swore to me you were going to stay a spinster and turn into a mad maiden aunt to all our children. When we have them, that is." He colored a little, perhaps at the thought of what he'd have to do in order to obtain these hypothetical children.

She scowled at him. "A girl can change her mind."

Jolyon crossed his legs at the ankles. His boots, unlike Jack's were lacking in shine. "And Mama said you had to marry someone rich in order to pay off Papa's debts, which Broxbourne surely is. Lucky fellow. I wish someone would pay mine off. Do you think your beau might do that for me, too?"

Irritated, Elenora shook her head with vehemence. "If Papa were not so addicted to gambling, I would not have to be marrying anyone. If I were you, Joly, I would give up the gambling as it will only serve to turn young ladies and their mamas against you. And no, I will not ask Jack to bail you out. It's bad enough that he's bailing out Papa."

She shuddered. "I find it quite mortifying that my engagement is purely a financial agreement." Did she? Well, she wasn't about to admit to anything else. Certainly not to finding Jack Deveril interesting. Although thinking him interesting didn't mean he was someone she might break her vow for. And anyway, he had such an air of supercilious entitlement about him, she couldn't possibly ever like him in that way. No, she could never think of any man at all as anything other than a friend.

"Jack, is it?" Matthew said. "I see you have it badly, Sis."

Fury rose. "I do not as you so crudely say 'have it badly.' Ours is a marriage of convenience only." And now she was defending the fact she'd just bemoaned. So confusing. "If I have to marry, then I would prefer it to be to someone who can help our family."

Goodness, her story was getting deeper and more complicated. Who'd have thought that the simple idea she and Jack had concocted last night would require so much elaboration? And the likelihood of it growing more tangled loomed ahead of her. Had she done the right thing in agreeing to this? At least Papa was no longer being dunned for what he owed, though. That was one achievement. In fact, as it was the achievement her engagement had been meant to bring about, she must surely now be absolved of further sacrifice. And she had no intention whatsoever of self-immolation on the bonfire of Joly's debts. The fact that he'd not learned from Papa's mistakes and Mama's unhappiness rankled.

Her brothers exchanged wary glances, as though they might be sheltering a secret neither wanted to share with her.

Oh well. "And you can stop looking at each like that. I already know Jack's a rake." There, it was out in the open now. "If that was what you were both wondering about telling me. I know all about rakes."

"You do?" Jolyon sounded disbelieving. "Are you sure?"

She frowned. "What do you mean?"

"We-ell," Matthew said. "From what I've heard, and I've not been in Town that long but rumor does get about, he has a mistress."

Jolyon nodded. "And she's not his first."

Matthew raised his eyebrows. "She's not?"

Jolyon sighed. "Of course she's not, you nincompoop. The man must be nearly forty. You don't get to that age, unmarried, without leaving behind a string of unsuitable liaisons."

Silence fell. Elenora and Matthew exchanged glances this time.

"Do you have a mistress, Joly?" Elenora asked.

His blush, deep and crimson and encompassing every square inch of skin above his cravat, gave her the answer.

"You do?" Matthew's eyes had gone wide. "You sly dog."

Jolyon had the grace to look awkward. "Not in front of Sis. Not for her ears. And don't tell me you haven't found a fancy piece in Oxford. I know how you fancy that actress."

"Do you think I'm stupid?" Elenora snapped.

They both shook their heads in unison, faces a matching shade of puce.

Elenora couldn't help herself. She had to giggle. "You should see your expressions. You're both very funny and no doubt consider yourselves as suitable husband material despite Joly having a mistress and Matthew having had liaisons with… with ladies of… of lesser virtue in Oxford. So in what way does that enable you to pass judgment on my betrothed? You should think of your Bible and remember the saying 'let he who is without sin cast the first stone.'"

Jolyon found his voice first. "I say, Sis, I'm sorry if I flew off the handle a bit. Just trying to look out for you. If this fellow suits you, then it's your choice. I'll be honored to welcome him into our family. And the last thing I'd like to be classed as is 'suitable husband material'—not for a long while yet at any rate."

"Me too," Matthew said, with a wide grin. "If he can make you happy, then we'll be happy too."

Elenora hugged herself inside. "You may rest assured, my dear brothers, that being engaged to Lord Broxbourne is making me very happy indeed." Which was practically the only true thing she'd told them. She rose to her feet. "And now I think I'd better change for dinner."

And with that she swept, she hoped regally, out of the library. Behind her she heard Matthew saying, "Now, what was she reading? One of those silly books on history she so likes, I'll be bound. And it is!"

Brothers.

CHAPTER TEN

B Y THE TIME Jack arrived back at his house in Portland Place, the lamplighters were out and the streets were a mix of pools of light and darker, shadowy spots which had to be hastened through. No sense in making a target of himself, despite his skills at self-defense. The cane he carried was a sword stick, something he'd had occasion to use more than once while abroad in the evenings. London, even in its most salubrious areas, was not a safe place at night.

People were still about, of course, but with the onset of darkness were more likely to be up to nefarious deeds than not. The scent of cheap tobacco smoke lingered in the damp air. Not a smell Jack was fond of, and he hurried his steps. It was not unknown for a gentleman out at night to be accosted even in a street like Portland Place. It didn't do to linger.

A carriage he recognized stood outside his front door, the four horses draped with blankets to stave off the chill and the driver hunched in his great coat on the front seat, a little red about the nose and miserable. He didn't require the coat of arms on the door to know that his mother had come to call on him. His father must have told her of his long-awaited engagement. Damn it, although he'd known he couldn't keep it a secret from her.

Once inside, he handed his hat, gloves and cane to Alcock and took the stairs two at a time. As he'd expected, his mother was in the drawing room on the first floor, seated in upright and righteous splendor on the blue chaise longue.

The Countess of Amberley, at three and sixty, was still a beautiful woman. Her once dark hair had gone steely gray, but her eyes, sharp and dark as her son's, had lost none of their acute intelligence.

She fixed Jack with a stare as steely as her hair. "Ah, Jack. I wondered how long I would have to wait." She did not sound happy. What could have given her cause for such a demeanor?

A little puzzled, Jack made a smart bow and approached where she was sitting. She held out a gloved hand for him to kiss, which he did. "Mama, how lovely to see you." How true this was would be revealed.

"Sit down." She patted the space beside her. "I have very little time as it's now so late, and Graves is outside with the carriage, waiting, as no doubt you have seen. The horses will be cold."

Trust her to think of the horses before her driver.

He sat down on a single chair opposite her. "As you are in a hurry, perhaps you might inform me to what I owe this unexpected visit."

"I shall get straight to the point. Your father tells me you have at last settled upon a bride."

He nodded, a little wary. "I have."

"And that she is a nobody, sans dowry."

"She is."

His mother's spine visibly stiffened. "Be honest with me, Jack. Is she a fortune hunter? Have you fallen into the clutches of an adventuress? It wouldn't be the first timc, would it?"

He let a smile touch his lips. "Really, Mama, is the former not a term reserved uniquely for men? And in what way do you imagine I would be taken in by an adventuress? Other than to take her promptly to my bed."

Her brow furrowed in threat. "This is not a laughing matter, Jack, and there is no need for you to be coarse. A woman can as easily be after a fortune from a rich husband as a man can be from an heiress. And from what I have discovered about this girl, she is no heiress." She must have spent the entire day in detective work, a dedication which had to be admired.

Jack sighed. "That's immaterial to me. I have enough for both of us and more to spare." Lying to his mother rankled. He'd always maintained an agreeable relationship with her. More so than with his father, at any rate.

She tutted at him, as she was wont to do in moments of annoyance. "Really, Jack, a girl whose family are plainly out for monetary gain is not a good match. And believe me, they are. I hear she's uncommon pretty, though. Which, no doubt, they thought would snare her the sort of husband they need. The sort of husband with a sizeable enough fortune to pay their debts. You, in other words. Your fortune."

The urge to defend Elenora from his mother's diatribe rose. "I would have thought by now you would have been happy to see me marrying anyone." He grinned. "Even a common flower seller."

Her eyes widened. "She is not… is she?"

Now he broke into laughter. "No, she is not a common flower seller, as your sources must already have informed you. She is the daughter of a baronet from Wiltshire. A good family with a long and unblemished ancestry behind them."

"A penniless rural baronet with a penchant for going deep in the card room, is what I've heard."

He had to give her this. "You are right on that, Mother. But I am not planning on marrying the baronet, and as far as I can tell on our short acquaintance, Miss Wetherby has no interest in cards." Wouldn't his mother be surprised if she heard what truly interested his betrothed? And the avarice with which she'd purloined his book. It would be fun to tell her, just to see the shock on her face. He felt like shocking her. Always a good thing to keep one's parents guessing.

She benefitted him with a reproving frown. "Do not be facetious, Jack, as it does not suit you and I find it irritating. I am perfectly aware that you are not betrothed to Sir Nicholas Wetherby, but your marriage to his oldest daughter will bring you into inevitable contact with the family. And I gather the eldest son is of the same bent as the father. A wastrel. They do not sound as though it will be a good connection."

The smile died on Jack's lips. "Hang on, Mother, I take issue with what you're saying. Just because you've reached the lofty position of countess and control Amberley Castle and Father's estates, it doesn't give you the right to condemn those less fortunate than yourself in such a high-handed fashion."

Her eyes narrowed, but she stayed silent for a moment. What was going on behind those eyes, so clever and calculating. He'd never been able to tell, and he couldn't now.

Whatever it was, she seemed to come to some sort of conclusion. "I see you will not be dissuaded. So, perhaps you can tell me about the girl and how you came to propose."

Jack swallowed. The exact circumstances should remain a secret—but had his father divulged some of last night's goings-on to his mother already, and would she know if he lied? "You don't know? Didn't my father already tell you? Or any of your other informants?"

She shook her head. "Your father was most irritating, as usual. He merely informed me that you had, on a whim, become engaged. He was smugly satisfied, as all he's bothered about is you producing an heir to his title. This morning. At breakfast. I mean, that he informed me at breakfast, not that you'd become engaged then." Her chest expanded as she drew in a deep, heartfelt breath. "I have to admit that I was quite surprised."

So his father had kept his promise, not a foregone conclusion by any means, where his mother, who could have stood in for the Spanish Inquisition, was concerned.

"I encountered her last night, at Father's ball."

She frowned. "I was there. Why was I not introduced?"

"You must have met her when she arrived with her parents and aunt. Everyone was introduced on arrival."

"She came with her aunt?"

"Lady Dandridge."

"Ah, Penelope." She sounded a trifle mollified, as though a connection to Lady Dandridge might mitigate the penury the rest of Elenora's family suffered. "I would remember if I'd seen Penelope arrive. Your father must have been greeting our guests alone while I checked the preparations." She huffed. "It's best not to leave it entirely to the staff, as things can so easily go wrong. Supervision ensures no mistakes are made."

So she hadn't met Elenora yet. Was that a good thing? The girl was such an original he couldn't be certain what she might say to his mother. Although, it might just be quite amusing... Perhaps he would invite Elenora for afternoon tea with him and his mother. "If you were busy with preparations, your lack of an introduction to my fiancée can hardly be laid at her door. Nor the door of her parents. Rather, at yours. You have a housekeeper to supervise the staff."

Lady Amberley was well known for her inability to resist interfering with the upkeep of any of her establishments. Her Town housekeeper, a woman Jack had known since his boyhood, had been heard to heave a deep sigh of relief when she retired to the country at Amberley Castle.

She bristled. "But there must have been a moment after you proposed to the girl, and let me tell you that proposing at a ball is not at all the done thing, when I could have been introduced. She met your father, after all."

Jack sighed. "If all you want to do is meet her, then that can easily be arranged. Come for tea on Thursday afternoon, and I'll invite Elenora and Lady Wetherby at the same time." But probably not Lady Dandridge and her daughter, nor those two rather plain younger sisters whom he'd observed eyeing him with definite fascination, tinged with a little scorn, when he'd visited. What did they have against him? Who knew with girls that age.

Mollified, his mother smoothed her skirts. "That will be most interesting." She paused. "Will little Edward be present?"

Jack froze, for once unsettled. He bit his top lip. "I think not. She need not meet him yet."

"If she is to be your wife, then she needs to. She needs to understand that she takes on more than just you."

Jack shifted uncomfortably, and not only because of the deception he was getting more and more involved in. "I don't think it would be a good idea just yet." Would it ever be? "I don't want to shock her." Although, was she the sort of girl who would be shocked by anything? He hadn't received that impression of her as yet. Despite her propensity to speak her mind, she seemed a level-headed and sensible young lady.

His mother nodded. "Perhaps that is wise. He might be better off if you sent him back to Broxbourne Park with his governess. The fresh air would do him good, and he is inordinately fond of animals, he tells me. Especially cows, for some unfathomable reason. Quite the little budding farmer."

"No." Jack shook his head. "I like to have him with me. He's not going to Broxbourne unless I go too."

His mother's mouth thinned as she pressed her lips together. "As you wish. But when his discovered presence causes trouble between you and your betrothed, don't say I didn't warn you." She stood up. "And now I need to go, or I'll be late to dine with your father. You know how he likes everyone to be punctual. Do you care to accompany me? I know he'd be pleased if you did."

Jack rose too but shook his head. "Thank you, Mother, but I prefer to remain at home this evening. You may pass on my regards to Father though."

When she'd gone, Jack rang the bell for Alcock. "I think I will take my supper in the nursery this evening." Perhaps today's events with finding Josie and taking her to Mrs. Sharpe's care had made him more aware of his own responsibilities. Perhaps he just wanted to see for himself that all was well up there. It would be, of course, for the nursery staff were of the best, and paid well for their devotion.

Two flights of stairs brought him to the generous nursery

floor, above which only the servants' quarters in the attic remained. Four doors opened off the wide landing—to the night nursery, the day nursery, the schoolroom and Miss Douglas the governess's room. As the clock in the hall outside the parlor had just been chiming five when his mother had left, and Miss Douglas would have finished the day's lessons, Jack pushed open the door of the day nursery and went inside.

A small, dark-haired boy was lying full length on the rug playing with a set of tin soldiers, and, over by the window, Meg, the young nursery nurse who had been one of Jack's first "rescues," was sitting beside a lamp darning a pair of stockings.

The little boy, clad in a navy blue skeleton suit, scrambled to his feet, a smile of delight spreading across a face very like Jack's in appearance. "Papa! You're home!" He ran into Jack's arms and Jack hugged him tight against his chest, breathing in the scent of small boy that soap was struggling to disguise. Such a contrast to the last child he'd held close as he carried her to Mrs. Sharpe's. With luck and good care, soon she would be as clean and well fed as this one.

He released the child. "Good evening, Edward. What battle is it you're recreating here?"

The child dropped to his knees on the rug and picked up one of the soldiers. "Bosworth Field. This is Henry the Seventh, and that over there," he pointed, "is Richard the Third, shouting for his horse." Henry VII had a decided bend in one of his legs as though someone had trodden on him.

Jack knelt down beside his son. "And who do you want to win? That's the important question."

Edward tilted his head to one side in thought. "We-ell... I know I ought to want Henry to win, and I know he did, but I'm not sure I like him much. And I'm not sure, either, that Richard killed the Princes in the Tower. Miss Douglas and me, we were talking about that in the schoolroom today, and she thinks it wasn't Richard. And Stanley, that's him over there, is going to be a traitor. So I don't like *him* at all."

Jack laughed. "That's my boy. You have the enquiring mind of a true historian, Edward. You're making me very proud. And as well as that, let me also commend you for your knowledge of Shakespeare." All of a sudden Edward's chatter reminded Jack of Elenora's. Both keen historians, even though Edward was as yet only seven. A precocious child, intelligent beyond his years. His chest swelled with pride even as he wondered if Elenora had been so as a child.

The little boy beamed. "Miss Douglas is teaching me all about the Wars of the Roses because I asked her to. It's so very interesting. When we were learning about the two princes, I imagined what it would have been like if I'd been Edward the Fifth, the poor little imprisoned prince. Stuck in the Tower of London. Although he wasn't in a cell, I don't think, like a criminal. He was allowed to use his bow and arrows. We read that."

"I named you for him, as the fate of the princes in the Tower is one of my interests."

Edward nodded. "I know, but they were victims, and I think I'd've preferred to have been named after King Richard. He was very brave trying to attack Henry all by himself. Edward was only a little boy and never did any fighting. He was too young, like me. But one day I'll be able to fight all right. I want to be a soldier for the king."

Jack stood up as the door opened and Thomas, one of the footmen, brought in a tray. "Enough of old battles, my little professor. Time to feed the inner scholar. I'm eating here with you this evening."

THE NEXT MORNING brought Jack back to Betterton Street. He'd promised Josie he'd return and make sure she was all right, and he wasn't a man who liked to break a promise. Especially not one he'd made to a child.

This time, Mrs. Sharpe herself opened the front door to his knock. A short woman whom childbearing had rendered rotund, she had about her the same aura of quiet peace that Jack had noted the first time he'd encountered her a good few years since, in the disreputable alehouse her husband had kept in the back alleys of Southwark. She'd taken off her habitual apron in order to open the door, and stood before him, neat, precise, yet above all, matronly. The perfect woman to run a home for vulnerable, rescued street children.

A welcoming smile spread across her pillowy cheeks. "Milord Jack." She bobbed a curtsy, something he'd asked her countless times to desist from doing. "I was wondering if you'd be back today. The little mite you brought us yesterday were convinced you'd come."

Jack smiled back at her as she stood aside to let him into the narrow hallway of number 23. To the right, a door opened into her inner sanctum—her parlor—kept only for the most formal of occasions and in order to teach her girls, all from the slums, how to behave in a decent household so they could obtain jobs as housemaids or shopgirls or even nursery nurses. Meg, who'd come from Mrs. Sharpe's a year ago, was proof enough of how her loving care worked.

Jack passed this door and headed for the back of the house where the warm and homely kitchen lay. Much his preferred location in Mrs. Sharpe's house, just as it was for the children.

However, as it was morning, all the children must be in the tiny schoolroom he'd had equipped in the front room of number 24, next door, being taught by the older of Mrs. Sharpe's two resident daughters. Only one of her charges remained, seated with young Lucy Sharpe at the kitchen table in front of the cozily burning range, each with a slate in their hands. It seemed his latest rescue's education had already begun.

Josie had undergone a transformation. The dirty, straggly hair of yesterday had been shorn to less than an inch in length— necessary to be rid of any parasites—and her face shone as though it had been well-scrubbed. Instead of rags, she wore a clean but shabby dress with a starched white pinafore over it. Her eyes, already not quite so sunken and shadowed, lit up with excitement as they fell on Jack. "You came back. I told 'em you would." Her voice held a definite hint of triumph.

Jack grinned at her, a small feeling of triumph sizzling through him as well, but for a different reason. Another child saved, or she would be saved by the time Mrs. Sharpe and her two daughters had finished with her. Much as he had saved them, once. "I said I would and I never break my promise." He sat down opposite the two girls. "I see Lucy is setting about teaching you to read and write already. Very useful skills, so you should work hard at learning them. If you can master those, then you should never be without work when you're grown up."

Josie held out her slate with pride. "I writ me name."

Jack took the slate and surveyed her embryonic autograph. "I think you are in need of a second name. Do you by chance recall what it is?"

She shook her shorn head. "Nope. I don't fink I ever had one. Lucy asked me, but I dunno."

Mrs. Sharpe, who'd been pouring tea from a huge kettle on the stove, brought some cups over and sat down beside Jack. "Like a lot of the girls here. They was never called by their surnames, milord, nor even their proper Christian names. Mostly they just got shouted at and called 'girl' or 'you,' I dare say. They don't know their real names. I think this one'll have to be another little Sharpe."

This would not be the first time she'd increased the size of her Sharpe brood.

Josie nodded with vigor. "I'd like to be Josie Sharpe, if'n you doesn't mind." She shot a shy smile sideways at Lucy, who put a motherly arm around her new sister's narrow shoulders.

She gave the child an affectionate cuddle. "And I should like to have you as another of my sisters. There's always room here for another little Sharpe."

Jack took a sip of his tea—hot and strong just the way he liked it.

Mrs. Sharpe nodded to Lucy. "Josie's done some good work this morning. Enough for her first day. Why don't you take her next door into number 24 and find her a storybook you can read to her."

"A story?" Josie's doubtful eyes swiveled from Mrs. Sharpe to Jack and finally to Lucy, who'd already got to her feet.

Lucy beamed at her protégée. "We have some wonderful storybooks Milord Jack's got for us. You come along with me, and we'll find a really good one and tuck ourselves in front of the fire next door, and I'll read it to you."

Once they'd gone, Jack turned to Mrs. Sharpe. "Any signs of mistreatment?"

She pulled a face. "A few nasty bruises. Undernourished, of course. Infested with lice and fleas. I burned her old clothes. She'll do. A bright little thing, if I'm not mistaken."

What a contrast to the life Edward led in Portland Place. It had been the way he'd become a father that had driven Jack out into the streets wanting to help the orphans of the slums. Only, despite his best endeavors, he'd so far been able to help so few. But at least he was doing something.

"I'm sorry I had to surprise you with her yesterday, but I couldn't have left her out in the cold like that. It's winter. You saw the way she was dressed. I had to bring her to you."

Mrs. Sharpe set her empty teacup down on the old oak table. How she could drink it so hot, Jack would never know. "You know I'll always find room for another waif if it's at all possible. I've got them all sleeping two to a bed as it is. You might be needing to take another house if you go on like this." But her chuckle proved she wasn't put out.

He drained his cup. "I could purchase you a bigger house somewhere else. Not rent any longer. Something more up to the task in hand. More bedrooms. Better than two houses knocked into one."

She smiled. "It's not so bad here. I know the neighbors, and they don't mind my girls. If we went somewhere else, there's some that might not like the idea of a lot of orphans from the slums in their midst. And I've at least three of the older girls ready to go into service—one of them's bright enough to be a shop girl. Real good at her reckoning. And another one's secured a job as a nursery nurse. Starts next week. That'll free up some space."

She poured some more tea. "We can manage here."

Jack picked up his cup again. "I don't want you to just 'manage.' I want you to have the resources to succeed and succeed well. That's why I installed you here. That and other reasons."

Mrs. Sharpe nodded. "And I'm eternally grateful to you for that, milord, I can tell you. I b'lieve he'd've killed me by now if you hadn't stepped in."

As this had seemed perfectly possible at the time, Jack didn't argue.

"'Twas the best day of my life when you stepped into our tavern and ordered yourself a pint of ale."

Jack stayed silent, but the image of that night, as dark and foggy as the ones that seemed frequent at the moment, leapt into his head. Mrs. Sharpe had been behind the bar, her husband drinking with his cronies. He'd noticed her black eye immediately, even though she'd combed her hair forward in an effort to hide it. The first evidence that she was married to a wife beater.

She cleared her throat and changed the subject. Perhaps she too was remembering that night and how close she'd come to death just a few days afterwards. "And how's your little lad doing?"

This brought a smile to Jack's face. "He's growing fast and is doing well at his studies, so Miss Douglas assures me. He's very fond of Meg as well. She's a wonderful nursery nurse. A credit to you. What matters most to me though, is that he's happy, and I do believe he is." He paused. "Just as I want all the children here to be happy." A lump rose in his throat. "To no longer fear going hungry and homeless and cold." How close had Edward come to that? If Mary had had her way... No, he wouldn't think about that. It was too painful.

Instead, he rose to his feet, talking fast to cover his discomfort. "I'm afraid this is but a fleeting visit, but if there's anything you need, don't hesitate to contact me. You can send Benjamin round to Portland Place whenever you want, never forget that." Benjamin was Mrs. Sharpe's oldest child and only son, who no longer lived in Betterton Street, but still called in several times a week to do odd jobs for his mother.

Jack held out his hand to his hostess and she took it in her own doughy one. "I should also inform you, I think, for you might well hear the gossip, that I am engaged to be married."

Mrs. Sharpe's eyes widened. No doubt, like everyone else, she'd never thought to see the day this happened. Jack was finding it quite pleasurable to surprise people in this way, even if the engagement was a sham. Shocking people was turning out to be more fun than he'd expected.

She kept hold of his hand, closing her other hand over it as well, her eyes sparkling with what looked like unshed tears. "Well, you could knock me down with a feather."

Jack laughed. "I won't try. And now I must leave you, as I have other errands to run."

Mrs. Sharpe gave his hand a squeeze before she released it. "And let me wish you all the happiness you deserve, milord. I'm right happy for you, that I am. And for your little nipper. He deserves a mother of his own to care for him." She paused, a hand going up to wipe her eyes. "I'm hoping she won't object to you already having a little lad, that is?"

Jack met her eyes as realization washed over him. He smiled. "No, somehow I don't think she will mind." Elenora wasn't that sort of girl.

CHAPTER ELEVEN

TWO DAYS LATER, days in which neither Elenora nor Petunia had done anything more than take a well-chaperoned walk in the park, a disturbing missive arrived. The whole family was at breakfast when Robert, one of Aunt Penelope's footmen, discreetly entered bearing a letter on a silver tray. She took the letter and read the name on it. "My goodness, it's for you, Fanny."

Papa, who'd just helped himself to a second plateful of kedgeree, came back to the table. "Not for me? Most odd. Who would be want to write a letter to Fanny?"

Aunt Penelope passed the letter to Mama, who broke the seal and unfolded it. Everyone watched her in expectation as she read. Her face, which had at first been curious, underwent several odd changes before finishing in an expression even Elenora had no difficulty in reading. Utmost horror.

Papa abandoned his kedgeree and leaned forwards, hand outstretched in an unsuccessful effort to seize Mama's. "What is it, Fanny dear? You're frightening the girls."

Mama's hand had flown to her mouth, and all she seemed capable of doing was passing the letter to Papa. He scanned it quickly. "Good heavens."

"What is it?" Aunt Penelope demanded. "Don't keep us in suspense, Nicholas."

"Girls," Papa said with terrible solemnity. "Your sisters have contracted the measles."

"The measles!" Mama squawked in corroboration. "Both of them. This is dreadful. Whatever shall we do? Elenora is in the midst of her season and freshly engaged. She needs to attend everything she's invited to. Oh, Nicholas, this is a catastrophe beyond all imagining, just when I thought everything was running smoothly." Then, as what could have been an after-thought. "My poor darling girls."

"I thought we'd all had the measles?" Elenora said. "I remember it well, although I was quite small at the time." Might they all have to return to Penworthy? How fortuitous, although she felt sorry for her sisters being the cause of it.

Papa shrugged. "I thought so too. How can Madeline and Phoebe have caught it again? I thought you could only have it once?"

Mama shook her head, her eyes filling with tears. "You're both wrong. The older children all had the measles when they were small children, but Madeline and Phoebe were not yet born, so they didn't catch it. What are we to do? I must go to my sick children. I can't stay here in Town. But Elenora must. It would not at all be the done thing to abandon her fiancé at this moment in time. Not when so freshly engaged. And she's been invited for tea at Lord Broxbourne's house this afternoon to meet his mama. I shall have to send a note of apology that she won't be able to come without me as her chaperone. Lady Amberley will think me so rude."

"Mama," Elenora said, with some asperity because she was already a little fed up with Mama's outburst. "I don't think it will matter one whit if I miss tea this afternoon and return to Penworthy with you to take care of my little sisters. I'm sure Lord Broxbourne will think highly of me for doing so. He must understand that my sisters come first." Which wasn't entirely true. Well, not true at all. But they were a very welcome excuse to depart for the countryside.

Mama shook her head in a mixture of shock and determination. "Nonsense. You can't do it. He's a man, and he won't understand. You have no idea how men think, Elenora, and I can assure you that they like to be the most important person in the hearts of their betrothed. He will not like to be pushed into second place." Her gaze fell on Augusta and Frances, who appeared to have shrunk down into themselves, perhaps in the hope of not attracting her attention. "I'll take Augusta and Frances with me. They are quite old enough to help nurse their sisters. Both of them have already had the measles, so will be immune to the infection. I gather you can only have it once."

A thought seemed to strike her. "And if you were to return as well, and then come back to Town, you might carry the infection back to Lord Broxbourne, afterwards, all unwittingly, and he might never have had it. That would be disastrous." She shivered, glanced round and her gaze fell on her sister-in-law. "No. You must stay, Elenora. Penelope must be the one to chaperone you about Town with Petunia. That will be for the best. There is the ball at Belmont house tomorrow that you simply must attend. Broxbourne is bound to be there and you will need to stand up at least twice with him. Penelope and I have already accepted, so my mind is made up."

Aunt Penelope's eyes lit up, and Elenora's heart dropped into her boots. "It would be nothing but a pleasure, Fanny. I will enjoy every moment of it. And so will Petunia."

Petunia fixed a smile onto her face. Ever since the engagement had been announced, she'd been distinctly frosty with Elenora. So much so Elenora had noticed, which was unusual.

"What about Papa?" Augusta, whose face couldn't hide her annoyance at being sent home to nurse her two little sisters, said. "Is he coming with us or staying in London?"

Mama looked to Papa, who harumphed a few times but said nothing.

"Well?" Mama asked, her eyes flashing. "Are you coming back to your sick daughters?"

Another harumph. Poor Papa. He was probably wondering

what the right reply to this was. Did Mama want him to return forthwith to attend to the two youngest members of the family, or did his duty lie in remaining in London with Elenora, where, admittedly, he would have unfettered access to the gambling tables, which wouldn't be a good thing with his newfound lack of debt.

Elenora glanced from him to Mama, then back again. "Why don't you go with Mama? Now I'm officially engaged, Aunt Penelope will be quite adequate to chaperone me. It isn't as if she needs to choose me a suitor, as that is already taken care of. I will be quite all right here with her and Petunia." And might not have to go to too many social events. The thought of spending more time in her uncle's old library, free of Mama's interference, was intoxicating.

Papa looked at Mama.

Grim faced, she nodded. "That's settled then. I shall rely on Penelope to chaperone you, Elenora, and you must pay strict attention to her advice. Now, Nicholas, you will need to organize our transport home straightaway. Speed is of the essence. And girls, you need to pack."

Elenora, a trifle despondent that she was the only member of the family remaining in London, abandoned her breakfast and went upstairs to help Augusta and Frances with their packing.

"It's so unfair," Augusta said, throwing her clothes into her trunk with a haphazard abandon that would have shocked Elenora's maid. "Not only have you inherited Papa's blonde hair and blue eyes, but, just because you were born before me, you get to come out first and go to balls and no doubt be invited to lots of soirées and maybe even a masquerade or two. And at your very first ball you catch yourself an earl's heir when you weren't even looking for one." She threw in her nightgown from the bed, in a tangle. "And now I have to go back to boring old Penworthy and look after Madeline and Phoebe who've had the cheek to catch measles just when Mama has finally taken us up to Town. I think they must have caught the measles on purpose."

Frances was sitting on her bed in front of her open, but as yet empty, trunk, elbows on knees, chin in her hands. "And we've had so little time here in Town. I'd so wanted to see the sights. And Aunt Penelope was going to hold a soirée of her own with recitals and all sorts of entertainments and she said we could both come. I was going to play the piano for her guests."

Augusta gave a snort. "I'm sure the people Aunt Penelope invites to her soirée will be immensely relieved they don't have to listen to your piano playing. I, on the other hand, had prepared a song to sing, which I'm sure they would have liked. Papa says I sing like an angel."

Elenora began packing Frances's clothes, as it seemed evident her sister wasn't going to do it herself. Unlike Augusta, she folded everything with care, mindful of how much work it would take for a servant to sort out crumpled gowns.

"An angel?" Frances retorted, getting into the swing of things. "He was being kind. No one would want to hear anything you sing as you bray like a donkey."

Augusta threw a shoe at her, which missed and hit a vase on the dressing table. It fell to the floor with a crash.

"Stop it," Elenora hissed. "Mama will hear, or worse, Aunt Penelope will. That was her vase and it might have been valuable. Stop arguing, both of you, and be assured, I would much rather be coming home with you than staying here."

Augusta stopped her packing. "You would?"

Elenora nodded. "I've achieved what was required of me, haven't I? A betrothal and a reversal of the family fortunes. You'd think Mama could let me abandon trying to fit into society. I feel like Cook's cat at home in Penworthy, trying to squeeze herself into a mouse hole after her prey. I don't fit."

Frances, ever more sympathetic than Augusta, got to her feet and put her arms around Elenora. "And I would stay here in your place, if I could. You can have no idea how happy your engagement has made me. I'd feared with the way you are, Gussie and I would never have had a chance of coming out until we were ancient."

Augusta scowled. "I don't know how many times I've told you not to call me Gussie."

Elenora frowned at Frances. "Was that meant to be a compliment?"

With a shrug, Frances bounced over to her trunk. "Yes it was. Now where did I put my boots?"

Elenora picked them up. "I'll put them in the trunk. I don't want you throwing them and breaking something else."

THE CARRIAGE DEPARTED a little after midday, after numerous false starts when Mama or one of the girls decided they'd forgotten something essential. Elenora, Petunia and Aunt Penelope waved them off from the front steps of the house until the carriage vanished amongst the rest of the traffic as it headed toward the Great West Road.

Aunt Penelope, who shared her looks with Papa in that she was tall and had once been fair-haired, turned to Elenora with an acquisitive glint in her eye that even Elenora recognized. "Well, just us three now, Elenora." She surveyed her new charge. "One could almost take you for my daughter and not Fanny's, we are so alike. You and Petunia could be twins."

Petunia, who despite being superficially like Elenora, was shorter and sturdier, shot her cousin a disapproving frown.

Elenora frowned as well. "You and I are not so alike, Aunt Penelope, for you are much older than me, your hair is nearly gray and you have wrinkles that I do not. And Petunia is fatter than me and her nose turns up at the end."

Aunt Penelope tutted like Mama was wont to do. "Your dear mother is quite right about you, young lady. You speak your mind far too freely. It is quite impolite... no, very impolite to pass comment on someone's looks. Especially in an unfavorable light."

Elenora's frown increased. "But you passed comment on mine."

"That was something quite different. And it is not polite to contradict your elders, either. So kindly do not argue. Now, we have a tea party to prepare for in Portland Place. Shall we go in?"

Elenora sighed. Why was it she could never quite understand what was the right thing to say? Why did she always get it wrong? Papa had drummed into her the importance of being honest when she'd been small, and yet, it seemed in polite society one was expected to lie, and that was thought polite. But lying didn't come easily to her, and she'd been unable to think of anything to say that would have pleased her aunt that hadn't been untrue. Perhaps it might be better if she didn't say anything. Yes, that was the wisest of moves. Silence, or at most, yes and no answers. How could that possibly go wrong?

Jack's house in Portland Place was one of a row of splendidly appointed town houses, each with large, shiny front doors opening onto a walkway over the basement level to the pavement. As Elenora and her aunt, for Petunia, in a fit of jealous pique, had claimed she had a megrim and taken to her bed for the afternoon, approached the door, Elenora peered down into the area below, where no doubt the kitchens were hidden, as they were in Arlington Street. Someone was baking a cake, the delicious aroma twisting up into the wintry air. The urge to escape down those spiral steps to hide in the kitchen with Jack's cook nearly overwhelmed her. Anything would be better than having to meet his mother.

Aunt Penelope tugged the bell pull, and the door immediately swung open to reveal an immensely tall, liveried footman. He bowed to them with an air of grandeur. "Lady Dandridge. Miss Wetherby." Clearly he'd been expecting them. He stood back to let them enter the house.

Elenora struggled to curtail her instinct to stare around in wonder. Of course, she'd been to splendid houses before, but this one was somehow different. This was Jack's house, and for some reason that meant something more to her. She needed to inspect it more closely.

Aunt Penelope tapped her arm. "Do not gawp, Elenora."

Elenora dropped her gaze to regard her own hands, but her eyes slid sideways, taking in the marble tiled floor, the portraits on the walls and the sweeping staircase. All on a far grander scale than Aunt Penelope's house, and of course, it went without saying more impressive than her own home at Penworthy.

"If you will come this way," the footman said, indicating the stairs, which were of dark oak.

"Thank you." Aunt Penelope followed the footman, and Elenora, indulging in her desire to stare while not under Aunt Penelope's eagle eye, followed behind. What a very impressive house. Mama would have liked it a lot.

At the top of the stairs, the footman led them to a door, opened it and went in. "Lady Dandridge, milord, milady, and Miss Wetherby."

Taking her courage in both hands, Elenora stepped into Jack's parlor, staring around herself at the stately décor of pastel shaded walls, elegant ornaments and tasteful paintings. However, in its very stateliness, it was not a comfortable room. Too much of an air of no one daring to put a foot wrong in it. If she lived here, she would remove some of the ornaments, or even the furniture and make it altogether a simpler room. But she never would, as this was only a sham engagement. For a moment she experienced an unexpected sadness that she'd never be calling this house her own. Which was quite ridiculous.

She switched her attention to the two people in the room. Jack, who'd been standing in front of the fire, and the woman sitting bolt upright on the chaise longue near him. His mother.

Jack strode across the room. "Lady Dandridge, I hadn't expected to see you, but the surprise is delightful." He bowed and kissed her hand, then turned to Elenora. Something about him felt different today, but she couldn't make out what. "Miss Wetherby, Elenora, you look charming."

This was true, as Aunt Penelope had insisted she wear one of her lovely new day gowns, made for her by Miss Collins in Lower

Grosvenor Street. Her aunt had persuaded her to admire herself in the mirror before she'd left, and she had to admit that the effect was pleasing. Although she'd done it for herself, not for Jack.

"I do, rather," she said, then wished she hadn't, as her aunt shot her a sharp stare and Jack's mother who had remained seated, arched a single eyebrow at her. "I'm sorry, I didn't mean to say that."

As this elicited a further similar reaction from the two ladies, it, too, couldn't have been the right thing to say. Too late, she remembered her vow to only answer with a yes or no. Better stick to it from now on.

"Penelope, my dear," Lady Amberley said, getting up now and taking Aunt Penelope's hands in hers. "So delightful to see you." She nodded to Elenora. "And I had no idea you had such a beautiful niece."

Elenora curtsied, keeping her eyes on the floor.

Lady Amberley lowered herself to her seat again. "Come, sit beside me, Miss Wetherby, and tell me about yourself."

Oh no. She was to be interrogated. No escape though. In trepidation, Elenora sat beside Jack's mother, very much on the edge of her seat, as Aunt Penelope took a sumptuously upholstered chair nearby, a slightly worried frown on her face. Did she think Elenora about to show herself up?

A quick glance showed Elenora Lady Amberley's cold dark eyes boring into her. "Your father is a baronet, I hear?" Such a frosty tone.

Elenora nodded. "Yes, Lady Amberley."

"Hampshire, I believe?"

"Yes, Lady Amberley." She'd clasped her hands in her lap and now kept her eyes fixed on them, firmly adhering to her resolution.

"You come from a large family, I hear?"

More than a yes or no answer required here. "Two brothers and five sisters, Lady Amberley."

"Do you play the pianoforté?"

"No, Lady Amberley."

Her ladyship harrumphed. "Do you paint?"

"No, Lady Amberley."

Out of the corner of her eye, Elenora could see Aunt Penelope who was looking more and more discomforted.

"What *do* you do, then?"

Oh no. But she couldn't lie. "I like to read, Lady Amberley."

Lady Amberley harrumphed again. "No need to 'Lady Amberley' me each time you reply."

"Yes, Lady—" Elenora stopped herself in time.

"So you are fond of romantic novels?"

Elenora shook her head. "Oh no, I never read novels. I prefer history books."

"History books?"

"Yes, history books. And I like to read some of the classics as well. Homer. Some of the Roman poets."

An indrawn breath. "You like to read them in translation?"

"Oh no. I taught myself to read in both Greek and Latin." She could feel herself scrunching up inside with embarrassment, but she'd been asked, and she couldn't lie. Her words were running away from her now, despite her resolution. Why wouldn't her mouth stop taking control of her brain?

"Good heavens. A veritable bluestocking." Lady Amberley was probably wondering how her son had managed to attach himself to such a person. Mama had told her enough times that bluestockings were not desirable as wives. Undercover of one hand, Elenora crossed the fingers of the other.

A silence ensued. Perhaps Lady Amberley couldn't think of anything else to interrogate her about. That, or she'd been shocked into silence. Elenora risked a peek at Jack, who was still standing by the window, a twinkle of definite amusement in his eyes. Was he laughing at her discomfort? Or at his mother's reaction?

Aunt Penelope reached out a hand to her old friend. "Perhaps the young people would like a few moments together, Lavinia?

And you and I might speak. I'm sure you're wondering how it is that I'm chaperoning dear Elenora and not her mother. It's a long story, I'm afraid."

Thank goodness for Aunt Penelope.

Lady Amberley seemed almost as pleased as Elenora was for this intervention. "What a good idea. Come, Penelope, and exchange places with your niece. We have a lot to talk about."

The two ladies took their places on the chaise longue side by side. For a moment, Elenora stood nonplused, unsure of what she was supposed to do. A gentle tap on her arm drew her attention.

"Come and sit by the window with me," Jack said. "Let my mother and your aunt renew their acquaintance undisturbed. And you can tell me why you have come with her and not with your mother."

Two seats stood in a window alcove. Elenora took one, and Jack took the other, their knees only inches apart. With an effort, Elenora looked him in the eyes. "I am to convey Mama's sincerest apologies to you. But we had word this morning that my two youngest sisters have been struck down with the measles, and my parents, and my two other sisters, have returned to Hampshire to tend to them." She paused. "You must understand that a mother's thoughts must be with her sick children." A direct quote from Mama.

"And you did not want to return to help?"

Was he a mind reader? "I did, of course, for I'm very fond of my sisters." Sort of true. "But Mama insisted that I stay. Had I not been engaged, I think she might have let me accompany her." She gave a little smile. "So, in a way, your idea for us to undertake this charade has caused me to remain in London. If we had not met as we did, I might even now be in the bosom of my family at home."

"Do you resent this?"

She shook her head slowly. "I would be lying if I were to say I didn't, but in truth, I fear that after my sisters recovered Mama would have had me back in Town at every ball again until I achieved the required success."

"You are the most honest girl I've ever met, I think."

She frowned. "That's not always a good thing. My family frequently have cause to chastise me for my honesty. I don't quite understand why it's seen as a bad thing by so many."

"You think it's not a good thing?"

"Not entirely. I have great trouble with the fact that I always say what is true, as Mama says not everyone wants to hear the truth. I cannot dissemble, which is another way of saying I find lying terribly hard to do. It can be most frustrating."

"For you or for your mama?"

She chuckled. "For both of us, but for her more than me. I cannot help it, but when something comes into my head, I fear I have to just say it. Whatever the consequences."

"Your honesty is refreshing."

She chuckled again. "I will tell you something, then. I had made a vow to say nothing, this afternoon, save yes or no. For fear of saying something your mother might disapprove of. Especially after what I said earlier."

His smile lit up his face, taking away the harsh lines that made him appear so devilish and making him suddenly appear much younger. "But you were speaking the truth, and you do indeed look quite beautiful."

"It is my lovely new dress that's done it."

He shook his head. "It's not just your dress, Elenora. You are a very beautiful girl."

She frowned. "My sisters are quite envious, although I don't know why. Being beautiful is another thing that's not so good."

"Why not?"

"Because it makes people look at you."

"And you don't like that?"

She nodded. "I can't bear it. Which is why a ball, or anywhere with a crowd, is such an ordeal for me. Not just because I'm a country nobody in Town for the first time, but because of the way I look and the fact that even when they're not, I'm convinced everyone is looking at me and seeing how odd I am."

"I don't think you're odd."

She shook her head. "Yes, you do. You called me an original. That means odd. I know I'm odd. I'm not like my sisters. I don't look like them, and I don't behave like them. We don't want the same things, they lack my… obsessions."

"You have obsessions?"

Elenora glanced back at the chaise longue, but Aunt Penelope and Lady Amberley appeared to be engrossed in one another's company. "Yes, I do."

"Pray tell."

Was that real interest in his dark eyes? She couldn't tell. "Well, you've already come across one. I love history with a passion."

He nodded. "That in itself is not odd."

"You can say that, because you're a man, and no one minds if a man shows an interest in intellectual pursuits. It is considered out of the ordinary, and unladylike, for a girl. And I'm not just interested, but deeply obsessed. I read history books all the time—mainly about the Ancient Greeks. In fact, I taught myself to read Ancient Greek—but don't tell Mama or she would be so cross. Mama thinks too much education for a girl is bad for her. She says men don't like young ladies to be cleverer than they are."

He smiled. "That might be true of many men, but it's not true of me."

She sighed. "Again, you can say that easily, but as ours is not a true engagement it hardly matters that you say you like a clever young lady. After this season and our engagement are over, and we return home, and Papa indulges in his newfound wealth and gambles again, sooner or later Mama will want me once more on the marriage market. And I doubt other men like you truly exist." She sighed a second time. "And do not forget I have four sisters who are queueing behind me to have their debuts and find themselves husbands. They will marry me off to some pea-brained member of the Ton who can't tell an Ionic column from a Doric."

He burst out laughing, and the ladies' heads turned to stare. He waved a hand. "It's nothing. I shall take Miss Wetherby on a tour of the house and allow you ladies to talk in peace. No doubt you have a lot to discuss." He stood and held a hand out to Elenora. "Come. I'm sure you'd like to see the rest of the house." He leaned toward her. "Or at the very least escape from this room. I only use it when my mother calls—the décor is all for her."

With only a momentary hesitation, she laid her hand in his and rose to her feet. "That would be lovely."

CHAPTER TWELVE

J ACK CLOSED THE drawing room door behind them with a satisfying click. If his mother couldn't be kind to Elenora then he would have to have words with her. However, the object of his pity didn't seem to be too indisposed by the catechism she'd been subjected to.

"I would love to see your library first," she said, steering clear of having to put her hand on his arm.

He didn't pressure her but led the way across the hallway to the double oak doors on the far side. He pushed open one of the doors. "It's one of my favorite rooms in this house."

"Libraries are always my favorite rooms, too." Following him in, Elenora halted and inhaled deeply. "I do think books, and particularly libraries full of them, possess the most delightful smell. They make me want to surround myself with them in big piles and just gloat over them. Magical. Yes, that's it. Books are magical."

An admirable sentiment. This was a girl who showed remarkable good sense. Not one of the vapid ninnies his mother had been accustomed to dangle, she thought seductively, under his nose from time to time. In all probability none of them had ever read anything other than the court social.

He stood back to allow her to look around, rightly proud of the size and content of his library. He'd spent the last twenty years compiling it. He would have to get his father to let him have the other two books in the series Elenora had borrowed. They were his books, anyway, as his father had bought them for him as a boy, so why they'd still been in his father's library he had no idea. A fortuitous circumstance, perhaps. And if they were here, she'd have reason to come back to read them.

This thought startled him. Why would he want her to come here any more than was necessary? After all, theirs was a sham engagement, and after the end of the season he need never see her again. And yet... this thought troubled him more than he'd expected. He must be getting soft in his old age. His friends would probably agree. But she was, as he'd already said, very much an original.

Elenora, still standing just inside the threshold, gave a suitably impressed gasp. "And you have so many books."

He nodded. "I'm proud to inform you that they're not just for show. I've read a great many of them." Most of the books, bar the ones he'd inherited when he took over the house, were ones he'd personally chosen for their content, and not just books bought by the linear foot to make their owner look intellectual.

"I should hope so too," Elenora said, but not in the tone of someone wishing to insult him. "I could never have engaged myself, even in deception, to someone who doesn't appreciate learning for the sake of learning."

He smiled. "You *are* an odd girl, Elenora. And you are quite right." She looked up at him. "But in the most enchanting way." What was he saying? That she had enchanted him by her honesty? He most definitely was going soft in the head.

She studied him for a long moment with a serious look in her blue eyes. "No one has ever called me enchanting before, not even because they thought I was pretty."

Rather a hole to dig himself out of. In a hurry. "Well you are, and if you can ever bring yourself to marry in the future, you will make some lucky gentleman very happy. I trust that if you do, you'll have the sense to choose someone who appreciates your quirks." My God, he was gabbling. What a fool he sounded.

"My quirks?"

He just might have dug himself in deeper. "The little things that make you into the girl you are. The things you think make you odd."

She frowned. "And it is *those* things you think are enchanting?"

How puzzled she sounded. Had no one ever told her that her frank honesty was endearing? Far better than the dissembling of a girl coached in the ways of flattery and flirting. Best to reward her by being honest himself. "Well… yes, they are. It's refreshing to talk to you." He felt heat rise unexpectedly from his neck up to his cheeks, and turned away. "Please, peruse my book collection to your heart's content."

She didn't appear to have noticed his discomfort, but took him at his word and hastened further into his library, running her slender fingers over the spines of the books as she studied their titles. What would it be like to have those slender fingers running over his arm? Or maybe over some other part of his body. He pulled himself up sharply. No. He was not going down that road with his thoughts. She was not the sort of girl to make a mistress out of, no matter how much he might be tempted by her looks and her charm. Even though he'd paid off her father's debts, he couldn't see the man tolerating it if he set Elenora up in her own establishment and made her his kept woman. And she had two older brothers, as well, who might not be happy about such treatment of their sister. Not to mention the fact that if she didn't want to be a wife, she would definitely not want to be a mistress.

He pushed these thoughts out of his head with deliberation, and turned his head away from the spectacle of such a pretty girl exploring the room he held most dear in the house and finding pleasure in it.

Footsteps sounded behind him on the stairs. Light, pattering footsteps. He spun on his heel. Edward reached the bottom three steps and jumped, landing with a thud on the rug, which slid forward, depositing him hard on his bottom. An annoyed cry shot out of him. Inside the library, Elenora's head turned.

Edward scrambled to his feet and brushed himself off. "Ouch. That hurt."

"What are you doing downstairs?" Jack asked, hurrying over to him. "And where is Miss Douglas?"

Elenora emerged from the library, a book in her hand, a questioning expression on her face.

"She's marking my Latin translation," Edward said, his eyes going to Elenora. "If she doesn't find any mistakes, she's going to take me to see the cows in Marylebone Park."

"Hello," Elenora said, smiling at Edward.

Edward performed a smart bow. "Good afternoon."

A silence fell. The need to fill it overcame Jack. "This is my ward, Edward Warren. Edward, this is Miss Wetherby."

Edward's eyes widened. "Is this the lady you're going to marry?"

Damn it. How had the child obtained this information. It couldn't have been via Miss Douglas, who was the soul of discretion. It had to be from Meg, his nursery nurse, a very chatty girl when she wanted to be. She'd probably gleaned this news in the servants' hall. She would need reprimanding, even though it was now too late. It would have been better had Edward never known about Elenora's existence. Unfair to get his hopes up of having a stepmother in his life. And the suspicion that Elenora might make a good one was strong.

"Yes, Miss Wetherby is the lady to whom I am engaged. I'm just showing her around the house," Jack said, not wanting to lie, and hoping Edward wouldn't slip and call him papa. He didn't want Elenora knowing his secrets, and Edward was one of them, and he also didn't want to lie to his son.

"I'm very pleased to meet you, then, Miss Wetherby," Edward said. "Would you like to come upstairs and see the nursery? I have a lot of really nice toys." His gaze went to the library. "And books. I spend a lot of time in the library." He held out a small hand to Elenora. "Do you like books?"

Jack shifted in discomfort. How unfortunate that for once Edward had ventured downstairs in the afternoon when usually he was engaged with his studies in the schoolroom. He should have spoken to Miss Douglas and impressed on her the importance of keeping the child out of the way on this particular afternoon. Too late now. Things could only get more complicated if he insisted on Edward leaving.

Elenora took away his opportunity to do that though. Smiling, she took Edward's proffered hand. "I should love that, Master Warren. Lord Broxbourne and I are avoiding having to sit in the drawing room with his mother and my aunt, so seeing the nursery would get us well out of their way. Lead on."

Jack cleared his throat and made a feeble attempt. "I'm sure, Edward, that Miss Wetherby isn't interested in seeing the nursery. She's just being polite."

She shot him an ingenuous smile, which, with what he knew of her, probably was exactly that. "Oh, I'm not. I would love to see Master Warren's nursery—and his Latin translation." She regarded Edward. "I had to teach myself Latin, I'm afraid, as my papa wouldn't allow me to learn it with my brothers. He doesn't think girls should learn the Classics. But I very much enjoyed the challenge."

"I'm not very good at it yet," Edward said, fidgeting a little in embarrassment. "I've only been learning it for a year. Just in case you're expecting my translation to be good."

The child seemed to have taken to Elenora straightaway, which was only going to make things worse when Jack had to tell him the engagement was over. But there was little he could do to prevent this now. Resigned to his fate, he followed Elenora and Edward up two flights of stairs and into the day nursery.

"These are my soldiers," Edward announced, indicating two rows lined up facing one another. "Yesterday, they were fighting at Marathon, and before that, Bosworth Field. Today, I think I'd like them to fight the Battle of Hastings." He picked one up, resplendent in the red coat of a modern warrior. "I just have to imagine them looking like Normans, I suppose. Miss Douglas drew a Norman soldier for me today so I know what to picture inside my head. I'm quite good at that. I'm not so silly as to think soldiers have always looked like they do nowadays."

Elenora dropped to her knees on the rug like a natural. "How splendid your imagination must be. I love history myself, and have always fancied performing a reenactment, only my brothers, who are older than me, were sadly lacking in any inclination to comply. All they liked to do with their soldiers was use their catapults on them, and see how many they could knock down."

Edward beamed. "Well, that sounds like fun too. But I love to have battles with mine, and I don't have a catapult. Miss Douglas says only naughty boys have them." He paused, as though a thought had struck him. "Were your brothers naughty boys?"

With a delighted laugh, she picked up a soldier. "Quite naughty, I have to admit, and still quite naughty now they're grown up." She held out the soldier. "This one could be William. He can't be called William the Conqueror until he's beaten the English under Harold, though."

Edward nodded. "Harold gets shot in the eye with an arrow. I'm afraid my soldiers have muskets so I have to imagine they're archers. Miss Douglas says imagination is very important." He paused. "Do you want to help me fight the battle?" A little blush colored his cheeks. "I was thinking that rug over there could be Senlac Hill. So I'm trying hard to be accurate. Papa says accuracy is of the most important with all things historical."

And there it was. Betrayed out of the mouth of a child.

Elenora looked up at Jack from her position on the floor, a puzzled frown for a moment marring her looks, then she turned back to Edward, no doubt weighing up how closely they resembled one another. She gave a shrug, as though it didn't matter. "I should love to help you fight a battle. Which side would you like to be?"

Jack leaned against the door. What was she thinking now Edward had given him away? Had that shrug been her dismissing the import of his son's words? Did she not care? Was she now wondering if he'd been married before? For a girl normally so outspoken, she remained surprisingly silent. Although not with Edward. Shortly the two of them were carrying on a noisy battle on the nursery rug, with soldiers falling like ninepins and loud noises of somewhat inaccurate explosions. "No cannon in 1066," Elenora shouted above Edward's battle noises.

"What noise do arrows make then?" Edward asked, as his one mounted soldier took out a row of foot soldiers. "King Harold is going to win this time."

The battle was nearly over when the door opened and Miss Douglas, a woman of dour middle-age, whose severe visage concealed a far gentler heart than could have been expected, came in. "My lord." She bobbed a curtsy. "Ma'am."

Elenora got to her feet and held out her hand, as though playing with Edward had loosened her tongue entirely. "Elenora Wetherby. You must be the famous Miss Douglas, and I see you have Edward's translation. Did he do well enough to merit his trip to see the cows?"

Miss Douglas's stern expression softened. "He did indeed. And if we are to get there and back before dark, we need to go now. If that is convenient, my lord?"

Edward scrambled to his feet, the battle forgotten. "Please say I can go, please, Papa." He swung round to Elenora. "I love cows and pigs and chickens and horses. When I'm older, I'm going to be papa's land agent at Broxbourne Park. So I have to learn lots about how to run an estate. Marylebone Park isn't like that. It's lots of farms. But it's got the nearest cows to us and it's only at the top of the road, so not far. And I love cows. They have such beautiful eyes."

Miss Douglas's eyes widened, no doubt surprised that Jack had allowed Elenora to learn his secret. Well, to discover it. Or was there a part of him that had all along wanted her to know? He nodded. "I'm sure the cows would miss your daily visit if you didn't go. Ask Cook for some apples to take for them. And put on your coat, Edward, lest you catch cold. And don't forget to hold Miss Douglas's hand at all times. The road is busy."

Edward hopped up and down with excitement. "Thank you, thank you." And he ran off with Miss Douglas.

Jack stood listening to his noisy departure for a few seconds before returning his gaze to Elenora, waiting for her to come out with her thoughts. Waiting, perhaps, for her disapproval of his secret. Although, probably that wasn't coming.

She was gazing into his eyes this time, as though all reticence about eye contact had vanished with her curiosity and with her game with Edward. "What a lovely son you have, Jack." She sounded as though she meant it.

"Thank you. He is a constant joy to me." How stiff his words sounded. How defensive.

She frowned. "But where did you get him from?" And how literal her question. Her bluntness could be disconcerting.

"You make it sound as though I went to a shop that sells children and chose him there."

She dimpled. "I didn't mean to. What I meant was, you haven't been married. I know that because Aunt Penelope told me. She knows everything about everyone in the Ton. She told Mama you are a confirmed bachelor, much as I plan to be a confirmed spinster. So where does a confirmed bachelor acquire a little boy? And I should say, that even before he called you papa, I could see he was yours as he looks so like you."

Jack sat down on one of the small table's two chairs. "If you sit down, I'll tell you. My mother advised me to be honest and tell you everything, as she thinks our engagement a reality, but I refused, mainly because I didn't think you needed to know. It seems Edward himself has forced my hand." But had he? Again, the thought that he'd wanted Elenora to discover his secret, or rather one of his secrets, arose.

Without a word, she sat down, still regarding him intensely as though it took a great effort to do so.

He cleared his throat, awkward as a schoolboy. "You will

know that I have had… mistresses. That is common knowledge amongst the Haut Ton. Lady Raby was my latest." He heaved a breath. "I should tell you at this point that my connection with her has been severed, in order to retain the impression of devotion to you that I would like others to see."

"You didn't need to do that on my account."

Did she mean that? Was there nothing about him that promoted any feeling in her against someone he might have a relationship with? And why was it he wanted her to feel that way? He'd think about that later. "Suffice it to say, that my connection with her is over. It is something I wanted, although it seems she did not. And before her, there have been other women. Not all of them in her situation. Not all of them ladies."

She was watching him now out of her candid blue eyes as though he was telling her the most fascinating story. She really did have the most beautiful eyes… the blue of bluebells in spring. He'd always liked bluebell time when he'd been a boy at Amberley Castle…

"Go on," she said. She possessed extraordinarily long, dark eyelashes as well. Unusual in one so fair.

"When I was younger I met an… actress. I thought her quite beautiful. We fell in love. It was not a mere dalliance on my part, nor on hers, or so I thought. But she was far beneath my station and when I raised the question of marriage with my parents, they forbade me from doing so."

"Why did you have to do what they said?"

An obvious question, but only when it came from her. Why indeed? "Now I look back on it, I don't know why I did. We have obedience to our parents ingrained into us from the very start, do we not? I wanted my father's approval, not his approbation. My mother was beside herself with shock that her only son should choose an actress as his bride. I swore I'd do it anyway, without their blessing. But my actress, Mary Warren was her name, refused to marry me. She vowed she could never come between me and my parents, and that she'd rather live as my mistress and have me on speaking terms with my parents."

"She sounds very selfless."

"She was."

"Was?"

He nodded. "Was. She died when Edward was born."

Tears glimmered in her eyes. "That is so sad."

He dropped his gaze to his hands where they lay on the table. "Yes."

Her hand moved across the table toward his, tentative and wary. "I am so sorry you lost Edward's mother." Her hand slid over his, small and warm.

Jack heaved a sigh. "It was a long time ago. Edward is seven now. I took charge of him after her death, as she had no immediate family, and found him a wetnurse, then a nurse, and now a governess. My mother was against it at first. She wanted me to put him in someone else's household to be brought up. She suggested he should grow up as the adopted son of one of our tenant farmers. But I'd given in to her once and was not to be bullied into it a second time." He looked up. "And in time, she's come to see him as her grandchild. I'm pretty sure she loves him."

"Well," Elenora said, "he *is* her grandchild. So I suppose if she didn't feel like that I might not be able to like her. She seems more than a little formidable. But if she loves Edward, then I am determined to like her, despite her questions."

"I suppose you see yourself as lucky that you won't have to deal with her beyond this season."

She frowned. "I suppose so."

An awkward silence fell between them. If only he hadn't spoken those final thoughts. If he could have taken them back, he would have. If they were going to make this sham engagement work, he needed to behave as if it was undertaken for real. "Perhaps we'd better go downstairs to the drawing room. We are, after all, alone together, and I'm not sure either my mother or your aunt would completely approve."

A smile lit her face, banishing the serious expression. "We are engaged, so I think every engaged couple is allowed a small amount of time alone." She glanced across at the fallen soldiers. "And we have two armies to chaperone us."

Jack stood up and held out his hand. "Most of whom are dead, don't forget. Let us go downstairs. Perhaps I could prevail upon you not to reveal what you know about Edward to your aunt? Or to your mother when you see her? I like to keep his presence not so much a secret, but more as quiet and unobtrusive. I don't want to give the gossipmongers more to gossip about me than they already have."

This time with less hesitation, she took his offered hand. "Your secret is safe with me. Although, if someone were to come out with the direct question 'does Lord Broxbourne have any children' I don't think I could lie for you. But I doubt anyone will ask such a question, so you may consider yourself safe."

And that would have to do.

CHAPTER THIRTEEN

THE DAY OF the Belmont House ball dawned all too quickly for Elenora. If only Aunt Penelope hadn't asked Jack to escort them. If only she didn't have to go. Everyone would stare at her, wondering how she'd managed to ensnare such a catch when no one else had succeeded, and she would want to sink into a puddle of embarrassment. It would be dreadful. She couldn't do it.

"I feel sick," she tried with Aunt Penelope. "I don't think I can go."

Petunia arched her eyebrows and heaved an impatient sigh from her seat on her bed. She'd been waiting there for a good fifteen minutes, her own maid having secured her appearance with more speed than Agatha was capable of. Especially as Elenora was in a fidget and no hurry to be ready.

Aunt Penelope laid a practiced hand on her forehead. "Nonsense, you look quite healthy to me. No temperature, and you have very pretty color in your cheeks."

Not what Elenora wanted to hear.

Petunia huffed as though exasperated. "That's what I told her."

They were all in Petunia and Elenora's bedroom, where Agatha had been struggling to arrange Elenora's hair to her mistress's approval, something Elenora had already decided not to give. She tried again. "I think I might be going to be sick." If only she were better at pretending, but she'd always found it far too stressful. Not as stressful as tonight was going to be though. At another ball. Who would have thought having obtained the desired engagement life would have become more difficult instead of easier? How unfair was that?

Aunt Penelope, who was dressed, coiffured and ready, just like Petunia, had come in to chivvy Elenora and Agatha along. "You ate a good breakfast of the same things as I did. It's just nerves, my dear, as it's your first time out as an engaged young lady. That's a big step for any girl." She glanced at her own daughter. "One which I'm sure Petunia will be taking before very long, as she has quite a fortune at her disposal."

Of course. Petunia was that desirable creature—an heiress with money, and Aunt Penelope had probably expected her to make a match before her impecunious cousin.

Petunia's expression became complacent. She'd been at pains to mention this several times already that evening.

Aunt Penelope fanned herself in distraction. "Now do hurry up, and stop worrying. All you need to do is raise your chin and look down your nose at those girls who haven't been as lucky as you."

Probably she didn't mean Petunia, although the temptation to do so was strong, given the way she'd been behaving since the engagement.

Aunt Penelope gave a little titter. "Getting yourself engaged to an earl's only son at your first ball is quite an achievement."

Had Aunt Penelope forgotten the circumstances of this engagement? Was she suffering from selective amnesia? She might not be so inclined to be smug if Elenora reminded her it had been brought about by her having been compromised. The inclination to remind her aunt rose, but Elenora stayed silent, perhaps wisely. Not that anyone in her family thought her wise. How right her aunt was about it being nerves making her feel like this. Only she was making a vast understatement. "I think I'm going to be sick right now."

"Pass her a bowl, Agatha."

Agatha obliged, holding the china wash basin in front of her mistress. Elenora made a few dry-retching sounds in the vague hopes her stomach would oblige, but it didn't. Drat it. Surely if she'd produced anything tangible her aunt would have allowed her to remain at home?

"There," Aunt Penelope said, a distinct note of satisfaction in her voice. "I told you there was nothing wrong with you. Now, slip your gown on and we can go downstairs. Lord Broxbourne has been waiting for us in the hall for the last ten minutes."

Elenora's spirits rose a tiny bit. At least she would be with Jack. Since she'd met his little ward, she'd revised her opinion of him somewhat. Any man who would take in his dead mistress's illegitimate child and clearly love him as he did could not be all bad. Could he? His child, in fact. He could so easily have followed his mother's first suggestions about who should care for the infant, and he hadn't. He'd kept him with him. A warm feeling for Jack's kindness trickled over Elenora. He wasn't the man everyone thought he was, and she was probably the only person who knew it.

If only Aunt Penelope knew that, as well. That would make her sit up and look. She smiled to herself as Agatha helped her into her ballgown. Another new one, this time in a pale silver satin, embroidered with tiny silver birds. Small, puffed sleeves sat slightly off the shoulder, and a sweeping neckline, combined with judicious use of stays by Agatha, created the impression of a decided bosom. A miracle what stays could do.

Taking her time, in the vague hopes that delaying the inevitable might help her, Elenora drew her gloves on, let Agatha drape a filmy cape about her shoulders that would not be enough to keep the cold off, and picked up her reticule and fan. Feeling like Marie Antoinette about to mount a tumbril on her way to the guillotine, she emitted a deep sigh. "I suppose I'm ready."

Aunt Penelope patted her arm. "No need to behave as if this is a punishment, you silly girl. You look a vision. If he had not already offered for you, I swear Lord Broxbourne would be fit to do so tonight when he sees you in this gown. It was an excellent choice of mine, if I say so myself." She stood back as if to better admire her creation. "It really won't be the ordeal you seem to be imagining, my dear. Your betrothed will be by your side as is his duty, and I shall be keeping an eye on you both, have no fear. You will be the belle of the ball, the toast of the evening, the toast of the season, in fact, as you are certainly the success of the season."

Elenora glanced at Petunia, whose face had taken on a mulish expression. Really, it was no wonder she was feeling jealous with the way her mama was extoling someone else's virtues and success. A pang of guilt washed over Elenora. She would have swapped places with her cousin in an instant, did Petunia but know.

She sighed. What a very good reason being lauded as the belle of the ball by strangers was for not wanting to go. She'd tried, but she'd failed. Short of flinging herself down the stairs in an effort to break something, she couldn't see any other way of getting out of this evening's ordeal. An ordeal that promised to make escaping this engagement at the end of the season all the harder.

With a nod of thanks to Agatha, she followed Petunia and her aunt out of the bedroom to the two flights of stairs to the hallway. On the first floor landing, she paused, peering down at Jack where he stood in the wide hallway with his back to her, ostensibly gazing at a portrait of Aunt Penelope's late husband looking portly and important, just as Elenora remembered him.

How tall and slim Jack was, and how smartly dressed. Quite the dandy with his dark hair styled into the Grecian and white stockings and tight silk breeches on, but also with the look of a military man about his bearing. She might ask him if he'd ever served in the army. Of course, he must have looked like this on the night she'd met him, but that memory had been erased from her mind. All she could recall of that night was him holding onto her dress so firmly it had torn, and then Mama and everyone bursting in on them. If only that wasn't the sole bit she could remember, she'd be happier.

Aunt Penelope, with a little, self-satisfied harumph, hung back, a hand restraining the grumpy Petunia, whispering, "Go down to him on your own."

On her own? Elenora hesitated, wishing herself anywhere but here. However, with Aunt Penelope behind her blocking any attempt at escape, she had no choice. She set her silver slippered foot on the top step, and as she did so, he must have heard her because he turned to look up.

Their eyes met and his rather severe expression softened into a smile. She hesitated, disturbed by both the smile and the strange look in his eyes. Why was he regarding her like that? Why was life so very complicated and filled with things she couldn't understand but others seemed able to?

"Keep going," Aunt Penelope hissed from behind.

Taking a deep breath, Elenora took another step, and then another, descending the staircase as slowly as possible, desperate not to trip on her long gown and looking where she was stepping rather than at Jack, but all the while conscious that his gaze hadn't wavered from her. Her cheeks bloomed with heat. Good heavens. It was bad enough having one person staring at her, how much worse would it be with a whole ballroom of people doing so?

She reached the bottom of the stairs, eyes still down.

"Elenora, you look beautiful." How deep and husky his voice was.

She dared a peek up at him. The smile had vanished and his face had taken on a deadly serious expression. At least, she thought it had… Long ago she'd realized how hard it was to read faces the way her sisters and brothers could, which was one of the reasons she watched people so closely. She tried to emulate their reactions where possible, but here she had no one's response to go on but her own. She tried a tremulous smile. "Thank you." She could return the compliment. That would be an easy reply.

"And you look most handsome and dashing tonight."

He reached out and took her gloved hand, bending his head to kiss her fingertips, all the while keeping his eyes on her face. Her heart performed a little, frightened flutter to add to all the other things she didn't understand. No man had ever looked at her like that before.

Aunt Penelope arrived beside her and Jack released Elenora's hand and executed a bow to her chaperone. "Lady Dandridge, as gorgeous as usual. My mother will be pleased to see you again so soon after your last meeting. She has decided to attend with my father."

Petunia cleared her throat.

"And Miss Dandridge. You look charming."

Elenora wasn't paying much attention to this. What had he said? His mother again? Oh no. The churning sensation in Elenora's stomach increased and for a moment she suffered the nasty sensation she might really be going to cast up her accounts—possibly all over Jack himself.

Aunt Penelope slid a supporting hand under her elbow. "Lord Broxbourne. I very much look forward to seeing Lady Amberley again tonight, and I'm sure Elenora does too."

Oh, but everyone was so polite. Elenora longed to tell them both the last person she wanted to ever see again was Jack's acerbic mother with all her catechism of questions. But she didn't. Hard as it was, she held her tongue.

"My carriage awaits you," Jack said, with a sweeping gesture of one hand toward the door where Hemmings was on duty waiting to open it for them. "Shall we depart?"

JACK OFFERED LADY Dandridge and Petunia his hand up into the waiting carriage, and, as they settled themselves, turned to Elenora. For a moment, he faltered. He'd thought her uncommonly pretty the first time he'd met her, but something about her extreme practicality had detracted from that beauty. Now, decked out like Cinderella on her way to meet her prince, she was exquisite. How would it be if she chose him to be her prince?

Pushing that rather disturbing thought out of his head, because it definitely wasn't what he wanted, he held out his hand.

She hesitated. Why was it she seemed to so dislike being touched? He kept his hand outstretched. Not because he wanted to force her into taking it, but because he very much wanted to feel her touch.

Her breasts rose and fell as though she were taking a deep breath to steel herself for something unpleasant. Damn it. Why did she still persist in finding his presence so distasteful? He'd thought the other day that things had warmed between them after she'd met Edward, but now it seemed they'd regressed to the start again. The urge to make her like him better, combined with a not unnatural annoyance that she didn't, had him almost snatch her hand.

He felt her resist and tightened his hold. Much as he had done with her dress, and perhaps for the same reasons. Despite himself, he wanted to get to know this strange young lady better. Whether she liked it or not.

Elenora shot him a sharp look, but allowed herself to be helped up the step and into the carriage. She sat down between her aunt and cousin, smoothing her skirts and keeping her eyes lowered. Had he not already known her better, he would have thought she was being demure, but he'd already worked out that demure was not an adjective to be used about Miss Elenora Wetherby.

He settled himself opposite the ladies, Hemmings put up the step and closed the door, and the carriage moved off.

Only a single lamp burned inside the carriage, and it was difficult to make out Elenora's face, not least because she was regarding her hands as though they were newly attached.

For some reason, though, Jack could think of no small talk to make, which was most unlike him. His mind remained a blank, as he studied Elenora and she studied her hands.

Lady Dandridge broke the awkward silence. "Will you be

going to the soirée at Lady Routledge's next week?"

That old harridan. Not if he could help it. "I have had an invitation."

"I have received one as well and will be taking Elenora and Petunia." She paused. "It would be most acceptable if you would be able to accompany us."

"In that case, I will do so." Damn it. Lady Routledge was such a nosy woman. If she sniffed a rat of any sort, she'd be on it like the terriers his grooms kept to keep the vermin down.

A somewhat strangled sound emerged from Elenora.

Her aunt turned her head. "What is it, my dear? Are you troubled about something?"

Elenora nodded. "No one has asked me if I would like to go."

Jack suppressed a smile. Good for her. An opportunity for him to help both her and himself. "If you would prefer not to, Elenora, I should be happy to invite you... and your aunt and cousin, of course... to dine with me in Portland Place that evening."

Lady Dandridge swelled like an angry pigeon. In Jack's experience, ambitious mamas, and Lady Dandridge obviously considered herself *in loco matris* right now, did not like to have their plans upset. And of course, she had her own daughter to marry off as well, a girl who was a paler copy of Elenora but who might shine were her prettier cousin not present. Dare he suggest that they should attend the soirée and allow Elenora to dine alone with him? Probably not. Alas.

"I should love to take dinner with you," Elenora said, her words tumbling out in her evident hurry not to allow her aunt to place an obstruction in the way. "That would be most agreeable would it not, Aunt? You would be my chaperone so I wouldn't be dining with Lord Broxbourne alone."

At least she had some idea of propriety, even if he didn't. However, her blue eyes had taken on a wide-eyed innocence that made Jack want to laugh out loud. This was a girl who could fight her own corner. A girl to be admired. If he had been looking for a wife, then she might have been just the sort he could have considered. The thought brought him up sharply. This was not what he should be thinking or, before he knew it, she'd have him in her clutches in reality. What a good thing they were both of one mind—against marriage, if each for different reasons.

As luck would have it, it wasn't far to Belmont House, and Graves was now slowing the carriage outside it, excusing Jack from having to continue the conversation and preventing Lady Dandridge from protesting.

A footman let down the step and Jack got out, the better to help his ladies descend. Time to go inside and face the grilling he was likely to get at his friends' hands as to why he'd suddenly decided to tie the knot.

"WHAT'S THIS I hear about you getting leg-shackled?" Lord Arthur Dugdale handed Jack a glass of whisky. "You'd better have a snifter of the hard stuff. I certainly needed one when I heard your news. Never thought I'd hear it said."

"It's all over Town," Sir Simon Westlake put in. "Everyone's talking about it."

"More to the point," Dugdale said. "What did La Belle Raby have to say about it?"

Westlake gave a snort that might have been laughter but also could have been horror. "If you told her face to face, then you're a braver man than I am."

Jack looked beyond his two friends, at where Louise was currently fawning over the young Duke of Routledge, whose mother she was old enough to have been. Just down from Oxford, he was lapping up the attention. "Suffice it to say, she was not amused."

Westlake eyed him up and down. "I don't see you limping or with any scars to speak of. You seem to have got off lightly." He sighed. "In one way, that is. But as you've hitched your horse to the marriage wagon, I think you've rather jumped out of the frying pan and into the fire. With both feet. You'll find out soon enough what being married is really like and be needing more of this nectar." He knocked back his own whisky in one gulp.

"She's an uncommon pretty girl," Dugdale said. "I must say that I can see why you succumbed."

"Being uncommon pretty doesn't mean she won't turn into a nag," Westlake said, glancing over his shoulder. "You will warn me if Amelia hoves into view, won't you?" He held out his glass for a servant to refill. "She's put a limit on how much I'm allowed to drink."

Dugdale raised his eyebrows. "I wouldn't have guessed."

Jack chuckled. "We both know how much you like her fussing over you, so stop pretending you don't. We won't wear it."

Westlake pulled a wry face. "Caught out, damn it." He paused, and a smile replaced the wry look. "Seriously though, old man. I wish you all the best. She's a gem. I can see that, and young enough to be molded into the sort of wife you really want."

They clearly hadn't met Elenora yet. Anyone less likely to be molded into any form she didn't want to take he had yet to meet.

"Do introduce us, Jack," Dugdale said. "I'd like a dance with your betrothed if that's all right with you. Need to see if she passes muster. I'm sure she will or you wouldn't have chosen her. I hear she's not got a penny to her name, so it must be love."

Ignoring the last part of this statement, Jack nodded. "She's with her aunt and my mother. Over there. I might as well introduce you now and rescue her from another grilling by my mother. Poor girl's already had one and she'll be grateful."

Elenora, seemingly demure and silent, was standing as he'd said with her aunt and his mother, near the door into the dining room where supper was being laid out. Petunia was conspicuous by her absence. Off dancing with some young man, no doubt. She looked a girl who shared her mother's ambitions. Jack led his two friends over and they made their bows.

ELENORA, WHO'D BEEN only half listening to the conversation

between the two older ladies, and had been trying to make herself as unobtrusive as possible, looked up as Jack approached. But who were these two men he had with him? Both of them older than Jack, surely? The sturdy one on the right had his sandy hair expertly combed upward, no doubt in a hopeless effort to hide his increasing bald spot, and was every bit as smartly dressed as Jack. The other, a tall, long-faced individual sported such high collar points he was having difficulty moving his head.

Jack introduced them as his oldest friends, and they bowed and kissed her hand, and Dugdale, the balding one, asked if she had a space on her dance card she could spare him. Her immediate reaction was to say no, but Aunt Penelope had turned her attention to the two newcomers and answered for her. There was nothing for it, she would have to dance with one of Jack's friends and avoid putting her foot in it. Although in what way this was worse than the other dances she'd had to take part in already this evening, she wasn't quite sure. Jack had danced with her only once, and the rest of the time she'd found herself so popular her dance card was now almost full. And she'd been right. Everyone was indeed looking at her. So much so she'd almost grown used to the mortification of it.

And now, Jack's friend was going to look at her as well and no doubt find her wanting. After all, wasn't that what friends were for? To find fault with the people around you. Or so she'd gleaned from observing her family.

At first, they danced in silence, as Lord Arthur Dugdale didn't seem to have much to say, despite staring at her the whole time as though she were an exhibit at a zoo and making her trip over her own feet and his in discomfort. It wasn't until the dance finished, and he offered to promenade her about the room, that he finally found something sensible to say.

"Wetherby." Dugdale tugged her hand through his arm with determination, despite her trying to tug it back. "Are you one of the Hampshire Wetherbys by any chance?"

His strong perfume was making her eyes water at close quarters. Thank goodness Jack didn't smell like that. Jack had just the faintest hint of perfume and a clean smell of soap about him, mixed with something she couldn't pin down. A much nicer smell than this heady aroma.

From Dugdale's expression, he must clearly be expecting an answer. "I suppose I must be. My family is from near Winchester. My father has a small estate called Penworthy not five miles outside of the city."

Dugdale seemed pleased with this information. He propelled her forward a few more steps. "Splendid. Now, tell me, Miss Wetherby, what d'you think of our Jack then?"

What a blunt question. The inclination to answer just as bluntly had to be controlled. With difficulty. "I like him well enough, my lord." Mama would be proud of her.

"A pretty answer from a pretty girl."

There wasn't really anything she could say to that, apart from thank you, so she didn't. Where was Aunt Penelope when she needed rescuing? Nowhere in sight. And no sign of Jack either. Inspiration dawned. She could ask Dugdale about Jack and thus prevent him from questioning her. "How long have you known Jack, my lord?"

His face lit up. "Since we were boys together at Harrow."

And it gave her something to talk about too. "My brothers both went to Winchester College."

"Splendid."

He did seem to like saying that.

Oh, how hard it was to keep a conversation going with someone who seemed to have a vacant space between his ears. Why on earth was Jack friends with such a dunce? It dawned on her, in a moment of unusual clarity, that perhaps here was a gentleman no more apt at conversation with a stranger than she was. Did he need some help, as she so often did? "Perhaps you could tell me some of the things he likes to do."

Dugdale blushed scarlet. Perhaps not such a good question to ask. "Er," he managed, floundering. "Hunting in the winter. A spot of pheasant shooting. The card table. That sort of thing. Same as most of us fellows." He waved a hand, looking desperate. What was it he didn't want to tell her? "Oh look, here's Westlake. Shall we join him?"

How pleasant to have met someone more tongue-tied in company than she was. Not a common occurrence for Elenora. Itching to remove her hand from Dugdale's arm, she let him lead her over to where his friend was talking to someone. Who it was, she couldn't see, as Westlake was in the way.

Westlake half turned, and his welcoming smile vanished, to be replaced with a rictus grin, as from behind him the magnificent Lady Raby appeared. The woman in the red dress with whom Jack had been dancing on the night she'd first met him. His ex-mistress, if he was to be believed, which he surely was.

Elenora felt Dugdale almost stop, then steel himself to continue as Westlake bowed to her. "Why, Miss Wetherby, I don't think you know Lady Raby, do you?" His voice rose an octave and perspiration stood out on his forehead.

Seizing the opportunity to regain her own hand again, Elenora dropped a sweeping curtsy. When she rose, she found Lady Raby's diamond-hard gray eyes fixed on her. Even she could tell those eyes did not hold any kind of camaraderie.

Lady Raby ran her gaze up and down Elenora, the faintest curl of her upper lip indicating that what she saw did not find favor. "Miss Wetherby, might I congratulate you on your triumph in snaring a man we'd all thought would never marry. An astounding accomplishment at only your first ball, I gather. And for one so young… and unencumbered with expectations."

Oh, if only she could slip away like a ghost in the mist, and not have to stand here fixing a smile on her face as though she'd contracted lockjaw. This woman did not like her one bit, and Elenora had no idea why. "Thank you, my lady."

Lady Raby put a gloved hand on Elenora's arm. "And now I must have Miss Wetherby to myself. You boys can run along. We shall be putting our heads together privately." She waved a hand at Dugdale and Westlake. "Off you go."

Jack's two friends exchanged panicked looks. She wanted to beg them not to leave her, but manners, for once, held her silent. They retreated, guilt written across their faces, abandoning her to what could only be her fate.

"Now," said Lady Raby with a self-satisfied smile. "Let us find a little alcove and get to know one another."

CHAPTER FOURTEEN

LADY RABY SEEMED to know Belmont House well. Still with her hand on Elenora's arm, a fact which was making her prey want to twitch free, she guided her into a sizeable, curtained alcove, equipped with a two-seater, velvet-upholstered sofa. She sat down, and her grip on Elenora's arm tightened as she compelled her down beside her. "Now," she said, her eyes narrowing. "Let us have our little talk."

Elenora swallowed. Whatever was this hard-faced woman, and there was no other way of describing her, about to say? However, a determination not to be cowed by her burgeoned. She lifted her chin and looked her in the eye. Admittedly with difficulty. "My lady?"

Lady Raby released her hold on Elenora's arm, and leaned toward her. "He's only marrying you because his father wants an heir to the earldom." Her voice was nothing more than a vicious hiss, and her eyes, those diamond-hard eyes, flared with hatred. Even Elenora could recognize that for what it was.

Before she could stop herself, she shrank back. Was this the sort of conversation one had with ladies one didn't know in alcoves at balls? Could Lady Raby, despite her title, truly be classed as a lady if she behaved like this? Beyond the curtained alcove, the sound of music and laughter and conversation receded as though suddenly far away. Nearly twenty years of country life had not prepared Elenora for an attack like this. However, honesty prevailed.

"I know." This wasn't quite a lie, as Jack's father most certainly did long for his son to provide an heir. Just it wasn't going to be through her.

Lady Raby's eyes narrowed. "A marriage of convenience, then." Not a question but a statement.

Elenora refused to allow her eyes to waver toward the ballroom, in search of help. The struggle was making her heart pound so hard she expected any moment for Lady Raby to remark on the noise. "Absolutely." If only someone would come. Anyone. But Lady Raby had chosen this alcove with care.

To her satisfaction, her honesty seemed to have taken Lady Raby aback. Perhaps she'd been expecting a fit of the vapors and tears. Well, she was going to be disappointed.

She soon regained her composure though. "And I daresay your parents have benefitted from selling off their daughter to the highest bidder." Spittle flew. "I gather you come from a large family—Lord Amberley will have seen you as good breeding material, I'm sure." She lifted her right hand and flicked Elenora's golden curls. "And pretty enough, I'll allow, to make getting that heir not an unpleasant task for Broxbourne."

This was insupportable. It was bad enough subjecting herself to occasional contact with those she knew, but strangers were not allowed to touch her. Elenora's hackles rose. Mama had drummed it into her enough times that she was just to nod and agree with anyone she met out of politeness, but this was too much. She couldn't sit there and take this woman's insults. Best to keep it polite though. "I don't think you should be speaking to me in this way." She invested her voice was as much regal haughtiness as Augusta liked to use when dealing with their youngest sisters.

Lady Raby's face darkened. Whereas Jack could look quite devilish, it was in the most attractive of manners, but this, this was frightening, or it would have been had Elenora possessed less backbone. How had she ever thought Lady Raby beautiful? Now, her face twisted into something ugly and malevolent, as though she were the wicked fairy from one of Elenora's childhood books. "It won't last, you know," she spat. "He'll pay you attention to start with, of course, because you're pretty enough, but once he has that heir in his nursery, he'll lose interest in you soon enough. And probably before that, when carrying the heir makes you fat and ugly. He'll be happy enough to leave you in the country and be back in Town with me." She bared her teeth, which were long and yellow like a wolf's, or at least they appeared so. "You'll see."

Of course, this woman had been Jack's mistress, not that Elenora had forgotten, but she'd always thought mistresses, if they'd ever crossed her mind, just moved on to the next man after they'd done with the first. That Lady Raby carried feelings for Jack was obvious. Had this woman approached her in anything but this way, Elenora might have felt sorry for her. He'd been forced to cast her aside—because he was now engaged. Briefly, the notion that he'd done so for her warmed her insides. But then the thought took over that perhaps he'd never seen his mistress as she was right now—a woman contorted so much with hate that she'd cornered the woman she saw as her rival at a ball. Was it love that had prompted this outburst, or was she just a woman scorned, jealous that someone else had, she thought, taken her place in Jack's life.

Elenora rose to her feet. "I'm sure you think you know what you're talking about," she said. "But you are wrong about many things. Jack and I might be engaged to suit his father, but we are at least on terms of friendship, and that is clearly more than you are. Good bye." She turned on her heel and plunged out of the alcove, straight into Jack's arms.

JACK HAD STARTED to look for her as soon as Dugdale and Westlake located him in the card room and informed him of what had happened. He'd excused himself to the other players on a matter of urgency and managed to escape the game he was part of. The thought of what Louise might say or do to Elenora disturbed him, although they were in a place as public as a ball, so hopefully etiquette would keep her silent. For the most part.

He was just heading into the ballroom, when Elenora catapulted out of an alcove on his right, straight into his arms. Out of instinct, he wrapped them around her, holding her for a moment against his chest, a warm feeling drenching him from head to toe. To his surprise, at first she made no attempt to free herself, but heads were turning, so he released her. And, over the top of her head, he saw Louise, still seated inside the shadowy alcove, her gaze fixed on his face, like a starving man might stare at a slice of bread.

What had Louise said? Elenora was trembling, her bosom heaving as though she'd run at least a mile, but from the flash in her wide blue eyes he could tell it was from anger rather than fear. He pulled her arm through his. "Come, let us walk together. I think you could do with some fresh air." He'd deal with Louise later.

Elenora for once made no objection, so he led her out onto the terrace at the back of the house where a couple of men were leaning on the balustrade drinking whisky in the dim light of some colored lanterns.

She shivered in the cold, and in a moment he had his coat off and draped around her slender shoulders. She looked up at him, but he couldn't see her face in the gloom at this end of the terrace nor tell what she was thinking.

With a long sniff, as though she were checking to see if it smelled, she drew the coat about herself. "Thank you."

"My pleasure." But my goodness, it was chilly. Better get this over with quickly before he froze in just his shirt sleeves. "What did she say to you?"

With a glance in the direction of the two other fellows, Elenora moved closer. The scent of her perfume tickled his nostrils. Inside, the band struck up Sir Roger de Coverley. If he wasn't engaged to her, and it wasn't all a hoax, and there weren't two possible witnesses, he'd have been tempted right now to take her in his arms and kiss her, for the fun of it. She was, after all, a very beautiful girl, and her quirky personality fascinated him.

Elenora kept her voice low. "She tried to warn me about you, is all, truly. But I didn't like the way she spoke to me. She was not polite at all." He could almost hear the frown on her face. "Mama took great pains to caution me, time and again, before we came up to London, that I should not argue with my betters or elders, but really, I had to tell her she had no place saying those things to me."

Jack frowned. "You didn't tell her the truth, I hope? She's not a woman I'd trust to keep a secret like that."

She shook her head. "Of course I didn't. I'm not stupid. I thought you'd worked that out for yourself." Indignation colored her voice at his implication. "But I did have to admit to her that it was a marriage of convenience, which I suppose it almost is. An engagement of convenience, if you want to be pedantic. So I wasn't telling a lie."

Jack breathed a sigh of relief. "You must ignore everything she says to you. She's a spiteful woman when crossed."

She moved closer still, ingenuous as ever. "I suppose she is... I mean was... your mistress, so perhaps she feels a little proprietorial about you." Now she sounded openly curious. No doubt she'd never come across anything so intriguing as a mistress. Sir Nicholas probably wouldn't have dared, any more than Simon would. Strong women could put a chokehold on a man's private life. Another reason for not wishing to marry. Why was it he kept having to repeat the reasons why he didn't want to? Was he reassuring himself in case he weakened at some point?

Elenora's shoulders rose in a shrug. "She did seem inordinately annoyed that you had got yourself engaged to someone like me, a nobody, although I think that whoever you had become engaged to, she would have hated them with a vengeance."

Refreshing as it was that she always spoke her mind, it was also embarrassing. He'd never had occasion to discuss his amatory liaisons with any other woman. His mother knew of them, in all probability, but wisely held her counsel. However, Elenora was a virginal nineteen-year-old with whom he should not be discussing his ex-mistress. However, honesty breeds honesty.

"I suppose I am forced to admit that I didn't treat her well in severing my association with her. I fear her feelings were more engaged than mine were." This was all far too awkward. "But she knew our liaison could never have come to anything, and it would have been impossible to continue with it after my engagement. *Our* engagement."

Her eyes caught the light for a moment. They appeared to be sparkling with curiosity. Was she enjoying this? Clearly so. "I think it quite fascinating that you have had mistresses. I've never before met anyone who has admitted to that, although I'm quite sure my two brothers are thus attached, or want to be." She chuckled, perhaps at a memory. "And it's perfectly splendid that you're able to discuss them with me, which makes me convinced that we are true friends now. Your friend Dugdale seems very fond of the word splendid. I thought I would borrow it from him." She paused, head tilted a little to one side, birdlike. "I was just wondering, though, if you had ever seen Lady Raby when she was truly angry?" She shivered. "I am not a girl normally shocked, but the look on her face was something quite unpleasant. And I'm being tactful." She chuckled again, a delightful low gurgle. "Not something Mama thinks I ever am."

Jack found himself tempted to join in her merriment. "Your lack of tact is something I find infinitely amusing. It's refreshing to be in the company of one so unrestrained by normal social mores."

She chuckled again as though this too was enjoyable. "But aren't you getting cold? I have your coat and you only have your shirt and waistcoat. Although both are very smart, I daresay that doesn't count toward their quality of warming you. Shall we go back inside? I have quite forgotten how horrible Lady Raby was now, and will steer well clear of her on the ballroom floor. In fact,

I should be quite happy to steer clear of everyone and go home. You already know I don't care for crowds, I think." She laid a dainty hand on his arm. "Would it be too much to ask if you would be so kind as to take me home in your carriage? Then, if you return, you can dance with Lady Raby and cheer her up a bit. She looked as though she needs it."

What a girl. He shook his head. "Your kind sentiment in suggesting I dance with her is wasted. I'm finished with Lady Raby. You saw her at her worst, as I did when I informed her of my engagement. Behavior like that is not the way to regain my attention, and she needs to understand that. I shall not be dancing with her again." He smiled, a bitter taste in his mouth. "Nor anything else. Rest assured. And even were I of a different frame of mind, it would not be acceptable for me, as a newly engaged man, to be seen to pay attention to the woman who used to be my mistress."

Her face caught the light and he saw her smile. "But you will still take me home? I can ask you this as we are alone, and engaged of course, but Aunt Penelope would be horrified. She thinks attending balls is the most important thing in the world for a girl and doesn't countenance any other opinion. And I, for one, do not like balls at all. Perhaps we can tell her I have a headache." Her face brightened further. "And if you tell her instead of me, then she will have to believe you. I've had my fill for one night of people staring at me. You can have no idea how embarrassing that is."

He shrugged, puzzled by her vehemence. "People often stare at me. I ignore them, and you would be best to do the same. But if that's what you want, I suppose we can but try. Come inside. I'll have to have my coat back before we go in, though."

She hesitated, an earnest expression on her face, clearly visible now they were nearer the doors. "You don't understand. And it's near impossible for me to explain. I know most people don't feel the way I do about crowds—about people in general. None of my sisters or brothers have the least difficulty with them, yet I find going out in public the hardest thing I have to do." Her eyes moved to the doors. "And this is very public and very crowded." She put her hand to her breast. "My heart is pounding with anxiety as it has been doing all evening long."

He turned toward her, one hand going up to her shoulder, the other lingering as though he wanted to feel for that rapidly beating heart. He didn't, of course. That would have had her flying for safety.

She didn't budge. "It's something I've struggled with all my life. Which is why coming out and having a season in London is such a burden for me. Every social event I have to go to is an ordeal because I know no one, and because I'm convinced, even though I'm told it can't be true, that everyone is staring at me." She paused. "It's hard enough for me to admit it here, to you, but I'm doing it because I think you might be able to understand me if you try." She looked down at her hands. "Your treatment of little Edward makes me think you are inclined to sympathy."

The urge to fold this delightfully honest young woman to his chest and soothe her fears away washed over Jack like a tidal wave. Why was he feeling like this? Never in his life had he felt an instinct like this one. Plenty of times he'd felt desire overcome him, but never the longing to keep someone safe. Apart from Edward, and the children he rescued from the streets.

He became aware he was staring at her like a moonstruck calf. Not a good idea. Time to say something. He had to clear his throat, but even so his words came out on the gruff side. "I believe you, Elenora."

Her face lit up. "Thank you, Jack." And before he could stop her, she'd stood on tiptoe and planted a light kiss on his cheek. "You know, I could really get to like you, Lord Broxbourne." And with that she shrugged off his coat and handed it back. As he was struggling into it, she was through the door and off onto the dance floor in search of her aunt. All Jack could do was follow her.

CHAPTER FIFTEEN

J ACK DID NOT go back to the ball after he'd escorted Elenora and
a rather grumpy Aunt Penelope and Petunia back to Arlington
Street. A journey notable for the fact that when Elenora got into
the carriage, she took the seat opposite her aunt and cousin rather
than between them, as she'd done on the outward journey. Jack
took the opportunity to take the seat beside her, although, as
Aunt Penelope was present, he kept silent. After all, Elenora was
supposed to be nursing a megrim. The fact that he quite wanted
to reach out and take her hand in his was more than a little
disturbing, which made him thankful for her chaperone's eagle
eyes keeping those impulses under control.

He escorted them up to their door and saw them safely
through it, as at that time of night you could never be certain of
safety even on your own doorstep. Several disreputable looking
men could be seen lurking in the shadows, out of the circles of
light thrown by the streetlamps, the smoke from at least one pipe
curling upwards to join the ever-present fog. He couldn't possibly
have abandoned three ladies to traverse the space between
carriage and front door alone.

With them safely inside, he returned to his carriage and had
Parker drive him home. The press at Belmont House had
somehow lost its attraction after the way Elenora had explained
herself. He couldn't imagine what it would be like to feel like
that, but a part of him wanted to do so, in order to relate more

closely to her. He'd stopped, by now, questioning his motives. And besides, without her there, the attraction had waned.

Parker halted the carriage at the steps up to his own double front door and Thomas came and let down the step, standing back smartly to attention. Getting home now, even if it was after midnight, would be a relief for his servants, some of whom couldn't take themselves off to bed before he returned.

The carriage rumbled off around to the back entrance of the mews, and Jack started up the steps to where Thomas was now holding the door open for him. As he did so, a slight movement caught his eye.

Someone was standing in the shadows a couple of houses down. A dark and for some reason familiar shape. Where had he seen that figure before? But whoever it was melted back into the darkness out of sight as quickly as Jack spotted him. Had he even seen him or had the figure been a figment of his imagination? And was he just on edge after having seen those lurking figures near Lady Dandridge's house? London was always like this—thronging with people who looked as though they meant you ill, and in all probability did. Maybe he was getting overcautious in his old age.

He shrugged and went inside.

His valet, Briggs, was waiting upstairs for him in his dressing room, possibly already alerted to his return by the secret house telegraph system whose workings Jack had yet to fathom. He bowed as Jack came into his dressing room. "My lord."

Briggs, a burly individual who would not have looked out of place in the boxing ring, had been with Jack since he was little more than a boy. Since he'd left Harrow to be exact. Jack's father had decreed that, as he was no longer a schoolboy, he was in need of a man to dress him and take care of his clothes. So Briggs, who had been one of his father's underfootmen, had been allotted the task. Something that had pleased Briggs, a Wiltshire boy with a yen to see London Town, no end.

And Briggs had probably seen a lot of London by now, as Jack, eager to kick over the traces and restrictions of life as a schoolboy, had almost immediately set up his own establishment in Portland Place.

Briggs helped him out of his coat. "Might I venture to remark that your lordship is returned unusually early. May I enquire after your lordship's health?"

Jack let him undo his cravat. "I suppose I am. My fiancée, Miss Wetherby, was feeling a little out of sorts, so I escorted her and her aunt home." Briggs, like all of his staff, had known about his engagement almost before he did due to that possible sixth sense they all seemed to possess. No doubt the servants in every house in London now knew as well, although hopefully not all the details. However, you never knew with servants.

"I trust she is not too indisposed," Briggs said, slipping Jack's waistcoat onto a hanger and straightening it with practiced hands.

Jack stepped out of his satin breeches and pulled off his stockings. "Briggs, have you noticed anyone hanging about in the street recently?'

Briggs paused in the act of picking up the breeches. "Many people loiter outside in the street during the day, my lord. After all, we're only a stone's throw from the poorer quarter of the city, with their tenements and beggars." His expression betrayed his own scorn for the loiterers and their origins.

Jack, standing in only his long shirt, shook his head. "No, I don't mean during the day. I mean at night, after dark. I noticed a figure in the shadows when I returned just now, and I'm sure the fellow saw me look his way and hid himself. If that isn't suspicious, I don't know what is."

"Do you want me to take a look out of the window now, my lord?"

Jack shrugged. "I daresay the fellow's taken himself off. He might have been out to rob me but thought better off it as I was so quickly inside the house. Even this street isn't safe, I'm afraid. You can look if you want to though. I'll just have a quick wash while you do."

Briggs disappeared into Jack's bedroom while Jack sloshed

warm water over his face. He'd have a shave in the morning. A quick brush with some tooth powder and he was nearly ready for bed. He was just pulling on his nightshirt when Briggs called softly. "My lord."

The bedroom was lit only by a lamp beside the bed—his reading light. Jack padded across the rug to the window where Briggs was peering out, keeping himself well back in case he should be seen. He waved an admonishing hand at Jack. "I think the fellow you mention is staring up at this very window right now, my lord, so have a care when you look out, or he might see you."

Jack exchanged places with Briggs and dared a peek. For a moment, he could see nothing, as the street, despite being furnished with lamps, was not well lit, and the man, for a man it was, was not standing near any of them. As before, a movement caught his eye. There he stood, leaning up against a wall at the corner of the next street, the smoke from a pipe wafting up being what had attracted Jack's attention. "I see him. Yes, that's the same man I saw earlier. Do you think you've seen him before?"

Briggs shook his head. "I don't think so, my lord. But it's difficult to tell in this light. He does seem to be persistent, doesn't he? I can see no reason for him to be loitering there unless he intends some crime, or he would be home to his bed by now, surely?"

Jack nodded. "If I wasn't already dressed for bed, I'd be sorely tempted to go out there and confront him. I don't like my house being spied upon." Did the man have anything to do with Louise? He wouldn't put it past her to set someone to spy on him and perhaps to beat him up, or worse, out of revenge. She was a woman of strong passions, as he well knew.

Jack stepped back from the window. "Perhaps you could go down and check Alcock has locked everything up, and warn him that we have someone lurking outside looking a sight too interested in us. Just as well to be cautious, especially at night. Although I don't think a burglar would risk entering a house as well occupied as this one, even after dark."

"I can stay up and keep watch, if you'd like me to, my lord."

Jack shook his head. "Nonsense, that would tire you far too much. Just get Alcock to make sure all the doors and windows are bolted, as I said, and warn the other servants to be on their toes. It's probably nothing at all, just a coincidence. He's more than likely waiting for someone and idly looking at the lighted windows of all the houses. And I'm probably worrying unduly. I expect he'll be gone soon, back to wherever it is he comes from."

Briggs bowed. "As you wish, my lord. Will that be all?"

Jack would have liked his usual glass of bedtime brandy but, with what he'd just seen, it might be best to keep his wits about him, whatever he'd said to Briggs. "Thank you, Briggs. You may go."

Briggs departed, bearing Jack's clothes and shoes to tend to later. As soon as he'd closed the door, Jack went back to the window. Sure enough, the man was still there, his pipe smoke curling into the cold night air. He must be determined at whatever he was about, because the night was freezing. He'd have to be on his way soon, though, or the lamplighters would be finding his cold dead body in the morning. Just a loiterer with nothing better to do.

Jack got into bed and picked up the book he'd been reading these last few nights—book two of the series he'd lent to Elenora. He hadn't read it for a long time and was curious to see what it was that attracted her. The thought that he'd really prefer it if he himself attracted her instead of his books arose, but was pushed back down. He wasn't immune to her pretty face and didn't mind admitting it. He'd always found pretty faces beguiling; what man didn't? Perhaps it would have been better had she been a little brown mouse like her mother and sisters. He opened the book. He wouldn't think about that now.

After he'd read the same paragraph three times and nothing had sunk in, he let the book fall back into his lap. The lamp flickered. Not the easiest thing to read by. And especially not when he was thinking about something else. About someone else. About Elenora.

He closed the book and lay back on his pillows, stretching his legs out. Briggs had put a couple of wrapped hot bricks in his bed earlier that evening and it was toasty warm. However, even that couldn't keep his thoughts from the girl he didn't understand.

Why was she immune to his charms? He was handsome, in a devil-may-care way, as more than one of his ex-mistresses, and other ladies of the Ton, had frequently informed him. Although she'd said he was old in that endearingly frank manner she possessed, he was certainly nowhere near her father's age. Forty was still two years off and he had maintained the trim figure of a much younger man. Unlike Dugdale with his little potbelly. And yet, a girl he was finding increasingly fascinating seemed not to have noticed his many attributes. In fact, she'd been more interested in his seven-year-old son. Perplexing.

He blew out the lamp and put his arms behind his head. Tonight was going to be one on which sleep would be hard to find. Not only were his thoughts full of Elenora, with her spun gold hair and intelligent blue eyes, but also every so often they returned to the figure lurking outside in the street, if only as a distraction from visions of Elenora. Shoving her image aside with determination, he concentrated on struggling to remember where he'd seen someone similar lurking, but failed.

However, inevitably, his thoughts returned to Elenora again. When she'd precipitated out of that alcove away from Louise's clutches, and he'd caught her in his arms, he'd suffered the sensation of never wanting to let her go. Which was quite uncharacteristic of him. He'd always prided himself on not allowing his heart to become engaged with whatever lady was his latest dalliance. And up until now, he'd succeeded. Until he'd met the little oddity that was Elenora Wetherby.

With a deep sigh, he rolled onto his side, the man in the shadows forgotten. How difficult was it going to be to get to sleep now he couldn't banish Elenora's face, with its furrowed brow of concentration, from his mind. Damn women to blazes. Damn Elenora and damn Louise Raby.

ELENORA WAS ALSO lying awake in Arlington Street. And she, like Jack, had thoughts only for the person she was engaged to. Aunt Penelope had fussed over her like an old hen with one chick when they'd reached home, insisting on a posset being warmed for her and sitting with her while she drank it in bed, something that had only elicited further resentful glares from Petunia. For some reason, her aunt had been far more inclined to believe Jack when he said Elenora was unwell than she had been when Elenora had claimed it herself before they left. Piqued at this discrimination, Elenora finally managed to rid herself of her putative nurse, and Agatha, who'd been waiting up for her, when the posset was all gone.

Aunt Penelope left with reluctance, Agatha with undue haste as she must have been exhausted and longing for her bed.

"It was very unfair of you to make us leave the ball early," Petunia said, as soon as they had the room to themselves.

Elenora, who'd been about to snuff out her candle, glanced at the other bed, wrestling with her conscience. "I had a megrim." Putting the lie into words rankled.

Petunia's brows lowered threateningly. "No, you didn't. You made it up, and that idiot you're engaged to believed you. Just because you don't like balls. You told me you couldn't tell lies. So that was a lie too."

Elenora bristled, seizing on the first bit as being the easiest to refute. "Jack's not an idiot."

Petunia harrumphed. "He must be to have asked you to marry him. Even though he compromised you, I bet he could have found a way out of it if he'd wanted to."

What was she supposed to say to that? Nothing she could think of. She'd just have to stay silent.

Petunia persevered. "How did you manage it?"

"Manage what?"

"To snare a man—an earl's heir, to top it all—on your debut into society? Did you deliberately set out to be compromised? I bet you did. I bet under all those innocent looks you give people you've been plotting this all along."

Oh dear. This was rapidly getting awkward. How had she missed how jealous Petunia was becoming?

"I, er, I don't know." Which in a way was quite true, as she had no idea how she'd fallen into the events that had led up to her engagement.

Petunia snorted. "There must be something you're hiding. I think you did whatever it was you did on purpose. No one gets engaged the first time they're at a ball. No one. Not even girls with huge fortunes."

By that she must mean herself, as her papa had left her with a goodly inheritance, something Mama had mentioned so many times it was engraved on Elenora's brain.

"Just lucky chance," Elenora tried, as that too was not a lie.

Another snort from her resentful cousin. "You must be just about the luckiest girl alive then."

This presented Elenora with another neat response. "I think you might be right." Or you could look at it that she was the unluckiest. It depended on which angle you came at it from. But she was indeed lucky that Jack had been so reasonable and suggested the sham engagement.

"I can't believe it," Petunia snarled, pulling her covers up to her chin. "I really just can't believe it. You're so undeserving. You don't even want to get married, and look at you—engaged to one of the biggest catches of the season." She turned onto her side, presenting Elenora with her back. "Put that candle out, can't you? I need to go to sleep."

With relief, Elenora blew her candle out and snuggled down into her bedcovers.

But sleep would not come. She wriggled down a little further and closed her eyes, but thoughts tumbled through her head as though they were in a whirlpool. Chief amongst them was the memory of how Jack had held her against his chest when she'd escaped from Lady Raby's dubious presence. And how she'd felt no inclination to struggle to free herself. This was a totally new sensation. His arms, tight around her body, had bestowed instead of agitation, a feeling of being safe and secure. Not that she'd been in any danger from Lady Raby. Well, probably not. Her face admittedly had taken on a rather threatening appearance. But a ball was rather a public place for a murder.

Why had she felt like that? For the first time in her life that she could remember? Try as she might, she couldn't work it out. A dim memory of a time when she'd been so small only one thing had stuck in her mind wriggled into her head. Of being held tight by someone, pressed against them much as Jack had pressed her against his chest. Had it been Mama? No, Mama always had such a scent of roses about her, a scent that Elenora could distinguish even at a distance. The various scents of different people had been something she'd noticed and classified them by all her life. And whoever had held her like that had smelled of carbolic soap.

She thought of Jack's smell and her heart did a little inadvertent flip. He smelled... nice. She had no other word for it. Or did she. He smelled... comforting. No, that wasn't it. He smelled... attractive. She drew a sharp breath. Yes, that was it, he smelled of something wildly attractive. Something that she wanted wrapped tight around her as she'd never wanted anything before.

Good heavens. She sat bolt upright in bed. Could it be that it wasn't just his smell she found attractive? And his strong arms holding her tight and secure? No, no, no. She wasn't about to go down this road. She was imagining all of this. It wasn't possible. She wouldn't think about him anymore.

She lay down again. But sleep had deserted her for good now. If it had ever been about to take her, that was. All she could see inside her head was Jack's handsome face, smiling down at her with his interested, yet indulgent expression on his face. Could it be that he liked her too? No, it couldn't. He'd said himself that he didn't want to marry, and his silly friend Dugdale had said as much as well—so surprised that Jack had become engaged. That was it, of course. He found her odd, as everyone did, and was amused by the frankness everybody else she knew disliked. And because of that, he was being kind to her. She must banish thoughts of the possibility of him liking her from her head. Neither of them were interested in marriage, and this engagement would end when the season did.

She turned over in bed. This was going to be a long night.

CHAPTER SIXTEEN

AFTER HIS DISTURBED night, Jack began the following day with every intention of steering well clear of Arlington Street and the intriguing Miss Wetherby. However, by the afternoon, this resolve had softened and he found his feet taking him there all by themselves when he'd really been intending to visit White's.

He knocked on the door and was admitted by Hemmings. "I'm afraid Lady Dandridge is not at home, my lord," he said in reply to Jack's initial enquiry.

Jack's spirits rose a notch. It would be nice to see Elenora alone without her chaperone's constant attendance. "Then perhaps you could let Miss Wetherby know that I have called?"

Hemmings showed Jack into the empty drawing room, and departed on his mission to find Miss Wetherby.

Impatient and fidgety, Jack wandered over to the window. Arlington Street, being a lesser thoroughfare, was not nearly so busy as Portland Place. A few gentlemen walking, canes swinging and a jaunty air about them, a woman selling some out of season red roses—he could have bought some for Elenora had he not been so preoccupied when he passed the seller. And standing only half visible on the corner of the street, his pipe smoke rising skywards, a man who could be the spitting image of the one he'd seen in the shadows last night.

In fact, he felt almost sure it was the exact same man he'd seen last night outside his own house. Or maybe he was getting paranoid due to lack of sleep. If he thought about it sensibly, London abounded with men propping up walls and smoking pipes. Most of them… well, a good number of them at any rate… probably for no nefarious reason whatsoever. And this man was probably nothing to do with last night's man and was one of the many innocent individuals abroad.

However… he glanced back toward the door. If he ran downstairs now, he might be able to catch the fellow and demand of him what he was doing following him around. That wasn't the behavior of a regular burglar, surely, or even a would-be pickpocket. They spotted their mark, did their work, and were gone before the mark even noticed. But if he did that, what would Elenora think if she came in here and found him gone?

He turned back to the window. The man had vanished. Well, that absolved him from precipitous action, at any rate, and probably indicated that his presence in Arlington Street was just by chance.

He rubbed his eyes. Had he imagined him there after last night? Was thinking about Elenora sending him mad? No, the man couldn't have been the same man as last night.

The door opened and the object of his thoughts came bouncing in. Elenora, that was, not the mysterious watching man. She appeared to be as full of vital life as if she'd not been out until all hours this morning and then pleaded a megrim in order to return home.

"Jack!"

At least she sounded pleased to see him. And she looked it, too. Which must mean she truly was, as she couldn't lie.

Putting thoughts of the strange man out of his head, Jack strode across the room to meet her, his hands held out.

She ground to a halt, eyes fixed on his hands, and too late he remembered how little she liked to be touched. Back to square one on that front.

He let his hands drop. "I'm sorry."

She drew her bottom lip in under her teeth and gave herself a little shake. "That is quite all right. I'm not offended at all. I know it takes people a long time to accustom themselves to my quirks."

"I wouldn't say it was just a quirk." He put his hands behind his back lest they stray toward her again, as a longing to feel her hands in his had arisen. "Tell me, Elenora, if you can, why it is you are so against being touched? It's something I would give anything to understand."

She frowned, her own hands laced together in front of her, and looked down. "In truth, my lord, I couldn't tell you, but I've always been like this. I believe it's all a part of my makeup and I can do nothing to change it."

He smiled at her. "Don't call me 'my lord,' Elenora, when you've been calling me Jack these last few days. We are engaged, after all."

She looked up, her eyes alive with sudden mischief. "And I rather doubt we should be alone together despite our engagement, but I assured Agatha, she's my maid, that I didn't need her as a stand in chaperone while my aunt is absent. Nor Petunia, who is at the piano in the music room in a temper again." She chuckled. "I think that had my aunt known you would call, she would not have gone out visiting herself. She wanted me to accompany her, but I made the excuse of my megrim to stay in bed, then got up the moment she'd departed. Days are too short as it is to languish idle in bed."

The rather pleasing image of Elenora in her nightgown tucked up in bed leapt into Jack's head, and warmth rose to his cheeks. What was this sudden aversion to thinking improper thoughts about a young lady? He'd never had this trouble before. In fact, he'd always found it entertaining. "I'm grateful your aunt has gone out, and that you deem me safe enough to talk to unchaperoned. I had hoped for a few minutes alone with you, if I'm honest. We are, after all, meant to be having a long engagement so we can get to know one another better."

Her cheeks colored, and, as if to distract him from this, she flounced past him and settled herself on the chaise longue, hands folded demurely in her lap, only the continual lacing of her fingers betraying her lack of equilibrium. Might it, dare he hope, be due to his presence? Or was it all a part of her character… her quirks?

He came and sat beside her. It would have been more proper to have taken one of the other seats, but he wanted to be close to her, and the fact that she'd chosen a seat with space for two made him want to believe she wanted him there.

She shuffled away from him a fraction.

He resisted the impulse to edge closer and take one of her hands in his. Temptation was a fickle thing. "Perhaps you might try and explain to me how it makes you feel when you're touched? To better help me understand."

Her face took on a thoughtful expression, as no doubt she struggled to formulate an answer. She opened her mouth as though about to speak once or twice without saying a word, only to close it again and give a little shake of her head.

"If I were to touch you… like this…" He set an outstretched finger on the back of her hand. "How does that feel to you?"

She snatched her hand back as though she'd been stung. "Like a pencil on slate. It sets my teeth jangling." She paused. "I never could use a slate and slate pencil in the schoolroom and got into trouble all the time with my governess."

A good description he could relate to. "And how does it feel if you touch me in the same way?" He offered his hand.

Her brow furrowed, but, her eyes curious, she laid her finger-tip on his, her touch as delicate as gossamer. She raised wide eyes to his face. "Different. Not so… scratchy."

He burst out laughing, and after a moment, she joined in. "Do you know, I've reached the age of nineteen without ever noticing that it's worse to be touched than to touch. How extraordinary." She gazed down at her hands as though in awe.

Jack returned his hand to his lap. "Edward was asking about you this morning at breakfast."

She looked up again, eyes full of interest for his son, if not for him. "He was? He's such a charming boy. I very much enjoyed recreating the Battle of Hastings with him on the occasion of our meeting. For one so young he has an intimate knowledge of the battle and its commanders. He reminds me a little of me."

This was safe ground. "He asked if you might come to Portland Place to see him again. He's anxious to talk to you about the battle of Stamford Bridge. And I suspect he wishes to coerce you into recreating it with him." And it was also grounds on which to induce her to visit, even if the prime reason she had was to play with his son.

"It's so interesting to meet a young boy with an academic bent," she said, her voice serious. "I have despaired of my family. None of them seem keen to set their minds to loftier pursuits than having fun. That is my brothers, I should say, both of whom have had the privilege to go up to Oxford and study, and both of whom have wasted the opportunity. Although it's perfectly possible to both study and have fun—as I do." She wrinkled her delightful nose. "Tell me. Were you up at Oxford, or perhaps Cambridge?"

He shook his head. "I was keen to… enjoy myself in a different way." He'd nearly said to sow his wild oats, but she would no doubt have known what that meant and might have been shocked. She seemed to be the sort of girl who picked up information like blotting paper, as she sailed through life. "I set up my own establishment in Town soon after I left Harrow." He smiled. "My mother wasn't all that keen for me to do so, but my father overrode her."

"But you will let Edward go to Oxford? He seems to me the sort of boy who would do well there. Better than my scapegrace brothers, at any rate."

Would he? Not everything he'd heard about university life had sounded praiseworthy, but Edward was not his father, and nor was he Elenora's brothers. "Perhaps. What about your sisters? I gather you have more than the two I met."

She made a moue. "Oh, they are quite boring but very sweet.

All they think about is preparing themselves for the marriage mart. Even the younger two who are only eleven and twelve—and covered in spots at this very moment, I suppose. None of them are keen to improve themselves with education beyond that which our governess, Miss Maggs, was able to provide. I had to do all my important learning by myself. Papa says I am an autodidact, which means I have taught myself most things. Mama disapproves, of course."

"I know what it means. I suppose you could say that I'm one as well, for I've learned more from the books in my father's library than I ever did at school. In fact, I'm not sure I will even send Edward away to school for fear it changes him. I like him too well to thrust him into the charnel house that is Harrow or Eton and see him either the victim of a bully or turn into one."

She nodded, enthusiasm shining from her face. "Indeed I fear you might be right, and I'm sure you know from your own time there." Her eyes narrowed. "Although you yourself have no air about you of either the bullied or the bully, which is puzzling. On such small acquaintance with Edward as I've had so far, I divined a thirst for learning comparable with my own. He seems to me to be a child to be nurtured and brought on like a hothouse flower, not exposed to the common rabble in the outdoor flowerbeds."

Jack burst out laughing. "I have to say that you are a very opinionated young lady."

She frowned. "Is that a bad thing? I cannot tell when you say things like that to me whether you mean them as criticism or praise." She sighed. "I cannot tell a lot of things, in truth, with other people too. I find it most frustrating when we've had visitors at Penworthy and Mama or my sisters point out one of them was sad, or out of sorts, and it's completely passed me by. It makes me feel guilty that I don't see those things, no matter how hard I try to learn from Mama and my sisters."

On an impulse, Jack reached out a hand to cover her clasped ones. For a moment she resisted, but he kept his hand in place and she gave up. "Please. Never change, Elenora, for it would be a bad thing indeed if you were to curb your nature to please others. You are very charming the way you are right now."

Color flushed her cheeks most becomingly, and her blue eyes met his, a question in them. "Are you telling me you like me being like this? Being odd? The things others want to change in me? The things Mama says are to be hidden?"

He nodded, swallowing down a lump in his throat. What was this? Emotion choking him? A hitherto unheard of feeling for Jack Deveril, that was certain. "I do. I like you very much."

Her eyes widened further, she licked her lips, bit the bottom one, looked down at her hands where his covered them and then raised her eyes to meet his again. "And I like you."

For some reason, Jack could think of nothing to say. She liked him, and she was gazing at him out of wondering blue eyes he could drown in. If he were to lean forward… he might press his lips to hers and steal a kiss… And she might not dislike it. Or she might leap up and run away and never want to see him again.

He released her hands and got to his feet in a hurry, pretending an inclination to walk to the long window and look out into the street. No sign of the man from earlier. "I came to enquire, on behalf of Edward, rest assured, if you would like to come to my house for tea this afternoon. Come back with me, that is, and take tea with Edward. And me. At my house." Good God, he was gabbling. He'd not done that in front of a girl since he'd been a lusty schoolboy at Harrow with his first conquest.

Elenora's serious expression melted into a smile. "I would love to, but I have no chaperone, and, nice as it is to sit and talk to you alone, I fear I cannot parade around the streets of London with only you and no chaperone, for all to see." She paused. "Well, I really believe I could, as what on earth could you do to me in broad daylight in public? But I know, because Mama has told me so on numerous occasions until it's engraved into my heart, that I should not be alone with a gentleman in that way. Silly as that rule is. And ridiculous as it is that here in the drawing room I'm probably in more danger than I would be if we were walking to your house. If you see what I mean."

Was she gabbling too? Dare he hope that the cause of this gabbling matched the cause of his gabbling? And why on earth was he thinking like this when it could lead to nothing, as neither of them wanted it to. Probably. No, definitely.

"What about bringing your maid?"

Her eyes lit up. "Of course! An excellent idea. Agatha can chaperone me. I'll go straight up to my room, and she can fetch my pelisse and bonnet and gloves." She bounded to her feet. "I am so looking forward to seeing Edward again." And with that she was gone in a maelstrom of impetuosity.

Jack stood beside the empty chaise longue feeling a little shell-shocked. She'd admitted she liked him, but had she meant it in the way he had? In many ways, she was such a child, yet in others, like an old professor. Would he call her a bluestocking? Perhaps, only her charm outweighed that rather pejorative description. Her enthusiasm for meeting Edward again both endeared her to him and engendered a hint of resentment. Was he jealous? Of his seven-year-old son? Surely not.

"WE ARE GOING to Portland Place, to visit Lord Broxbourne," Elenora told Agatha when she'd responded to the urgent tug Elenora had given the bell pull. "I need my warmest pelisse as it's so cold outside. And you are to come with me as Aunt Penelope is out. I suppose I had better leave her a note of explanation or she'll think I've done something improper. I'll tell her you're with me, then she'll know everything is perfectly above board."

While Agatha sorted out the necessary warm clothing, Elenora wrote the note to her aunt.

Dear Aunt Penelope, I have gone to visit Lord Broxbourne and taken Agatha with me so you have no need to worry about the Propriety of my visit. We are to take tea together and no doubt he will escort me home. As I have Agatha with me, you may rest Assured that I will come to no harm. And besides, he is my

Betrothed so that makes this acceptable. Mama will not object, I am certain.

Your obedient Elenora

Possibly a little longer and more convoluted than necessary, but she wanted to be clear so her aunt would understand she was safe. With it clutched in her hand, and with a warmly wrapped Agatha trailing behind her, she descended to the drawing room again, passing the music room from which the sound of Petunia's rather aggressive piano playing emanated. She found Jack pacing up and down by the window. "I'm ready," she called from the door.

He turned toward her, a slightly worried frown on his forehead. Had he changed his mind? Her heart, which had been doing a bit of pounding that had nothing to do with rushing about to get ready, sank a little.

But when he saw her, his worried expression dissipated and he strode over, as happy as he'd seemed, or so she thought, when she'd raced off upstairs. The small worry that her racing off had bothered him, rather than decorously walking as advised by Mama and Aunt Penelope, arose. Did he think her terribly fast? Was that even what being fast was? So literal? She had no idea.

They went downstairs together with Agatha following behind, and Elenora gave her hastily scribbled note to Hemmings before he opened the front door for them. Beside her, Jack paused, seeming to be skimming his gaze over the people on the street. As if he'd set his mind at rest about something, he held out his arm to her. She took a deep breath and slipped her hand into the crook of it, feeling his muscles beneath the good wool cloth of his coat and noting how touching him no longer felt so scratchy and off-putting. How strong he must be. Her treacherous heart gave another lurch at the thought as she remembered his arms around her at the ball. Whatever was it doing that for? He was only a man, after all.

The walk to Portland Place didn't take long, as Elenora liked to walk briskly due to the cold, and Jack seemed happy to measure his longer stride to match hers. She did catch him once or twice looking back over his shoulder. After the third time he did it, she decided to ask him about it. "Why do you keep doing that?"

"Doing what?"

"Peering back over your shoulder. Do you think Agatha might fall behind or get lost? She's used to walking at Penworthy. I walk a lot down there and she's usually with me."

"I didn't realize I was doing it."

"Oh." She peered over her own shoulder at Agatha, whose rosy cheeks had blossomed even redder in the cold.

"I'm sorry. I'll stop doing it."

She smiled. "It's quite all right. I'm sure she's flattered that you're worrying about her." Or was he? She took another look over her shoulder, peering past Agatha's sturdy form, but nothing untoward caught her eye.

At the house in Portland Place, Elenora dispatched Agatha to the servants' hall with a haughty wave of her hand. "I shall be perfectly all right by myself now we are here and no one can see what I'm doing." The import of these words sank in. She chuckled. "Not, of course, that I intend to do anything you or my aunt or my mama would disapprove of. You may go and take tea and cakes with Lord Broxbourne's servants and have a gossip, as I know that's what you like to do."

Agatha, a little nonplussed, departed toward the kitchen with alacrity.

"Now," Elenora said with satisfaction at having rid herself of her chaperone so easily. Far more easily than she could have been rid of Aunt Penelope with her ridiculous notions of responsibility for her. "Can we go up and find Edward please?"

Three flights of stairs brought them to the nursery floor, where they discovered Edward playing with his young nurse in attendance. He jumped to his feet when he saw Elenora and ran to make a neat little bow to her. "You came, Miss Wetherby. I was so hoping you would so we could fight another battle. Miss Douglas has been teaching me about what poor King Harold had to do before Duke William's invasion of England. I refuse to call him king, as for me, Harold was the true king and William just a usurper. Only I wouldn't call him French—he was Norman and they have their origins in Scandinavia. Miss Douglas told me that this morning."

"Goodness, you're the most well-informed boy I've ever met," Elenora said. "And I notice you do like to side with the kings who were usurped. My brothers were both dunces compared to you. I've never been able to get them the least bit interested in history other than to play at being knights in armor so they could fight each other."

Edward's face took on a slightly guilty expression. "If I had a brother to play with, I think I'd like to play at knights in armor too. But I don't. Unless… you and I might do so one day? I mean… just with wooden swords, not real ones. In case we hurt each other."

So he could be a playful small boy as well as a little intellectual. Elenora burst out laughing. "I should warn you that I often bested my brother Matthew who is only one year older than me. But yes, if your papa can provide us with wooden swords, then we can fight."

"And shields," Jack said.

Edward nodded with vigor. "Yes, shields too. With coats of arms on them."

Jack laughed. "Just as you command, my liege lord."

Edward clapped his small hands together.

Elenora joined in their laughter. "And yes, I would love to reenact a battle with you again. I believe your papa said you were most interested in the battle of Stamford Bridge, which came before Hastings if I remember correctly."

He jumped up and down on the spot, still only an excited little boy. "Yes, oh yes. That's just what I want to do. Miss Douglas has told me all about it." He turned to Jack. "Will you play with us too, Papa?"

Jack was still smiling. "I suppose I could. So long as you don't make me be the baddie again. You do have a habit of picking the winning side every time."

Edward fairly crowed with delight. "If you like then, you can be Harold Godwinson and the Anglo Saxons, and I will be Harold Hardrada. Miss Wetherby can be Tostig Godwinson, who is very meanly fighting against his brother on the side of Hardrada. You don't mind being such a turncoat, do you Miss Wetherby?"

Elenora burst out laughing. "Not one bit, but do call me Elenora, as calling me Miss Wetherby all the time makes me feel as though I'm about a hundred."

Edward beamed. "I don't think you're *that* old. I'll go and get my soldiers. Meg made me tidy them away yesterday." He shot a glare at the nursery maid, who was again employed in mending his clothing. With two older brothers, Elenora well knew how boys the world over could get holes in their clothes at the drop of a hat. Girls too, if she was honest.

She dropped to her knees on the rug, and peeked up at Jack. "Come on then, Harold Godwinson. You must get down on the rug with your opponents and try to beat us. Be warned, that as your treacherous brother Tostig, I shall play dirty and try to change the course of history by winning."

Edward came back with some of his soldiers clutched to his chest and tossed them in a rather cavalier fashion onto the rug. "Norwegians, I think. Those're mine and Elenora's. I'll get you some Anglo Saxons, Papa."

"They look more like French soldiers to me with those blue coats," Jack remarked as he too got down onto his knees and picked up one of the small warriors. His comment went ignored. Edward must have an excellent imagination.

Elenora watched Edward as he went back for more soldiers, of which he seemed in possession of a good supply, a warm feeling she wasn't quite used to welling up into her heart. A feeling of being included, of belonging, of fitting in. Not something she'd ever felt within her family, not even with Papa. She was going to enjoy this afternoon.

CHAPTER SEVENTEEN

THE BATTLE WAS short but sweet, and Jack, in his guise as Harold Godwinson, managed to keep history on its true course and win. Harold Hardrada and Tostig died in heroic fashion, knocked over by a wooden bowling ball Jack rolled across the rug at them. Edward, in high dudgeon, protested that huge balls like that weren't historically accurate, he didn't think, and thus his father had cheated, but the whole thing ended amicably, and Harold Godwinson was dispatched southwards toward Hastings and his ultimate ocular fate.

Just as they were finishing, Miss Douglas, who must have finished marking Edward's work and planning the next day's, came bustling in, all good-humored efficiency. She was a thin stick of a woman, with her graying hair scraped back from her face almost aggressively, but Jack would never have employed her had he not been certain of her gentle heart. "Good afternoon, my lord, Miss Wetherby. If you'll excuse me, it's past time for Master Edward's walk, and although he finds historical reenactment so interesting, he mustn't miss out on his fresh air every day."

Jack, who'd removed his coat during the battle, scrambled to his feet, pretending he hadn't noticed the barely disguised smile of approval on Miss Douglas's stern but kind face. She liked him to show an interest in his son, which wasn't something he could do as often as he would have liked, and he guessed at her approval of

Elenora as a possible stepmother for his son.

A small pang of guilt that this was just a deception, and he was depriving Edward of something he deserved, coursed through him for a brief moment. That he had to depend on the kindness of servants as stand-ins for the care of a mother seemed suddenly unfair. Not that Edward knew what he was missing, though.

He smiled. "Of course, Miss Douglas. We don't want to interfere with the smooth running of the nursery and schoolroom. Go and fetch your hat and coat, Edward. Gloves and scarf too. It's cold out and, thanks to us, your walk is running late. Off you go."

Edward, his defeat forgotten, beamed in delight. "Can we go and see the cows again, Miss Douglas?" He turned back to Elenora, effortlessly including her in his little coterie as though she'd always been a part of it. "I love cows nearly as much as dogs, Elenora, but I'm not allowed a dog." He paused, a frown marring his brow. "Or a cow. Would you like to come and see them with me and Miss Douglas? She says they're all going to be having calves soon and I can hardly wait. But Papa says they're going to turn Marylebone Park into a Town park like Hyde Park but only for a few people, and there're no cows in Hyde Park. Which I think is a bad thing. Only people on horses and a big pond. Although I like horses too and at Broxbourne Park I have a pony of my own. And there're lots of cows."

Jack burst out laughing. "Stop, stop, stop. Elenora is staying here with me. You could talk a horse's hind leg off, young man. And you know you can't have a dog here in London. Unfair for a dog, and as for a cow… If you're good, I'll take you down to Broxbourne Park in the spring and you can see all the cows you want. We'll even choose one of the new calves for you to have for your own and feed with a bottle. And there are plenty of dogs down there, but for going out to shoot pheasants, not having in the house."

Edward mock pouted. "The kind of dog I'd like is one who'd sleep on my bed, not in a kennel." He shot Elenora a pleading glance. "Maybe you'll come tomorrow and you can see the cows then? I'd like that. Yes, I'm coming Miss Douglas." He ran off after his governess, his booted feet clattering on the oak floor.

Jack extended a hand to Elenora, who was still sitting amidst the detritus of battle. Indecision flashed across her face before she took it and let him pull her to her feet.

He kept hold of her hand, and, to his relief, she made no effort to snatch it back. Was that because she was getting used to his touch and might even like to have him hold it? He could but hope. "I did intend to take tea in the nursery with Edward, but as we've put poor Miss Douglas quite out of order with her timetable, and nursery tea will be late, perhaps you'd like to take it with me in the drawing room? I hear Cook has made some fine cakes."

Elenora smiled, those beautiful eyes shining. Alas, most likely at the thought of cake. "I should love that. I've had such a wonderful afternoon. You're very lucky to have Edward. He's such a..." She paused as if deep in thought. "An unusual little boy." Praise indeed from an equally unusual young lady.

To his surprise, and delight, she still didn't try to recover her hand, so Jack held it a little more firmly and headed for the door. She came with him, perforce because she had to as he had her hand, but perhaps also because she wanted to. Still hand in hand, they descended two flights of stairs to the drawing room, and Jack rang the bell for tea.

Still with her unprotesting hand clasped in his, he guided her to the chaise longue and they both sat down. Silence fell, but it wasn't an awkward silence, for once, and Jack felt no urge to break it. Instead, he enjoyed the warmth of her soft hand in his own, her fingers gently curved around his. How was it that such a simple thing as this could give so much pleasure? None of his other relationships had begun like this... No. He must not gull himself. This was not the start of a relationship. At least not the sort he was used to. If anything, it was the cementing of a friendship they would have to sustain for the length of the season.

Wasn't it?

Tea came, with the promised selection of cakes, and he was pleased to note that Elenora was not a nibbler, despite her delicate frame. She liked cakes and she tried every one of Cook's offerings, even to the extent of licking her fingertips and picking up the crumbs off her plate. Like a little girl. Another new sensation came to him as he watched her, as his heart swelled with… what was it? Not that little word, no, it couldn't be. But contentment washed over him like a warm balm as he listened to her excited chatter. This was what it was like to truly get on with a woman for no other reason than friendship. Or was he gulling himself?

Their conversation lent itself in no way to encouraging how he was beginning to feel, but nevertheless remained relaxed, varying from discussing the *Antiquities of Athens* books to the newly released *Specimins of Ancient Sculpture Aegyptian, Etruscan, Greek and Roman; selected from different collections in Great Britain* by John Samuel Agar. Once Elenora had professed her longing to visit Egypt for herself, time flew by as Jack told her all about the Dilettanti Society, to which he belonged, and of which John Samuel Agar was also a member, and from which the author had harvested most of the specimens mentioned in his book.

Time fairly flew, and darkness had fallen outside when their tête-á-tête was interrupted.

The door into the hallway swung open so hard it banged back against the wall, and Alcock came staggering in, red in the face and supporting a battered and filthy Miss Douglas around the waist, one of her arms drawn over his shoulder.

What the hell? Jack was on his feet in a second, the plate he'd been holding on his knee clattering to the floor in a shower of crumbs, lumps of cake and broken pieces of china. Miss Douglas had lost her bonnet, her hair hung in a bedraggled mess, and her once prim and pristine gown and pelisse were both smeared liberally in mud. Blood streaked one side of her face, which was swollen and a mottled gray in color. She looked near to fainting.

But Jack's first thought was not for the governess. His voice rose in uncontrollable panic. "Edward. Where is Edward?"

He was dimly aware of Elenora jerking to her feet beside him. More galvanized to common sense than he was, she hurried to Alcock and Miss Douglas. "Sit her down here. Where is the brandy? What's happened?" She drew Miss Douglas down onto the chaise longue she'd just vacated, mud from her dress smearing unheeded across the velvet upholstery. "Alcock, quickly fetch the brandy. I fear Miss Douglas is going to faint. Or smelling salts. Mama always has smelling salts to hand when she thinks she's going to faint. Put your head between your knees, Miss Douglas."

"Where is Edward?" Jack repeated, his voice as icy as his frozen heart. His mind churned as the possibilities jangled through it: an accident with a carriage, his son lying mangled in the street, thieves who'd attacked Miss Douglas and left Edward, who, brave as ever, had tried to defend her, dead in the street. In every scenario, Edward was dead. Or why else was Miss Douglas, in such a terrible state, here alone? She would never have left him had he been alive.

Miss Douglas squinted up at him out of one eye, the other being swollen shut. "They took him, my lord. I tried to fight them off, but they took him." Her voice shook and tears streamed down her face. "They were too strong for me. I couldn't save him." Her head fell forward and Elenora put a comforting arm across her back. A little tentative, as though she were doing something she knew she ought to do, not something she wanted to do. Odd, the things one noticed when a crisis arose.

He clenched his fists. "Who took him. Quick, woman. And where? And how long ago?"

Miss Douglas shook her head, wincing with the pain. "Near the cows. We went to see the cows as Master Edward requested, and he's been such a good boy today. Not that he's ever anything else." More tears fell and Elenora thrust the delicate lace handkerchief Mama made her carry into her hands, quite inadequate for the job at hand.

"The cows were farther round than usual, as we were late. We normally find them near the gates into the park. I shouldn't have let him go to look for them. I should have said no as it was getting dark, but he was so polite in the way he asked, and I'd promised him. I didn't think we could come to any harm. There were shadows under all the trees. The shadows became men before I noticed. Two, maybe three, I think. One of them seized Edward, and the other two fought me off. Beat me with sticks as I tried to snatch Edward back. When I fell, one of them kicked me in the stomach." Her hand went to her waist and she winced again.

"I could hear brave Edward shouting at them to leave me alone. He tried his best to save me, the brave boy. Then one of them hit me on the head with something." Her fingers went to the cut on her forehead and the fast growing black eye. "When I came to my senses, I was alone in the dark, lying in the mud where they'd left me. Edward was gone." She looked up at Jack, dabbing at her nose and eyes with the already soaked handkerchief. "Those dreadful men have taken Edward, my lord, and it's all my fault. As soon as I could stand, I hurried home."

Elenora patted her on the back. "It wasn't your fault, Miss Douglas. You were a woman alone, and they were three against just you. No woman could have fought them off."

Trust her to be ever practical when all Jack wanted to do was get hold of the woman and shake her and shout at her for not protecting his son. Even though he knew in his heart that it wasn't her fault. It was his, for allowing Edward out with only a woman to keep him safe.

He paced to the window and back. "I'm going after him."

Elenora looked up from her awkward nursing of Miss Douglas, who had bent forward again with her head between her knees. "Then I'm coming with you. But shouldn't you send for the Bow Street Runners or the Watch? If three men have taken him, you can't go after him on your own. I can help."

What? Was the girl mad? Brave but mad. He shook his head. "You can't. It might be dangerous. No, I take that back. It will be dangerous. God only knows what these men have snatched Edward for. You must stay here and look after Miss Douglas. She needs a woman's touch."

Elenora was on her feet again, her face set, eyes fiery. Anyone less likely to administer a gentle woman's touch he had yet to meet. "And leave little Edward in the hands of evil kidnappers?"

She stamped her foot. "No. You can't make me. I'm your fiancée, not your wife. You have no right to tell me what to do. Alcock, can you fetch my maid from the kitchen where she's no doubt enjoying tea and cake with the servants to sit with Miss Douglas. No, better still, you take Miss Douglas down to the servants' hall with you, and look after her down there. Tell my maid I'm putting her in her charge. I think she keeps smelling salts in her reticule. Make sure Miss Douglas gets a little brandy and some hot tea with lots of sugar in it. A steak for her eye. I'm going with Lord Broxbourne to find Edward."

Jack stared at her, reluctant admiration filling him. What ferocious bravery she possessed, ready as she was to go out into the dangerous dark of a London night, on foot, with him. Who was he to say her nay? His momentary indecision evaporated. "Get your pelisse and bonnet then. Gloves too. It's going to be cold." He turned to Alcock, who was already helping Miss Douglas to her feet. "And send Thomas round to Bow Street magistrates immediately, and on to rouse the Watch. We need all the help we can get."

Downstairs in the hallway, as Elenora pulled on her pelisse and the thick scarf he'd found her, he shrugged himself into his caped coat, the two inside pockets heavy with two of his pistols. Loaded, of course. With Alcock busy with the injured Miss Douglas, and Thomas already on his way round to Bow Street, no one was there to see them leave.

As THE DOOR closed behind them, Elenora realized at once just how dark the streets of London were at night. Of course, she'd been out at night before to attend those awful balls, and sometimes at home in Penworthy, where they had no benefit of street lighting. But now, even though the lamplighters had been round, the night seemed darker than it had ever done before, and much more threatening. Surely that must only be in her head?

A typical London fog, thick and all-enveloping, swirled about the glowing orbs of the lamps, making the far ends of the street vanish into misty darkness. She swallowed. Had she done the right thing in insisting she should accompany Jack to try to find Edward? Then she remembered the trusting look in the little boy's eyes as he'd greeted her. And the fact that their game of soldiers might well have led to him being abroad at a time when he should have been safely tucked up in the nursery having his tea. Yes, she'd made the right decision. And she couldn't possibly let Jack go out on his own into the night. She owed it to him to make sure he was all right as well, as though he and his son were now her responsibility. She wouldn't think about how she might feel if something happened to either of them. That these men who had stolen Edward were dangerous was a foregone conclusion.

Jack reached out a strong hand and seized hers. She hung on tight, for once thankful for human contact. And it was Jack, after all. Somehow, contact with him had ceased to be so abhorrent in this emergency.

"This way," Jack said, gripping his cane like a weapon in his free hand and setting off in a half run along the broad pavement. Heading north, he dashed between the pools of fog-shrouded light the lamps threw across the wide street. The widest street in London, to be exact. Something that leapt unbidden and randomly into Elenora's head, as many things did, and had to be dismissed.

To either side of them, cozy lights glowed in the windows of the tall houses, as the inhabitants went about their business inside their warm, safe homes. Whereas out here, in the cold and darkness, danger came creeping out of every shadowy corner to pursue them on ghostly feet.

She had to run to keep up with Jack's long strides, rather regretting the tightness of her stays which were not conducive to strenuous exercise. They passed Weymouth Street, opening up to left and right, and kept going. The next street, Devonshire, lay close to the end of Portland Place where the fenced grassland that made up Marylebone Park and her farms began. Jack turned right into it, hurrying her along until they came to Portland Road where he turned sharply left, heading north. "This way. I've been here myself once or twice with Edward to take him to see his precious cows. They belong to Kendal's Farm. It's up here."

Ahead, the trees that marked the edge of the Park rose, darker than the night sky, looming higher than the houses they bordered. Dark and threatening, as what streetlights there had been died away. Only the moon, thin and feeble in the night sky, and partly obscured by a thin veil of fog, served to light their way as they left Portland Road behind.

Jack slowed to a walk, his head turning from right to left. Elenora copied him, hoping against hope that Edward would come running out of the gloom, battered and frightened but safe. He didn't.

She clutched Jack's hand freely now. If she were to let go, she might never find him again in the dark. She was reminded of some of the novels Augusta liked to read, the plots of which she had recounted to Frances and Elenora in all their gory details in the cozy familiarity of their beds at home in Penworthy. Well, not precisely gory in the literal sense, but quite sensational with some of the adventures the heroines got up to. How Augusta came by them, Elenora had no idea, but she had a secret hiding place where she kept them. Why was she even thinking about them when real danger threatened here? No, had already threatened and won.

Jack stopped in the graveled road. "This is the New Road west to Paddington. Here's the fence line. I should have asked whether they went left or right to find the cows. *Cows.*" Jack's voice dropped, sounding disgusted. "Bloody cows. How can something so mundane have led to this?"

The ground beside the wooden-railed fence was uneven and, in the dark, Elenora kept stumbling. What a good thing she had sturdy boots. A distant lowing carried on the cold night air. "Up ahead. Cows. I hear them."

This only served to make Jack increase his speed, a dangerous thing in itself in such darkness. She stumbled along with him, more than once being kept upright just by the strength of his arm. Was that a timber yard to her right, the heaps of logs piled high behind a sturdy fence? This was countryside now, not London Town, something in which she felt more at home, even in the dark.

The cows soon came into view, a little group clustered near the fence line, their white markings showing up in the darkness like milky beacons. Their warm breath rose into the night air to make filmy statues that mingled with the thickening fog and vanished. Most of them were sitting down, as cows are wont to do at nights. How peaceful they looked, as though nothing bad had happened right under their noses.

Jack halted, staring at the cows. He released Elenora's hand, and she took the opportunity to lean on the fence and get her breath back.

"Edward!" His voice boomed into the night. "Edward! Can you hear me?"

The lights still glowing in the streets now seemed far away and alien, cut off by the fog. Out here, in the remains of what had once been forest and now was farmland, Elenora felt she could have been back in Penworthy or even out on the Downs at night, which she and Matthew had once done and got into fearful trouble for. The city was a long way off. Was Edward lying here unconscious somewhere? Unseen?

One of the cows mooed gently, as though answering Jack's shout, her voice a soft, reassuring sound that was thick with lies.

They'd seen what had happened, but they could tell Elenora and Jack nothing.

Elenora pushed herself off the fence. She must look for clues. And they might be on the ground underfoot. A difficult undertaking in the darkness. Overhead, as though they'd heard her silent prayer, the fog thinned to reveal the moon again.

"Edward!" Jack was standing in the center of a little clearing of trees at the side of the road, his figure clear as the moon emerged, his head flung back, listening hard after every call. No answer though.

A carriage clattered past, wheels rattling in the ruts and lamps shimmering front and back, its passengers oblivious to their quest.

Elenora stumbled over something soft and nearly fell to her knees. For a dreadful moment, her heart lurched almost into her mouth, if that were even possible. Was it a body? Taking her courage in both hands she bent and groped with her hands. Something soft... and woolly. A scarf. She gathered it up and pressed it to her nose. It smelled of small boy and carbolic soap. It had to be Edward's. And beside it, something else, round with a stiffness to its wide brim. A hat. Old and no doubt smelly—she could feel the grease of long wear inside the rim with her fingers. She held this to her nose, as well. About it hung the distinct smell of tobacco and tar.

"Jack, over here." She stood up, clutching both items to her chest.

He was with her in a moment. "What is it?"

She thrust the hat and scarf into his hands and by the dim moonlight saw him stare down at them, his face contorting. As she had done, he lifted the scarf to his nose. "It's Edward's."

"And the hat? Could it belong to one of the men who took him?"

Slowly, Jack inclined his head, his eyes dark pools she couldn't read. "It could." He hesitated. "And I think I recognize it. I think a man's been following me. I've seen him a few times but, like a fool, dismissed it as coincidence." He sniffed the malodorous hat. "The man I saw wore a hat very like this one. A sailor's tarred hat. I know many men in London probably wear hats like this— old sailors and those on leave from their ships. But the man I saw smoked a pipe continuously. Again, many men do just that. But I saw this man more than once, and I refuse to accept it as coincidence." Bitterness filled his voice, perhaps at not having taken more notice of this man before.

Elenora put her hand on his arm. "Someone was truly following you?"

"Yes. I'm sure of it… now."

The crackle of paper sounded as Jack screwed up Edward's scarf in his fingers.

Elenora grabbed it out of his hands. "What's that? I heard paper crunch."

Jack snatched at the scarf but Elenora was unfolding it. Sure enough, someone had pinned a dog-eared piece of paper to its center. She peered at the ill formed writing. "I can't read it in this light."

He took it from her, pulling her back toward the nearest fog-bound streetlamp. "Oh my God."

"What is it? What does it say?"

In silence, his mouth set in a hard line, he handed it to her.

hes my boi now

She looked up. "His boy? Edward? What does this mean?"

Jack's angry hands squeezed about the hat, deforming it, as he shook his head. "I have no idea, but it seems whoever's taken Edward thinks to goad me. No need. I'm already fit to kill on sight."

Elenora glanced over her shoulder at the pressing darkness. "What are we going to do?"

Jack grimaced. "I'm going to get him back, and I'm going to make the bastards who've done this wish they'd never crossed me. But first, I need to find some help. I know someone with connections who might be able to help me find who has Edward and come upon them from behind. If they can be persuaded to help, that is. We didn't exactly part as friends, but he has the whole of the rookeries at his fingertips. He knows everything that goes on within his manor." He seized her hand. "Come on."

AT ABOUT THE same time as Jack and Elenora were finding the scarf and hat on the edge of Marylebone Park, Aunt Penelope, who'd returned home from her visit just before dark to find Elenora's hastily scribbled message that she'd gone to Portland Place with Jack, was just beginning to feel anxious about her charge's continued absence.

She rang the bell for Hemmings, who promptly arrived in the drawing room, his face a picture of imperturbability as he bowed to her. "You rang, my lady?"

She nodded with unaccustomed vigor. "What time was it that my niece went out with Lord Broxbourne? The precise time, that is."

Hemmings's brow furrowed as he thought. Perhaps she was asking too much of her busy butler. But no, his face cleared. "I believe it was a little after two, my lady, as the clock in the hall had just struck the hour."

"And the time now is?" Why ladies didn't carry pocket watches, she had no idea. She could certainly do with one but had nowhere about her person she could stow it. And there was no clock in the drawing room because her late husband had ordered it taken out. He'd never liked to be controlled by a clock. She made a mental note to have the servants find it from wherever it had been stowed and reinstate it.

Hemmings, however, was as good as a clock. "Just gone half past five, my lady. Dinner will be served shortly, if you would like me to send Johnson up to help you dress." The fact that Elenora had not yet returned seemed to have escaped him.

Aunt Penelope shook her head. "No. Inform Cook that dinner will be delayed until Miss Wetherby returns." She tutted in anxiety. "And can you send one of the footmen—Robert will do—round to Lord Broxbourne's to escort Miss Wetherby home as it's now been dark for an hour. I don't want her walking back with just her maid to protect her. The streets aren't safe nowadays." She tutted again, dropping her voice to a mutter. "Really, Lord Broxbourne shouldn't have allowed her to stay out so long. Although perhaps he is bringing her back in his carriage. There is that." She looked up. "Off you go, Hemmings. The sooner we have her back, the sooner we can have dinner."

CHAPTER EIGHTEEN

JACK LED ELENORA on down London's lamplit streets deeper into the foggy recesses of the city she'd probably never have guessed existed. He kept one hand firmly on his cane, ready to react should anything untoward happen. The reassuring weight of the pistols in his great coat pockets, a pair of half-stocked saw-handled dueling pistols by Parker that his father had given him when he came of age, bumped him as he hurried along. Showing admirable sense, she kept close to him, her fingers tightly intertwined with his own. Good. He'd known she possessed commonsense, and this proved it.

The way to Betterton Street led them through some of the less salubrious parts of London. The big houses of the rich, like his, were frequently cheek by jowl with those of the poor, their cramped homes clustering in behind the huge expensive ones, often close to the mewses at the backs of the big houses. It was possible to go from wide open modern streets to the rookeries that had existed since the time of Good King Henry in as much time as it took to run downstairs in his own house.

And these streets, even though they weren't within the rookeries as yet, were not safe at nights, particularly not for a woman. He'd already decided he'd be leaving Elenora with Mrs. Sharpe, however much she protested. The pistols banged his leg again. Thank goodness he'd had the sense to bring them with him, despite the panic still coursing through his veins. And he had his trusty sword stick in his hand, ready to be drawn at a moment's notice.

He glanced over his shoulder, more wary now it was too late. The irony of that almost made him laugh, but it would have been a bitter, angry mirth. Anger at himself and his stupidity. Which Edward was paying for.

Having lived mainly in Town since he was eighteen, which was now nearly twenty years, he well knew the hazards that could befall the unwary if they ventured out after dark, particularly into the streets they were now entering. Narrower streets, lined with terraced redbrick houses, where lights only glowed in a few meager windows. Streets whose dirty cobbles were uneven and lit but intermittently with the feeble glow of the old oil lamps. The new, better gas lamps had not yet reached these less-favored sections of the city.

They passed an alehouse on a corner. The sounds of a piano being played, and of raucous revelry and shouting, spilled out onto the cobbles through the open doors, as a man lurched drunkenly out and nearly crashed into them. The stink of alcohol came with him, but luckily he swayed away to cast up his accounts in the gutter, where no doubt others had done the same before him. Many times, from the stink.

Elenora shrank closer to Jack, eyes wide with shock. A back street alehouse would not have been a sight she'd be used to, however sanguine her outlook on life. Jack hurried her on, leaving the man to his noisy voiding of his drink and dinner.

He slowed at the end of the street, looking left and right as a gong farmer and his noisesome cart trundled past. "Where are we going?" Elenora asked, her hand to her nose at the stench of the man's load. "Where is this person you think might be able to help us find Edward?"

Jack pulled her across the road to avoid the stinking cart. "I keep a house in Betterton Street. A woman runs it for me."

Her eyes flew wide. Was she leaping to conclusions? Most likely.

He shook his head as they hastened on, leaving the gong farmer behind. Another alehouse loomed ahead. "No. It's not what it sounds. You will see. We take in children off the street—orphans, and even those cruelly treated by their parents, sometimes. The woman, Mrs. Sharpe, was born in the gutter herself as most of her charges were, but hauled herself up out of it by her own endeavor, and with a little help from me. She's a kind and matronly soul and looks after the children well, preparing them to have a useful role in life. She cares for them. I pay for it. Saving them from the gutter at my expense."

"How can she help us?" Elenora, who seemed to have taken this confession in her stride, was panting now from the exertion. Her stays wouldn't be helping her. A ridiculous thing for a girl to wear when undertaking exercise of any sort. He must remember she wasn't used to charging about London in the middle of the night.

"She has many connections still with the underworld from which she came. And so do some of the children in her charge. Her adult son especially." Yes, Benjamin was the one he wanted to talk to. If he was there. At twenty, Mrs. Sharpe's firstborn lived and worked elsewhere, but had more than one foot remaining in his old life having been too old to change when Jack had rescued his mother and siblings from his father. But he was a good lad at heart, even though Jack suspected, despite his holding down a job in the docks, he also led a life less law-abiding with his father.

He thought of Josie's pinched, gray face and shorn hair. "Do not be misled into thinking the children I've rescued will be like Edward or your sisters. These are children who've been bred like rats in the rookeries, for whom thieving has been a way of life in order to stay alive. They're hard work to bring round to the decent life we offer them, and we haven't always succeeded. Some return to the only way of life they've known." Always difficult when that happened, making him feel as though he'd failed that particular child. Worse if it was one of the girls. A boy might return to thieving, but a girl almost always went back to selling her body on a daily basis.

Nearly there now. "We do our best to persuade them to stay, but, for some, their old life lures them back. However, we do have our successes. And the children who return to the rookeries, who I won't call failures, still view Mrs. Sharpe with favor. They keep in touch, and thus she has a network of informants who can help her rescue other children when the need arises. It's complicated."

She was gazing up at him, still wide-eyed. "Good heavens. You appear to have a side to you I'd never have guessed at."

He hadn't been meaning to try to impress her. His other life, a life none of his family or friends knew anything about, had become so much a part of him he'd ceased to think of the way others might see it. Or if he had, it had been to suspect others might think him mad. It didn't seem as though Miss Elenora Wetherby was of that opinion.

The name Betterton Street appeared, illuminated by an oil lamp. "She lives down here. It's not the best of streets, but it's not a slum. I learned early on that it did not do to transplant slum children into a life of comfort in too respectable a street. They were not made welcome in the first house I acquired, and nor did they take well to living in a genteel area. We had to move them here. They fit in better where they are close to their roots, but not so close as to make it too hard to escape them."

THE HOUSE JACK indicated lay halfway down the street, lights showing in its ground floor windows, bright and homely and promising. Elenora stared up at it from the street, the image she'd thought she had of Jack part of a spinning turmoil inside her head. If only they could find Edward there now, but that was an impossibility. If only this unknown foster mother of street orphans might know something that would help. In her heart, she didn't believe this possible, either, but optimism kept her silent.

Jack rapped on the neatly painted front door with the head of his cane, as she moved closer beside him on the step, not liking the feeling of empty darkness that lurked behind her back, as though waiting to pounce. This was a part of London she'd never even guessed existed. A part of London where a girl like her, in her expensive new gown and pelisse, was sorely out of place.

After a few moments, the door opened a crack and a wary, middle-aged face peered out at them. This must be Mrs. Sharpe herself, not sending one of her charges to answer the door after dark. "Milord Jack." The woman's voice was rough, but kind, and more than a little anxious. She opened the door wider, revealing a narrow passageway that must lead through the house to the kitchen at the back. "Whatever brings you here at this hour?"

"An urgent mission," Jack said. "This is Miss Wetherby, my… betrothed."

Mrs. Sharpe stepped back, her face softening into a welcoming smile, although still with her initial wariness fringing it. "What am I doing, keeping you on the doorstep. Come inside out of the cold, Miss Wetherby, my lord. Come inside right now."

Jack led Elenora inside and the door closed behind them. Mrs. Sharpe opened another door on the right which proved to lead into a small, cluttered parlor. Two young girls were sitting sewing by the light of two bright oil lamps in front of a small coal fire. They looked up at the newcomers in curiosity. "Milord Jack," the older of the two said, rising to her feet and bobbing a curtsy. A poke in the shoulder got the second one to do the same. Her 'milord' just a mutter.

"Daisy, Ruth, good evening," Jack said. "May we have the room to ourselves?"

The two girls, who must have been about ten and twelve, dressed smartly but plainly in somber gowns and starched white pinafores, scuttled out, abandoning their sewing. If they were anything like Elenora, then that would be with relief. She took a quick peek at their work, but the neat stitching put her own efforts to shame.

"Do please sit down," Mrs. Sharpe said. "If you've come again to enquire about how Josie is doing, then I can report to you that she's settling in well, the poor wee mite. I've put her in a room with Beth and Sarah. They're kind girls and a little older than her. Sarah has taken her under her wing."

Who was Josie? All these names meant nothing to Elenora, but she could hazard a guess. How many orphans was Jack supporting? It sounded like a lot. Still waters run deep, as her old governess had been wont to say. How had she not guessed this about Jack with the way he was with his son? What a suit of armor he wore, letting people think he was nothing but a heartless rake. And yet here he was, spending his money on children who until he'd met them had possessed no hope, no chance of betterment.

A feeling of inadequacy that she'd never considered how children might be living such a different life than the one she and her siblings led sank over Elenora as she took a seat on a straight backed chair. Even when Papa had gambled all his money away, they'd still not ended up destitute as these children had been—without homes or food or someone to care for them. Until Jack had come along.

Elenora sank onto a stiffly upholstered chair, but Jack remained standing, his whole being bristling with urgency. "For once I'm not here to enquire about the welfare of your charges. Not tonight. I need your help, Mrs. Sharpe. A terrible thing has happened. My son has been snatched by I know not who. For what reason also escapes me, but the man who has taken him, is, I fear, someone who has been following me about in my daily life. I glimpsed him a few times but thought nothing of it, like a fool. Only too late did I work that I was being followed and spied upon. One of those times was here, outside this very house."

Mrs. Sharpe's soft brown eyes narrowed and sharpened in an instant. "Your little lad? Taken? When?"

In a few crisp sentences, Jack told her what they knew, which wasn't much, and about the ill-written note pinned to Edward's scarf.

Elenora clasped her chilled hands, suppressing the desire to hold them out to the heat of the fire. "We have to get him back. Jack thinks you might be able to help us."

Mrs. Sharpe sat down with a thump on one of the other chairs. "How can I do that? I would if I could, but I don't know how. Have you sent for the Runners? The Watch? Tell me what you need from me. You know I owe you my life and those of my children, too."

This was dramatic stuff. Had Jack really saved her life? And her children's?

Jack caught Mrs. Sharpe's hand in his own. "You have connections from your old life. I know Benjamin still has dealings with his father—your husband. And, due to his father's... affiliations, he would be able to find out what whispers there might be of a sailor intent on stealing a child from Portland Place. And where he has that child hidden."

Mrs. Sharpe's brow furrowed in concern. "You well know I have nothing to do with that vagabond no more." Her grammar had noticeably slipped. It must be a learned thing, a deliberate abandonment of her roots, in an effort to improve herself and distance herself from them.

"It's my child we're talking of." Jack stood very still, staring down at the woman. "I've helped enough children in my time for it now to be the time for others to help my own son."

"Please," Elenora said, not quite sure what she was pleading for. "You're our only hope." Was she? London was a huge place and how could one woman hold the key to finding a veritable needle in a haystack?

Mrs. Sharpe hesitated a moment, then gave a curt nod. "Very well. Let me get Benjamin. I'll send him to find his father. As you say, he still keeps in touch with him."

As soon as she'd departed in search of this Benjamin, Elenora turned to Jack. "What does her husband do that is so bad she doesn't want to see him? And how did you save her life?"

Jack tapped his cane on the side of his boots. "He was a cruel and violent husband to her, as many men of his type are, but he was and is also part of the criminal underworld, in a well known and powerful gang. The most powerful gang in the rookeries. I came to her aid quite by chance and saw what he was doing to her. And what he would do to their children. She escaped him, with my help, when she realized he was about to coerce her children into his world of crime. She's raised all of them to be better than him, but Benjamin, her oldest and the only boy, who now works in the docks, found it hardest to break the link with his father."

Elenora started at the sound of the door opening again, as Mrs. Sharpe returned with her son.

Benjamin was nothing like his mother. Whereas she was short and round with an apple-wrinkled face and kind brown eyes, Benjamin must surely have favored his father. Tall, spindly and narrow faced, with nondescript mouse-brown hair, and eyes that could have been described at best as shifty, he was the sort of young man you might pass on the street and never notice but who might pick your pocket of all you possessed. He wore what must be his work clothes still, and carried a soft cap clutched in both his bony hands.

"Milord, Miss." He executed a somewhat wary bow, as his mother prodded him further into the room and closed the door behind them.

"I've told him what's happened," she said, folding her arms across her ample bosom.

"You wants me to go find my pa," Benjamin said, his voice lacking any hint of the enforced refinement his mother had acquired. "To get him to find out what's become o' your lad."

Jack nodded. "And I want you to take me with you."

The boy's rather too close together eyes narrowed, much as his mother's had done, but with cunning rather than intelligence. He gave a snort of clear disdain. "I ain't takin' you into St Giles. T'ain't no place for a nob like you. Someone'd slit your throat soon as look at you, just to steal your fancy boots."

"You'll take me with you," Jack snapped, "and help me find

my boy." He patted his coat pockets. "And I'm not going unarmed." He looked over his shoulder at Elenora. "I can't sit here and wait. I have to be doing something. And whoever has him means to keep him, I'm guessing, after what he wrote in that note."

Mrs. Sharpe leaned toward her son, keeping her voice too low to be heard. The young man shook his head, she muttered again, and as if in anger, he finally nodded. "Be it on your own head, milord." His gaze ran over Elenora appraisingly, lingering on her bosom.

Her hackles rose.

"I'll take you to The One Tun, milord, my pa's dive. And good luck to you if he's in a bad mood. He's never forgot how you took my ma from him, I'd best warn you now. Tells me about it ev'ry time I sees him. And as fer the lady—she ain't coming, that's for sure. She'll have to stay here with Ma, or I ain't goin'."

Elenora opened her mouth to object, but Jack got in there first. "Agreed. She will stay here with your mother and sisters, where she's safe."

"I won't," Elenora managed to get out, indignation rising. "If you're going, then I'm coming too."

Jack glared at her. "Your personality has its good points, Elenora, but stubbornness is not one of them. You will stay here in safety. This boy is correct. If he's taking me into the rookeries, and in particular to The One Tun, then it's no place for a young lady of your upbringing. Mrs. Sharpe will look after you. Wait here for me."

Mrs. Sharpe laid a hand on Elenora's shoulder. "Best do as milord says, Miss. For your own sake. Women're not safe on the streets of St Giles in daylight, never mind after dark. We'll wait here for news together."

Frustrated, all Elenora could do was nod agreement.

In Portland Place, Robert, Aunt Penelope's footman, Robert,

had by now arrived on the doorstep and been greeted by the harassed Alcock, who had just come upstairs from the kitchens where Cook and Miss Wetherby's maid had been attending to the wounds of Miss Douglas. There'd been a heated discussion as to whether a doctor should be called, which Miss Douglas had won, in insisting that apart from bruises, she was perfectly all right. *A right trooper, that one*, as Alcock's father, who had served in the army, would have said.

He opened the front door to find a rather annoyed Robert on the doorstep. He'd not wanted to traipse round to Portland Place in the dark on a rather embarrassing errand as he was certain it would be pointless and only serve to annoy Miss Wetherby, who all the servants had already classified as 'an odd one.' If she wanted to spend long periods in the company of her betrothed, then who was he to stop her?

Alcock, on being informed why Robert was here, found himself suddenly bereft of words. His lordship had certainly gone out, as he had said he would, and he had also certainly taken Miss Wetherby with him, without her maid as chaperone. And he, Alcock, should perhaps have taken the liberty of pointing out how improper this was. As his lordship did seem to have a rather loose grasp on what was or was not proper where young ladies were concerned. But he hadn't, because he'd been caught up in the care of poor Miss Douglas, whom he rather liked, and he'd allowed his lordship to slip out of his grasp. With Miss Wetherby.

He was then presented with the dilemma of whether to tell Robert the truth about what had befallen young Master Edward, which would involve revealing the child's relationship to his lordship, hitherto a well-kept secret. As a consequence, Alcock dithered.

Robert, tired after a long day, grew annoyed, but held his tongue as a good footman should even with a butler from a different establishment. However, his face betrayed him. Alcock, tired and grumpy with his master's proclivities, gave in and told him everything. And with the alarming story committed to memory, Robert, accompanied by a suitably anxious Agatha, began his journey home again, trying to work out how he was going to break news of her niece's disappearance into the back streets of London to his mistress.

CHAPTER NINETEEN

B ENJAMIN EQUIPPED JACK with a battered old cocked hat before
they left, insisting his smart top hat would be out of place.
Elenora had to agree with this, as even with this greasy monstros-
ity on his head, Jack, with his height and bearing, still looked
every inch the gentleman and would stand out all too well where
Benjamin was taking him. Fear that he wouldn't be safe nearly
overwhelmed her, but was overcome when she pictured Edward,
terrified and alone with the rough men who'd snatched him.

Once Jack had the hat, Mrs. Sharpe prodded Benjamin out of
the little sitting room, leaving Elenora, still seated near the fire,
alone with Jack. Somehow, even though she'd been alone with
him much of the afternoon and on the rush here, this lack of
chaperonage now felt much more serious. She swallowed down
her anxiety for Edward, and wondered what the situation called
for her to do.

As the door closed behind Mrs. Sharpe, Jack took a few steps
toward her, the expression on his face for once uncertain. He had
the cocked hat tipped back at an angle that could have been called
jaunty, had not the situation they were in been so serious. Despite
her worries, she couldn't help but notice how handsome he was.

On an impulse, Elenora rose to her feet as he approached her,
unclasping her cold hands. She offered no resistance when he
reached out and took them in his, the feel of them strangely
warm and reassuring. If only he didn't have to do this, but she

knew better than to try to persuade him not to.

A frown settled on her face. If only she were a man herself, and could go with him to protect him, for she was certain above all things that he would need protection. And how odd it was to find within herself that instinct to protect someone who looked more than capable of protecting himself. And he was going in the company of a young man who knew the slums intimately. Surely he would be safe? Common sense, though, suggested he would not. She had to swallow again, as that persistent lump kept on rising to her throat no matter how hard she tried to quell it.

He drew her closer to him, his thumbs running over the backs of her hands in a disturbingly intimate gesture that once she would have shied away from. Now, she gazed up into his eyes, fighting the instinct to let her own drop to his mouth, as how much easier would that have been? How cheating. She owed it to him to look him in the eyes.

She surprised herself by what she could see. His handsome face was etched in pain, his eyes anxious, but something else lurked there too.

He licked his lips. "I'm going into danger tonight, as you well know. And I want you to know how much I appreciate your wish to aid me. I cannot take you with me, Elenora, not only because you are a woman, but also because I value you too highly. I cannot put you in the same danger as Edward."

He valued her? She blinked a few times in confusion, unused to the notion of being valued. Did her family value her as this man, so recently a stranger, did? Perhaps only as the instrument of preventing their financial ruin. Jack could have no such ulterior motive.

"I wish I were a man, so I could come with you." The words tumbled out.

The smallest wry smile twisted his lips. "I am heartily glad you are not." He hesitated as though for once unsure. So unlike the man she'd been coming to know, the forthright, determined man. This was a different individual altogether. A man unsure of himself.

With difficulty, she kept her eyes on his, curious as to what he would say next, aware that he had something he very much wanted to unburden himself with.

The smallest of smiles twitched his lips. "For I could not do this if you were a man." And he leaned toward her.

She had the briefest of moments as the realization that he intended to kiss her dawned. Not enough time to dodge, even, and present him with her cheek. And anyway, did she even want to if she could? What would a kiss from him be like?

Then his lips found hers, and the kiss, quick and hard, was over in a second. His lips were cool and out of instinct, she closed her eyes for that moment as she felt them press against her own closed ones. And then he was gone, leaning back away from her but still retaining her hands in his, eyes claiming hers.

Good heavens. Her eyes flicked wide in shock and her breathing quickened, for no one had ever kissed her before, not like that, on the lips. Her sisters had not even dared to kiss her on the cheeks. She'd made it well known to them she wouldn't like it. Ever. And yet this had been… nice. She couldn't, for the moment, think of another word to describe it. "Thank you." That response felt decidedly inadequate, once said, and heat swarmed up her cheeks.

The wry smile returned. "Thank you for allowing me to do so. And when I return, with my son, I should like to kiss you again, if that would please you?"

She couldn't find an answer. No words would come. All she could do was stare at him, quite forgetting how hard it was to look someone in the eye. And nod. Just the tiniest of nods, as she couldn't be certain of what she wanted. Only that she'd liked him kissing her and that repeating it might spoil it.

He released her hands. "Mrs. Sharpe will keep you safe."

The door banged shut behind him and she was alone in the tiny, cluttered sitting room.

The clock on the mantlepiece ticked so loudly it seemed to fill the small space, each tick echoing back at the next and bouncing around the papered walls.

He'd kissed her. A man, not any man, but Jack Deveril, the rake, had pressed his lips to hers. In a kiss. And she'd liked it. Her heart hammered at the restriction of her stays, thudding rhythmically hard and fast like never before, and she was still breathing fast. As though she'd been running, or more than that. Racing. Her legs suddenly weakened at the knees, and she sank down again onto the chair she'd just vacated, the heat of the fire unnoticed.

The door opened and Mrs. Sharpe bustled in. "A nice cup of tea with sugar is what you need, my dear," were her first words. She leaned out of the still open door. "Ruth, make yourself useful and brew a pot of tea for Miss Wetherby, and bring it into the parlor." She turned back to Elenora. "You've gone white as a sheet, miss. What you need is something to eat, I should think. Did you have any dinner tonight?"

Elenora could only shake her head. Was she about to disgrace herself and faint? Something she'd never done in her life, not even when she'd missed a meal at Penworthy due to some escapade. Mama had always advised her to take smelling salts with her wherever she went, but her reticule was sadly lacking in those supplies as she'd always pooh-poohed Mama's words.

She'd never thought of herself as a girl given to fainting fits. Unlike Augusta, who indulged in them far too frequently for all of them to be genuine. She gripped the arm of the chair until her knuckles whitened and took steadying breaths. Had being kissed done this to her? Surely not? Was she as base and simple a creature as the vapid girls in Augusta's favorite romance novels? Brought to this state by the touch of a man?

The kettle must have been hot, because the older of the two girls who'd been in the little parlor earlier soon arrived with a tray covered in a white lacy cloth and laid out for tea. When she'd set it on the round table beside one of the fireside chairs, Mrs. Sharpe dispatched her off to find bread and butter and cake. An air of distinct disappointment about her, shoulders slumped and tread leaden, the girl, who must have been Ruth, departed.

Mrs. Sharpe poured tea into two elegant china cups. "Do you take cream?"

Elenora nodded, busy trying to take unobtrusive but steadying breaths, her mind still a whirl.

Having added a generous serving of cream from a pretty china jug that matched the cups, Mrs. Sharpe handed a cup to Elenora, who took it with a trembling hand. The cup rattled so in the saucer Elenora had to set it down on the small table by her chair. Hopefully, her hostess hadn't noticed.

Mrs. Sharpe, giving her guest a knowing glance, took the opportunity to stir several large spoonfuls of sugar into the teacup, unasked. "I can see you've had a shock, miss. This'll put you to rights."

Elenora managed a weak smile, shocked at how enfeebled circumstances had rendered her and chiding herself for not having more backbone. "Elenora. As we are to be thrown together tonight, I feel I should make you free of my name." Why not? Mama would be shocked at her bestowing this liberty on someone of Mrs. Sharpe's class, but who cared? Mama would be shocked at everything that had gone on this afternoon and evening, so why not shock her a bit more? Besides which, how would she ever find out this part of it?

Her hostess looked flattered at the suggested familiarity. "Why, thank you very much, miss, I mean Elenora. Martha's my name and you're very welcome to call me by it, especially with you being engaged to his lordship. I never thought I'd live to see the day. It's a blessing you are. A blessing. He deserves to be happy and I'm sure you'll make him so. You take a sip of your tea while it's hot, Miss Elenora. The sugar'll do you good."

"Thank you, Martha." Elenora sipped the hot sweet tea and did indeed immediately feel better. Odd how something so simple could have such an effect. But Mama always said tea was a pick-me-up in difficult times, and it seemed she was right. Elenora drained the teacup. "Might I trouble you for a second cup? I fear I'm quite thirsty after our hasty journey here through the streets."

Martha's kind brown eyes widened. "You come along the streets? In the dark? From his lordship's house?"

Elenora nodded. "There was no time to call for his carriage, I suppose. We came as soon as we heard Edward had been snatched." Fresh anxiety for the little boy coursed through her. "And I think Jack, Lord Broxbourne I mean, most likely didn't want to turn up at your door in his carriage." She managed to avoid the obvious for once—that his carriage would have looked out of place on this working class street. Or were they in the slums? Never having been in real slums, she had no idea. Although this street had appeared neat and tidy, which was not how she'd ever pictured slums.

Martha nodded, sagely. "His lordship thinks of everything."

Ruth returned with a plate of large slabs of cake and one of thickly buttered bread, the few crumbs adhering around her mouth attesting to the fact she'd taken the opportunity to fortify herself in the kitchen. She bobbed a neat curtsy and made no effort to leave, but stood there, trying hard, perhaps, not to stare at Elenora.

"Sit down, Ruth," Martha said. "And make yourself useful with that mending."

Clearly delighted that she was to be allowed to remain, Ruth did as she was told and picked up her discarded sewing, but Elenora could recognize a girl making a pretense of work when she saw one, having done so herself so many times. What Ruth was really doing was being nosy.

"I'm that pleased to find his lordship's found himself a lady," Martha said, as she refilled Elenora's cup a second time. "I've long said that's what he needs. A mother for his little lad and brothers and sisters for him too, one day. 'Tisn't right for a little lad to grow up with no other children around him."

Elenora bit her lip, deciding to ignore this suggestion that she should provide Jack with children. The cake looked most inviting, and she was beginning to recover from the shock of being kissed. Martha, who must have been a mind reader, held out the plate. She took one of the large slabs of pound cake. Her favorite. "This is excellent cake. As you divined, I haven't eaten since a small snack at noon. I'm feeling much better now, thank you, having drunk your excellent tea."

Mrs. Sharpe took a piece of cake herself. Her figure betrayed the fact that she probably was fonder of eating cake than she should have been. "Now," she said, settling back in her seat, "perhaps you might like to tell me all about yourself, Miss Elenora. I'm getting to be an old lady now, and I don't get out of this house often, what with all the children in my charge. So I always likes to hear about other people, and now I know as you're to marry our Lord Jack, I'd like to hear about you. If you don't mind, that is."

Elenora managed a smile. No, she didn't mind at all, and perhaps talking would go some way to preventing her from worrying about Jack and Edward as she was doing right now. She set down her cup on the table, and dabbed her mouth with the corner of her napkin. Where to begin?

Ruth, whose ears must be fairly flapping, bent her head over her sewing, but Elenora caught her eyes slanting sideways. No doubt all of this would at some point be relayed to her friends here in Betterton Street.

JACK AND BENJAMIN had left via the back door of the house, out into the little, stone-slabbed yard where the privy stood. Unlatching the gate, they let themselves into an alley, nowhere near so clean as the road itself, that ran behind this row of houses and the one backing onto it. A rat scuttled out of their way, and somewhere farther down a cat, who should have been chasing the rat, meowed plaintively. In the distance a dog barked, closely followed by a second, as if in answer.

"This way, milord," Benjamin, who was holding a lantern, said.

Jack fell in behind the boy. "Best not call me that where we're going. Jack will do just fine." The boy nodded but said nothing, loping along like some long dog out after hares with Jack as the owner running him.

Betterton Street, despite its lower middle class pretensions, lay close by the rookeries of St Giles. Within minutes, they'd left behind the rows of neat brick houses and quiet streets which clerks and schoolteachers and office workers called home. St Giles, renowned as the most deprived area of London and from which Jack had rescued most of Mrs. Sharpe's young charges, had changed little since Medieval times. As more people had flocked from the country into the city, it had only grown more congested. Whole families lived in single rooms with damp running down the walls, and whole buildings shared a single outdoor privy. Jack had been here before, of course, in the course of his activities in saving his orphans, but rarely in the dead of night and the cold of winter.

The stench, despite the cold, clogged his nostrils with an evil miasma of overflowing cesspits, piles of discarded rubbish and the general dirt of thousands of human beings crammed into a space better suited to hundreds. Rats scuttled everywhere, and worse things he couldn't see.

Every time he came here, Jack was struck with how terrible a place it was and couldn't wait to be out of it. If hell were to be found on Earth anywhere, it had to be here. Only now, this had to be where the men who'd taken Edward would have retreated to, secure in the knowledge that it would be nearly impossible for Jack to send Bow Street Runners after them. The Runners were brave, but not brave enough to enter the warren that was the rookeries of St Giles and the Devil's Acre, down near Westminster Abbey. Jack would have to do that by himself. With Benjamin's help, and hopefully with that of his father, who had his ear to everything that happened in the rookeries of London. If Reuben Sharpe didn't kill him first.

Benjamin trod the filthy lanes as if born to them, which of

course, he had been. When Jack had helped Martha Sharpe escape the clutches of her husband, eight years since, Benjamin had been a half grown boy of twelve, already entangled in his father's web of crime, and it had been hard work to twist him free of it and into respectable employment at first at Smithfield Market, then later the docks. But he was strongly attached to his mother still, and had not, as far as Jack knew, reverted back to his old life. Although he'd kept in touch with his villainous father so that might well not be true.

Although the hour was not as yet late, the rickety wooden houses that grew like so much dirty fungus to either side of the lanes showed little light. Here and there a murky oil lamp hung to light their way along the foggy streets, and only the taverns on every corner seemed to show signs of occupation. Music and shouting tumbled out of their doors and into the streets, and sometimes drunken customers too. Down side streets dirtier and darker than the lanes lurked the destitute, the beggars, the prostitutes and thieves, all of them ready and waiting to fleece and rob any gentleman who might unwarily venture into their territory.

Jack kept a tight hold on his cane, glad of the pistols hidden in his coat, but either Benjamin's presence kept them safe, or the people they passed were too lost in their own miseries to care.

Ahead loomed the shadowy bulk of Westminster Abbey, towering high above the mean streets that surrounded it. "We're in the Devil's Acre now," Benjamin said over his shoulder, his voice a raspy whisper. "That's where Pa's based nowadays. Keep close, Jack."

How could this fetid conglomeration of buildings, running with filth, exist a bare stone's throw from something as glorious as Westminster Abbey? And Westminster Palace as well, along the banks of the Thames, had all of this lurking at its back whilst those in government, with their top hats and their carriages, went about their daily business all unknowing, or more likely ignoring, the immense suffering they'd turned their backs on. That people should have to live like this stuck in Jack's craw as much as the stench of their homes did. Worse than the way the pigs were kept at Broxbourne Park. So much worse. No wonder they resorted to crime to feed themselves.

"Here we are, sir," Benjamin said. "The One Tun."

A dilapidated inn sign showing the dirty image of a barrel hung motionless above the street, where the buildings on either side leaned toward one another so much the sign almost touched the house opposite.

"This is where we gotta go. This is my pa's alehouse."

Jack nodded. Into the den of the man he'd bested eight years ago. A man who would not be happy to see him return. In fact, a man who'd promised to kill him if he ever saw him again. But that had been eight years ago…

CHAPTER TWENTY

THE HOT STENCH of unwashed mankind met Jack at the door of The One Tun. That and the noise of the occupants. Even this early in the evening, they must have been there for some time, for drunken shouts filled the air, mingling with screams and screeches from the women, doxies all of them. Thank God he'd saved little Josie and her fellows from a fate such as this.

The beamed ceiling hung low, and Jack was glad he no longer had his tall top hat. He took off his grubby cocked hat and, holding it to his chest, followed young Benjamin through the crowd as he elbowed his way toward the bar. To right and left stood tables crowded with the source of all the noise, the knives and forks chained down. What sort of a place needed to prevent the theft of eating utensils in this way? And did they ever wash them in between uses?

Despite the hat, it bore in upon him that he stood out the way a woman in a ballgown would have done in White's, that bastion of male dominance. Every head turned to stare and, as he progressed behind Benjamin, silence fell as if from the wake of a boat to spread out behind him. These were a people deeply suspicious of anyone who wasn't a part of their world, and Jack could not have looked more so had he tried. The temptation to glance back over his shoulder or from side to side burgeoned, but he fought it off. He must betray no lack of confidence in front of them, or they would pounce on it.

Benjamin reached the bar, by dint of everyone falling back as though afraid to catch some disease of the rich Jack might be carrying, and leaned upon it in an attitude of casual arrogance. His sharp, street-wise face fitted in here as though he'd been born to it. Which he had.

"Ben Sharpe," the innkeeper said, without pausing in his wiping out of tankards with a less-than-clean rag. He was a swarthy individual with bushy brows that met above his nose and a thatch of matching dark hair hanging so low over his forehead as to have almost joined in. A rash of dark stubble covered his lantern jaw, and a couple of gold teeth glinted in his mouth as he spoke. "What brings you down here to *The Tun?*" But his gaze was on Jack even as he posed the question.

The silence in the room bristled with tension, suspicions bouncing around the walls as though given living substance. If Jack looked over his shoulder, he'd find the customers pressed up close behind him in open threat, probably fingering whatever weapons they had about them. Was everyone in the tavern agog and listening?

"Come to see my pa," Benjamin announced. "I b'lieve as he can help this cove." He gave an expressive shrug of his scrawny shoulders. "If he's a mind to, that is."

An indrawn gasp at Jack's effrontery hissed around the low rafters.

Everyone was indeed agog and listening to his business.

Jack had never felt quite so intimidated. His sword stick would be no use whatsoever against so many, and his pistols were hidden in an inner pocket and, if an emergency arose, could only take out two at most. A quick glance around at his audience showed him that most of the women had melted away, and in their place a motley array of characters as threatening as the innkeeper were standing, eyeing him with suspicion. Most worryingly, all had set aside their tankards of drink, and a good few of them clutched knotted staffs in their equally knotted hands. One of them gripped a piece of rope on the other end of which a scarred bullterrier strained, piggy eyes fixed on Jack as though he were a piece of prime steak. Or a rat.

The innkeeper rubbed his sizeable nose, from which sprouted hairs as dark and bristly as his eyebrows. "Your pa know you're comin'?"

The crowd edged half a step closer.

Jack determined not to give them another glance.

Benjamin shrugged again. "I don't know what business you think it is o' yours, Tom Havelock, but so far as I'm concerned, 'tain't nothin' to do wi' you. I've gotta speak with my pa, an' you ain't stoppin' me."

Havelock drew himself up to his considerable height, puffing his chest out. "Mr. Sharpe don't give an audience to jus' anyone, and well you knows it. You can go in, young Benjamin, and no question. I ain't arguin' with that. But this cove's a swell'un by the look of him, an' he don't go in unless he states his business an' gets searched, or I'll be in trouble with the guv'nor."

A battle of heavy stares ensued, but Havelock carried the day, as age and experience triumphed over brash youth. Benjamin shrugged yet again, as if to imply his setback was of no importance. "Awright then. If you has to know. My gen'leman cove thinks my pa might know somethin' to help him find his little nipper wot's been taken 'gainst his will."

A young woman in a low cut scarlet dress that might once have graced a more salubrious establishment than this one, shouldered her way to the front of the audience of men. Auburn hair hung in unruly curls down her back. At any other time she would have aroused Jack's interest, but not now, for more than one reason. "His little nipper, eh?" She surveyed Jack from head to foot, a speculative look in her eyes. "A swell's little nipper, no less. What's Reuben Sharpe got to do with nippers? He ain't got nothin' to do wiv anyone as'd snatch littluns, nor no bands of pickpockets, if that's what you're implyin'."

"No one said he did," Benjamin snapped. "Keep yer nose out, Molly Bragg. Ain't nothin' to do with you, neither." He turned back to the innkeeper. "He's here, then, I s'pose?"

The innkeeper pulled a face not unlike that of the scarred bull terrier. It didn't improve his appearance any. "He's in the back room, where he always is. But I got to search your swell cove before he can go in."

Another shrug. "Help yerself then. It ain't no skin orf my nose."

Havelock shot Jack a challenging look and stumped out from behind the bar. Like Jack, the top of his head brushed the low, soot stained roof beams. "Arms out."

What Jack would have liked to have done was plant the man a facer to knock him flat, but that would have got him nowhere, possibly even killed by the looks on the faces of his audience. So what he actually did was to lift his arms while the man ran his beefy mitts over his body. Not unexpectedly, he found the two dueling pistols straightaway.

"Wot's this then?" He held them up delicately between thumbs and forefingers, like a duchess with a teacup, fixing Jack with a low-browed scowl. "Thinkin' of goin' in to see the gov'nor armed, were you?"

"I always travel armed when I enter the Devil's Acre," Jack said, enunciating his words clearly for the benefit of the watching crowd. "I'd be a fool not to."

"Then I think I'll keep 'em here for you, while you're seein' the guv'nor. He don't take to coves who bring weapons to the table. Hidden weapons." He laid the two pistols on the bar.

Jack fixed him with a hard stare. "They'd better be here when I return for them."

Havelock gave a snort. "If I says they'll be here, then here they'll be. You think we're all thieves in The One Tun?"

Best not to answer this one, as that was exactly what Jack was thinking.

Benjamin straightened his skinny limbs and pulled himself up from his position lounging at the bar. "Then we're goin' in." He turned to Jack. "You'd better come wi' me right now. I daresn't leave you alone in here." He grinned, showing his crooked, yellowed teeth. "I don't think this lot likes the look o' you too much."

In agreement on that, Jack followed Benjamin as he edged through the surly, still threatening crowd, who seemed less inclined, now, to move than ever, toward the far side of the tap room. There, a low door lurked in a shadowy corner, guarded by two enormous men, their beefy arms folded across their wide chests. By their cauliflower ears and broken noses, they looked as though the fighting ring was their preferred milieu. Probably bare knuckled fights like those Jack had gone to watch and bet on in his reckless youth.

Both of them surveyed Jack out of hostile eyes for a moment before the one on the right unfolded his arms as though this were a great chore. He wore a dirty, collarless shirt, the sleeves rolled up to above the elbow to exhibit a tangled mass of tattoos. With a curl of his hairy upper lip, he tapped on the door with the delicacy of a duchess, while never taking his watchful eyes from Jack's face.

"Enter." A deep rumble of a voice Jack well remembered answered.

The tattooed man jerked his head at Jack and Benjamin, and with one muscle-bound arm, pushed the door open. Jack had to duck to pass through it. Even Benjamin, who was small and wiry, had to stoop to avoid losing his own jaunty cap.

The room Jack entered was small and square and hung like the taproom with low beams overhead that brushed the top of Jack's head. A coal fire blazed in the hearth and in the center of the room sat a solid oak desk, much gouged about on top and most of its polish gone. Behind the desk reclined a mountain of a man who made both Havelock and Jack look slight, and who, like them, would have found it difficult to stand upright in the room. Time had not been kind to him. Not only was he tall, but in possession of a huge gut that he'd not had when Jack had last met him eight years since. The buttons of his brocade waistcoat strained across it, intent on giving up the challenge to hold him in. In front of him, on the table, lay the remains of his dinner—a well-picked chicken carcass.

"Jack Deveril, or I'm a niffy-naffy feller. Well, strike me down." The man's piggy eyes, nestling within flaccid, pouchy cheeks, ran up and down Jack in obvious assessment. "The years've done you well, I see." His greasy lips curved in a smile. "I didn't think you'd dare venture into my neck o' the woods ever again." He coughed into a voluminous handkerchief. "Although I've heard about your exploits snatchin' children off the streets. Rumor has it you've been cookin'em and puttin'em in pies."

He gave a great guffaw which ended wheezily in more coughing. Was that blood on the handkerchief?

Jack fought to hang onto his self-control. His son's life depended on his comportment now. He mustn't put a foot wrong. "Well, here I am."

The two burly guards had shouldered their way into the room behind Jack and Benjamin and their meaty, solid presence rendered the room airless and claustrophobic. Did they imagine Jack might try to harm their guv'nor even now, with all those men out in the taproom just feet away? He wasn't an idiot.

Reuben Sharpe wiped his mouth and waved a dismissive hand at them. "You can wait outside. My boy's enough guard for me tonight. And me an' this gentleman're old acquaintances." He nodded at Benjamin. "You got your barking irons, boy?"

For answer, Benjamin tapped his waist where his loose coat covered the top of his trousers. "I don't come out wivout'em, Pa." The two guards, faces wreathed in disappointment that they weren't to be involved in the battering of such a swell cove, and whatever profits that might generate, retreated, and Benjamin closed the door behind them.

Reuben nodded, a satisfied grin spreading across his face, and Jack had pause to wonder if it had been a good idea to entrust himself to Benjamin's tender care. The boy had spent more than half his life in his father's company and been nearly a man grown when his mother had escaped that life, and was also used to going about armed. Perhaps his present employment was all a sham. It didn't do to take people at face value.

Reuben pushed aside the plate of bones. "Warren said you'd come."

"Warren?" Jack frowned. What did Sharpe mean by that? It wasn't lost on him that Warren had been Mary's surname and thus it was Edward's as well. But who was this Warren and how was he someone Reuben Sharpe knew? Mary had told him she'd had no family to turn to, and that she'd been quite alone in the world. It seemed Reuben Sharpe was already well acquainted with Jack's reason for being here. That would save some time.

"Know the name, don'tcha?" Reuben was enjoying this, his eyes dancing with malicious fervor.

Of course he did. Jack's mind leapt back to the day he'd first met Mary Warren, ten years ago. She'd been singing in a tavern, in Limehouse, when he'd come in with some friends for a dare. It hadn't been the sort of establishment men of the upper echelons of the Ton were wont to frequent, but he and his fellow young blades had taken it upon themselves to visit every tavern in London between them. The Angel, Limehouse, had been on Jack's list, and back then it had happened to be the tavern run by Reuben Sharpe.

Mary had been the evening's entertainment. As Jack and his friends had settled with their tankards of ale, she'd taken to the makeshift stage, such as it was, to sing *Farewell and Adieu to you Spanish Ladies*. An aptly chosen ditty, which had fitted her dockside audience who joined in with the rousing chorus with gusto. Most of them, as Jack found out later, were sailors who'd been, or still were, part of the force fighting against the French.

Jack and his friends had raised their glasses to her and sung as lustily as the denizens of The Angel, but Jack had only had eyes for the singer.

Mary had been the most beautiful girl Jack had ever seen, with her wild black hair cascading about her almost naked shoulders, her slanting cat's eyes and her luscious red lips. A look of the exotic about her, but an accent that was pure Welsh valleys. Young and full of bravado, with a heart already swelling with love, he'd raised his own tankard of ale in salute to the beautiful young singer and the brave sailors who surrounded him. And that had been the start of the relationship that had led to her death two years later.

"Who is this Warren?" Jack asked. Was he mistaken in his belief that Mary had possessed no relatives? She'd been gone so long, now, it was hard to recall. And her death in childbirth had left him so racked with despair his reaction had been to shut out all memories of her. Only her child had remained, consigned, at first, to a wetnurse chosen from amongst his tenants at Broxbourne Park and only later part of his life in London.

But Reuben wasn't about to reveal all his secrets straightaway. He leaned forwards suddenly, pointing a stubby, dirty-nailed finger at a rickety chair. "Sit yerself down, why don'tcha? Milord." That last word came out as a sneer, the effect somewhat marred by another fit of coughing. This time it was obvious he was coughing up blood. Of course, consumption—with his pasty almost gray skin and hollows around his eyes, it was clear the man had that death sentence of an illness.

Jack eyed him in speculation for a few seconds. But, if he wanted to find out what was going on here and retrieve his son, he'd best do as he was asked. He sat down, and Benjamin retreated to the door, which he leaned against, arms folded across his scrawny chest.

"That's better." Reuben wheezed a chesty cough again, this time producing nothing. "I got a lot to say to you."

Jack resisted the inclination to say, "Well, get on with it then," and stayed silent.

Reuben rubbed his stubbly chin. "I can't say as I ain't got no axe to grind wi' you, my fine lord, because I has. And you well knows it. You prigged my wife'n'fam'ly more'n eight years back, and I ain't a man as takes that lyin' down." He grinned, flashing an array of brown teeth and a couple of gold ones at Jack. "Though I'm a man as likes to take his time with things like revenge. No rushin' in like a bull in a china shop for Reuben Sharpe. I'm a man as likes to savor his revenge when it comes. A patient man, that's me."

That this was revenge had occurred to Jack as soon as Sharpe had mentioned Mary's surname. Whoever this Warren who'd taken Edward was, he must have known she'd worked for Reuben in the past. And eight years ago, when Jack had helped Martha Sharpe escape her bully of a husband with her brood of terrified children, Reuben had sworn Jack would live to regret it. The man was right. He'd waited a long time to hit back, if that was what this was. And perhaps the arrival of this man Warren had triggered this.

"You have my son?"

"Do I?" Reuben smiled. "You thinks I do, most clear. But do I? What would I want wiv a lad like him? A twig off the grand trunk of milord Jack Deveril? A small an' snivelly twig, at that. Cries like a baby, so I'm told."

Jack held his tongue. If he spoke now, he might end up leaping over the table and seizing the man about his doughy throat.

Reuben smirked. "Another has your boy, not me. Another who has a right to him in law. He come to me for help, seein' as the last he saw of the boy's mother was in my tavern in Limehouse. Seein' a way to make you pay, I agreed." He coughed again, his whole body wobbling with the effort. "And seein' as I don't have much longer on this Earth, I thought as it were high time I fulfilled my promise to you. And made you pay for stealin' my wife away from me. So me and this other cove, this Warren, we're working together on this. You're dicked in the nob if you think I'm goin' let you have your brat back fer nothin'."

Jack's fists clenched.

"You owes me bad, fer what you did eight year back. You prigged my fam'ly and deprived me of their use. A man's wife is his property, same as his dog and his business, and you took my wife away from me. Now, with Warren's help, I've done the same to you." A self-satisfied smile crept across his sweaty face.

"What is it that you want?" the words came out through Jack's gritted teeth.

Another smirk graced that ugly face. "What does anyone want from a wheyfaced nob like you?" He laughed. "Money. Me and Warren wants money from you, or you'll never see your boy agin. He wants money for what you took from him, and I want money for what you took from me. Same thing." He coughed again, bloody spittle on his lips. "Only I wants money that I can't take with me—for my boy." His eyes went to Benjamin where he still stood leaning against the door. "To set my boy up in honest business, and to look after my little ones that I've got from my second wife."

Whoever had provided Sharpe with further children could hardly be his wife, as he'd never divorced Martha Sharpe or Jack would have heard about it. He forbore from pointing out that Benjamin already possessed an honest occupation working at the docks. "Who is this Warren, then? Tell me, and I might believe he exists and this is not all down to you."

Reuben stuck his fingers in the pockets of his waistcoat, a difficult undertaking due to his enormous girth, and leaned back in his seat, a toad of a man whose great tongue might well come snaking out to snatch a fly from off the ceiling at any moment. Repugnant, evil. "He's your doxie's husband, that's who. Back from sailin' the ocean blue in the king's navee. Back to find his wife gone, stole from him by a swell cove with too much blunt to know what to do with. The wife Able Seaman Warren loved, what should've bin waitin' for him on his noble return. But he comes home to find her gorn from where he left her, dead, in fact, and all that's left to him is her little lad. A lad that should by rights be his. A lad what bears his name and what you stole."

Jack's stomach lurched. "Her husband?" He couldn't keep the shock out of his voice.

Reuben grinned. "Aye, that's addled your pate for you, my

fine lord, I c'n see. Din't tell you that, did she, when she was climbin' her way up through the theaters you'd introduced her to? Via your bed. Usin' you as a ladder to success. Kept her man quiet, p'raps thinkin' he'd never be comin' home. Happens often enough with sailors—they dies for lots of reasons thousands o' miles from home. Their wives don't never know what happened to'em. Thought she'd get away with forgettin' him. Well, now he's back, and he wants a cut of what should be hers by right and therefore his. Payment for services rendered, call it."

"I don't believe you."

Reuben appeared unmoved by this statement. "B'lieve what you likes. He has the boy—his boy by law as he were born while she were wed to him. He's keepin' him if you don't settle wi' him, quick like." His face contorted into a leer. "An' I hear he's goin' back to sea wi' the boy if you don't pay up."

Her husband. His Mary, the woman he'd thought the love of his life had been living a lie. Causing him to live a lie. He'd spoken to her of marriage, content to go against his father's wishes for his love of her, and she'd lied to him. She'd said she had to put him before herself, that she could never bring him down to her level and disgrace him before his family. And every bit of it had been a lie. She couldn't have married him if she'd wanted to, and she'd let him think her reasons for refusal noble.

The pedestal he'd relegated her to after her death came crumbling down as images cascaded through his head. Her shock, when she'd found out she was pregnant, the difficulty he'd had persuading her not to resort to a back street abortionist, the badly disguised anger she'd shown when her increasing girth had halted her singing career. Of course, he'd said she should go back to it after the baby was born—his baby—but she'd never been able to do that, dying in a welter of blood on the bed in the house he'd bought her.

She'd been a liar.

But that didn't alter his love for her child. His child. The child who, along with Martha Sharpe, had prompted his own altruistic endeavors. The child who could have grown up backstage in a theater and in tawdry rooming houses with his mother, who instead had grown up on a viscount's country estate and in a mansion in the city. He'd think about Mary's perfidy later. Right now he had to get their son back.

"How much does he want?"

Reuben licked his lips with relish. "You can ask him fer yerself. He's upstairs. Been stayin' here for a week while he took a spyglass to the lay of the land. Told him it'd be no good goin' face to face with the likes of the gentry. Told him the only way was to come at you sideways and force your hand." He held up his own pudgy hand as Jack half turned toward the door. "Hold yer horses. The boy ain't with him, an' if he don't get back to the boy, safe an' in one piece, you'll not be seein' the lad again. Mark my words. You keeps your hands off of him."

Jack's shoulders rose and fell as he fought to control himself. He had to stay calm. He had to, for Edward's sake. He must mean nothing to this man who called himself Mary's husband other than a meal ticket to untold riches. The man would not care if the boy died. He was not his true father, whatever the law said.

"Very well. Take me to him."

Reuben nodded at Benjamin. "First room at the top o' the stairs. You go in with him. I don't trust him not to cause a mill. I'm trustin' you to watch him for me, boy."

CHAPTER TWENTY-ONE

AT ABOUT THE same time as Jack was being led upstairs by Benjamin Sharpe to meet the husband of the woman he'd once thought the love of his life, Robert, Aunt Penelope's footman, was returning home with sluggardly steps. He was not looking forward to having to break it to her that the tender shoot she was in charge of, her only brother's eldest daughter, had been whirled off into what sounded like the darkest corners of the underworld by the well-known rake who was her betrothed. He, like all of Lady Dandridge's servants, had already formed the opinion that Miss Wetherby had made a mistake by getting herself entangled with a man of such deep and disreputable infamy. And now they'd been proven right.

His only comfort was that he was returning in the company of Miss Wetherby's maid, Agatha, who was more terrified than he was. She'd committed the unforgiveable crime of allowing her young mistress to slip between her fingers in the most uncaring way, and Robert could only see dismissal looming before her. From her slumped shoulders and trailing feet, she shared his opinion. Hopefully, once she'd been given her marching orders, Lady Dandridge would be too upset to sack him too. Which in any case would have been unfair. Although Robert was familiar with the phrase "don't shoot the messenger," in his experience the messenger was always a good one to blame.

They let themselves in through the mews at the back of the

house into the servants' hall, where they found an agitated Hemmings waiting for them. To Robert's horror, the butler insisted on taking both of them upstairs immediately, without even the opportunity for a fortifying snifter, to where Lady Dandridge, attended by her own maid with plentiful smelling salts, was waiting in the drawing room.

As Agatha appeared to have been struck dumb, it fell to Robert to relay the situation. Out came the smelling salts.

"Oh, good heavens above. Where on earth has he taken her?" Lady Dandridge finally managed to gasp, her voice barely above a horrified whisper, as she waved her maid away. Discovering that her niece's betrothed, despite her prior knowledge of his less than perfect reputation, had been nurturing an illegitimate child in his household, like a cuckoo in his nest, had proved the worst shock of all, and Hemmings was immediately asked to pour her a generous glass of brandy.

Robert could not answer this, for no one in Lord Broxbourne's house had known where his lordship had headed off to so precipitously, in the company of Miss Wetherby. He shuffled his feet in embarrassment, praying silently for a deliverance that took its time coming.

Hemmings, once her ladyship was sipping her brandy, dismissed Robert and the trembling Agatha, still both in a state of employment, and turned his attentions to his distraught mistress. "Please don't upset yourself, my lady." He kept his voice level and emotionless, something he'd learned to do long ago with the volatile Lady Dandridge. "Miss Wetherby seems to me the sort of girl who can look after herself."

Her ladyship shot him an anguished glance. "That is what I am afraid of."

ELENORA WAS RIGHT at that moment becoming more than a little restless in Martha Sharpe's parlor. Having fortified herself by eating several more slices of the excellent pound cake and washing this rather unsuitable dinner down with a good half-dozen cups of strong sweet tea, she was feeling ready to face all eventualities. The thought that Jack had gone off without her into the depths of the slums had begun, with her rising spirits, to trouble her more and more. She should never have allowed herself to be so easily dissuaded from accompanying him.

"I think, Martha," she said to her hostess, with some asperity, "that you need to tell me the whole story behind this, for I suspect there's more to it than either you or Jack has divulged."

Martha glanced at young Ruth, whose ears must have been on high alert. "Time for you girls to get ready for bed, I'd say. You go and tell my Betsy and Lucy to get the little ones in their beds for me. And you big girls can have some hot cocoa in the kitchen. I'll be up later to tuck you all in and hear your prayers."

Ruth's rather thin mouth set in a discontented line, but she set her sewing down and with an abrupt curtsy, took herself off. No doubt all these other girls Martha had mentioned would be waiting agog to hear what was afoot from their spy in the camp.

Elenora set down her empty teacup. Where to start, now they were alone? At the beginning. "What sort of an establishment, exactly, do you run here?" Best to be upfront and clear from the start, and the fact that it appeared to be full of more girls than one mother could possibly be responsible for bringing into the world seemed something that needed delving into, despite Jack's brief explanation.

Martha shifted uneasily. "I'm not sure his lordship'd want me being free with what he does here."

As if that wasn't suspicious in itself.

Elenora shook her head, determined not to be put off. "Nonsense. I am his betrothed, and the fact that he brought me to you in his search for his son must prove to you that he holds me in his confidence. So therefore I should be in yours." She bestowed a beaming, and falsely positive, smile upon her hostess and leaned forwards in her seat. "So, pray tell me all about it."

Martha bridled a bit more. "It's a long story, Miss Elenora, and goes back years."

"Start at the beginning then. You will find I am all ears. And it seems, at this moment, that we have time for you to tell me everything."

Martha nodded, although with a show of reluctance. "I first met his lordship when he came to the tavern me and my husband, Reuben, were running in Limehouse. A lot of young bucks liked to come there and drink, down with the rough trade. To see the other side of life to what they're used to in their big houses to the west. After, when I was safely out of it, he told me it was something called a 'rite of passage.' I thought he was no different to the others, doing it for a dare, I'd say. But that night…" She hesitated as though she might be reaching a bit of the story she didn't want to divulge.

"Warts and all," Elenora said, a phrase she'd long wanted to use. "Tell me everything. Leave nothing out. Nothing at all."

Martha nodded, a resigned expression settling on her face. "That night we had a singer in the tavern. Young girl fresh arrived from Wales. Her name was Mary Warren."

Edward's mother, of course.

Curiosity consumed Elenora. She had to know this story now. She had to find out about the as yet mysterious young woman who'd found her way into Jack's life and out of it so abruptly. "Go on."

Martha sighed. "She was lovely to look at. Like one of those china dolls you see in shop windows up west. I always wanted one of them when I was a littl'un. Never got one, but that didn't stop me wanting one. Black hair down to her waist, skin like…" She searched for a word. "Like a pearl, all glowing and fresh. Eyes that sparkled and a figure any man would want to call his own."

"And did Jack call her his own?" Although she already knew the answer to this. Was that a nub of jealousy forming in her heart? Mary Warren had been the love of Jack's life and given him his adored little son. He'd made it clear how much he'd loved her. Or had he?

Martha nodded. "She lit onto him soon as she saw him. Recognized him for what he was and saw how smitten he was, too. Her ticket out of the rookeries. A girl as lovely as her could go a long way with a rich benefactor, and she knew it. Either that, or she'd have ended up on the street, selling her body to the highest bidder. And she could sing too. Like a lark, I'd've said. Later on, folks called her the Welsh Nightingale, when she was famous and singing in those big theaters up west."

"But what does she have to do with you running this house?"

"It's how I got to know his lordship. Through Mary. And how he got to find out how unhappy I was with Reuben."

"Why were you so unhappy?"

Martha dabbed her eyes with the corner of her apron as though the recounting of her story cut her to the quick. "Oh, when we first were wed, and he were young and handsome, he was kinder to me than any man I'd ever met. He could be a charmer when he wanted to be, could Reuben. My ma and pa said I was marrying beneath me, but, like a fool, I wouldn't listen to them. We were both young and in love, but love doesn't last, Miss Elenora, take it from me. If it ever exists, which I've had cause to doubt in my life."

She sniffed. "And I didn't know, back then, that he was getting himself involved with the Limehouse gang." She shook her head. "The money was nice, of course, and he wasn't backward in buying me pretty things when I was young, and pretty things made me prettier, but then I found out where it was comin' from. Well, we had words, and more, because I thought I knew him and had found I didn't... That was the first time he beat me senseless." Her matter of fact words dropped into the cozy sitting room with a thud that echoed.

Elenora swallowed. A man, Martha's husband, who must once have promised to stand by her and care for her, had beaten her unconscious for daring to raise an objection to his criminal ways. She wasn't such a numbskull to think that sort of thing didn't go on between husbands and wives. She'd seen a few wives of Papa's tenants sporting bruised faces before now. But this was closer to home, somehow. "And did Jack find out what your husband was doing to you?"

"He saw. Not the beating, which wasn't the first I'd had from Reuben by a long chalk. No, Reuben was always careful to lay into me somewhere no one'd see. He didn't like having no witnesses. Not even in front of our younguns. No, Jack saw me after, behind the bar, with my face all swoll up and sore, my ribs broke, only no one to take no notice of the bruises. No one save Jack. The folk in The Angel, that was our tavern's name, they saw, but they knew Reuben and they said nothing. Turned a blind eye. Turned two blind eyes. If any of 'em had said something, they knew they'd've received the same. Or worse. Reuben was getting himself a reputation, by then. He was well in with the Limehouse gang and no one goes against them. Not then and not now."

Her matter of factness shocked Elenora. What could she say to Martha's tale of suffering? And this courageous woman had allowed her precious son to take Jack to meet this man, whom she'd escaped from. To walk into the danger of the rookeries to save Jack's child. Bravery could lurk in the most unexpected places.

Martha wiped eyes which had grown watery and moist. "I didn't think a swell cove like your Jack would've cared, but he did. He got me away from Reuben, with my children, and set me up in a little house. Safe away from him. I don't know what he said or did, but Reuben didn't come after me. Jack'd got Mary well away by then in a nice little house up west, but he'd kept coming back to The Angel—I think to keep an eye on me. I think Mary asked him to. She knew, you see."

She paused. "That's why Reuben bares him such a grudge. He thought Lord Jack stole me away to be his doxy." She chuckled. "Stupid idea when the lad had already got Mary, fresh young thing that she was, but Reuben's a jealous man, and he don't forget if someone's bested him. No, he's happy to bide his time, that one. His favorite saying's that revenge is a dish best served cold." She shivered.

"Does Jack know this?"

"He does."

And yet he'd gone with Benjamin into the lion's den. Or the wolf's den, for Reuben Sharpe did not sound like a proud and brave lion. What was that strange and ugly animal, looking as though it had been made from the bits left over when God had created all the rest, that she'd seen on display at Astleys? A hyena. Reuben Sharpe sounded like an ugly hyena.

"And Jack has let you have this house ever since?"

Martha nodded. "I work for it, you mark my words. Don't you go thinking I'm a sponger. I'm not. He saw my girls, and Benjamin too, and he realized there's children out there, in those back streets, all over London, in need of the sort of care a good woman can give a child. Littl'uns with no mothers, no blankets to keep them warm of a night. No food to fill their bellies. When he finds one, most often little girls as they're the most at risk, he brings them back here for me to mother. I've twenty girls here right now, the newest from just a few days ago. They get an education, enough to see them employed as something other than street sellers or whores. No girl leaves here without having a job of work to go to as a maid or a shopgirl."

Elenora felt tears stinging her own eyes, a most unusual experience as she normally found crying an impossible achievement. She would have taken out her handkerchief, had she not already given it to Miss Douglas. As it was, she had to be content with her sleeve.

Martha reached out and patted her hand. "Excuse me being familiar, Miss Elenora, but you seem such a nice young lady, and interested in what Lord Jack gets up to. I believe he started this house, this home for the little orphans he finds, partly because of helping me, but also because of little Edward. Let me tell you the lad's story too, to make the square. Then you'll know everything."

Elenora bit her lip. "I keep thinking I shouldn't have let Jack go on his own. That he's going into danger with this man who was, is still I suppose, your husband, and the more you tell me, the more I think I'm right. We should go after him."

Martha shook her head. "We can't. I can't go back there. Not ever again. I swore it to myself eight years ago. And I can't let you go there. It'd be more than my life was worth. Lord Jack'd never forgive me. Let me tell you about Edward."

Elenora fought to control the urge to leap up and run out of the tiny room that had suddenly become claustrophobic. "Go on."

"Lord Jack, he fell hook, line and sinker for young Mary the moment he clapped eyes on her. Fell hard and fell strong. And she saw he was what she needed. I don't like to speak ill of the dead, and she's long dead now, but she used him all right. I'm sure she had feelings of some kind for him, I could see that, but he, well, like I said, he was smitten. He'd have done anything for her. Under his patronage, she was soon singing and dancing across the finest stages in town, singing to the Prince himself, even. They called her the Welsh Nightingale. Did I tell you that already? She was Welsh, you see, and they say all the Welsh can sing. Music's in their blood."

This was a different side to the story from anything Elenora had heard before.

"Then she found she was with child. You'd have heard her screaming and carrying on if you'd been out at sea in a ship on your way to France, I can tell you. Loud enough to scare every raven in the Tower. Loud enough to wake the dead. She didn't want that bairn getting in the way of 'her career'."

Not wanted Edward? Elenora thought of the bright and lively little boy with his love for history… and cows. Of how he stretched himself along the rug with his soldiers and how his small, booted feet kicked in the air with delight. Of how Jack watched him, eyes full of love. A father's love.

"But she died when he was born, like God had heard her and been spiteful. She didn't want the babe, so he took her away from him."

"I knew that bit. That she died."

"Jack was in a rare taking. We thought he'd go mad with grief. I don't think he ever has got over it. That's why he saves what orphans he can find. Thinking that each of them could have been little Edward, or perhaps, Mary herself. He couldn't save her, so now he saves other children."

"And that's why he doesn't want to marry anyone." The words were out before Elenora could stop herself.

Martha's honest brown eyes widened. "Doesn't want to marry? Why, he's got himself engaged to you. You'll be marrying and giving Edward the mother he's never had before long. And brothers and sisters too, if you're blessed."

Somehow, it felt wrong to lie to this woman who'd just unburdened her chest to her so fully. Elenora licked suddenly dry lips. "I can't lie to you Martha. Jack and I are not really engaged." The whole story came tumbling out.

Martha listened, and when Elenora finished, she took both her hands in hers. "My dear, you don't shock me. Nothing can after you've lived with a man like Reuben. But I'll tell you this— Lord Jack has it in his eyes that he cares for you. I saw it tonight, and I'm never wrong. And you—well, I see love in your eyes when you're thinking of him like you are right now. I'm not sure this engagement is the sham you think it is."

Elenora gazed into Martha's kind brown eyes, something strange kindling in her heart. It might have been hope. "You really think so?"

Martha nodded. "That's a man in love I've seen tonight, but a man who doesn't yet know it."

"And me?"

"And you're the same."

CHAPTER TWENTY-TWO

ENJAMIN LED JACK up a creaking spiral staircase to the rooms above the tavern crowded in under the eaves. A long, low ceilinged corridor ran along the back of the building with a few shabby doors opening off along one side, from behind which came the definite sounds of people participating in sex. Havelock's unfortunate women at work. Would he have put his daughters into this profession to make money out of them if Jack hadn't stepped in to save them? Probably.

Opposite these doors, high up, mean and filthy little windows stared out at the far-too-close, and sagging, rooftops of the building next door. For someone who professed to see his father only rarely, Benjamin seemed to possess an intimate acquaintance with what lay behind these doors, for he steered Jack past them with brash confidence and a knowing smirk.

At the final door, Benjamin halted and glanced back at Jack, the smirk replaced by a cocky grin on his ratty face. With one hand, he pushed it open.

Jack stepped inside.

The room contained a single narrow iron bedstead pushed up against one wall, close under the sloping ceiling, and beside that a rickety table on which stood a lantern. Seated on this bed was the man Jack had seen watching his house, devoid now of his lost sailor's hat. As Jack came in, this man rose to his feet, and Jack was able to look him up and down in the harsh lamplight.

He stood taller than the scrawny Benjamin, but not so tall as Jack, and his build was on the light and wiry side, although well camouflaged by his loose sailor's clothing. An air of secretive strength hung about him, honed, no doubt, by his years at sea. He stared back at Jack out of eyes puckered by long years squinting into the sun and wind on board a ship, and his skin had that desiccated, weathered look Jack had seen on the old tars of Limehouse and beyond many times before. Impossible to hazard a guess at his age, but to Jack, the man looked prematurely aged by the harshness of his life.

Jack made no preamble. "Where is my son?"

Warren, for it had to be he, gave a shrug of the shoulders as though that scarcely mattered. "Now then, boyo, no need to get all arsey." A definite Welsh twang to his voice. He could be someone who'd known Mary, but had his lovely Mary attached herself to this venal creature in her youth? Impossible to imagine. The man was most likely lying, and Mary hadn't been. He wanted to cling to that idea, even as inside himself he knew she had been.

Behind Jack, Benjamin had closed the door and was now leaning his narrow shoulders against it, much as he'd done in his ailing father's office. Was he here to make sure Jack didn't hurt Warren, or to make sure Warren didn't hurt Jack? Whose side he was on seemed a moot point now. Had he ever made the break from his good for nothing father or had he been gulling his mother and Jack all this time, fooling his hapless sponsor concerning his new life? What did any of that matter now?

"What have you done with my son?" Jack asked.

"Don't you mean *my* son?" Warren said. The singsong lilt that had made Mary's voice so attractive sounded out of place and coarse in his. Alien. Jack itched to plant him a facer. He clenched his fists by his sides and stood silent. That could wait until he had Edward back. Then he'd deal with this cockroach.

Warren smiled, showing crooked, yellowed teeth with big gaps where some had been lost, to scurvy, no doubt. A single gold incisor flashed. Gold earrings decorated the lobes of his fleshy ears, and around his neck hung a gold necklace, peeking from between the collars of his shirt and blue sailor's coat. Unwise to go about the Devil's Acre showing off your riches like this. The man must be confident no one would touch him. Confident, perhaps, in the patronage of Reuben Sharpe.

"I'll ask you once more. Where is Edward?"

"That what you call him, is it?" Warren ran a grimy finger along the groove of his chin. "Well grown the way he is, he'll make a likely cabin boy when I take him back to sea wi' me."

"I want him back. He's not your son."

Warren threw a scornful glance at Benjamin. "You've fed the brat better than you have this one, with his trap stick legs, I can see. Oh yes, I know all about how you've treated my mate Reuben." He laughed, a hoarse, grating sound like a saw. "You make a habit of stealing other people's wives, he tells me. If I weren't so pissed with you, I'd thank you for taking such good care of my boy."

"He is not your boy." The urge to seize the man by the throat waxed strong. It was only with great difficulty that Jack kept himself under control.

Warren grinned, and his gold tooth flashed. "In the eyes of the law, he's mine all right, boyo. Mine to use as I want, to take where I want, to put in work as I want. And he's big enough to put to work in one o' they cotton mills up north in Manchester, if I've a mind to it. Or down a mine. I've been up there, seen those mills. They'll snap him up and pay me for it. He's mine to sell as I want. To the highest bidder… of course." He winked at Benjamin. "Think your man here can be the highest bidder?"

Benjamin said nothing, his face a study in uninterested nonchalance. Hedging his bets, damn the boy.

Every bone in Jack's body cried out that it would be wrong to give this man money, that he shouldn't submit to this blackmail, that he should find some other way to get Edward back. But he couldn't. If Warren was indeed Mary's husband, then Edward was legally his child. To this man, Edward was nothing more than a ticket to riches, and if those riches didn't arrive, Edward's life would be worth nothing. At the very least, Jack had to appear to be compliant. For now.

"How much do you want?"

Warren seemed much given to smiling, flashing that gold tooth with abandon. Even with Reuben Sharpe's patronage, Jack knew the man couldn't be certain no thief wouldn't stick a knife in him for that tooth and the necklace and earrings. "That's better, boyo. I knew you'd see the light." He ran his fingers through his thatch of shaggy, straw-colored hair. "Only there's not just me wants recompense now. There's my mate Reuben downstairs, who helped me find you and my boy. Glad, he was, to be offered the chance to get one over on your high and mighty lordship."

He grinned yet again. "All I knew when my ship docked back in London was my Mary had been working the alehouses here in London when I left with my ship for the Antipodes. Last I saw of her, she was workin' The Angel in Limehouse, for your friend Reuben. Luck brought me back to Reuben's door, and luck threw us together with one end in our hearts. Yours."

He chuckled. "See? He's got his own axe to grind, you mark my words. He tells me you prigged his missus and took her along with mine. One wasn't enough for you." His eyes narrowed to slits. "Make a bit of a habit of priggin' other people's wives, do you, boyo? All Reuben's regulars know the story. There weren't no shortage of volunteers to help me snatch my boy back."

Jack said nothing. Telling this man how Reuben had beaten his wife would make no difference. He'd probably beaten Mary himself when they'd been together, or she might not have left him. Although, of course, as she'd kept her married state secret, she'd never revealed anything to Jack.

"I don't just want money for giving up my boy," Warren said. "I want compensation for the loss of my wife. For the earnings she should've been giving me. Reuben told me she was raking in a fine fortune singing for the gentry in theaters up west. You owes me for that. And for her loss when you let her die birthin' my boy. And my mate Reuben wants the same for his wife. You deprived him of her services these eight years past." He paused and gave an earthy chuckle. "Now, what do you suppose, boyo, is a wife worth to a man? And his children. Reuben's lost all his children, hasn't he young Benjamin? Savin' this one, I hear."

Benjamin shifted a little but said nothing.

Oh, how much Jack didn't want to give this grasping man money. To give neither of these extortionists a penny. To see them both in Newgate Jail, or transported to Botany Bay. Though, for preference, hung. Outside Newgate Jail, in public.

"How do I know he's still alive? I need to see Edward for myself."

Warren shook his head. "Not happenin', boyo. I'm no flat to be gulled by you. No money, no boy."

An impasse.

"Prove to me he's safe, then."

Warren's ferrety face crunched in a frown. "How'm I to do that, d'you s'pose? Without showin' you my hand? D'you think I'm an idiot?"

Jack jerked his chin at Benjamin. "Show Reuben's son my boy is safe. Living. Without proof he is, I'm not prepared to give you a single penny."

Benjamin straightened up.

Jack dug his nails into the palms of his hands. He was depending now, on Benjamin being on his side. For all he knew, Edward was already dead, and if Benjamin came down on the side of his father and Warren, he might lie and say he'd seen Edward. But he wouldn't think like that. He had to believe his son still lived. He had to put all thoughts like that from his head as they only bred fear, and he couldn't falter in his resolve.

Warren shrugged. "All right. You wait here, and I'll take Reuben's lad to the boy. Then he can tell you he's safe, and we can settle on a price."

Either Warren was confident Benjamin would lie, or, more likely, or to be *hoped* more likely, he had Edward stashed somewhere not so far away, still alive but a prisoner. That had to be it. The germ of an idea was forming in Jack's head.

Jack nodded. "And make it quick."

Warren grinned again and that bloody tooth flashed. "We'll take as long as we like, boyo. You're in no position to order me about. You sit yourself down here and wait, and while you're here, you think about what you did to me and Reuben."

The room was small, and Warren had to pass close by Jack to reach the door. The strong smell of pipe tobacco hung in the air about him. Jack had to fight once more for his self-control. If he gave in now, all would be lost.

Without a backward glance, Warren and Benjamin departed, the door closing with a bang behind them. Their footsteps died away along the dirty corridor. At least they'd left him the lantern.

In the comparative silence that followed, broken only by the muted sounds of congress in the surrounding rooms filtering through the thin walls and nagging at his ears, Jack surveyed the rest of the room. The battered table with the lantern stood beneath a window thick with cobwebs and dust. Apart from that, the only other furniture was the rickety bed, strewn with dirty blankets. If he'd been going to stay, the last thing he'd have done was sit on that bed. But he wasn't going to stay.

He must be quick.

He pulled the rickety table away from the window and seized the catch. It didn't want to open. The old, dirt encrusted metal was rusted solid, but Jack's fingers were desperate. Warren and Benjamin would be in the taproom by now, pushing through the crowd and heading for the front door. He scrabbled at the catch, nails breaking as he fought to open it. If he didn't get out in time, he'd never see which direction they'd gone in.

At last, after what felt like forever, it gave, and the window creaked open a bare crack, letting in the smoky fog of the slums, a thick miasma of polluted air. No wonder Reuben Sharpe had the consumption. Jack forced the window wide and put one leg through it. Below lay the shadowy yard of the inn, silent in the freezing cold, cobbles dirty and damp. Remembering to pick up the lantern by its wiry handle, he said a thankful goodbye to The One Tun's dubious hospitality.

As a tall man, although not heavily built, the window was a tight squeeze. For just a moment, he felt his body jam, but with a convulsive wriggle, he prised himself free to wriggle round to hang by his hands, still clutching the swaying lantern, from the crumbling sill and drop down into the noisesome yard below.

Now, where was the door Warren and Benjamin would be exiting?

In Betterton Street, Martha had gone to tuck her brood of youngsters into their beds and make sure they said their prayers, leaving Elenora sitting alone in the little parlor, nibbling her nails to the quick. This was a habit her mother had forced out of her as a child by dint of painting the offending fingertips with something bitter, but it returned with a vengeance in moments of stress. Now, she couldn't stop herself.

The walls of the room seemed to press in on her, every detail of their decoration imprinting itself on her mind: where the wallpaper curled loose in the corners, the worn patches and small burned spots on the rug in front of the fire, the crumbs on the tea tray and the smell of coal smoke in the stuffy air. She glanced at the window, but only foggy darkness lurked out there, threatening and featureless.

Jack had been gone such a long time. Was she to sit here all night waiting for him? Suppose he never came back? Suppose this was all a trick by whoever had taken Edward just to get Jack into his power? She folded her hands in her lap in an effort to stop chewing at the nails. Mama would be furious when she saw the state they were in. Elenora was even a little bit angry with herself for succumbing to her old habit. Would gloves prevent her?

Her eyes roved the crowded room yet again. The furniture

was too close together, chairs and tables jammed in, with too many ornaments on every surface, as though with respectability Mrs. Sharpe had gone quite mad with emulating her social superiors. Nothing like Aunt Penelope's neat and spacious home, and a thousand miles from the faded opulence of Penworthy.

Where was it Jack had gone? Benjamin was taking him to The One Tun, a tavern in the Devil's Acre. A common tavern in what sounded like an extremely dangerous part of the city. Such an odd name for any location. Not that Elenora had any experience of taverns or their names, nor the parts of London where they might be found. Jolyon and Matthew probably did though, and Matthew, who was closest to her in age, and for whom she'd always been a confidante, had more than once told her about his forays into the Oxford backstreets whilst he'd been at university in that town. Not that he was there any longer though, with this latest misdemeanor of his. He'd not been specific this time about his supposed crime, but knowing him, she could hazard a guess.

Jolyon and Matthew.

Of course. Why hadn't she thought of this sooner? She could ask for their help. What time was it? Would they be at Jolyon's lodgings? Probably. Too early for them to be out at some soirée, gambling and flirting with the young ladies. She had to get a message to them. They, the playmates and co-conspirators of her Penworthy youth, would know what to do. And they might even have pistols or know where to get them.

She prided herself in not being a missish girl in any way, and had never been one to sit about whilst others took action. Jack needed help, and she might be able to provide it. With the assistance of her brothers. If only she'd thought of them earlier.

But how? This tavern lay within the backstreets of London, a place she'd never been to before. However… Her eyes narrowed and focused. The girls here in Betterton Street must have been there, for that was where they'd come from. They'd been born into those mean streets, and only rescued from it by Martha and Jack, so surely they remembered their old haunts.

She got up and, on silent feet, padded to the door. She would try the kitchen.

The corridor passed a steep and narrow staircase to the upper floor before opening into a warm and cozy kitchen.

There, she found three girls seated around a well-worn kitchen table, drinking steaming mugs of hot chocolate. None of them was Ruth, who would anyway have been far too young for this adventure, and all of them, although younger than Elenora, looked old enough to perhaps have outside work they'd returned home from. She breathed a sigh of relief. Martha must still be safely upstairs getting the younger ones to bed. Hopefully, a long-winded operation.

All three girls stared up at her from their seats with open curiosity, although without any shock at seeing someone like her in their house. No doubt young Ruth had spread the word.

"I need your help," she opened with.

They looked the sort of girls she'd seen working as kitchen maids, or sewing seams in dressmaker's establishments, here in London, or behind the counter in a shop. A little rough around the edges, dressed in clean but not smart dresses, with their hair confined in neat plaits down their backs; their homely, freckled faces reminded her of the dairy maids at Penworthy, only pastier in appearance. "Yes'm?" asked one, whose mousy hair had released pretty, curling tendrils around her forehead. She couldn't have been more than a year or two younger than Elenora.

"I need someone to take me to The One Tun tavern and to take a message to my brothers in Jermyn Street."

They regarded her in shocked silence. They must know where she meant, probably regarding both locations.

She pressed on. "Do you know where the tavern lies?"

All three nodded, eyes wide.

"What d'you want to go there for?" asked the first girl, who appeared to be the oldest and their ringleader. "That's not a nice place for a lady like you."

"It's a matter of life and death. I need to help Lord Broxbourne. Jack. My betrothed. He's gone there on his own. Well, with only Benjamin Sharpe to keep him safe."

The girl, the one with the mousey hair, set down her empty cup of cocoa and drew her fingers across her lips to wipe them. "Lord Jack? What's he gorn there for? Has he gorn barmy in his old age?"

Elenora ignored the suggestion that Jack was old, even though it was what she had at first also thought. He'd ceased to be that a long time ago for her. "To rescue his son who's been kidnapped by some terrible villains."

The girls exchanged anxious glances, betraying no surprise that Jack possessed a child. "What d'you think you're goin' to do?" one of the other two, a younger girl with a good crop of spots, asked. "You're a girl for a start, an' you don't know the rookeries like we do."

Stupid question. "I want to help him, of course."

"By doin' what?" the first one put in, sounding incredulous. "A girl like you... goin' to The One Tun..." She pulled a dismissive expression. "You don't know what you'd be gettin' yourself into, down there. Those streets aren't for the likes o' you."

"I don't s'pose you've ever been further than your own front door, or Rotten Row in Hyde Park, at the most." This came from the third girl, smaller than the other two and sporting a decided squint that made her look shifty. Or perhaps she *was* shifty.

Elenora bristled. These girls clearly were taking a dim view of her abilities, no doubt due to her appearance. If only she'd been wearing her old clothes from Penworthy, although even they were much smarter than the girls' workaday apparel. "I came here on foot from Portland Place, Lord Broxbourne's house, quite safely."

"Not on your own you didn't," the first girl said. "I saw you comin' in orf the street. You was with his lordship. And anyways, these streets're nothin' like the Devil's Acre." Her eyes narrowed. "What's he to you, then? You his doxy?"

This was not going as Elenora had envisaged. The girls sounded somewhat less than helpful. Aggressive, even, and this last felt like an insult. "He and I are engaged to be married."

Eyebrows rose en masse.

"He's got himself leg-shackled at last, has he?" The first girl gave a snort of laughter. "Well, if you've got him ready to be yoked, you're to be admired. We didn't none of us think we'd ever see the day."

The little squinting girl leaned over to her friends. "She *is* very pretty." Her hushed whisper carried.

Elenora looked from face to face. "Will one of you, or perhaps all of you, for safety's sake, please take me to the tavern where Jack has gone? Please? I beg of you. He's been gone too long, and I'm very worried."

The first girl looked upwards at the ceiling. "Ma Sharpe'll be mad with us if we do."

Her two friends nodded.

A light glinted in the girl's gray eyes. "But if we *all* go, that'd be four of us, countin' her ladyship here. Ma can't be mad with all of us at once, an' she won't be mad with'is lordship's lady friend." She grinned. "His intended."

"And I'll tell her I made you do it," Elenora said, hoping she'd be given the chance to do so, and this wouldn't be the last time she saw the house in Betterton Street and Martha Sharpe.

The three girls stood up as one, the first girl their spokesman. "We'll do it, miss. Together. Because you're marrying our Lord Jack. And because we want to help him like he's helped us. Not one of us'd be here now if it weren't for him."

Her friends nodded.

Elenora held her hand out. "Thank you, but first we need to get to Jermyn Street and persuade my brothers to come with us. And I'm not a 'her ladyship.' My name is Elenora. Ellie, in fact, to my friends."

The first girl took her hand and shook it with vigor. "Ivy's my name, and these two're Rosie and Peg." She glanced upwards at the ceiling again. "We'd best get out of here now if we're going to. Before Ma finishes gettin' those little heathens upstairs to say their prayers. Can take her a while. Come on."

✦

CHAPTER TWENTY-THREE

JACK COVERED THE light on the lantern, just in case, and groped his way across the dirty yard he found himself in. Thank God for his top boots. His feet were sloshing through mud and… other detritus he didn't like to try to identify. The smell was appalling. All around the yard, buildings leaned over it as though desperate for their sagging roofs to meet in the center. Something ran across his foot, using it as a stepping stone through the mud, and made him jump. A rat, or possibly a cat. It was gone before he could identify it. Thank goodness.

The dim light of a distant oil lamp illuminated the gateway that led out into the street where the tavern stood. That people lived in such squalid conditions horrified Jack, but he had to push that out of his head. He'd seen it all before, of course, but that didn't prevent him being shocked to the core by it every time. By the iron spike of the lamp, a woman lounged, her skirts dragged up to her thighs to reveal blotchy skin above filthy, gartered stockings. "Want someone to give you a good time?" she wheedled. "Only a shillin', milord." She sounded very much the worse for wear.

Shaking his head, Jack looked past her toward the tavern door. It banged open on its ancient hinges, and a drunk came staggering out to lean up against the opposite building where he let flow a stream of steaming urine. Where were Warren and Benjamin? Had he missed them? Surely Warren would have gone to inform Reuben Sharpe of his mission before leaving the alehouse? Not that Sharpe could accompany him. Jack doubted if the man could walk six feet in his condition.

Jack slunk into a shadowy recess and waited. The woman by the lamp post heaved a sigh and moved off into the fog, her halting footsteps echoing through the night. Josie's pinched little face danced before his eyes. At least he'd saved the girls at Mrs. Sharpe's from a similar fate to that poor woman's.

He didn't have long to wait. Only half a minute later, Warren and Benjamin emerged from the tavern, the boy carrying another lantern. Without a second glance, Warren headed straight toward Jack, who had to flatten himself back into the shadows, glad he'd hidden his own lantern's light. They passed within six feet of him, oblivious to his presence.

Jack gave them a short head start, then headed after them.

Before he'd gone three paces, six figures emerged from the darkness, surrounding him. Four of them were wearing dresses.

"Jack!" Elenora seized his free hand.

"Milord Jack." By the dim light of the prostitute's vacated streetlamp, he recognized the faces of the three oldest girls who lived with Mrs. Sharpe. And two quite short young men he didn't think he'd ever clapped eyes on before.

He took an anxious look over his shoulder into the fog. "I can't stop. I have to follow those two men."

"I'm coming too," Elenora said.

"Us as well," Ivy said.

"And if you're going, so are we," the taller of the two strange young men put in, his voice giving away his anything but native origins, as did his smart top hat.

"Who the hell are you?" Jack managed to get out, before Rosie interrupted him.

"If you're follerin' some cove, then you'll be hard to spot if you're in a crowd of us girls."

Peg just nodded and seized Jack's arm.

He had no time to object. Besides which, they were quite

right in their estimate that being a mixed party would draw less attention. The one good thing was that they could keep the distance between them small, as if Warren looked back, all he'd see was girls intent on giving some upper class men a good time. But who were these two strangers who seemed mysteriously au fait with his mission? He didn't have to wait long for an answer.

"These are my brothers," Elenora, who had a tight and proprietorial hold of his left arm, explained. "Ivy has Jolyon, and Rosie has Matthew, who is nearest me in age. I decided we needed their help and when it was all explained to them, they were delighted to accompany me and my new friends."

"Good evening to you, Lord Broxbourne," Jolyon Wetherby said, mercifully keeping his voice low but betraying by his jaunty tone that he saw this as some kind of jolly adventure akin to he and his friends daring one another to go and drink at taverns in Limehouse. Which it was not.

"Glad to make your acquaintance," Matthew chimed in. "And glad to render our assistance. Do anything for our sister. She's a good'un."

Peg was still firmly attached to Jack's other arm, so he had no way of resisting the onward impetus of the two girls. However, this didn't stop him from being angry. "What part of stay behind safely with Mrs. Sharpe did you fail to understand, Elenora?" And why hadn't her scapegrace brothers sent her packing back to safety? Were they madmen?

She tightened her hold, perhaps suspicious that he might try to send her home even now. "I sat in that little parlor with your Mrs. Sharpe worrying about you, going off on your own into the backstreets the way you have. And in the end, I could stand it no longer. I came to the conclusion I had to do something. I couldn't let you go on your own." She shot him a glare made crystal clear as they passed under another streetlamp. "And as you're neither my father nor my brother, and you're not even really my fiancé, you don't have any right to tell me what to do."

The affrontery of the girl. But wasn't that why he liked her so much? The way she didn't beat about the bush but jumped straight in with what she was thinking? The dangers of her forthrightness bore down on him. "These streets are more than dangerous for a girl like you, and could well be for your brothers, too."

"For everyone," Peg, who must have been listening, put in.

Jack nodded. "She's right."

"Safety in numbers," Elenora said, with defiance. "There are four of us girls, and now we have Joly and Matt, three of you gentlemen. And my brothers both have pistols like you, and have given me one which is safely stored in my reticule, which is happily just the right size for it. Ivy said we should be safe if we have pistols."

Only of course, Jack no longer had his pistols, nor much likelihood of ever seeing them again.

"Ivy doesn't know."

"Ivy does," Ivy put in. "Who was dragged up round here, Milord Jack, you or us?"

"You shouldn't have encouraged her," Jack snapped. "She's not like you girls. She doesn't have the wisdom of the streets you all do."

"Wisdom of the streets, is it?" Rosie mocked. "That's what you're callin' it now."

Jack fumed. But he couldn't deny that four girls together were a lot safer than one or even two on their own. And when you added in three men as well, all armed, even if he now only had his swordstick, that made their odds of safety much higher. He peered through the thickening fog. The alley had narrowed and was going downhill, Warren and Benjamin just shadowy figures in the gloom. Were they approaching the Thames?

THE WAY THROUGH the maze of dirty backstreets had confused Elenora's country sense of direction and she now had no idea which way she was facing, so when the alley they'd been traversing suddenly emerged onto the damp and foggy embankment of the River Thames, she came to an involuntary halt, pulling Jack to a stop as well. The smell of mud and… other far less savory things… rose up in an almost tangible barrier to hit her in the face.

"Tide's out," Ivy remarked as she tugged Jolyon along the narrow path beside the river. Up ahead the slinking shapes of the two men Jack had set himself to follow flitted from one pool of smoky light to the next, like wraiths in the mist, their lantern bobbing. Who were they and where were they heading?

Beside her, Jack hurried his pace and she had to almost run to keep up with him. Little Peg was running in truth. Then, as if suddenly hitting a wall, Jack ground to a halt, and Jolyon and Matthew and their girls almost cannoned into him. "Get back." The two words emerged from his lips as a barely breathed whisper. Elenora flattened her body against the wall on her left, holding her breath and far too aware of the noisy tumult her heart was making.

The two men, one of whom, now they were a little closer, looked as if he might be Benjamin Sharpe, had stopped where a tumbledown warehouse overhung the muddy riverbank as part of a deserted wharf, and at last taken time to peer over their shoulders.

Ivy nodded at the warehouse. "I know this warehouse. We're in Devals Wharf, just off Abingdon Street." Her warm breath made shadowy statues in the cold air. "It's fallin' down now and outta use. I know the gangs used to use it to store stuff they'd prigged. What's the bettin' they still do? There's lockups in there where you could hide anything you wanted. A boy, easy."

She glanced from Jack to Elenora. "No one there'd ask any questions, nor do nothing to save a boy locked up in there. An' plenty of people wi' nowhere else to sleep're probably in there all right. They used to crawl inside of a night for a bit of shelter." She gave a dismissive shrug. "Done it meself a few times before I met Lord Jack an' he took me to Ma Sharpe's. If they've got the lad stashed in there, he'll be upstairs where there's a few rooms you could lock, what was once offices for the wharf. Like I said, be easy to keep someone there a prisoner."

Had she been kept in there herself, as a prisoner? When she'd been little more than a child herself? The possibility made Elenora's blood freeze in her veins, accompanied by the thought that she herself had led a very sheltered life, never dreaming that people lived in this terrible way. Never again would she take for granted the luxury of her family's life. Mama had thought herself poor because Papa had gambled away their money, but this was what being poor truly was. Sleeping in a disused warehouse on the banks of the River Thames in fear of your life.

How long had it been since these back alleys were the haunts of her three new friends, and for how long had they been living respectable lives with Mrs. Sharpe? She'd ask them later, if there was a later.

Her left shoulder was pressed up against Jack's body, his imposing bulk reassuring. The practical part of her was glad of this, although she also felt a yearning not to have to feel beholden to a man for her safety. That she could look after herself without his help. That, in fact, he needed her. Whatever would Mama say now, if she could see her here cowering in the shadows while two villainous denizens of the slums conferred. That Benjamin was villainous, she'd already decided.

A door creaked and the two figures disappeared into the dark cave of the warehouse.

Elenora stood on tiptoe to whisper in Jack's ear. "Now what?" A curl of his hair tickled her nose and the scent of sandalwood caught in her nostrils. How could a man smell so… what was it? Tantalizing. Yes, that was it. She'd never smelled anything quite so alluring, and to her surprise it had turned out to be the scent of a man. How very odd.

He turned toward her, much closer than he'd ever been, apart from when he'd kissed her. His breath was warm on her cheek. "We wait."

"Want me to foller 'em?" Peg asked. "I'm small an' no one'll notice me. I was always good at that."

Jack shook his head. "No. Too dangerous. I think we've found where they have Edward hidden. If we go blasting in after them, they'll have chance to hurt him. So we'll wait for them to come out and jump them. I'm assuming Benjamin to be on our side, but we can't be certain. Don't hurt him. Just hold him down. There are seven of us and only two of them so we should have the upper hand. After that, once we have them in our hands, we can go in and rescue Edward."

"A good plan," Jolyon whispered.

Matthew heaved a sigh as though he'd have liked to have stormed the warehouse all guns blazing.

Elenora bit her lip. It did indeed sound like a good idea. But only if the capture of Warren didn't make a lot of noise and there weren't a lot of people guarding Edward. Would there be, or wasn't this more likely to be a one man enterprise? She had no idea. And from out here in the dark, how were they to know? Perhaps they should let Peg do her spying.

"All of us?" Ivy asked. "We'll go in together?"

Rosie nodded. "If Warren's still alive, one of us'll have to stay and guard him." She lifted her skirts to reveal the top of her boot, from which the bone handle of a knife protruded. "I c'n do that if you want. We're all armed. As usual."

"'Cept her." Peg nodded at Elenora. "I bet she don't have no knife hid in her boots nor anywheres else."

Miffed at their dismissal of her lack of preparation and more than a little shocked that they'd clearly been armed like that while they were at work, Elenora pulled the small pistol out of her reticule. "I do have this, and make no mistake about it, I know how to use it."

"Well, strike me down with a feather," Ivy hissed. "Where'd you get that from? Was it in there all along? Do fine ladies go about with pistols in their bags?"

Elenora shook her head. "Matthew slipped it to me. And I think some ladies do."

"You sly cove," Rosie whispered to Matthew, to whom she seemed to have taken a shine. "Never saw you do that. And she's tellin' the truth? She knows how to use it?"

Matthew, eyes shining in the dark with untoward excitement, nodded. "I can assure you my sister is a crack shot. Better than me and Joly."

"You got your toasting iron?" Ivy tapped Jack's cane and he nodded.

A toasting iron? What did she mean by that? Elenora soon found out, as Jack slid a long, deadly looking blade from inside the cane. She'd heard of sword sticks but never seen one before. Perhaps a wise thing to carry if you were a young blood roaming the less salubrious areas of London of a night. Maybe all young men had them. Older ones too. Although neither Jolyon nor Matthew possessed such a weapon. Perhaps she should suggest they get one each.

Elenora checked her pistol was loaded, which, of course, it was, but you should always check if you intended to use it to defend yourself. She'd learned that early on. She hadn't grown up in the country close to her two older brothers without having joined in with their pursuits whenever she could, whenever Mama was otherwise engaged with her sisters or visiting friends. She weighed the pistol in her hand. It was smaller and lighter than any she'd handled before when she and her brothers had been target shooting in the woods. "I forgot to ask you, Joly, why you have such a small pistol about you."

"It's called a Queen Anne Pistol," her brother whispered. "Or a Muff Pistol, if you will, as so many ladies keep them hidden within their muffs in case they're attacked. That's why it's so small. Not particularly accurate, but enough to put an assailant off if you point it at him."

Elenora examined the decorative silver handle. That this had belonged to a lady, she had no doubt. But who? Could it belong to some lady her brother knew… well enough to have her pistol in his house? She'd quiz him about that later. "I see it's loaded."

"I'm not walkin' behind her, if you don't mind," Ivy said, and her friends muttered agreement. "Don't want to be shot in the back by mistake."

Jolyon grinned. "She won't shoot you by mistake. She's not an idiot. I can vouch for that."

Jack nodded. "Don't fire it unless you have to, though. Now, all of you, hush. And wait in the shadows until you get my signal."

They had all by now retreated down a small alley full of muck and rubbish and no lighting, which was just as well, as right then the two men emerged onto the street again and started their way, the light of their lantern illuminating a circle around them. That the lantern carrier was Benjamin was now obvious.

As they drew level with the alley, Jack stepped out of the gloom to stand in front of them, legs planted wide apart, the sword glittering in his hands.

Everything in the next few seconds happened at top speed, yet, oddly, also in slow motion as though all the participants were wading through treacle.

Benjamin must have seen how the land lay immediately, for he fell back six rapid paces, hands up in the air in defense, the lantern swinging wildly. "I seen your boy, milord. He's not been hurt."

Warren shot him a furious glare, his hand going to his belt. It came up with something dark clutched in it. Jack lunged forward with his sword, a terrific bang reverberated around the old stone buildings and the sword found its mark, driven deep into Warren's chest. The lantern fell from Jack's left hand, clattered across the cobbles and went out.

Warren's eyes widened in something between terror and shock, and Jack wrenched the sword free. The kidnapper stumbled to his knees on the dirty cobbles.

Had Jack killed him? Elenora's free hand shot to her mouth. Had she just seen someone killed? The hand holding her own pistol dropped so the weapon was pointing at the ground.

"Oh my Gawd," Rosie said.

Time moved back to normal speed.

Warren toppled forward face down, a pool of blood spreading around his body, black and glistening in the dim light of Benjamin's lantern.

Jolyon bent and put two fingers under the man's jaw. "He's dead as a doornail."

Elenora looked at Jack. His hand was gripping his left upper arm, his fingers stained with blood. "He shot you!" She ran to him, forgetful of the man he'd just killed.

He shook her off. "It's nothing. He just winged me. We have to get Edward. Whoever's inside will have heard the shot. Quick before someone hurts him."

Benjamin held up his lantern. "There's a lot of folks in there sleepin' but no one was in with the boy. The door's locked, so I think he's safe."

Jack waved him forward. "Show us the way."

The boy, his colors now firmly pinned to Jack's mast, held up his hand and bent over Warren's body. "Like I said, the room he's in is locked. Here's the keys." He tossed a sizeable bunch to Jack, who caught them deftly, his bleeding arm forgotten.

As one, Jack's little army, now increased by one, headed for the warehouse doors, Elenora staying as close to Jack as she could, her eyes transfixed by the ragged tear in his coat and the dark stain of blood on it. But he was right. It wasn't affecting him at all, so it had to be just a flesh wound. Much as Matthew had sustained that time Jolyon had shot him by mistake while the three of them had been out after pheasants.

The thought that she was now in a part of London where violent self-defense was required had Elenora's breath coming fast and her heart pounding, but that she was also part of a gang raised her spirits.

At the door into the warehouse, Jack held up a hand. With a finger touched to his lips, he gently pushed the door. It swung open in front of them.

He held out his sword in front of them. "Keep behind me."

Elenora followed him in, along with Jolyon and Matthew. The girls, evidently still mistrustful that she might accidentally discharge her firearm into their backs, brought up the rear.

Once, this warehouse must have been part of the roaring trade in commodities that passed through London, but time had taken its toll, and the spaces that had once held spices and tea and coffee and silks from all over the world now lay empty of all but heaps of rubbish.

Only they weren't heaps of rubbish. They were people.

From under piles of rags, pale faces peered and eyes glittered in the feeble light of Benjamin's lamp, most of them uninterested in the arrival of yet more people to disturb their sleep, some wary, some angry, some resigned to interruption.

"My goodness." Elenora couldn't keep the shock out of her voice. "I can't believe people have to sleep in this dreadful place."

Jack caught hold of her hand. "Don't look."

But she couldn't avert her eyes.

Benjamin stopped in the center of the room, the light from the lantern spilling out across the fetid floor toward the cowering shapes of the sleepers. Grunts and groans echoed in the darkest recesses, scuttling noises sounded, and the stink of unwashed humankind clogged Elenora's nostrils. "Up them stairs. The room at the top."

Jack caught her arm. "Upstairs, then."

A rickety wooden staircase leaned against the farthest wall, the handrail broken and some of the treads missing. Above, darkness lurked. Darkness and silence.

CHAPTER TWENTY-FOUR

AT THE TOP of the stairs lay a narrow, dirty corridor, hung with cobwebs and devoid of windows. Two mean doors opened off it, both so old, what paint they'd ever possessed had peeled away long ago. The light of the lantern Benjamin was still holding showed Jack that someone had slashed a daub of paint across the notice on the first door that had once said 'Manager' and underneath it had painted, in big, uneven lettering, 'GUVNER'. The second door, though, stood naked of any sort of paint, but possessed of a rusty padlock.

Benjamin fumbled out the bunch of keys, the lantern light wavering. "I'm not sure which key it was."

"Get on with it, man," Jolyon growled.

Jack didn't wait. He took a breath and shouted. "Stand back from the door!" His booted foot shot out and struck the door a resounding blow. The old wood caved in before his onslaught, splintering into several pieces. Most of it clung to its rusty hinges, but some of it fell broken to the floor, attached to the padlock. Inside lay darkness.

Jack followed the remnants of the door into the room beyond, pulling Benjamin after him, the lantern swaying back and forth. Behind him, his co-conspirators crowded in.

The room was tiny, little more than a store cupboard, perhaps once used as a secure lockup when this had functioned as a working wharf. Furnished only with a pile of dirty rags in one corner, it stank of musty decay. Benjamin's lamp threw flickering light onto the pile of rags. Sitting on them, his knees drawn up to his chin, was Edward, unbearably small, white-faced and drawn, cowering back against the cobwebby wall and blinking like a myopic mole in the lantern light.

Elenora, quicker to react than Jack, put out a hand to the lantern, lowering it in Benjamin's hands. "He can't see it's his father." Then she was past them both, down on her knees on the stinking rags with the little boy, reaching for his hand, all reticence about touch apparently gone. "It's me, it's Elenora and your papa. We've come to save you."

For a moment the little boy regarded her out of eyes that were pools of darkness, then, as if suddenly awoken, he flung himself at her, his arms fastening about her neck, his face against her shoulder.

Jack, his heart swelling with relief, saw her flinch at the contact, probably far more than she'd experienced for a long time, but she made no effort to disentangle the terrified child, who clung on with the determination of a limpet to a rock. The little boy seemed not to have noticed her discomfort. "Elenora," he sobbed. "I knew you'd come. I knew you wouldn't forget about me like the horrible man said you would." As if she was the only one who'd effected his rescue. A nub of jealousy rose in Jack's heart, that he was being sidelined by a woman. But Edward had long needed the love of a woman... a mother... other than the redoubtable Miss Douglas.

From behind Jack, one of Mrs. Sharpe's girls made a clucking sound, like a contented hen. None of them had ever met Edward, yet all the girls knew about him—a secret he'd never kept hidden from them. And they knew it was due to Edward's birth they owed their own security nowadays.

Elenora seemed to be nonplussed about what to do with her hands. They flapped for a moment before she must have resigned herself to human contact, unusual as she found it. They went tentatively around Edward's slender body, holding him to her, then tightened, as though she might be enjoying the new sensation. A beatific expression slid across her face, her eyes closed, and she nestled her head against Edward's as he sobbed into her shoulder.

"We oughtta go," Ivy muttered, glancing over her shoulder at the broken door. "It's not far back to The One Tun, and the fellers there'll be finding you gone from there before long and puttin' two and two together and makin' five. Won't take much fer them to work out that you follered that dead cove and Benjamin."

"Hold me tight, Elenora." Edward's small voice came, muffled from its position against her body.

Jack tapped her on the arm, remembering the atmosphere of open threat in Sharpe's taproom. "We don't have time to delay. Ivy's right. We have to get out of here. When Sharpe finds me gone from his alehouse and the window open, he'll raise his customers in a mob to come after me. Us. They'll forget about extortion and they'll come straight here and find Warren's body. None of us will have a chance. Now. Give him to me."

Benjamin coughed. "They won't find that feller if we gets rid of the body."

"Good idea," Ivy said, as though disposing of bodies came naturally to her. Perhaps it did. "Into the river with him. Tide'll take him before morning. Even if his body's found, nobody'll connect it with us. Come on."

Jack hesitated, but not for long. Too many questions would be asked if Warren's body was found by the Watch run through with a rapier. Not the weapon of choice for the gangs of the Devil's Acre.

The three girls returned to the smashed doorway, and he turned to where Elenora was still holding tight onto Edward, blind to the fact she was sitting on that fetid pile of rags.

She looked up at him over Edward's head, and he held out his arms. "Here. I'm better able to carry him than you. He's not small."

With a look of strange reluctance, and some difficulty as he was firmly attached, she relinquished her hold on Edward and Jack took his son in his arms. Edward, his sobs finally lessening, transferred his clinging hold to Jack's neck. Jack settled him on his hip. "Downstairs, now."

They crowded out into the mean little corridor and approached the rickety steps, Ivy now carrying the lantern. They weren't alone. Two figures occupied the half-landing, creatures from a nightmare, grotesque and threatening.

"Where d'you fink you're goin'?" one of them growled. The lantern light flickered over a cudgel embedded with six inch nails.

Jack hesitated, encumbered by Edward and unable to reach his sword.

Before he could do anything, Elenora had stepped in front of him, her pistol levelled at the men. "Get out of our way or you'll regret it. I am considered an expert shot." Not a tremor shook her hand and she kept her voice calm as she pointed the small pistol at the man with the cudgel. What a woman.

Jolyon and Matthew stepped forward. "As are we." Both of them had pulled out their own pistols, bigger and more deadly looking than the one they'd given Elenora. These they also pointed at the two men, delighted grins on both their faces as though they were enjoying the danger of their situation.

A pistol had also appeared in Benjamin's hands, and this he swung back and forth over the darkness below, where the sleepers had lately lain. "Not one o' you lot make a move or I'll fire. I might not be able to see yous, but I'll get one of you for sure."

All three girls had their knives out, the thin blades flashing in the lamplight. Did Mrs. Sharpe know they went about secretly armed like this?

Their would-be assailant's eyes settled on the pistol in Elenora's hand, then slid past to those in her brothers'. For a moment, they hesitated, before, as one, they stepped back, retreating down the last few steps, keeping their gazes fixed on Elenora, perhaps the one they thought most likely to shoot them by mistake. She followed them down, keeping well back. Sensible girl. Anyone would think she'd done this before.

Jack followed her and her brothers and, behind him, his female army, knives in hand, followed him. With one hand, he kept Edward's head pressed against his shoulder lest he should see the horrors of the warehouse. If he hadn't seen them already.

The lantern threw a pale circle of light around them, and, as they reached the foot of the stairs and the two men withdrew, illuminated the denizens of the warehouse. From out of the shadows and the piles of rags, they'd crept, dirty, unkempt, hollow eyed, in what seemed a seething mass of inhumanity, like something from Danté's Inferno. How many people called this place home? Amongst the drawn faces of men and women were those of children, eyes sunken, dressed in rags no better than what they were sleeping on.

"Mistress Princum Prancium's got a barking iron," one of the men from the stairs said, reversing into the crowd. "And I fink she means to use it."

"Too right I will," Elenora snapped. "Don't for one minute think I won't."

"There's more of us than there is of them," the second man snarled. "Or are you lot lily-livered cowards?"

Hard to tell if they were. Desperation could drive a person to reckless action.

Four pistols against maybe fifty people. Not good odds. But the girls had their knives.

Jack set Edward on the floor, pushing the child's hand into Ivy's empty one. "Hold him tight." He drew his sword and held it out in front of him. "And I have this to prick you with."

The other two girls stepped forward, the light glinting on their knives. Rosie spoke, her voice a sneer. "And we've got these to gut you with. We won't go down wivout takin' a load o' you hedge birds wiv us."

"Who's to be first, then?" Peg asked, jabbing with her knife.

"Yeah, no one messes wiv our nobs," Rosie added.

The crowd, swollen now as the other rough sleepers had arisen, shrank back toward the wall. It seemed none of them was prepared to be a sacrificial lamb.

Neither, it appeared, were either of the two men with the cudgel.

"Outside, now." Jack jerked his chin toward the door.

Ivy, still holding Edward's hand, stepped sideways toward it, and her friends followed her.

Jack turned to Elenora, who still had her pistol levelled at the crowd of hostile faces. "Out, Elenora, when I tell you."

She shook her head. "I have my pistol. We go together."

Bloody woman.

Jolyon, eyes still dancing with enjoyment, caught her arm. "Go outside and guard the boy. Give Broxbourne your pistol first. That'll be four of us with pistols. And find something to bar the door with to stop them following us."

Sensible suggestion. Jack nodded to him, and, for once, Elenora did as she was told and handed Jack the small pistol. Far too light for a man, but threatening, nevertheless.

Their would-be assailants had taken a few steps forward as the girls retreated out of the door. Jack swung his slender sword in an arc, pointing the pistol at them, and they fell back. None of them possessed the bravery to test him out. But would they try to follow?

"I have no argument with you. But I do with the men who trapped my child here. I know you know who was behind this and are afraid of him, but if you try to follow us, I'll see you all hanging from outside Newgate Jail for conspiracy to kidnap. Leave us be, and I'll not mention where I found my son, only that he was taken by Warren with Sharpe's help."

Would they believe him? Would this mean anything to them?

He and the other three had reached the door. Hopefully Elenora had found something to block it with.

"Get outside and see if your sister's found some way to lock this door. Benjamin and I will hold them back. Ivy knows the way out of here."

"We're not leaving you," Matthew said.

"Not a chance," added Jolyon. "You're to marry our sister and we have to keep you safe for her."

Bloody chivalric pair. The suspicion that neither of Elenora's brothers were taking this seriously burgeoned. Were they a pair of idiots? Couldn't they tell the mood of this crowd of poverty-stricken and desperate people?

Elenora appeared in the doorway. "Found something. Quick. Get out now." She glared at the ragged crowd. "Come after us and you'll regret it. My brothers will blow your heads off without a second thought. It'll be like shooting rats in the barn."

What a woman.

Jack believed her. And most importantly, so did the crowd.

The man with the cudgel held up his arms in front of his fellows. "She's a right vixen. Let'er go. Tain't worth riskin' our lives over." As the mood of the crowd deflated, Jack, Benjamin and Elenora's brothers retreated out of the door and he slammed it shut behind them.

Peg and Rosie slid an ancient but still solid beam into place across the door.

Jack hesitated. There was still the matter of Warren's body. However, the Wetherby brothers seemed to have that well in hand.

"Grab his legs, he's heavier than he looks," Jolyon said, indicating Warren's body lying where they'd left it. "Can't leave any evidence behind us."

Matthew grabbed the legs and the two young men heaved the inert mass to the edge of the wharf.

"Tide's out, damn it," Jolyon grunted.

"I told you it was before. Chuck him onto the mud," Ivy snapped. "Tide'll be in before long and roll him down to the sea if we're lucky. Now, stop dawdlin' and run."

Elenora ran, aware that beside her Jack had hold of Edward's hand again and the child was running between him and Ivy, his little legs pounding through the darkness and the mud. Fog swarmed in all around them, damp and cold and cloying in her straining lungs, bringing with it the stench of soot and dirt and the filthy waters of the Thames.

They ran for what seemed like forever, her feet slamming against uneven cobbles or splashing through mud and other liquids she didn't want to discover. The soaked skirt of her gown flapped cold against her legs and moisture formed on the wool of her pelisse.

"I can't run anymore," Edward gasped before long. Jack sheathed his sword in its camouflaging stick and scooped him up in his arms, and they ran on, keeping as silent as they could, only the sound of their breathing rasping in the cloaking fog. At least that might stop anyone pursuing them. Or at any rate, finding them in it.

Ivy, who was leading the way now, led them through a winding maze of narrow, dirty alleyways and streets. They passed through shadowy courtyards overhung with tumbledown buildings and lines of smut-covered washing, where scarcely any light showed from filthy windows.

Elenora, whose sense of direction had been thrown akimbo early on, had no way of telling which way they were going until, at last, they emerged as if from a nightmare, onto a street whose lamps made it seem like daylight after the dark gloom of the slums. Fog still clouded the street, but it was not a slum, there being decent, red-brick houses in a row, their faces calm and welcoming. Not yet the streets Elenora knew as home, but nearer to Betterton Street in form.

"This way," Ivy said.

Although he was now carrying Edward, Jack still had the swordstick in his hand, and both her brothers still gripped their pistols. They might be out of the slums, but that didn't make them safe. Hadn't Mama told her often enough that the streets of London, wherever you were, could not be considered safe after dark? And it must be getting late now.

Twenty minutes hurried walking brought their party back to Betterton Street, but it appeared they were not going in. Jack set a sleepy Edward on his feet. "You girls and Benjamin go in. I have you all to thank for tonight, for fetching Elenora's brothers with their pistols. I couldn't have done this alone, even though I thought I could." His gaze slid to Elenora. "You are all very brave."

The girls exchanged glances. "It were nothin' compared wiv what you've done fer us," Ivy said. "Otherwise, it'd have bin us you'd have seen in that warehouse, sleepin' rough, sellin' ourselves for the price of a meat pie."

Peg and Rosie nodded. Had any of them been forced to do that in their past? Before Jack had rescued them? And what about all the other girls still in that position? Elenora shuddered.

"Will you be safe, milord?" Ivy asked. "We can come back wiv you if you needs us to? Or Benjamin can."

The look on that young man's face said that he'd had enough of escorting nobs about the dangerous backstreets of London.

Jack shook his head. "Elenora and I have her brothers to see us home. Have no fear. Although your knives would be a handy addition to our munition. You've seen us out of the Devil's Acre and that's all you needed to do. I have my sword and I'll give Elenora back her pistol, just in case, and her brothers are armed to the teeth. We'll be safe. You'd best go inside and explain to Mrs. Sharpe where you've all been." A smile lit his face. "My brave soldier girls."

"I'm cold," Edward said.

Ivy had her shawl off in a moment and was wrapping it around his shoulders. "There, my little lord, that should keep you warm till you gets home and into your bed." She dropped a kiss on his curly head.

Edward smiled and made a little bow. "Thank you, miss."

The girls went inside, not without noticeably longing looks at Jolyon and Matthew, who seemed to appreciate their attention, and Jack scooped up Edward again. "Back to Portland Place."

CHAPTER TWENTY-FIVE

Portland Place had never looked so welcoming, although
rather worryingly a carriage stood in the street outside, the
driver's shoulders draped in a thick blanket against the cold. A
wave of relief that they'd made it back unmolested washed over
Elenora as they approached the front doors. As if their return had
been foreseen, these doors swung open and Alcock appeared,
haloed in bright light but managing, nevertheless, to look very
harassed. As well he might. Behind him loomed the unmistakably
upright figure of Lady Amberley, her expression heavy with
approbation.

Oh no. Not Jack's mother. What on earth was she doing here
at this time of night? But Elenora had met more intimidating
people tonight than she'd ever imagined possible, and even
though she no longer required a pistol to deal with this one,
determination rose in her heart. Whatever Lady Amberley had to
say, she could face it. She tucked the aforesaid pistol away in her
reticule, in case Lady Amberley might think she intended to shoot
her with it.

Jack stood back and allowed Elenora to pass inside in front of
him, then carried Edward into the wide front hallway. Jolyon and
Matthew, sober-faced now, probably at the sight of Lady
Amberley's expression, sidled in behind them, keeping well back
as though afraid of entering the line of fire. Their pistols had also
vanished into some inner pockets of their great coats.

"My lord! Miss Wetherby." Alcock's voice held a mixture of the same relief Elenora felt and a strong degree of remonstration. A little more than one would expect from a butler, but then, he'd probably had an extremely trying evening.

A further reason for his discomfiture emerged from the door on the right hand side. A portly man in a slightly shabby blue coat and carrying a walking stick emerged, his unusual white top hat tucked under his arm. Behind him followed four more fellows, all in drab navy blue uniforms from top to toe, apart from their black boots and hats. Elenora needed no telling that these were the Bow Street Runners Jack had sent for before their departure.

The portly gentleman made a bow. "John Townsend from Bow Street, at your service, milord." His gaze fastened on little Edward still cradled in his father's arms. "Although it looks to me like you've righted this problem for yourself."

Lady Amberley snorted her disapproval, rather like a bull preparing to charge. "Jack." That one word from her held many things: disapproval, enquiry, anger, surprise, and annoyance that someone had stolen her thunder by making such a dramatic entry on the scene.

Jack set Edward on the tiled floor and the little boy immediately reached out a hand and caught hold of Elenora's skirts, much as his father had done in the library in what felt like another world. Only Edward was wary, not commanding. "Don't leave me." He buried his face in the dirty fabric. Was he hiding from his grandmother? Her frosty demeanor was not at all welcoming, so he couldn't be blamed if he was. Elenora hadn't known either of her own grandmothers but, at a guess, Lady Amberley was not the most openly affectionate of women where small boys were concerned.

What to say to Edward? She'd never been beseeched in such imploring tones and her heart, unused to feeling like this, went out to the little boy. Her sisters would never have dared appeal to her like this. They knew all too well her lack of emotional response, her 'thoughtlessness' as they put it. Which was unfair, as in reality it wasn't that she didn't feel anything, but far more that she found it impossible to show what she did feel. Too awkward. Too embarrassing if she got it wrong. Best to err on the side of no reaction at all.

But with Edward it was different. She'd just have to shove aside everything she'd known until now, every impulse telling her she couldn't be a source of comfort for a child, and rise to the occasion. Because Lady Amberley certainly wasn't about to fill that role just now, and Edward needed someone.

She bent and put her arms around him. "I won't leave you, don't worry. Let's get you upstairs to the nursery. And Alcock can organize something nice for you to eat, and a hot drink too. You must be starving. And I rather think a bath would be in order." She wouldn't look at Lady Amberley's forbidding face. She wouldn't. But, out of the corner of her eye she could see how that formidable lady had fixed her son with a gimlet glare. However old you got, it seemed, you were not above your mother giving you a telling off.

"Will someone please explain to me what is going on?" her ladyship's voice cut through the atmosphere in the hall like a well-sharpened knife as she glared at Jack. "Your servants tell me you have been into the slums. Mr. Townsend here tells me you sent for his Runners after my grandson was kidnapped."

She threw a glance at Edward, his face now against Elenora's shoulder as she knelt before him. "And to top it all, you took your betrothed, Miss Wetherby, with you into the slums. A young lady of respectable birth. Unchaperoned." Her gaze fell on Jolyon and Matthew. "And who, pray, are these two... gentlemen?" She sounded very much as though she wasn't sure that was what they were, as their originally smart apparel had been much dirtied by their flight through the backstreets.

Jolyon made a flamboyant bow, and Matthew followed suit. "Jolyon Wetherby, Lady Amberley, at your service. And this is my brother, Matthew." He hesitated before evidently deciding that more of an explanation was needed. "Elenora is our sister."

Elenora gathered Edward, who was a tidy weight, into her arms and stood up. "I'm taking Edward up to bed."

No one seemed to be taking any notice of her.

Lady Amberley's gaze, still on Jolyon and Matthew, sharpened. "And how did you come to partake in whatever this expedition has entailed?" Her elegant nose wrinkled. "For it is quite evident that wherever you have been it was not somewhere clean."

Jack appeared, for the moment, to have been struck dumb. Unusual for him. Did he go in awe of his mother as Jolyon and Matthew did with Mama? Papa too, if truth be told. Lady Amberley seemed keen to prove herself as forceful as Lady Wetherby.

Edward, now reassured that his new friend wasn't about to abandon him, seemed to have recovered some confidence. He put his arm around her neck, drawing her closer so he could whisper. "You're right. I'm starving. I haven't had my supper. And that horrible man said I didn't need any when I asked. He said I was fat." His voice rose in indignation at the insult, but he also gave a little shiver at the memory. "Can I have hot cocoa?" His small hand was sticky and hot on her neck and made her want to twitch away his touch. She suppressed the urge. He was only a child. A child who'd undergone a terrible experience. She mustn't let her foibles upset him when he needed comfort. And besides, it wasn't so bad as all that.

"Of course, you shall have hot cocoa. I'd like some myself. It's a great restorative after an adventure such as the one you've had. I'm sure your cook is still up and can make us some." Perhaps she could make his ordeal sound as though it hadn't been so bad. Cast it in the light of a boyish adventure. If she was lucky.

A reassuring twinkle sparkled in his eyes. "And can I have cake, too?"

She nodded with vigor. "As much as you like. In fact, you shall have whatever you wish. Alcock can go and tell them in the kitchen."

Lady Amberley tapped her finely shod foot. "I'm waiting for an explanation."

Jack stowed his sword stick in the stand by the door, along with one or two walking sticks. "Mother, this is nothing to do with you. What are you even doing here this late at night?"

"Lady Dandridge sent me a message regarding her niece." Lady Amberley directed a meaningful glare in Elenora's direction. "Something garbled about kidnappers. I could make neither head nor tail of it until I arrived here, and even after speaking with Mr. Townsend and your butler, nothing is clear."

Alcock managed to keep an admirably straight face. Jolyon and Matthew looked as though they rather wished they'd parted company with Elenora and Jack out in the street and were edging nearer to the door. Mr. Townsend and his Runners might well have felt the same.

Lady Amberley sailed on, regardless of her audience. "Penelope must have been having a fit of the vapors when she wrote it. I came here straightaway and found you gone and Miss Wetherby as well, and Alcock tells me the governess you employ for my grandson was attacked near Marylebone Park. In the dark, of all times, as if the woman didn't realize how dangerous it is to be out after dark."

She drew breath. "And my grandson was taken by ruffians. You should terminate that woman's employment forthwith. I can't have my grandson cared for by a fool."

Elenora's brow furrowed and she held on tighter to Edward. Not if she could help it would poor Miss Douglas be dismissed. The woman had fought to save Edward against several men and been beaten for her efforts. Best to say nothing at the moment though. She just wanted to get Edward upstairs and into a bath.

Perhaps Jack guessed how she was feeling. "If you don't mind, Elenora, could you take Edward upstairs." He turned to Jolyon and Matthew. "I fear the hour is late and there's much for me to sort out here. Allow me to thank you for your assistance tonight, of both your sister and of me. Perhaps we could meet at

White's, tomorrow?" And finally to his mother. "Might I escort you home, Mother? Elenora will take care of Edward. I feel you and I need to talk. Alcock, can you get Thomas to escort Miss Wetherby back to Arlington Street when Edward is in bed? Thank you."

Elenora, Edward snuggled in her arms, started up the stairs as her brothers almost fought each other to be out of the door first.

Mr. Townsend of the Runners stepped forward. "Lord Brox-bourne. As you have your boy back, do you wish us to take further action?"

Elenora turned her head to watch and listen better, thinking of the body they'd heaved into the Thames. Would Jack be in trouble if they knew he'd killed the kidnapper?

Jack's gaze came to rest on her, his eyes troubled. Then he looked back at Mr. Townsend. "No, I have my son back and Reuben Sharpe hasn't long for this world. When I saw him tonight in his lair, he was coughing blood—in the later stages of consumption. The Devil's Acre isn't a safe place for any Runners to enter, and I couldn't justify putting your men in danger. I'm just content to have my son back home."

Mr. Townsend gave a smart salute. "As you wish, milord, but remember that if you change your mind, we're at your disposal. Just send your man round with a request and we'll be here."

Thank goodness he wasn't going back after Reuben Sharpe. Elenora heaved a sigh of relief and continued on up the stairs to the night nursery.

No one was in it, but a warm fire glowed in the hearth as if Edward's speedy return had been expected with confidence. Elenora rang the bell and, within minutes, Meg, the nursery nurse, was helping to carry buckets of hot water upstairs to fill a bath for Edward.

While this was going on, Elenora sat on the end of his bed holding him on her lap, his little arms still firmly wrapped around her neck as though he feared to let her go. He needed that bath. Six or seven hours locked in that room with only a pile of filthy rags to sit on had left its mark and she had to wonder if he'd need delousing too. If *she'd* need delousing. Even if Jack would need it too. Her skin and hair itched at the thought and she wriggled her shoulders, longing to dunk her body in hot water as well.

When the bath was half full, Meg, all soft, comforting warmth and kindness, took her small charge and removed his offending smelly clothes without protest from him. "They can be burned," was all Meg said, tossing them with evident disdain into an empty bucket. He must have been exhausted, but the hot water revived him, as did the forcible washing of his hair in carbolic soap. Several times. It seemed Meg had the same worries about what had hitched a ride home with him as Elenora did, and Edward's complaints about soap getting in his eyes rose unheeded to the stuccoed ceiling.

From the other side of the screen Meg had put up for Edward's modesty, Elenora listened to sounds of splashing and good-humored banter from her charge. He, at least, seemed to have bounced back with rapidity, the rigors of his captivity forgotten. At least he hadn't been held there for long.

She looked down at herself. The hems of her dress and pelisse, the latter of which she'd removed in the warm nursery, were so thick with mud and dirt as to be irredeemable, and the rest of her apparel was liberally splattered with things unmentionable. Perhaps they'd need burning like Edward's clothes. And if Edward smelled, then so did she.

The nursery didn't possess a mirror, but she could imagine what her face and hair must be like. She unfastened her bonnet and discarded it on the floor with her pelisse. She could never wear that particular bonnet again, ingrained as it was with the stink of the slums. But what could she do about her appearance? Nothing. She stifled a yawn and tried hard not to think of what Mama would say, and how shocked Aunt Penelope would be. Lady Amberley was bound to tell them both what she'd discovered. But did she care?

Oh well. What was it her old governess had liked to say? *It's no use crying over spilled milk.* So true. She would just not think about things like that. It was too… irritating.

Edward at length emerged from behind the screens in a clean nightshirt and with his curly hair wet and wild, and Meg trying to catch him to dry it with a towel. "You can't get into bed with it wet, Master Edward, you'll catch a chill. Everyone knows that if you go to sleep with wet hair you get ill."

"Very true," Elenora said. "My mama says exactly the same." Edward bounced onto the bed, a different child from the one Jack had carried back from the slums and who'd huddled close to Elenora for comfort. She held out her hands for the towel. "If you won't let Meg do it, will you let me dry it for you?"

Meg handed over the towel without any ado. "Shall I run and get a bath ready for you in the guest bedroom, miss?" Her speculative gaze ran over Elenora's filthy gown and boots. "I'm thinkin' you can't be goin' home like this or you're goin' to shock whoever you meet."

Elenora sighed as she began to rub Edward's hair. "Very true, but I have no other clothes to put on. If I have a bath, what am I supposed to wear afterwards? I can't put these things back on again and nor do I want to. I'm of half a mind to suggest they'd better go in that bucket for burning, along with Edward's clothes, only my aunt paid for them and she might be a bit annoyed at the waste."

Edward bounced up and down in excitement, making it hard for her to keep rubbing his hair. "I know, I know. You can wear my mother's old clothes. Papa has some of them still in her room. I'm not supposed to know, but I go in there sometimes and sniff them, in case they still smell of her." He beamed. "I'd very much like you to wear my mother's clothes because you're going to be my new mother now you're to marry Papa."

Hot color rose to Elenora's cheeks, the discomfort of living a lie that was going to hurt Edward almost unbearable. But would wearing the long dead Mary Warren's clothes be a good idea? "I don't know…"

Meg clearly thought it was. "That's arranged then. I'll go and get the housemaids to fill a bathtub for you in the best guest room, and make sure the fire's lit. And I'll find out where Master Edward's supper's got to." And she was gone, leaving Elenora more than a little shocked.

"It's quite all right," Edward said, peering up at her from inside the towel which she'd stopped rubbing his hair with. "I'm sure my mother's clothes will fit you. She has some very pretty gowns. Nicer than the ones the ladies who pass in the street wear. You'll look pretty in them. I think she must have looked very pretty, but Papa says there aren't any portraits of her. So I don't know what she looked like." He paused. "I wish I did." He clapped his hands in delight. "And when you've had your bath and I've had my supper, will you come back and read me a story?"

Elenora didn't answer but rubbed harder at his hair as they waited for the promised cake and cocoa to come up from the kitchen.

Chapter Twenty-Six

A T Amberley House, his mother waved him into her parlor and sent her butler for a tray of port. "I think we all need a pick-me-up after tonight, don't we?"

Jack stood by the fireplace until the port was delivered and his mother was pouring generous glasses for them both. She shot him a sharp glare. "Do sit down, Jack. Your restlessness is grating on my nerves. Whatever is it that's dragged you away from your just returned son? Whatever it is, it must be important."

Jack eyed the empty space beside his mother on the chaise longue and opted for the single upright chair next to it, noting the frown she gave his dirty boots, but ignoring it.

"Well?" she said, never one to clutter conversation with preamble. "And what have you done to the sleeve of your coat?"

His hand went to where Warren's bullet had grazed his arm. "Caught it on a nail." An easy lie. Probably not a good idea to tell his mother someone had shot him.

She grunted. "You need to be more careful. The coat is ruined. Now. What did you want to talk to me about?"

He'd better get it out now, if he was going to. "It's Elenora."

His mother's pencil thin eyebrows arched. "You've seen the light? Changed your mind about your engagement when you saw what kind of a girl she is?"

Jack shook his head, annoyed at her assumption. "Not at all. Nothing of the sort. No." Why wasn't he able to come out with it? He was brave about everything else. As was Elenora. "Quite the opposite."

Her already sharp gaze sharpened further. "And what do I infer from that garbled statement?"

There was nothing for it. He'd have to tell her the truth. "I find that quite unexpectedly, and contrary to my intentions, I've fallen in love with her."

"Good heavens." His mother came from the era of arranged marriages for whom falling in love was not expected. "That is a turn up for the books."

"I know."

She fixed him with her usual gimlet stare. "And what do you expect me to do about it?"

He shrugged, and the throbbing in his upper arm, which he'd been ignoring, increased. He'd have to get his valet to clean it up later. "I ought to explain my predicament more clearly."

"Yes, I think you should."

Where to start? "Our engagement up to now has been a sham."

His mother's eyebrows headed skywards, but she remained silent, watching him.

"It came about because I inadvertently compromised her at your ball. Father and Elenora's parents caught us alone in the library. I was sewing up her dress. On my knees in front of her."

"Sewing up her dress?" His mother's voice rose.

He nodded. "I had been sitting quietly in front of the fire, out of the press of guests, when she came in. She didn't know I was there until she came to the fire to sit down, and her interest in history, and her choice of book to read goaded my interest in her. The only way I could think of to persuade her to stay was to grab her gown. It ripped. They're made of such damnable flimsy fabric."

"I see."

"And Father and her parents were not alone. By bad luck, Lady Routledge was passing at just the wrong moment. As they opened the door and saw me with Elenora, I could see the glee in that harridan's eyes that she'd caught me out at last. The only answer to save Elenora's reputation was an engagement. Of course, I had to offer for her, and I did, but she turned me down with unexpected vehemence. Quite off-putting for the ego to be rebuffed with such determination."

His mother's eyes widened, no doubt at the thought her precious only son, heir to an earldom no less and with a sizeable fortune of his own, had been refused. "She turned you down?" Again her voice rose.

He nodded. "She did. But I had a good idea. She needed an excuse to avoid her mother's matchmaking efforts, and I needed one to keep you and my father from pestering me to marry and produce an heir. I persuaded her into a sham engagement. One we could quietly agree to annul at the end of the season. One that would give us both some peace from pestering parents."

She regarded him in stony silence, possibly digesting his description of her and his father as "pestering parents."

"The problem is," Jack said, soldiering on in the face of so stern a countenance, "that I have fallen in love with a woman who has told me in no uncertain terms that she intends never to marry."

His mother sighed. "And do you think that in any way your feelings might be reciprocated? I see that is what you would like to happen. This modern idea of having to be in love to marry. Very bourgeois and middle class. Your father and I hardly knew one another before we married. Our parents arranged it for us. I think we met six times before the wedding day."

He shrugged. "I like to think she might be coming to like me." He paused, unsure whether he should admit this to his mother. "She allowed me to kiss her. And said I could kiss her again, once Edward was rescued."

She raised her brows again but didn't seem too shocked. "And have you?"

"No. Not yet. But I want to."

His mother sighed. "I think, my boy, that you would do well to declare your intentions to the young lady. She sounds a remarkable young woman if she was prepared to head off into the slums with you, even though I strongly disapprove of her actions as headstrong and foolhardy. Do you not think that was the action of someone who cares for you?"

"For Edward, maybe. I don't know about me."

His mother gave a snort. "How old are you, Jack? How many love affairs have you had? Oh, don't look so shocked. A mother always knows these things. And you haven't the wit to tell if this girl loves you back?" She harrumphed. "Allow me to tell you something. I saw the look in her eyes tonight when she was standing on the stairs with my grandson, watching you. If I were you, my boy, I would be honest with the girl. I think you might find her reaction favorable."

IT WAS AFTER midnight when Jack finally returned to Portland Place, although the streets were by no means empty. London never seemed to sleep. He should have been feeling a sense of satisfaction that Edward was once more safe in the bosom of his family.

But he wasn't.

He was thinking not of his son, but of Elenora and the way she'd sprung to his aid that evening. In fact, he couldn't get her out of his mind, try as he might. The feeling was pleasurable, but mingled with unease that if he spoke to her, he might find her opinion of marriage unchanged. What would he do then? The realization dawned that a second refusal of marriage from her would feel like the end of his world.

On tired feet, he trudged back along the silent, foggy streets, conscious of the fact that ahead of him lay a house that would be devoid of the strangely fascinating presence of Elenora Wetherby. She would have returned home to her aunt by now, Edward would be asleep in bed, and only a few of the servants would still be up. His shoulders sagged with weariness after the exertions of the night, but also at the thought that he wouldn't be seeing Elenora. In fact, once her mother and aunt found out about where she'd been with him tonight he'd be lucky if they ever allowed him anywhere near her again. Her aunt would be packing Elenora off down to Hampshire to rejoin her family, washing her hands of a decidedly difficult to handle young lady.

What wouldn't he give to be returning home now to Elenora's arms. The thought was delirious. Was he mad? Yes, he was tired, but was he tired enough to let his mind wander in this direction? And would she even welcome his embrace with her odd dislike of being touched? And yet, she'd let him kiss her. And his mother seemed to think she had feelings for him. If only they were the sort of feelings he wanted her to have.

They reached his house and even before he'd set foot on the steps, Alcock had the front door open, his face flushed with relief. Jack had never known his normally imperturbable butler to display so much emotion. Perhaps he'd thought the men Jack had rescued Edward from had returned to wreak their revenge on the man who'd deprived them of their ransom. Jack handed him his hat and cane. "Thank you, Alcock. I'm sorry to have kept you up so late. You can send all the servants to bed and tell them I'll thank them personally in the morning for their service."

Jack glanced down at his boots. Filthy. Holding the stair rail he lowered himself to the third step and stretched his legs out. "But before you go, Alcock, could you possibly do me the favor of helping me with my boots? I know it's not your job, but you're the only one here, and I'm too tired to do it myself."

A small smile lit the old butler's face. "I'd be honored to assist you, my lord."

A few minutes later, his dirty boots discarded, Jack started up the wide staircase in his stockinged feet, each step an effort now tiredness was pouring over him in wave after wave. He needed to check Edward was sleeping soundly, so he kept on going to the nursery floor, where a single light burned on the wide landing.

Crossing to the night nursery door, he turned the handle with caution lest it squeak, and pushed the door open a crack. A candle flickered on the table beside the bed, throwing its warm light across the figures snuggled together in the bed, a book lying open beside them. For a moment his heart gave an ungainly leap—was that Mary cradling the child she'd never known? Then he saw that the figure he'd taken for a ghost had blonde hair and could not be Mary. Edward lay sleeping sweetly in Elenora's arms, his head against her shoulder, his dark curls spread upon the pillow beside her blonde ones.

Jack stared, his heart still pounding from the shock. Was he glad it wasn't Mary there with his child? A child she'd never wanted. The woman who'd lied to him throughout their relationship. He'd been a fool where she'd been concerned. In his heart, he'd known she was using him, but loving her had made him easy for her to manipulate. And manipulate him she had. But she'd left him with the best thing in the world—Edward.

His gaze lingered on the woman in the bed. What was Elenora wearing? Not the clothes she'd run through the slums in. She'd snuck beneath the quilts of Edward's bed perhaps to comfort him, but he could see the silk of a peignoir he knew all too well. Someone had offered her a change of clothes, and the clothes were Mary's. His heart did a further leap, although he couldn't have said why. Was he angry she was wearing Mary's night attire? And what was she still doing here? The impropriety of the situation settled on him heavily. Someone should have taken her home rather than allow her to spend the night looking after his child. Not that her reputation wasn't already in tatters.

He frowned. He could hardly wake her now and take her home. That would be just as bad. He looked at his fob watch. Gone one. His only hope for her reputation would be if he wasn't here in the morning, and could deny having been present overnight, but that was a faint hope indeed. He'd go to White's and sleep there, in a chair if he had to.

He closed the door as quietly as he could and padded to his room to find clean clothes. Without the help of Briggs it would take him longer than he was used to, but he forbore from calling on his sleeping valet at this hour. All around him the house lay silent and peaceful. The servants would all be in bed, sleeping until they had to rise at five to lay the fires in all the rooms. He'd best be gone before they woke.

Once in his room, he stripped off all his dirty clothes, longing to be able to take a bath and rid himself of the stink of the gutter. No time. Leaving his things in a heap on the floor, he pulled on clean breeches, boots, and shirt and hurriedly fastened his cravat about his neck. Briggs would be horrified at the mess he made of it in his haste, but he was too tired to take trouble with it. Then, having put on a clean coat, swordstick still in hand, he descended to the front hall and let himself out. Let everyone believe he'd never been here. Alcock would swear to it, he knew.

The door closed with a soft click behind him, and he set off toward St James's Street. It wasn't much over a mile so wouldn't take him long. His energy returned, he swung his cane as he walked, his clean boots tapping on the pavement. Elenora had not gone home. She'd stayed. That had to mean something, surely?

⁕

CHAPTER TWENTY-SEVEN

WHITE'S PROVED A singularly inhospitable place to sleep. Jack found a chair near the fireplace and settled into it, but sleep would not come. One of the discreet waiters, on duty all night long, brought him a brandy, but even that didn't help. As the sun was just trying to pierce its way through the fog that hung perpetually over London in the winter months, he gave up all pretense of trying to sleep and set off along St James's Street in the direction of Amberley House. Fresh advice from his mother was required in the light of his discovery of Elenora sleeping in his house.

He found his mother, not unnaturally, still in bed. "Go and tell her I need to see her. Again," he said to his parents' elderly butler. "It's a matter of urgency, and I can't wait."

Westfield started up the stairs with Jack in hot pursuit, and knocked with diffidence on her ladyship's bedroom door. A minute later Jack was inside and Westfield had departed, muttering under his breath at the way young people behaved nowadays and that no one would have dared to call before eleven when he'd been a young man.

Lady Amberley had been given scant time to adorn herself with a warm knitted shawl and was sitting up in bed looking irritated at being disturbed. One of the maids must have crept in earlier, before she woke, because a good fire was burning in the grate. Jack strode to the windows and pulled back the curtains, letting in what little light a February morning was forced to share.

"Mother."

"Jack." She sounded tetchy. "To what do I owe the pleasure of this extremely early visit? So soon after your last one. I'm not used to such frequency." She eyed him with asperity. "Should I assume that you are worried I'm about to depart this mortal coil? What wouldn't wait until this afternoon?" Her tone was frostier than it had been last night. Or was that early this morning?

Jack grabbed the chair from her dressing table and set it beside the bed. "You look charming, as usual, Mother." He sat down.

She waved a dismissive hand at him. "Flattery will get you nowhere. Get to the point, because now you've woken me, I need tea and toast, which Westfield has gone to tell my maid to bring and, once that arrives, I expect you to leave. I am not at all used to being disturbed at this hour and you have put me right out for the rest of the day. Now, what is it you want?"

"I am in a little bit of a fix."

"When are you ever not?"

"Frequently. My life has run with excellent regularity since Edward's mother died. When have I ever come to you for help?"

"About eight hours ago."

"I wasn't counting that."

"Well, I was. Whatever it is, do hurry up and get it off your chest. Are you off to speak to the girl now?"

Jack swallowed. "I need more of your advice."

She tutted. "Go on. I suppose you'd better tell me."

Jack swallowed. "You recall our conversation about Miss Wetherby."

"Of course, I do. I'm not senile."

"Well, things have rather moved on."

"And what is that supposed to mean?"

Jack wriggled in a discomfort he wasn't used to. "After I left you last night, I returned home to Portland Place and went up to check on Edward after his ordeal."

"Yes?"

"Miss Wetherby, Elenora, had not gone home to her aunt's house."

His mother's delicate brows arched. "She was still there after midnight?"

Jack nodded.

"I suppose it's too much to hope that she had her maid with her as a chaperone?" Her tone was more than sarcastic.

Jack remained silent, knowing full well that Elenora's maid had returned to Arlington Street some time earlier that evening.

His mother sighed. "Of course she didn't. I hope you provided her with a suitable escort and sent her home forthwith."

Jack remained silent. Again.

Realization dawned in his mother's dark eyes. "You didn't? What were you thinking of? You let her stay? In your house? The house of a known rake? By herself? Overnight?" Her voice rose with each utterance in the most alarming way, reminding Jack of when he'd been brought before her as a boy and forced to admit his misdemeanors. Which had been many.

"She was already in bed. So to speak."

"In bed?" He hadn't thought her voice could get any higher, but she proved him wrong.

"You went into her bedroom while she was *in bed*? In a state of deshabillée?"

He'd better get this off his chest quickly before steam started coming out of her ears. "No. She'd clearly been reading a bedtime story to Edward and fallen asleep with him. I went to the nursery, as I told you just now, to check on Edward, and I found her curled up with him. Asleep."

He paused, the image dancing before his eyes tantalizingly. "I couldn't have disturbed her for it would have disturbed Edward too. And he needed his sleep after his ordeal."

His mother fanned herself with one hand. "So you let her spend the whole night in your house? With you? Good heavens, Jack, do you possess no sense of propriety?"

Jack bridled. "It didn't happen quite like that. When I saw she was still there, I took myself off to White's and spent the remainder of the night there. The servants there can vouch for that. One of them brought me a glass of brandy as I couldn't sleep. I was not under the same roof as her."

His mother shook her head in what looked like despair. "Very correct of you, after a night of such inveterate incorrectness. However, I think what you've just told me solves your little problem with your Miss Wetherby. You will have to marry her now, whether she loves you or not, and rub along as best you can. Her parents and my dear Penelope will stand for nothing else. There'll be no backing out of this engagement at the end of the season. The girl has spent the night under your roof. Whether you were there or not is immaterial. She will be ruined if you don't marry her within the week."

Jack put his head in his hands. This wasn't how he'd wanted to win Elenora's heart. He needed her to love him back, not feel backed into a corner like this. "What do you advise?"

His mother drew her shawl more closely about her shoulders. "I suggest you get round there straightaway and propose proper marriage to her. And go and get a Common License and marry the girl immediately before the gossipmongers of the Ton get hold of this story. She'll come round to it, I can assure you. Girls always do."

ELENORA WOKE TO the sound of heavy rain on the window. Papa would be cross if he couldn't go out for his daily ride around the estate and that would make him grumpy with her and her sisters. She snuggled further into the warmth of her covers, putting off the moment when she'd have to get up. But who was this in bed with her? Could it be Phoebe who'd dared slip in beside her? Only Phoebe was thick-skinned enough to ignore Elenora's often repeated warning words about coming into her bedroom.

If it was Phoebe, then she was snoring, and that was intolerable.

Incensed at the cheek of her sister to creep into her bed during the night and on top of that to snore, Elenora sat up in bed with a jerk.

This was not Phoebe.

For a moment, Elenora couldn't work out who it was before realization dawned and she recognized Edward's sleeping form and remembered she wasn't at home at Penworthy. His snoring sleeping form. She must have fallen asleep last night. She hadn't meant to. Her memory surfaced about everything that had happened yesterday. She'd come in after her bath to make sure Edward was happy, and he'd asked her to read him a story. She'd climbed onto the bed beside him and he'd snuggled in close as she read, warm and cozy, and as far as she could remember, she hadn't reached the end of the story. They'd both been so very tired...

She must have fallen asleep. It had been an exceedingly stressful day, after all.

Dim light filtered in around the heavy curtains, so it must be past dawn, which, as it was February, meant it must be after eight o'clock. The fire in the hearth had gone out, and now that she was sitting up, the chill bit into her shoulders. The elegant peignoir she'd borrowed had little substance but she pulled it closer about herself, nevertheless.

The full import of her situation sank in. She'd spent the night here, in Portland Place. In a man's house. The house of a *single* man, no less, with no woman to give her stay any hint of propriety. Her betrothed, it was true, but that counted for nothing. Young ladies, especially not those clad in fancy nightgowns and peignoirs that were not their own, should never spend the night in a man's house. Alone. Not even the house of their betrothed. She looked at Edward's sleeping face, so like his father's. Technically, she wasn't really alone. She had a chaperone. Of sorts. Even if he was only seven years old.

She glanced about the nursery. She couldn't stay here. She had to get home. But before she did that, she had to find some clothes. She could hardly go home in a silk peignoir. Where was Agatha? Should she ring the bell for one of the servants? Oh dear, she seemed to have got herself into more of a pickle than ever. No, she wouldn't ring the bell. She'd manage by herself. The fewer people who knew she was here, the better. Easier said than done, but best undertaken now, before she quailed. Facing an irate, possibly apoplectic, Aunt Penelope was not going to be fun.

She slithered out of bed and found the pair of silk slippers she'd worn last night on the rug. Good. She slipped her feet into them, pulled this pesky peignoir close, and tiptoed across the nursery on silent feet.

No one in the corridor, thank goodness, but with all the curtains closed, deep gloom reigned, as though not only she and Edward, but the whole household, had slept in late.

She ran to the top of the stairs, the slippers flapping. Edward's mother, she couldn't call her by her name, too horrid, must have had bigger feet than she had, and peered down into the chasm that was the stairwell. Still no one. She had to find her way back to the guest room she'd taken her bath in last night and retrieve her clothes. But hadn't she inadvertently suggested to Meg that they should be burned, like Edward's? That would be a catastrophe. She'd be stuck here with no clothes to her name. Mama would probably lock her up in a tower like Rapunzel and throw away the key.

A hope came to her. Might Lady Amberley perhaps still be here? If she was, that would lend propriety to her visit. Well, it might. The thought hit her that she'd now done far worse than had been suspected on the first night she'd met Jack. If she didn't marry him now, her reputation would be ruined, for this was sure to get out. Someone would talk. Servants were renowned for spreading gossip to the servants in other houses, and it was then just a brief hop before everyone in society would know about her indiscretions. Perceived indiscretions.

She might actually have to marry Jack. Was that such a bad thing? The thought that it wasn't sent a warm glow to her stomach. But he didn't want to marry her and, knowing what it was like to have someone try to force one into matrimony, she wasn't about to be party to making him. She had to sneak out before he woke.

She hesitated at the top of the stairs, Jack's face rising before her eyes. He'd kissed her. And what was more, he'd said he wanted to do it again. So, did that mean he liked her? If only she were better at judging what others were thinking, life would be so much easier. But he was a rake. A man all of whose relationships had been with women of loose morals. Maybe he wanted her to become his mistress? The thought wasn't unpleasant and brought a hot flush to her cheeks as she imagined what Mama would say to that. Probably swoon. She bit her lip. And if he liked her, wasn't it true that she liked him. A lot. More than a lot. She swallowed, her hand gripping the stair rail. Did she want him to marry her? A question she refused to answer. Did she want to be his mistress? Good heavens, was she actually thinking the answer to that might be yes? A tingle ran down her body at the very thought. And she didn't feel guilty about it. How naughty.

But this was getting her nowhere but cold. She ran down the stairs to the landing below and quickly found the guest room. The filthy clothes she'd taken off yesterday lay spread on the bed. Someone had worked a miracle on them and the mud was gone, although both gown and pelisse now looked as though they'd be more suitable on a denizen of the slums. But, as her old nurse had said, beggars couldn't be choosers. If she wanted to get home she'd have to put these on, repellent as the thought was.

It took her a good half hour to negotiate the stays and ties on her slips, petticoats and gown. Never had she more needed Agatha's deft fingers, but she still didn't dare ring the bell for help. It might be better if no one knew she'd stayed the night. In fact, there was no "might" about it. It would without question be better.

However, this was to prove impossible, because when she crept out of the guest room, settling her battered bonnet on her head, the first thing she did was bump into one of the house-maids. The one who'd brought all the hot water up for her bath the night before.

"Ooh, miss." The girl, clutching a basket of coal and kindling, staggered back a few steps. "I'm sorry. I didn't think no one would be up yet. Not after last night."

Elenora put her finger to her lips. "You haven't seen me. Just go on about your work and forget me."

Puzzlement flooded the girl's homely face. "Forget I seen you?"

Trust her to come across the only housemaid with the brain of a flea. "Yes. I'm not here. Get on with your work."

The girl's jaw sagged. Elenora experienced a strong urge to put her finger under it and close her mouth for her. Instead, she abandoned the gawping girl and hurried down the next flight of stairs. Foiled again. Alcock was in the front hall. Lurking. She was sure butlers had a propensity for lurking, otherwise how would they always be on hand to open doors? She only spotted him when it was too late to retreat. Damn and blast it, and other things too. She'd gained a working knowledge of words her mother would have been shocked at from her brothers. She'd have to brazen it out.

"Good morning, Alcock." She reached the foot of the stairs and approached the door.

"Miss Wetherby. May I be of assistance?"

"I am returning home and will be quite all right, thank you."

Alcock's face clouded. "Shall I send for the carriage, miss?"

"Good heavens, no. I shall walk."

"I'm afraid it's raining hard and his lordship would not like you to catch a chill. Nor walk home alone and unattended. Please allow me to order the coach brought around." His tone was insistent. Almost an order.

She could stand and argue with Alcock, or she could meekly acquiesce. The latter alternative won. "Very well." She sat down on an upholstered chair. "I'll wait here for it."

Alcock seemed a little surprised at her insistence on remaining in the hall, but, satisfied that he'd done what his master would have wanted, disappeared, no doubt to inform the grooms and coachman that their services were needed.

Elenora fidgeted on her seat. She could get up now and head for home on foot. It wasn't far and she was sure she could find her way. Well, now she came to think of it, not quite sure. How dreadful would it be if she got lost? She was just thinking she'd brave the rain before Alcock returned, when one of the footmen, who must have also been lurking out of sight, materialized out of thin air, or so it appeared, and hurried to open the front door.

On a gust of rainy air, Jack hurried into the hallway.

JACK HAD BEEN hurrying back from Amberley House on foot, when the rain began. Without his greatcoat, he was soon wet through, but this didn't stop him. He had to get back before Elenora woke up and realized what a faux pas she'd made by falling asleep in Edward's bedroom.

As he reached his front door, he gave himself a shake to dispel some of the rain from his hat, and strode up to the door. As if by magic, it swung open, and he hurried into the dry to be faced with Elenora, seated in a chair at the foot of the stairs, dressed in her pelisse and bonnet of last night. He ground to a halt and behind him someone unseen closed the door.

Elenora jumped to her feet in shock, one hand going to her mouth.

For a long moment he regarded her in silence. She was even more beautiful than he remembered, although the sight of her asleep in bed had been delightfully disturbing.

Jack broke the silence first. "Elenora."

"Yes?" Her blue eyes were wary.

"I need to talk to you."

"You do?"

He nodded. "Upstairs. In the parlor. Not here."

Her eyes went to the door as though she was considering

making a run for it. He stepped up to her, took her gloved hand, and tucked it into the crook of his arm. "Now."

She made no attempt to escape, so he started up the stairs, acutely aware of her close proximity and her bent head. Was she looking at her feet?

Someone had lit the fire in the parlor, and it was cozy and warm. Keeping his hold on her hand, Jack closed the door behind them and turned to face her.

They were only feet apart.

"Do you mind looking at me?"

As if this were a near impossible request, she raised her head and briefly looked into his eyes. Hers were the bluest he'd ever seen them, but puzzled and uncertain, even a little afraid. She dropped her gaze to his mouth, warm color surging up her cheeks and making his heart a little more hopeful.

"Perhaps you'd like to remove your coat and bonnet?"

For a moment he didn't think she would, but it was warm in the parlor. She undid the buttons on her pelisse and slipped it off, quickly followed by the bonnet. Her golden hair haloed her face in a cloud of unruly curls no maid could have touched that morning.

"At Mrs. Sharpe's," he said, aware of a halt in his voice, "you let me kiss you."

She nodded, the color in her cheeks deepening.

"And when I asked you if I could do it again, when we'd saved Edward, you said I could."

Her eyes rose to meet his again, and her lips parted as her breath came quickly in the most desirable fashion. Longing for her coursed through him. If he were to put his hand between her breasts, such a tempting proposition, would he feel her heart pounding as his was? "I did." Her voice was a timid whisper. How unlike her usual confidence, but how like her to be scrupulously honest.

"May I claim that kiss now?"

She licked those rosebud lips. How could a girl be this beautiful? This alluring, and yet this naïve as well? The smallest nod.

He mustn't frighten her. Conscious of her dislike of being touched, he made no effort to take her in his arms, but instead just bent his head to hers. Their lips touched, she flinched but made no attempt to draw back, and her lips parted under his. He felt her gasp of what had to be pleasure and suppressed his own groan. How he wanted to press her to his chest and cover her with kisses, but this would have to do—at first.

He drew back. Her breasts in her lowcut gown rose and fell as though she'd been running, and a little smile played around her lips. She met his gaze. "I rather think I liked that. Would you mind doing it again, so I can check my first impression?"

He felt his own lips make a smile. "Delighted to be of assistance."

This time the kiss lasted longer, and he dared to let his tongue probe her mouth as it opened wider under his. Again came the tiny flinch, and to his surprise, her hand rose to touch his arm. The kiss deepened. His tongue touched hers. She gasped and her tongue retreated before it returned, curious. They parted.

"I was right the first time." She was almost panting. "I very much like being kissed by you."

Jack's heart swelled so much if he hadn't known better, he'd have thought it would burst. Another baser part of his anatomy joined in. "It's customary for the gentleman to take the lady in his arms when he kisses her."

"I know."

"Would you mind if I did that?"

She had to consider that. "I think I might like it a great deal. I have a feeling it won't be scratchy at all. I think I like to be hugged tight. I noticed that at the Belmont ball when you held me after Lady Raby had been so nasty."

With as much gentleness as he could muster, Jack drew her into his arms, at first just holding her pressed against his body, enjoying the feel of her closeness, acutely aware that she must be able to feel his obvious arousal. Then she raised her head. "I thought you said this was part of kissing?"

He chuckled, himself breathless with desire for her. "It is. But I'm afraid to put you off, with the way you dislike being touched."

"I think, although I can't be sure, that I might have overcome my dislike of being touched… by you, at any rate." She tapped his chest. "No scratchy feeling I want to escape. Nothing. Nothing but… a sort of hot feeling as though someone has poured hot water over me. My whole body is unaccountably hot." She paused and frowned, as though discovering a secret long hidden. "In fact, I think I like you touching me and it's that which is making me so hot." One hand fanned her face. "How odd is that, when all my life I've found other people's touch so irritating?"

"Be quiet," Jack said. "You do too much analyzing of how you feel." And he bent his head to kiss her once again. This time, as they lost themselves in the kiss, their tongues met with no hesitation, dancing over one another and Jack could feel his arousal growing. Her arms went around him, pulling him closer, and one hand rose to his head, her fingers in his hair.

Good God, she was enticing. An innocent and so different from any other girl he'd known. His own hand slid to cup her breast, and she made no effort to resist.

At last, panting, they parted. She looked down at his hand and he quickly let it drop. "Don't stop." She was panting harder, her cheeks rosy. "I find I like that." Her voice held wonder. "I think I'd like you to do it again."

He pulled her closer once more, and his hand went to her breast again, feeling the softness of the flesh as he drew down the neckline of her gown.

"Hold me tight and kiss me again." Her whisper shivered through him. He bent his head and found her mouth, responsive now, as though keen to explore this new experience to the full.

"Don't stop." Desperation in her voice.

Somehow, they were on the chaise longue and she was underneath, her gown awry and her breast half exposed. He mustn't allow himself to get carried away. This was his betrothed, not someone he intended to make his mistress. But she was entering into her newfound love of touching with a vengeance, as though born to it. Her hands seized his hips and pulled him tighter against her body. What did she know of lovemaking? Nothing, and yet it seemed instinct had told her she wanted him.

He pulled away, the shock of what he was doing slamming into him. "I can't."

She smiled up at him, blue eyes wide with innocence. "I think you can."

His arousal was not diminishing, despite his efforts to think of something else. "We're not married. It would be wrong." Would it? Wasn't this what he'd always done? Was he suddenly such a prude? But this was Elenora.

"You are my betrothed."

How uncomfortable his tight breeches felt.

Her hand went to the buttons on his fall. "I know you want me."

He shook his head. "I do, but not like this. I want it to be on our wedding night, not hurriedly like this, driven by lust."

Her blue eyes shone. "Our wedding night, Lord Broxbourne? Is that another proposal? And are you telling me that this is lust I'm feeling? I did wonder what it might be like, but never thought I'd feel it. The young ladies in Augusta's books claim to feel it."

Whatever sort of books was her sister reading? "Nothing but lust."

Her eyes narrowed. "And love?"

He nodded, his self-control returning. "Bound up in it."

She righted her disarrayed gown, not making much of a success of it. "And is what I'm feeling for you love?"

"I hope so."

She pursed her lips. "And are you telling me you love me?"

He swallowed. "I am, and I do. I have done for a while now, I think. You're a woman who is hard to resist. Will you do me the honor, Elenora, of being my wife? So we can continue what we've started here?"

A slow smile spread across her face. "I believe someone once said to me that a lady is allowed to change her mind. I think it was Mama. And I should like to tell you that my opinion of marriage has changed somewhat." She put up a hand and touched his cheek. "I think I would like to be a married lady, after all."

"And I think," Jack said, "that we had better get ourselves a Common License and be married as soon as possible. I don't think I can wait more than a few days to have you to myself."

Elenora smiled. "And I think you might be right." Her eyes flicked wide open. "And we'd better tell Alcock I no longer need the carriage."

CHAPTER TWENTY-EIGHT

ELENORA LOOKED DOWN at her hands and her short-chewed nails. If Mama had been able to come up from Penworthy for the wedding, she would have been horrified at their state. But she hadn't, as Phoebe had taken a turn for the worse and Mama refused to leave her, even for her oldest daughter's nuptials, which were, perforce, more than a little hurried.

Which had to be a good thing, as her presence would have only served to irritate both Elenora and Jack. Elenora because Mama would be clucking away like a hen with one chick at how well she'd engineered the match, which she hadn't. Jack because he didn't tolerate fussy women, not even if they were the mother of his beloved. He'd confided this to Elenora when she'd apologized for Mama's absence.

And now, the wedding was over. She and Jack had been married in the rather imposing church of St James in Piccadilly, by the Reverend Gerrard Andrewes, not far from Arlington Street, and only around the corner from Jolyon's lodgings. Which had meant that on Elenora's side there had been Aunt Penelope, a singularly green with envy Petunia, and both Jolyon and Matthew, who had persisted in offering up conspiratorial winks to Jack throughout the service.

Of course, Jack's parents had been there as well—the white-haired earl and his intimidating wife, although after a week of getting to know her prospective mother-in-law, Elenora was no longer finding her quite so overbearing. At least that was what she'd told Jack.

They'd returned to Portland Place for the wedding breakfast, none of which Elenora had been able to touch, and now their guests had departed and they were alone.

Elenora fought to control the impulse to start nibbling her nails again. If only Jack had not been so determinedly decent a week ago. In the heat of the moment, with her blood heating in her veins and every nerve singing with desire, she'd have been happy to have continued and given herself to him. But he'd pulled back, insisting on them waiting for their wedding night. And, for the last week, that night had been growing to monstrous proportions in Elenora's head, taking on a personality of its own. A frightening, off-putting personality.

She'd tried once or twice to rekindle the way she'd been feeling about Jack as they'd kissed on the chaise longue, and failed. Would those feelings ever recur? And what would her wedding night be like if she continued to feel like this? She thought about Jack all the time, but she just couldn't rekindle the way she'd felt about him last week, and it was beginning to frighten her. Above all, she didn't want to disappoint him.

She was about to find out, and this time, unlike a week ago, her heart was pounding from fear, not from desire.

Jack closed the bedroom door behind them. He'd dismissed Elenora's maid and his own valet, and his parents had taken Edward home with them. The room, his room, which she'd never seen before, felt terrifyingly empty of anything that might mollify her fears.

From behind, he put his hands on her shoulders. She was wearing the new gown Aunt Penelope had insisted they order for the wedding, gold silk rustling about her body and leaving her shoulders bare. His hands were hot on her skin. Almost, she shook him off, out of instinct, that scratchy feeling resurfacing for a moment.

His thumbs massaged her back and her breath came quickly.

She did like his touch. She did. The scratchy feeling vanished. Phew. That at least hadn't changed. But could she ever manage to feel the way she'd felt a week ago? Or was that something gone and forgotten, only to be given that once? Something they should have taken advantage of at the time.

His hands slid down her to her arms, raising goosebumps of anticipation. Maybe… just maybe… "You have the most beautiful skin."

If she didn't look at him, she wouldn't have to think about this.

His fingers traced a fiery line across her back above the bodice of her dress. What was that? The fire whispered down into her stomach, turning it over. Yes. She liked that. Remembrance of the way he'd touched her a week ago came slipping back and a warm feeling started in her stomach, and dived lower.

Warm breath on the back of her neck. The touch of lips. He was kissing her neck.

A part of her she didn't have a name for suddenly became the center of her focus.

His kisses trailed across her back, down her right arm, and his hands slipped round to caress her breasts. She closed her eyes. If she opened them in this strange bedroom, the magic would die, and magic it was indeed. The magic from last week, returning.

All week they'd been like strangers with one another, which hadn't helped, only coming together in the company of Aunt Penelope, who'd kept Elenora close and well-guarded after her adventures. No kisses, no loving looks, no touches possible. And now… could they go back to what they'd had a week ago? Could she?

What was love, after all? He'd said he loved her, and he'd said what they'd both been feeling had been lust. Was it love or lust cascading through her body right now? How was one supposed to tell, and did it even matter if one couldn't?

His lips found her throat, soft and gentle, as he pressed his body against her back. "Oh, Elenora, I've been longing for this day for so long."

Then, everything had been natural, as if the order of things need only be followed and all would be well, even to the point of giving herself to him before they were married. Until he'd stopped them. Tonight, it felt contrived, planned, lacking in the spontaneity they'd had before. Expected. So how could it be the same?

His fingers slid down inside the front of her gown and found her breasts, sending trails of desire through her entrails. Perhaps... perhaps you *could* have those feelings more than once?

"Let me undo your gown for you."

Eyes still firmly closed, she stood still while he undid the fastenings and let the gown pool in a golden heap of decadence around her feet. She heard his indrawn breath and felt his fingers fumbling with the ties on her petticoat. That too rustled to the floor. Now she only wore her stays and slip.

He gave a little, throaty chuckle. "I'm thought to be very good at unlacing stays."

Of course. All those mistresses would have given him that skill. If her mouth hadn't been bone dry, she might have commented on this.

He had hers unlaced more quickly than Agnes had ever done, and they followed her gown and petticoat to the floor at her feet.

He was breathing hard now as his hands settled on her waist and slid upwards across her stomach, the filmy muslin no barrier. His touch seared her skin, but not in a way she wanted to shake off. When he reached her breasts, cupping one in each hand, a little moan escaped her lips and she leaned back against him, her head resting on his shoulder, his cheek against hers, his musky, masculine scent in her nostrils.

"I want this to be right," came his whisper.

Her heart was soaring. You *could* feel like this more than once, and it wasn't difficult to do. His touch had done it to her. The ridiculous thought that if they went out together to a ball or dinner, and he touched her hand, even, she might feel like this in public, brought a chuckle to her throat.

"Come. Let's go to bed."

She obeyed, lying back on the pillow, heart pounding, and keeping her eyes shut as the unmistakable sounds of him undressing came to her. His boots clattered away. Was that his coat being thrown to one side? The mattress shifted as his weight moved onto it. He was so tall… so naked, his skin so warm under her touch. Her fingertips brushed against his chest, finding little curling hairs and nothing else. He'd even removed his shirt.

She could sense him leaning over her, his face hovering above hers. "Tell me I can kiss you."

"You have been already." Her voice was croaky with dryness.

His throaty chuckle came again. "That was your body. Now I would like to kiss your lips."

For answer, she reached up a hand and slipped it around the back of his head, drawing his face toward her. Their lips met, fire tingled through her like molten lava to her central core, and a gasp of shock escaped her. Their tongues met, the kiss deepened, and she arched her back toward his body, feeling the length of his arousal pressed against her stomach. A little tremor of fear ran through her.

Jack released her mouth. "Don't be afraid. I would never hurt you."

"Don't stop," she whispered. "Whatever you do, don't stop this time, or I might change my mind, and I don't want to."

Jack slid his hand down her stomach toward the dampness between her legs. "Don't worry, I have no intention of stopping this time, Lady Broxbourne."

THE END

About the Author

After a varied life that's included working with horses where Downton Abbey is filmed, riding racehorses, running her own riding school, owning a sheep farm and running a holiday business in France, Fil now lives on a widebeam canal boat on the Kennet and Avon Canal in Southern England.

She has a long-suffering husband, a rescue dog from Romania called Bella, a cat she found as a kitten abandoned in a gorse bush, five children and six grandchildren.

She once saw a ghost in a churchyard, and when she lived in Wales there was a panther living near her farm that ate some of her sheep. In England there are no indigenous big cats.

She has Asperger's Syndrome and her obsessions include horses and King Arthur. Her historical romantic fiction and children's fantasy adventures centre around Arthurian legends, and her pony stories about her other love. She speaks fluent French after living there for ten years, and in her spare time looks after her allotment, makes clothes and dolls for her granddaughters, embroiders and knits. In between visiting the settings for her books.

Social Media links:
Website – filreid.com
Facebook – facebook.com/Fil-Reid-Author-101905545548054
Twitter – @FJReidauthor